PRAISE FOR *HONOR*

and other novels by Lyn Cote

"A wonderful story of a brave and strong woman, *Honor* is both a sweet romance and a lesson on the importance of doing what is right. The historical detail is fascinating and the characters are rich and real. Highly recommended!"

GAYLE ROPER, AUTHOR OF *AN UNEXPECTED MATCH*

"Cote skillfully and deftly combines period details with a touching, heartwarming love story in a thought-provoking tale that will have readers eager for the next book in the Quaker Brides series."

MARTA PERRY, AUTHOR OF THE LOST SISTERS OF PLEASANT VALLEY SERIES

"In *Honor*, Lyn Cote has given her many faithful readers another story of suspense, surprise, and love that will hold their attention from beginning to end."

IRENE BRAND, BESTSELLING AUTHOR OF *LOVE FINDS YOU UNDER THE MISTLETOE*

"... A moving and emotional tale of self-forgiveness and compassion. Complex characters and good pacing make the story entertaining."

ROMANTIC TIMES ON *THEIR FRONTIER FAMILY*

"In her new series launch, [Cote] demonstrates her skill at creating strong female protagonists in compelling stories that will captivate historical romance readers."

LIBRARY JOURNAL ON *THE DESIRES OF HER HEART*

"*The Desires of Her Heart* is a riveting historical romance that takes you to a time and a place not often written about. Ms. Cote's characters are unique, and each one takes on a personality of its own."

TITLETRAKK.COM

"*Her Healing Ways* is a wonderful love story. . . . Cote knows what will keep readers interested in the story and uses this knowledge throughout."

ROMANTIC TIMES

Honor

Quaker Brides

LYN COTE

Tyndale House Publishers, Inc., Carol Stream, Illinois

Visit Tyndale online at www.tyndale.com.

Visit Lyn Cote's website at www.lyncote.com.

Honor

Designed by Stephen Vosloo

Edited by Danika King

Published in association with the literary agency of Browne & Miller Literary Associates, LLC, 410 Michigan Avenue, Suite 460, Chicago, IL 60605.

Scripture quotations are taken from the *Holy Bible*, King James Version.

Honor is a work of fiction. Where real people, events, establishments, organizations, or locales appear, they are used fictitiously. All other elements of the novel are drawn from the author's imagination.

Library of Congress Cataloging-in-Publication Data

Cote, Lyn.
Honor / Lyn Cote.
pages cm
ISBN 978-1-4143-7562-5 (sc)
1. Single women—Fiction. 2. Quakers—Fiction. 3. Man-woman relationships—Fiction. 4. Arranged marriage—Fiction. I. Title.
PS3553.O76378H77 2014
813'.54—dc23 2014013147

Printed in the United States of America

20 19 18 17 16 15 14
7 6 5 4 3 2 1

To Mrs. Doris M. Crawford,
one of my first African American teachers
and the one who took the time to teach me to write, RIP

Chapter 1

HIGH OAKS PLANTATION
TIDEWATER, MARYLAND
AUGUST 1819

Each time her grandfather struggled for another breath, Honor Penworthy's own lungs constricted. She stood beside the second-story window, trying to breathe normally, trying to catch a breeze in the heat. Behind her, the gaunt man lay on his canopied bed, his heart failing him. How long must he suffer before God would let him pass on?

Outside the window stretched their acres, including the tobacco fields, where dark heads covered with kerchiefs or straw hats bent to harvest the green-speared leaves. High Oaks—to her, the most beautiful plantation in Maryland. She felt a twinge of pain, of impending loss.

"The edict was impractical. And your . . . father was a

dreamer. But at least he had the sense to realize his irrational decision must be kept secret. Doesn't that tell you not to carry it out?" Each word in this last phrase slapped her, and each cost him.

Unable to ignore this challenge, she turned. In her grandfather's youth, the Society of Friends had dictated that all Friends should free their slaves. "My father remained Quaker." She said the bare words in a neutral voice, trying not to stir the still-smoldering coals.

"I remained a Christian," he fired back. "My forebears chose to leave the Anglican church to become Quaker. I chose to change back."

He'd made that choice because the Episcopal church didn't press its members to emancipate their slaves. All of the other Quakers in the county had left except for a few older, infirm widows—women who'd lost control of their land to sons. As a single woman, however, Honor could inherit and dispose of property legally.

Honor returned to his bedside. At the sight of her grandfather's ravaged face, pity and love surged through her.

As she approached, her grandfather's mouth pulled down and his nose wrinkled as if he were tasting bitter fruit.

Torn between love for her father and for her grandfather, she didn't want to fight with him, not now. "My father loved thee," she said to placate him.

"That is beside the . . . point. He should *never* have asked that promise of you. It was cowardly." He panted from the exertion.

Honor gazed at him levelly. The memory of her father's

untimely and unnecessary death still had the power to sweep away her calm, but one couldn't change history. Her grandfather's comment could lead them into harsh recriminations. And it proved that he knew he'd done wrong and had chosen the wide way, not the narrow gate. She chose her words deftly. "I believe that my father was right."

Grandfather's mouth tightened, twisted, not only because of her recalcitrance but also from a sudden pain. He gasped wildly for breath.

If only it weren't so hot. She slipped another white-cased down pillow under his chest and head, trying to ease his breathing. She blinked away tears, a woman's weapon she disdained.

"How will you . . . work the land without . . . our people?" he demanded in between gasps.

"Thee knows I cannot. And that once they are gone, there will be no way I can hold the land." She said the words calmly, but inside, fear frothed up. Freeing their slaves would irrevocably alter her life.

He slapped the coverlet with his gnarled fist. "This estate has been Penworthy land for four generations. Will you toss aside the land your great-great-grandfather cleared by hand and fought the Cherokee for?"

Honor felt the pull of her heritage, a cinching around her heart. "I know. It weighs on me," she admitted.

"Then why do it?"

He forced her to repeat her reasons. "I gave my father my promise, and I agree with him."

Her grandfather made a sound of disgust, a grating of rusted hinges. Then he glared at her from under bushy, willful brows. "Things have changed since your father left us. Did you even *notice* that our bank failed this year?"

The lump over Honor's heart increased in weight, making it hard to breathe. "I am neither blind nor deaf. I am aware of the nationwide bank panic."

"Are you aware that we've lost our cash assets? We only have the land and the people to work the land. *And debts.*"

"Debts?" That she hadn't known.

"Yes, debt is a part of owning a plantation. And I'm afraid last year's poor crop put us in a bad situation even before the bank panic."

Honor looked into her grandfather's cloudy, almost-blind eyes. "How bad?"

"If you free our people and sell the land, you will have nothing worthwhile left."

A blow. She bent her head against one post of the canopied bed. The lump in her chest grew heavier still. "I didn't think emancipation would come without cost."

"I don't believe you have any idea of how much it will cost you." Disdain vibrated in each word. "Who will you be if you free our people and sell the plantation? If you aren't the lady of High Oaks?"

She looked up at the gauzy canopy. "I'll be Honor Penworthy, child of God."

"You will be landless, husbandless, and alone," he railed. A pause while he gathered strength, wheezing and coughing.

Honor helped him sip honey water.

"I don't want you in that vulnerable position," he said in a much-gentler tone, his love for her coming through.

"I won't be here to protect you. You think that Martin boy will marry you, but he won't. Not if you give up High Oaks."

Alec Martin had courted her, but no, she no longer thought they would marry. A sliver of a different sort of pain pierced her.

The floor outside the door creaked, distracting them. Honor turned at the sound of footsteps she recognized. "Darah?" she called.

"I want to see her," Grandfather said, looking away.

Honor moved quickly and opened the door.

Darah paused at the head of the stairs. She was almost four years younger than Honor's twenty-four, very slight and pretty, with soft-brown eyes and matching brown hair.

"Cousin, come here. Our grandfather wishes thee."

Darah reluctantly glanced into Honor's eyes—at first like a frightened doe and then with something else Honor had never seen in her cousin before. Defiance?

Darah slipped past her into the room. "Grandfather?"

He studied his hands, now clutching the light blanket. "Honor, leave us. I wish to speak to Darah alone."

Why? Worry stirred. She ignored it. "And I must see to a few of our people who are ailing." Honor bowed her head and stepped outside, shutting the door. She went down the stairs to gather her medicine chest, remembering that later she must meet with the overseer. The plantation work could not be put aside because her grandfather's heart was failing. She tried to take a deep breath, but the weight over her heart would not budge.

Honor hated to see her grandfather suffer, and she hated to disappoint him. But her course had been set since she was a child. She shuttered her mind against the opposition she knew she would stir up.

❁

Later that afternoon, Honor was walking down the path to the kitchen when she glimpsed her cousin Darah stepping into a carriage farther down their drive. Was it the Martin carriage? "Darah!" she called. "Where is thee going?"

Though she must have heard, Darah did not even turn. Honor watched the carriage drive away. Why had the Martin carriage come for her cousin? Honor and Alec had not been a couple for several months now, but he still entered her thoughts at will.

Her maid, Royale—a year older than Honor and more beautiful than her, with light-caramel skin and unusual green eyes—met her on the path. She asked after one of Honor's patients. "How the baby doing?"

"Better." Honor handed Royale the heavy wooden medicine chest. Moving under the shade of an ancient oak, she pressed a handkerchief to her forehead, blotting it. "Who is with my grandfather?"

"His man is sitting with him."

"Then I can take time to cut flowers for Grandfather's room." Honor dreaded going back into the room and awaiting death.

Royale bowed her head, wrapped as usual in a red kerchief. She always seemed to want to hide her golden-brown hair. "I'll bring out your flower basket."

They parted, and Honor headed farther from the house

toward the lush and sculptured garden. The daisies and purple coneflowers would be in bloom.

The heaviness she'd carried since the bank panic, and since she had parted with Alec Martin, had become a tombstone over her heart. A sudden breeze stirred the leaves overhead, sounding like gentle, mocking laughter.

Honor tried to concentrate on cutting the flowers, and only on that, but failed. She tried to envision her future and failed at that, too.

❖

"What about me?"

The familiar voice startled her, and she looked up from the flowers she was cutting. One thing Honor had always liked about Alec Martin was that he didn't bore her with idle social chatter. She thought she understood his abrupt question. He had no doubt heard her grandfather was nearing death and wanted to know if this affected her decision not to accept his proposal.

Alec leaned against a maple, his dark horse grazing nearby. He was as handsome as ever—lithe and of medium height, with wavy black hair. The urge to run to him nearly overpowered her. Yet his words held her in place.

"You are so lovely, Honor, even in this situation."

His praise brought back sweet memories of his compliments about her flaxen hair and fair complexion. He'd called her beautiful. She felt again his lips on hers. Sudden irrational elation blossomed within, and she moved forward, seeking his comfort. "Alec."

"Is it true?" he asked.

His sharp tone stopped her.

"Are you still determined to free your people?" He picked up a fallen branch and began to whip the air with it. "Destroy High Oaks?"

His question and his savage movements rendered her mute for a time. In her naiveté, she'd allowed Alec to court her. But six months ago, when her grandfather began to fail, she'd revealed her secret resolve to liberate her slaves. And it had broken them apart.

Watching his slashing motions, she held on to her composure. "Thee knows quite well," she said at last, "that I am."

He threw away the branch and advanced on her. "Why? Freeing your people makes no logical sense." His voice increased in intensity and anger with each step he took. "It's just a woman's weakness, and I never thought you would be so foolish. It's time you grew up, Honor."

The unveiled fury in Alec's tone alarmed her. He sounded almost dangerous. *My nerves are strained; that's all.* And then, recalling Darah and the Martin carriage, "Does thee know where Darah is?"

Alec brushed aside her question with an irritated shake of his head. He reached her and gripped her arms, and the cut flowers fell from her hands. "Why are you doing this? If you didn't want to marry me, why not just say so?"

"Thee isn't making sense, Alec Martin," she said, reverting to the formality they usually observed in the company of others. "My decision to honor my father's wish has nothing to do with us." *Or it shouldn't, not if thee truly loved me.*

His grip became painful. She struggled to pull free, but his grasp only tightened.

"Thee will leave bruises," she snapped. "Let go."

With a throaty growl he released her, and she staggered backward.

"I'll go, but just remember this is all your doing, not mine. I intended to marry you and join our two plantations. With your grandfather's gold, we would have been able to salvage everything." He stalked to his horse and mounted. "And we could have been together as we should be. Just remember—this is all your willfulness, your fault, Honor!" He tossed her one final fiery glance and then kicked his horse into a gallop.

His words jumbled in her head until she couldn't sort them out. She realized she was rubbing her arms where he had gripped them. Until now, she had never seen the slightest bit of temper from him—not toward her, at least.

Royale ran to her side. "Miss Honor, please come." Her voice was shrill. "Miss Darah's maid is packing her clothing!"

Honor could only stare at her.

Insistent, Royale nudged her toward the house, leaving the fallen flowers behind. Raising their hems, the two of them hurried inside and up the stairs. But in Darah's room, the maid would only tell her that Miss Darah and she would be staying nearby with Alec Martin's aunt.

"But Grandfather is . . ." Honor's voice failed her.

"Miss Darah will come to visit," the maid said, avoiding Honor's eyes as she folded all of Darah's possessions neatly, packing a trunk and valises.

Honor stared at the young woman. Though her heart was in tumult, her mind was clear. Darah was leaving because she did not want to be associated with Honor and what she meant to do.

And Darah was going to stay with Alec's aunt. Honor didn't have to be brilliant to know exactly what that meant. So that was the way it was going to be. Matters would not work out with Alec. Her last thin lace of hope dissolved.

For a moment she pressed a hand over her heart, longing for peace, for the ease of swimming with the current rather than against it. But she couldn't go against her conscience, against her father's dearest wish.

And her father had counseled her with Luke chapter 12: *"Suppose ye that I am come to give peace on earth? I tell you, Nay; but rather division. . . . The father shall be divided against the son."* And now she against her family and even the man she'd once thought would be the father of her children. *"Your fault"* echoed in her mind, mocking her.

❖

Less than a week later, Honor stood at the graveside alone—or that was how she felt. A large crowd of neighbors and distant relatives had come to see Charles Whitehead Penworthy laid to rest in the family cemetery on a hill overlooking the plantation. Honor's black mourning dress and bonnet soaked up the August heat and the dazzling sunlight that was more appropriate for a wedding than this funeral.

Darah stood on the other side of the grave, staring

downward, and had not once looked in Honor's direction. Alec lurked behind Darah among the mourners, his curled hat brim shielding her from his gaze. No one had spoken to Honor except for the Episcopal priest who was officiating. And he had said as little as possible.

"Ashes to ashes, dust to dust," the priest intoned. He sprinkled some earth over the coffin, which was being lowered into the grave.

Honor's self-control melted. She could not hold back the sobs, not even with her handkerchief pressed over her mouth. Not only was she losing her grandfather, whom she'd loved, but also Darah, Alec, and her life here—everything.

The mourners turned from the graveside and headed not toward the house as expected, but toward their carriages.

This brought Honor up short. A buffet had been prepared in the house, as was customary. "Isn't thee staying?" she blurted out.

The crowd halted, but none turned to her. Their backs erected an unbroken wall.

The priest, by her side, cleared his throat. "Miss Penworthy, your intentions are known. Perhaps you need to reconsider. Freeing your slaves is an act of willful disobedience to your grandfather. He discussed this with me on his deathbed. Won't you change your mind and not do this dreadful thing?"

Sorrow turned to shock and then to boiling anger. Honor shook with it. "Thee has made thyself clear." Then she glared into his face. "It is better to obey God than man."

A collective gasp swept the mourners, and they all

hurried away from her, the women lifting their skirts and nearly running.

The priest sent her an acid glance and hastened after the others. Even Darah, on Alec's arm, left with everyone else and without a backward glance.

Honor watched them go, her tears falling.

"Miss Honor," Royale said, appearing beside her, "come to the house."

Honor let Royale urge her down the hillside, but she soon became aware that another set of mourners followed them at a respectful distance. She halted and reversed to look at the slaves, who had gathered apart at the graveside. They would soon be free. Why not begin now? "Thee are invited to the big house. Refreshments have been prepared."

Their faces registered shock. Except for the house servants, such as Royale, the other slaves had never entered the big house.

She motioned toward them, trying to smile around her tears. "The food will go to waste. Please gather on the porch to enter the dining room for the buffet."

At the front of the crowd, her aged butler was startled but recovered presently. "You heard Miss Honor. Please follow me. And watch your manners."

Their people, numbering over a hundred, cast worried glances at her as they trailed after the butler, grouped in families.

Royale touched Honor's arm, tentative comfort.

Honor pressed her hand over Royale's, feeling the weight of grief on her shoulders. If she had the choice, she would have sunk to the green grass and closed her swollen, painful eyes. "Go on and help. I want to spend a few moments at my grandfather's grave."

Royale squeezed her hand and walked toward the house.

Honor watched her go, then returned to stand beside the new mound of earth. Grandfather had been buried next to the grandmother Honor had never known. Nearby lay her own father and alongside him her mother, who had died giving birth to Honor. She gazed at the graves, and moments passed. "I hate to leave thee," she whispered.

❁

Lying on top of the rose-colored silk coverlet of her canopied bed, Honor woke at Royale's touch.

"Miss Honor, the lawyer Mr. Bradenton here to see you."

"What time is it?" Honor sat up, trying to clear her fuzzy head. The heat of the day was suffocating. She reached for her fan.

"It be near half past three o'clock."

Almost two hours after the funeral luncheon had ended. Had the lawyer come already for the formal reading of her grandfather's will? Her heart sagged, and she let her hand drop. "How do I look?"

"I best fix your hair." Royale offered Honor a hand and led her to the vanity, where Honor sat.

The commonplace occurrence of Royale dressing her hair soothed Honor's ragged emotions. When Royale was done, Honor caught her hand and pressed it to her cheek in thanks. "Soon thee will be free," she murmured.

Royale smiled but only in obedience, her eyes troubled.

What is she thinking? Honor rose and headed down the stairs.

The butler met her at the bottom. "Miss Honor, Mr. Bradenton brought Miss Darah with him, and they are waiting in your grandfather's office."

The news that the two had come together felt ominous to Honor. "Thank thee." She walked to the small office at the back of the first floor and entered. Mr. Bradenton was ensconced behind her grandfather's desk, and Darah perched on one of two chairs that had been placed opposite the lawyer. Loss stabbed Honor. Her grandfather belonged at that desk.

Darah did not look up but focused on the lawyer's lined face.

Honor sat beside her, but never before had she felt so unwelcome or awkward in this room. "Darah. Mr. Bradenton."

He nodded sharply once and began reading without any preamble of polite conversation. "The last will and testament of Charles Whitehead Penworthy. 'First, I leave a message for my granddaughter Darah. Marry wisely. You have a propensity to take people at their word. You should not.'"

The lawyer paused to pierce Honor with a withering look. "'Second, to my granddaughter Honor Anne Penworthy, who is wise and foolish at the same time. Honor, since you intend to squander it, I am taking away your inheritance. Darah May Manning, not you, will inherit High Oaks.'"

At first Honor couldn't think; then came a roaring in

her ears. Finally a coldness drenched her from her head down to her toes. "But Darah isn't his heir. She is the daughter of my mother's sister."

Mr. Bradenton raked her with disapproval. "Your grandfather summoned me a few days ago to change his will—and chose Miss Darah as the only other young person even distantly related to him. Miss Darah's mother was a distant cousin of the Penworthys."

The lawyer's face hardened. "Your grandfather said that you insisted on keeping your ill-considered promise to your father to free your people upon inheriting this plantation. So Charles changed his will and disinherited you. You can of course go to court, but I doubt any judge in Maryland will counter Charles's wishes as stated and duly signed."

"May I see the will?" Honor asked, unable to believe the lawyer.

He handed the parchment to her.

She took it. At first she couldn't focus her eyes, but at last the words became clear. It was true. Her grandfather had disinherited her in favor of Darah. The coldness drenched her again. Her hand shook as she returned the will to Mr. Bradenton.

Through it all, Darah had not moved, had barely breathed. Her calm attention focused on the lawyer. *She knew.* Betrayal dug its teeth into Honor.

Mr. Bradenton lifted another page. "There is a third stipulation. Honor, you are allowed to take your clothing, your mother's jewelry, your father's personal Bible, one hundred dollars in gold and silver, and your maid, Royale.

That is all." He turned to Darah. "You are instructed not to give her anything else, or you will lose the inheritance."

Darah nodded, just a flicker of acquiescence.

The man pinned Honor with his gaze. "Your grandfather said that since you hold *with such little regard* what your family has labored over a hundred years to amass, you should leave with just enough to keep you from penury. You are a disgrace to your grandfather and an affront to every other landed family in this county." His voice quavered with disapproval.

Honor wanted to speak, but the words jammed in her tight throat. Her coldness turned to heat, anger at this betrayal.

In his lifetime, the land and the people had been her grandfather's. But they should have passed, unhindered, to her—the grandchild, daughter of his only son. However, without one word to her, he had altered his will. Her grandfather had not played fair. He'd gone behind her back and thwarted her.

She tasted hot bitterness on her tongue.

As if propelled, she rose. "Thank thee, Mr. Bradenton. I will begin packing. I'll be in my room, Darah, if thee wishes to discuss anything with me." She walked from the office. Outside, she had to stop and lean against the wall to still the emotions that rampaged through her.

Royale was waiting nearby for her. She came to Honor and walked with her toward the stairs. Halfway up the staircase, she whispered, "I was listening. We thought your grandfather would do something like this."

Honor swung toward Royale. "Thee did?"

Tight-lipped, Royale nodded. "You should have told your grandfather what he wanted to hear and then did what you wanted after you buried him."

The brazen words shocked Honor to her marrow. Royale had not spoken so baldly in her presence since they were children. Honor could not have lied to her grandfather. Yet how could he, in turn, have so callously disinherited her? Hurt throbbed with each beat of her heart.

She walked beside Royale up the grand staircase and into her room, where she sat on the chair beside the window. She wondered if Darah would come up or lack the courage to face her.

Honor had her answer soon enough. She recognized the footsteps mounting the stairs. Darah entered her bedroom without knocking, then stood staring at Honor. "You can still change your mind."

What naive, silly words. And people called *her* foolish. Honor rose to face Darah. "Can Grandfather still change his mind? Can I regain my inheritance?"

"You can change your mind about abolition. People will forgive you. You'll find someone to marry and be happy. Why do you have to take the hard way?"

Honor felt a grinding inside her like rough metal rubbing against rough metal. "Thy words are apt." She quoted Matthew: "'Wide is the gate, and broad is the way, that leadeth to destruction, and many there be which go in thereat: Because . . . narrow is the way, which leadeth unto life, and few there be that find it.'" She folded her arms and, not wishing to add more weight to her words, gazed down at the floral hand-tied rug. "I choose the narrow way." She softened her voice. "Is that not the way thee wishes too, Darah?"

"You are so self-righteous." Darah's hands clenched the ribbons of her reticule. "But what you want to do is wrong. What would our people do without us to care for them?"

Honor gripped tightly her self-control. "How can thee say that? Who raised us when our mothers died? Royale's mother, Jamaica, did. Did she lack understanding or ability?"

"Even animals can make good mothers," Darah retorted.

Honor's hand itched to slap Darah, and the urge shocked her. Their slaves were deemed children by most, but Honor's father had taught her to view them as people who differed only in the color of their skin. She couldn't let Darah's scorn go unchallenged. "Jamaica was as wise as she was loving to us. How can thee belittle her?"

Darah looked as if she were crushing hard words between her teeth. "You will not listen. You think you know better than anyone else."

"I think differently. If people didn't know in their souls that what they say about slaves needing us is a lie, what I believe wouldn't cause them such anger." Her father had taught her that too.

Darah shook visibly with outrage.

Honor changed tack. "What was it that Grandfather said in the will—for thee to be careful whom thee weds? Is thee indeed planning to marry Alec Martin?"

"Yes, I am." Darah's chin lifted. "You don't want him."

Regret, remorse pooled inside Honor. Her feelings for Alec had been strong, but how could a woman who freed her slaves marry a man who kept his? There was no middle ground for them.

"Do you still love him?" Darah asked in a softer voice, uncertain, reaching for Honor's hand but not taking it.

Now Honor looked her in the eye. "No. It has been over between the two of us for months. I came to my senses and told him the truth." Saying those final words cost her more than she had expected. Her long-standing attachment to Alec could not be dismissed, discounted, or denied. Not yet.

"What will you do?" Darah asked.

"Weeks ago I wrote to a relative of my mother's in Pittsburgh. As soon as I hear from her, I'll pack and leave with what has been allowed to me."

Darah appeared to want to say more, but what was there to say? She left the room, weeping.

From her window, Honor watched Darah enter Mr. Bradenton's carriage and drive away down the avenue of stately oaks.

Like a bellows losing air, Honor sank onto the chair, suddenly weak. Her mind jumped from thought to thought—from Grandfather to Father to Darah to Alec. She leaned backward and let tears flow from her eyes. First she must let the heartbreak and sorrow and betrayal have their way, expend themselves.

And then, when she could think instead of feel, she must pray that her mother's cousin in Pennsylvania would welcome her for a visit.

Honor had thought her future course was laid out. She would free her slaves, sell High Oaks, move to Pennsylvania with modest wealth, spend the rest of her life in good works. Independent-minded, she had doubted marriage would ever have a place in her life.

But one hundred dollars in gold and silver did not mean wealth of any kind, especially since she must help Royale establish herself too. Fear threatened her, but what choice did she have now? She'd been shunned by the living and betrayed by the dead.

Chapter 2

SEPTEMBER 2, 1819

The coach jerked to a stop, throwing Honor and Royale forward. "All out, Pittsburgh!" the coachman shouted from his seat above.

Choking dust swirled in through the windows, and Honor began brushing off her face and dress. After leaving Maryland on a clipper and then two weeks of being jolted over the Allegheny Mountains, she felt trampled like tobacco fields after hail.

Her one hundred dollars had been flattened also by traveling costs for two. And now the trip was done and she faced starting a new life here—not only for herself but also for Royale, a chancy undertaking.

As the other passengers grumbled and stumbled out of the coach, Honor closed her eyes, seeing her last glimpse of High Oaks, hearing the farewell wailing of the people she'd thought she would free . . .

Honor stilled, grappling with the hurt her grandfather had inflicted. He'd cleaved her heart, slicing away home and family.

The burly, unshaven driver urged her and Royale down from the coach. Touching the cobblestoned street, she swayed a little as she had when they'd left the vessel that had sailed them to Philadelphia on the first leg of their journey.

"Miss Honor!"

Honor swung around at Royale's cry.

A man had claimed Royale's elbow and was whispering to her, tugging her away.

"Please unhand my maid," Honor insisted, pulling Royale free.

The man disappeared into the crowded coach yard. A lady and her maid traveling without male protection, they'd both been circumspect and cautious. But unfortunately this wasn't the first time men had behaved in an overly bold manner toward Royale. "Keep close to me," Honor muttered into her ear.

Royale nodded, her head bowed.

They needed to reach the protection of family. Honor attracted a young boy with a two-wheel cart from a gaggle of such. Soon their trunk and three valises were loaded onto it. The boy placed himself between the shafts and got the cart creaking toward 22 Sixth Avenue, where Honor's mother's second cousin, Miriam Cathwell, lived. "It's not far," the boy said. "Less'n a mile."

Honor and Royale walked side by side behind the cart. How would Miriam Cathwell view Honor's straitened circumstances? Receiving a wealthy relative was different from being burdened with a poor one.

A stranger barreled out of an alley, nearly colliding with the cart. Honor pulled Royale closer and skirted around the man.

A rifle in hand, he stared after them, his stubbled face intent and sour.

Honor picked up her pace. Every slight breeze of the hot September afternoon wafted up another foul smell. She pressed a lavender-scented handkerchief over her nose as she glanced over her shoulder. The man with the rifle was following them, actually tracking them. She quickened her step, drawing nearer to the cart and Royale.

"There be a lot of black smoke round here," Royale said, glancing up at the smudged sky.

"Iron," the boy said in a tone redolent with pride. "They make iron here. We even got an arsenal for guns and cannons and such."

In a sudden burst, the man sprinted forward and halted in front of the cart. "Hold up."

Honor drew herself up. "Sir, why is thee blocking our progress?" Men and women around them stopped, openly gawking.

The man spit and pointed at Royale. "She got a manumission paper? I'm looking for a runaway mulatta gal."

Honor's throat constricted. A slave catcher, the lowest of the low. Indignation trapped her words.

"I got my paper." From a concealed pocket under her

apron, Royale produced the notarized paper Honor had written.

The man yanked it from Royale and stood perusing it. He read aloud her description in a mocking, disrespectful tone. "'Royale, a Negro woman with light skin, light-brown hair, and green eyes.'" He took his time inspecting Royale, insulting her.

"Royale is free, not a runaway," Honor said stiffly. "Please return her paper."

The man spit again and made no move to give back the document. "You the one who freed her?" This time he spit words at Honor.

"I am." Honor held out her hand, demanding the paper. "I have witnesses—" she glanced around at the crowd that had gathered—"that thee has accosted respectable, free women on a public street."

"She is correct." An older gentleman with a beaver hat and cane stepped out of the crowd. "You had the right to ask to see the girl's manumission paper. Now give it back to her and be on your way."

People crowded closer, the men moving forward, and Honor felt the press of their disapproval of this slave catcher.

He slapped the paper into Royale's open hand, turned on his heel, and shoved through the crowd. Royale quickly concealed the paper again.

Resting a reassuring hand on Royale's arm, Honor curtsied to the older gentleman. "I thank thee."

He bowed his head. "Slave catchers congregate around coach yards and the wharves. Be sure to keep your maid close at these places." He walked away, and that released the rest of the gawkers.

With a grunt, the boy lifted the shafts and started the cart forward again. Honor's heart still thudded in her throat as she hurried to catch up with the cart. Royale drew closer still to Honor, her face again downcast. Would Royale be welcome in Miriam Cathwell's house? If not, where could they go? How could she keep Royale and herself safe?

Sixth Avenue came at last. Honor welcomed the sight of the modest but obviously respectable street of one- and two-story frame houses, some with flowering window boxes. *Which one—?*

A woman in her middle years rushed out of a house ahead, waving a white handkerchief. "Is thee Honor Penworthy?"

"Yes, I am," Honor said, hurrying forward, relief tingling through her.

"And I'm Miriam Cathwell," the woman said in a thin voice. Her old-fashioned high-waisted dress revealed a frail frame. Her skin possessed a transparent quality, and deep lines etched the corners of her mouth and eyes. Miriam did not look to be in high health.

Halting, Honor felt momentarily guilty for adding to the woman's work. *What choice was left to me?*

"Ever since thy letter arrived," Miriam continued, "I have been on the watch. I am happy to greet thee." Miriam's smile was truly a welcoming one, igniting her face with a glow.

The expression drew Honor forward. Curtsying, she accepted the woman's thin hand. "I'm so glad . . ." Her voice faltered, but she forced herself to go on. "This is my maid—I mean, Royale," she stumbled. Was Royale her maid still?

Miriam extended her warm smile to Royale, who curtsied with a bowed head. "A cup of tea will help thee both. Come in." Miriam gestured for the young women to enter. She turned to the boy. "Thee can leave the baggage inside the door. My son will carry it upstairs."

Honor paused to pay the boy and thank him. Then she stepped through a side door that opened to the large kitchen. Miriam led them into the neat, cozy, whitewashed room. To the left of the fireplace, white dishes sat on shelves over the counter, where a deep-brown pottery basin and matching pitcher sat. The homey place began soothing Honor's ragged nerves.

A scant cook fire burned in the hearth, a black cast-iron kettle hanging over it on a hook. Pots and pans hung above the mantel, and a settle occupied the other side of the hearth. One door opened onto this main room. As Miriam rinsed and then filled a teapot with boiling water, she waved the two of them toward the simple round oak table in the center of the room.

Honor was pleased that Miriam had welcomed Royale to her table. That wasn't common. In most inns on their journey here, Royale had been sent to eat outside the kitchen. Now the two of them sat together gingerly, still tender from days on the hard coach bench.

"Before my son and grandson return from their errand, I want to explain our situation," Miriam said, looking pensive.

What did she mean by "our situation"? A fresh wave of tension tightened Honor's neck. "As thee wishes."

"There are three of us: my son, Samuel; my grandson, Eli; and I," Miriam said, filling the sugar bowl. "Until Samuel contracted a virulent fever at only eight years of age, he could hear and speak. He recovered, but the high fever took his hearing."

Honor didn't know how to reply to this.

"I be sorry," Royale murmured.

With a long sigh, Miriam joined them at the table. "If the Father wishes Samuel to be deaf . . ." She shrugged. "Still, it has separated my son from God and from others. While it is true that his deafness was God's will, why do people say that and then treat him as if he were responsible for this loss? Or as if it was a judgment on us?" Miriam's words became tinged with bitterness. She scratched a dry patch on her arm that appeared red and irritated.

Honor waited, hoping to discern the point.

Miriam surfaced from her preoccupation. "Samuel has a fine trade. As his late father was, he is a glassblower at a factory nearby. I wanted to prepare thee because he won't speak except with his hands." She glanced at the steeping teapot and tried to rise but appeared suddenly weaker as if she'd used up her reserves.

"Let me." Royale rose to finish making the tea.

Honor remembered to smile her thanks to Royale, who did not have to serve them, then turned to Miriam, saying the only thing that came to mind. "I've seen that once before. One of the slave children on a nearby plantation was born deaf. He and his mother devised signs so he could communicate."

"I 'member that boy," Royale said.

"Well, when Samuel became deaf," Miriam continued, "I wrote letters to different places of learning. Eventually I found a man in Philadelphia who had visited monks in Europe. Some of these monks had taken vows of silence and spoke with their hands. Mostly it's a way to spell out words, with a few additional signs that express common phrases such as 'How is thee?' I was able to learn the hand language and teach it to Samuel, who had already learned his letters before the illness."

"I see," Honor said politely.

Royale set the pot and tea strainer on the table.

"Some people—most people—are put off by his deafness," Miriam admitted as she pointed Royale to the white cups dangling from hooks on the wall. "They treat Samuel as if he's lost his sense along with his hearing."

Apparently Miriam hoped preparing Honor and Royale would prevent them from acting this way.

"You got a grandson, too?" Royale said, quietly setting the cups and saucers on the table.

Once again, Royale's new habit of speaking out of turn surprised Honor. No, that wasn't right: not "out of turn." Honor pressed her lips together, thinking. It was just that servants never spoke unless spoken to or unless they brought a message. *But Royale is no longer my servant.*

"Yes, God blessed me with two sons," Miriam said, her face lifting, then falling. "However, last spring, cholera took my son and his wife, leaving my only grandson, Eli, orphaned with us. He just turned three years old."

Honor murmured sympathetic phrases, but in truth she just wanted to lie down to rest and weep, to shut her eyes and forget.

At Miriam's request, Royale lifted the trapdoor to the root cellar and brought up a pitcher of cream. Soon the three of them were stirring sugar into their tea.

Honor knew she must be as forthcoming as her hostess. She tested her tight lips to see if she could speak naturally. "Cousin Miriam, my situation has altered. When I first wrote—" she focused on her spoon as she stirred the creamy tea—"I thought that I would be left with a modest inheritance, an independence, so that with thy guidance, I could purchase a small home and then devote myself to good works."

Miriam paused, her cup held near her mouth by both hands, trembling ever so slightly. "What has happened?"

The woman's warm tone reassured Honor. Still, she turned her head slightly away as she gave Miriam a succinct summary of what had come of her plan to free the slaves.

Miriam set down the teacup with a clatter. "That's dreadful."

Airing her difficulties further sapped Honor's strength, and her chin dipped. "I'd appreciate it if thee did not share this with anyone else. It is too painful to . . . Now I need to find a way to provide for myself. As I see it, the only two avenues open to me are as a governess or a lady's companion. But I have no idea of how to pursue either of those."

"And I got to find work as a lady's maid," Royale added.

Honor stared into her cup, seeing her grandfather's face and trying to hold back tears.

Miriam took a moment to compose herself. "I don't think Royale will have much difficulty in finding a position, but . . . Honor, those positions—governess and companion—are scarce here. Why doesn't thee consider marriage? That seems to be the most obvious solution."

Honor nearly gagged in revulsion, sour acid washing up her throat. Marry? This soon after Alec's betrayal? And out of necessity, without love? *No.*

Interrupting them at this opportune moment, one of the largest men she had ever seen entered the kitchen. Swinging a little boy down from his shoulders, he nodded to Miriam. Then he walked to the basin, where he washed his own hands and the child's.

When he didn't greet Honor and Royale or wait to be introduced, Honor knew he must be the deaf son. She studied him. His back was straight, and he had powerful shoulders and large hands. His reddish-brown hair was cut short but not fashionably so, waving around his nape.

The man turned, and a shaft of sunlight from the high window across from him gilded his hair. A few years older than her, he had fine, regular features, brown eyes, and a square jaw. His attractive face was set in lines that, while not disapproving, were at least unapproachable.

"This is my son, Samuel Cathwell," Miriam said. "And my grandson, Eli." The little boy hid behind his uncle.

Honor greeted Samuel as if he could hear her. But she was fascinated by Miriam's swiftly moving "talking" fingers. This sign language appeared much more intricate than the one she'd once observed in Maryland.

Soon they were all gathered around the table. Eli perched on his uncle's lap with his head against Samuel's shirt. Honor was amazed to see such a little child simultaneously speaking aloud and signing to his uncle. Whenever Eli thought Honor wasn't looking at him, he peeked at her.

In contrast, Samuel did not even look in her or Royale's direction. Honor tried not to stare at him, but she wondered what it felt like not to be able to hear or speak. *At least I haven't been struck deaf and dumb.*

Miriam poured more tea and set out a fragrant blueberry cake and slices of bread and cheese. Honor tried to eat like a lady, but it was the best food they'd had since leaving home. Her appetite awoke, and she had to resist the urge to lick her plate. Evidently guessing this, Miriam chuckled and brought more food to the table.

❁

So his distant cousin had arrived from Maryland at last. At this intrusion, resentment chafed Samuel. When people found out he was deaf, they usually tried to act as if he were invisible. He, in turn, had long ago perfected keeping his face expressionless.

Samuel sent an aggrieved glance at his mother. He'd urged her to send her regrets to this distant relative. Mother needed to conserve her energy and her strength for their move. But she'd refused to listen to him, and now here were these strangers at their table. He fumed.

Then, with surprise, he noticed the cousin lifting her

hand and talking to his mother. He observed his mother demonstrating the sign asking how a person was. In amazement, he watched the cousin, Honor, mimic this gesture, then turn to him and, with a hesitant smile, repeat the sign.

Gooseflesh sprang up on his arms. Very few had ever tried to learn how to greet him in sign. He stared at the young woman, really seeing her this time. She was pale with almost-white blonde hair, a fair complexion, striking green eyes, and golden brows. She had a long neck, dainty wrists, and slender, delicate hands. She was lovely but reserved. Then he realized the lady was blushing, her hand frozen in midair. A frisson of awareness crackled between them.

His mother tapped the table to gain his attention. "Reply."

Hiding his gritted teeth, he begrudgingly raised his hand and signed, "I'm well. You?"

His mother translated and showed the cousin how to reply in kind.

"I'm fine," the lady signed, then stared down at her plate, still blushing.

Samuel lifted his cup to conceal his mouth, twisted with irritation. He felt stirred up, unsettled inside. And he resented it. With quick slashes, he signed to his mother, "The land agent will come soon. You have invited these women to stay with us. Have you told them we leave for the Ohio Territory as soon as this house sells?"

His mother gazed at him, pleading for time. He refused to go along with her. "Tell them. They have a right to know."

Samuel watched his mother speak and sign this to

their guests. The lady's reaction was plain to see. She went whiter and bowed her head.

His mother's gaze scolded him.

He replied in sign, "She had to be told."

"But not the first time she sat at our table. Thee has not been kind, Samuel."

When did anybody make the attempt to be kind to him? Then his own words slapped back into his face. This woman had tried to be kind. Samuel drained his cooled tea, wrestling with his confusion. What did it matter? This attractive woman wouldn't have any trouble finding a husband, and one wealthy enough to afford to hire her maid.

❖

After supper, Samuel led Eli out to play catch in the small back garden. Royale offered to help Miriam clean up. When Honor realized how exhausted Miriam appeared, she rose and joined Royale at the sink. "I'll help."

Royale turned to her, looking surprised.

"I'm sure I'm capable of drying dishes," Honor murmured. She had often glimpsed this chore in the kitchen and butler's pantry at High Oaks.

"I thank thee both. The clean cloths are in those drawers," Miriam said, gesturing toward a low oak sideboard. "I should go lie down on my chaise longue in the parlor. When the kitchen is tidy, I should be able to show thee up to thy room."

Thy room. Honor and Royale exchanged glances. They had shared a bed as children. But after they'd put up their hair and let down their skirts, the gap between lady and maid had intervened.

Refusing to let her discomfort show, Honor found the dishcloths and stood beside Royale, drying each dish with care.

"What you think about them moving west?" Royale said in a low voice.

The question triggered another jolt of alarm. "I didn't expect that we would stay here long," Honor said, focusing on the cup in hand.

"I think Miriam be right—you not gonna find a job as a governess or companion," Royale said, handing her another cup. "I know you don't want to think of getting married, but you best start thinking that."

Honor didn't drop the cup, but her stomach dipped. She took her time drying it and hanging it back on its hook. She had set Royale free, and now Royale was at liberty to speak to her like this. But it was an adjustment, especially when she said words Honor could not bear. "I can't even think about marrying yet." Just saying the word caused her stomach to take another dip.

"You been through a lot, I give you that." Royale's voice radiated sympathy. "But you and me got to do what we got to do." Royale's tone turned sarcastic. "We coulda stayed in Maryland like Darah said—" then her tone shifted to practical—"but we moved here, and everything is different now. We got to be different too."

Honor accepted another wet cup and rubbed it hard, wrestling with herself. "I can't," she whispered. "I can't."

Royale offered her another cup and stared at her. "A woman do what she got to in this world of men."

Honor grasped the cup. The final word, *men*, brought the man of this house to mind. No doubt Samuel Cathwell felt awkward around strangers. That had prompted her to ask Miriam to teach her some sign language. But was that the true reason he did not want them here? Or was it personal?

And his insistence that she be told the house would soon be for sale—it had struck her like a bludgeon, as he must have intended. She dried the cup with a vengeance and slapped it onto its hook, where it rocked dangerously.

"Way will open," that was the old Quaker saying. And one must open for her and Royale. Soon.

❖

As Samuel Cathwell—home again from work—hung his hat on a peg by the door and sat down at the table, Honor recalled from earlier the feeling of the delicate glass vase. Tall, clear amber with an elaborate ribboned rim.

Slipping from her wet hands.

Watching it fall. And hearing it shatter on the stone kitchen floor.

Downcast with regret, Honor moved to sit in the chair opposite him and beside Miriam. Honor began slowly to sign the words of apology that Miriam had taught her. "I am sorry. I was cleaning." She watched her own hand, not daring to glance at him. "I broke the vase. I am sorry. It was beautiful." She realized she was beginning to babble and rested her hands in her lap, waiting for his response.

Samuel sat, his arms crossed, confused by mixed reactions. The prized vase he'd made for his mother—broken. This pretty lady learning sign language. *Why? We're leaving, and she is staying.*

His mother, who had been sitting at the table when he came in, rapped the tabletop and signed, "Where are thy manners, Samuel? The young woman has apologized."

He looked to his mother. "And will she understand me if I sign?"

"She has spent the afternoon learning the signs for the letters and simple phrases. Please sign slowly, and she will understand."

Irritation rubbed inside him like sand on raw skin. He swallowed down his reluctance to speak to this stranger. "It was an accident. I am not angry."

But he was angry. His irritation gnawed at him, penetrating deeper. How often did he have the energy or time to make something of beauty? At the factory he made simple molded bottles in bulk. He had spent hours after work crafting that glass vase for his mother.

"I'm sorry," Honor signed, adding again, "It was beautiful."

Her repeated compliment caught him around the heart. She meant it, and it released something within him. A warmth flowed through him, and he couldn't look away. The afternoon sunshine glinted on her fair hair. The curve of her elegant neck reminded him of the neck of the vase. He imagined brushing his palm down her soft neck—

Stop.

"Samuel, both Honor and Royale did the shopping

today and have given the parlor the first deep cleaning it's had in months. Please thank them."

He noted Honor had been watching his mother's hands but looked a bit mystified. "Thank you," he signed, "for helping my mother."

She bowed her head. "Welcome."

He nodded—quick, curt, done. Her efforts to communicate with him only sharpened afresh his feeling of separation from those who could hear and speak. It didn't make sense, and he liked this perplexing confusion even less.

Rescuing him, Eli ran inside, the black girl in his wake. Eli signed, "Let's go play ball?"

Rising, Samuel scooped the boy into his arms, making his escape to play in the shady garden. Nonetheless, at the door he couldn't stop his head from turning for one last look at Honor.

❖

A few days later, Honor and Royale walked to the pegs by the door and donned their bonnets, preparing to face this new city, to seek employment. The door to the parlor opened, and Miriam came out from resting on her chaise longue. "I wish thee good fortune."

A man looked in at the open front door. Samuel, who had been sitting at the table, rose to gesture in a middle-aged man, who then entered and doffed his hat.

"This is the land agent who has come to list our property for sale," Miriam said.

Honor was tempted to stay and hear what the land agent said, but she was not so impolite. Besides, she and

Royale must find the nearby employment agency a neighbor had recommended. Leaving the door open as they left, they set out into another sunny, warm day, soon passing Seventh Avenue. They had only a few blocks to walk to 102 Tenth Avenue, the Superior Employment office.

Royale walked by Honor's side, and even though Honor was distracted by watching the street signs, she became aware of Royale's nervousness. *Eighth Avenue.* "I don't think thee will have any difficulty finding a position."

"I'm not gonna take just any position," Royale muttered. "I got to be careful."

Honor pondered this as they continued. *Ninth Avenue.* She glanced pointedly at Royale, asking why.

"I don't want to work in a house with any master."

The unpleasant incidents on their journey here jolted back into Honor's mind. With her lighter skin, curly brown hair threaded with gold, and unique green eyes, Royale had garnered the wrong kind of attention. Honor slowed her pace. *Tenth Avenue.* "I understand."

"Do you?" Royale's voice was suddenly harsh, cutting. "Didn't you never wonder why we have the same eyes?"

Honor's steps nearly faltered, but to keep up with Royale, she moved forward to the Superior Employment door.

The two entered and paused to let their eyes adjust to the lower light inside.

"May I be of help?" A man with a narrow goatee rose with some hesitance from where he sat behind a small desk in the small office.

Honor drew on her reserves of confidence. "Good day.

I am Honor Penworthy—" she stopped before she said *of High Oaks*—"lately of Maryland."

Royale's words ran through her mind: *"Why we have the same eyes."*

"I am looking for a position as a governess or lady's companion," Honor said.

"And?" the man prompted with a glance at Royale.

"Royale has been my lady's maid but now must look for another position also. I can give her an excellent reference."

"Why we have the same eyes."

"And do you have references?" the man asked.

This startled Honor. When had the lady of High Oaks needed credentials? She shook off her pique and humbled herself. "This would be the first time I've sought a position. A death in the family makes the change necessary." Honor would give no more information. Revealing this had cost her enough.

"I see." He frowned, his goatee quivering as if he were talking to himself.

Honor waited, enduring his assessing study of both of them.

"Why we have the same eyes."

"I'm afraid employment opportunities are limited at this time." He recited these words as if he'd already worn them threadbare. "The bank panic this year caused many of my clients to reduce staff. I'm afraid I have too many applicants for too few positions."

Honor suffered the blow in silence. "May we leave our names and the address where we are staying in case something comes available?"

"Of course. Please be seated." The man motioned toward two chairs and took his own seat. He drew out paper and asked Honor to write their information down, looking shocked when Royale filled out her own paper. Honor's father had insisted Royale take lessons with Honor, even though it was against the law.

"Why we have the same eyes."

❖

After taking the land agent through the house and surrounding property, Samuel signed the documents specifying the agent's commission for showing and selling their real estate. Before the agent left, he placed a white placard reading For Sale in the front parlor window.

Samuel donned his hat and headed for the door. He would be late for work as it was.

His mother tapped the floor with the kitchen chair to catch his attention, and he turned.

"Thee must face my ill health, Son," she signed. "I will not be going to the Northwest Territory. Thee must admit this."

Samuel's mind shut out her words. He was taking his mother and Eli to a place with clean air and water. His mother's health would improve. After kissing her cheek, he left for the manufactory. Nonetheless, a heaviness he couldn't budge lay over him.

❖

Feeling squeezed by disappointment, Honor managed to flee the employment agency with dignity. Ahead, a bench in front of a store beckoned her. She moved toward it as if wading through water. Royale's words, spoken just before they'd entered the agency, could no longer be avoided. She waved for Royale to sit beside her. "What was that comment about our having the same eyes?"

Chapter 3

THE NARROW BENCH hard beneath her, Honor was distantly aware of Royale beside her, head bowed. People passed. More demanding images from Maryland flitted through her mind, a thousand clues she'd never noticed or questioned. Flashes of Royale's mother in tears or hiding tears. Honor's grandfather and father speaking in raised voices, silenced when she, only a child, ran into the room.

A growing presentiment held Honor mute. Finally she shot to her feet. "We can't talk about this here."

Royale stood also but would not face her. "We go home then?"

Go home? We can never go home. Honor grasped Royale's elbow. She steered them through the jostling throng, suffocating in the heat and smell and noise. More memories tried to shove their way into her mind; she slammed the door on them.

Arriving on Sixth Avenue, Honor averted her eyes from the For Sale sign in Miriam's window. Through the open door, they stepped out of the sun and halted. Eli was sobbing in the parlor. They hurried to him. Miriam lay sprawled on the faded floral carpet, and Eli knelt beside her, patting her arm and crying, "Gramma. Gramma."

Honor's heart wrenched. She dropped to her knees, fearing the worst. But the woman was still breathing. "Miriam?" Honor murmured.

Miriam's paper-thin eyelids fluttered. "I fell," she muttered.

"Miss Honor," Royale warned sharply.

Honor followed Royale's gaze. Copious blood stained Miriam's dress and apron. She leaned close to Miriam's ear. "Is thee still bleeding?"

With a shake of her head, the woman moaned, sending chills through Honor.

Honor drew in a calming breath and slowly let it go. "I'm here."

"I'm having a bad spell." As if on cue, Miriam twisted with conspicuous pain. Snatching Honor's hand, she dragged her downward, closer, and said, "Take Eli out. I don't want him to see . . . this."

Honor squeezed the dry, clawlike hand and turned. "Royale, please keep Eli and bring down my medicine chest."

Her face tight with sympathy, Royale was already leading Eli out by the hand. The little boy went along but until the last moment refused to turn his head away. Royale shut the door quietly.

"Let me help thee up," Honor said. Rising, she took both of Miriam's hands and then drew her up, shocked by how easy it was.

Miriam leaned against her, breathing fast. "Help me sit on the wooden rocker. I don't want to stain the chaise."

Honor led Miriam to the rocker and set the footstool under the woman's feet.

With Eli clutching her skirt, Royale carried in the scarred wooden medicine chest.

Honor thanked her with a glance. "Perhaps tea?"

Royale picked up the whimpering child and hugged him against her. "Let's make tea for your grandma, Eli. That will make her feel better."

The child leaned his head against Royale's shoulder, staring sadly at his grandmother again till the door shut.

Honor set the chest on the side table near Miriam. "I have experience tending the sick. What is thy ailment?"

Miriam closed and then opened her eyes. "Honor, I regret . . . I am dying."

"No," Honor said instantly.

"Please . . . I don't have the strength to argue. Samuel refuses to believe. Look at me. Am I well?"

No, thee looks deathly ill. Though she'd met Miriam only a week ago, Honor knew she was not a woman who would exaggerate. Honor felt panic rise within her like a sail catching the wind.

Another bout of pain attacked the woman.

Honor gripped Miriam's hand. Suddenly words were pouring from her lips. "'Though I walk through the valley of the shadow of death, I will fear no evil: for thou art with me.'" An urgency tingled within, the rest of Psalm Twenty-Three flowing through her and out.

Miriam stared at her in anguish, gasping for air in tiny hitches.

Honor ended with "'Surely goodness and mercy shall follow me all the days of my life: and I will dwell in the house of the Lord for ever.'" She trembled with the power of the words.

Her spasm easing, Miriam gasped, "Amen. Honor, thee has come in the nick of time."

Honor didn't understand, but she leaned closer. Miriam's hair was sliding from its pins. Honor stroked the hair back from the woman's face and repeated, "What is thy ailment?"

"The doctor said . . . cancer in my female organs."

Honor blanched. A death sentence. Not meeting Miriam's eyes, she opened the chest. "I can give thee some laudanum to ease the pain. How long . . . ?"

"The doctor—I've not more than a few weeks . . . longer."

Honor nearly folded up inside. Nonetheless, she forced herself to measure out a modest dram of the opiate. Supporting Miriam, she helped her sip it. Then she sat on the chaise across from Miriam, who looked barely able to hold herself up. In the quiet house, the kitchen clock ticked, ticked. Eli cried out to Royale and she soothed him in a low voice. Another spasm hit Miriam.

Honor winced, enduring it too. "Should I send Royale for a doctor?"

Miriam shook her head no. "He would merely give me more laudanum."

Honor's nerves tightened, tightened till Miriam's spell ebbed. Then she offered the only comfort she could. "Can thee drink tea now?"

"Yes." Miriam closed her eyes, resting her head against the high back of the chair, panting from exertion.

Honor went into the kitchen. On the stone floor, Eli was playing with wooden blocks, bathed in sunshine from the window, a bright contrast to the gloom hanging over them.

Royale was lifting the steaming kettle from the hearth. "What wrong with her?" she whispered.

"Cancer," Honor replied in kind. Her mouth was so dry she had to swallow in order to continue. "She says she's dying."

Royale set down the kettle hard. "What is that baby and that deaf-mute gon' do without her?"

Honor bowed her head. What was there to say? The two of them fixed up a tray, and Honor carried it in to Miriam.

The day passed. Royale cared for Eli. Honor sat with Miriam, measuring out small sips of laudanum. Between onslaughts of pain, Miriam taught Honor more of the hand language. It distracted both of them. But underneath it all, uncertainty strained Honor's nerves. What had Royale yet to reveal? How would Samuel react to Miriam's sudden decline?

At last Honor heard Samuel come home. Entering the parlor, Samuel paused, scanning the scene—Miriam only half-awake from the drug, the bloodstains that had darkened to brown. Honor stood, clasping and unclasping her hands, wound as tightly as a pocket watch.

Finally he bowed his head toward her as if in thanks. Though reading and spelling words in sign was becoming easier, she could not sign to him all she thought, so she merely gestured, "Welcome."

Worry for this family and pity for this man tangled inside her. Honor wished to comfort him. But she had none to give. There was none to give.

❖

Honor and Royale had managed to lay out a cold supper and clean up afterward. Then, downstairs with the curtains drawn, Royale gave Miriam a sponge bath while upstairs Honor helped Samuel undress Eli for sleep in the small bedroom the two shared. The little one in his thin cotton nightshirt was clingy and cranky. Settling on the rocker, Honor lifted him onto her lap.

Samuel sat on the bed across from her, signing to Eli, trying to reassure him. Honor did not miss the sadness she read not only on the man's face but on every part of him. He looked as if he'd been pounded by mallets. The urge to touch him in comfort nearly overwhelmed her.

Regardless of Samuel's efforts, the little boy began to weep, and he buried his face into Honor's shoulder.

She tried to soothe him, rocking him and softly singing children's songs she remembered. She'd never comforted a child before. A new tenderness blossomed within. She kissed the top of his head and rested her cheek there.

Finally Eli fell asleep.

Samuel signed and, half-standing, motioned that he would lay Eli in his small bed.

Honor held up her hand and signed awkwardly, "Wait—till he sleeps sound." She wished she were more polished in her sign language, but at her words Samuel resumed his seat.

Now that Eli slept, Honor found herself alone with a man in a bedroom—something that had never happened before—and odd sensations rippled through her. Samuel was so imposing a figure, yet so gentle, so vulnerable now. The prompting to help him could not be ignored. The sooner he began to accept the truth, the sooner he would be able to deal with it. "Miriam is ill, very bad," she signed.

Samuel looked away as if rejecting her words.

She lightly tapped his knee with her knuckles. "Do not say no. We will help thee."

"I can't lose her," Samuel signed at last.

I lost my grandfather and my home—everything. Her heart throbbed with these words. But making no reply, she cuddled the child closer, giving and receiving comfort.

"If only I can get my mother to Ohio," his fingers insisted, "she will get better."

False hope would lead nowhere. For either of them. Honor found she could read his signing, though forming her own fingers into the words was an arduous chore. "She is not well enough."

He surged to his feet and began pacing in the small room.

Drawing back, Honor rocked the sleeping boy, witnessing Samuel's anguish. Now she understood Miriam's words: *"Thee has come in the nick of time."*

Though she could help this family for a time, Honor

could see no way forward for herself. Once Miriam died, she and Royale would have to leave. An unmarried man and woman could not live under the same roof without an older woman as chaperone.

❖

Later Samuel carried Miriam to her bed. Honor told him to wake her if Miriam needed her. She and Royale entered their room. As soon as the two of them were alone, what lay between them reared up. They avoided each other. And neither spoke till they were in bed and no light but the moon glowed.

All day, even in the midst of worry over Miriam, Royale's words had streamed through her mind like a circle of ribbon. Honor braced herself. "Now tell me," she whispered.

"Your grandfather be my father."

The air went out of Honor's lungs. She closed her eyes and her mouth, struggling to conceal her reaction.

"He be my father, and he didn't leave me one word or one thing for my own," Royale said, hurt in each word. "Or set me free in his will."

Honor found Royale's hand and gripped it. She whispered the only comfort she could offer. "He knew I'd set thee free."

"But I wanted *him* to set me free. Don't you see?"

Honor did. "He betrayed both of us. Did he love us at all?" That last sentence bubbled up from deep inside.

All her life she had loved her grandfather, and she'd thought he'd loved her. But he had turned out to be a man she didn't know at all.

"You can count on me," Royale said, her voice stronger. "'Cause I know I can count on you. You said you would free me, and even when you lost everything to Darah, you kept your word."

"I was raised to keep my word." *By a grandfather who was capable of betraying his own flesh and blood.*

Honor realized that Royale was weeping. She pulled her closer. "Don't worry. Way will open." The Quaker phrase mocked her.

"I don't know that. But I know I'm sticking with you."

Honor's eyes moistened at this.

"You got to think of marrying, though. Nobody need a governess or companion, and I don't want to work in a house with a master. You marry, and we can stay together."

Panic at the thought of marrying a near stranger swept through Honor. "Royale, I can't. Not now."

"Miss Honor, I already told you. We do what we got to. If it's between starving and working with a man in the house, then I'll do it. But better we stay together. We all we got left."

Unable to draw up words, Honor lay staring at the faint shadows on the ceiling. She must try again to find a haven for both of them. Royale had spoken the truth: they had only each other. Then she listened to the summer night in the city, the voices and footsteps of other people wafting through the open windows.

Samuel's tortured face flickered in her mind. She ached for him. He'd already lost so much, and now he would lose not only his mother but his dream of a better life in Ohio. Life had been so easy for her in Maryland, but it had all been an illusion. Did they all live just one step from disaster? *Oh, Lord, help.*

❖

SEPTEMBER 12, 1819

When another First Day came, Miriam was again too ill to go to meeting. Her friend Jemima Wool, white-haired, petite, and dressed in sober gray, arrived to walk with Miriam. Honor and Royale set out with her instead, taking turns holding Eli's pudgy hand. Honor opened a light-blue parasol against the blazing sun. Her black mourning dress and bonnet soaked in the cloying heat.

Last week Honor and Royale had both been too daunted to face a group of strangers, and Honor still did not feel like entering a meetinghouse full of people she'd never met. But she and Royale needed a place to live, jobs to support them—and soon. Fear sped her pulse as she walked sedately between Jemima and Royale.

"Miriam looked some better this morning, don't you think?" Royale asked.

Honor tilted her head to one side, peering around the parasol, realizing that Royale might be resisting the truth just as Samuel was.

Walking under her own gray parasol, Jemima kept up a gentle flow of words about the meeting and Pittsburgh.

Honor fanned herself and tried to observe the pleasantries.

"There it is!" Eli finally called out, pointing half a block ahead toward a white clapboard building with green-striped canvas awnings above the windows.

Honor smoothed her plain, modest dress and hoped she presented a cool and ladylike appearance in spite of the heat. Certainly positions might exist among the members of this large meeting, positions for her and Royale that would not require them to go through an agency.

They mounted the few steps into the shady interior of the unadorned building, its coolness a relief. They trailed Jemima to the women's side of the large room, filled with the hum of quiet conversation.

A tall, commanding woman with wisps of iron-gray hair escaping her plain bonnet stepped in front of them. "The black girl must sit on the rear bench."

The words stung. After Miriam's acceptance of Royale, Honor hadn't expected this. She should have. In Maryland, the slaves who had become Quakers sat separate in the balcony of the meetinghouse.

Still holding Eli's hand, Royale headed toward the rear bench, her head lowered.

Immobilized, Honor helplessly watched Royale's humiliation. *We're related by blood, but only the color of our skin matters—even here.*

Jemima nudged Honor into the nearest row. "Dorcas could have been more gentle," the older woman murmured.

Honor dropped onto the backless bench in a daze.

The meeting began with a quiet time of prayer. Then men and women rose at the prompting of the Inner Light—the Light of Christ—to quote Scripture or give insights. Finally Jemima rose and introduced Honor, and she was welcomed into the meeting. After a closing prayer, everyone gathered in the aisles and on the steps, greeting one another and exchanging news.

Royale, with Eli in hand, slipped outside, but Honor forced herself to stay and chat with women who came up to greet her individually and in small groups. She tried to connect names and faces, but both flowed through her mind like water through fingers.

"I'm looking for a position as a governess or lady's companion," she repeated. "And my maid is seeking a position too."

Her requests were met with polite surprise and delicate inquiries of what had brought her to Pittsburgh. But no leads. No one knew of anyone seeking either a governess or a companion. No one required another maid.

"The times are bad," Jemima said, summing up all the commiseration and rebuffs.

"I'm also interested in abolition." Honor posed this to the group of ladies around her. "Are there any other Friends here working toward that?"

Again the response was lukewarm at best. Emancipation was laudatory but had nothing to do with this meeting. Pennsylvania was a free state.

Then, even more unwelcome, first one and then another gentleman presented himself to Jemima to be introduced to Honor. One was a young attorney and another a middle-aged businessman. Each asked where she lived and if he might call on her. Each question caused her nerves to tense.

Jemima reminded them that Honor was in mourning and added that Miriam was not well enough for visitors.

Both men in turn bowed solicitously over Honor's hand, and from their expressions, she feared she would be seeing them again anyway.

Jemima patted her hand. "'Tis hard to be among strangers."

Honor's smile was merely a coating on her lips, and Samuel's anguished face glimmered in her mind. For some reason her fingers fidgeted as if they wanted to practice the signs Miriam continued teaching her.

Finally Jemima walked beside her down the steps, stiff from sitting so long. From the shade where they'd been waiting, Royale and Eli joined them.

"Miriam has been faithful to this meeting her whole life," Jemima said as they started home on foot. "It is a shame that her older son Samuel stopped coming to meeting. People didn't make the effort to learn how to speak to him in that hand language Miriam found. And it has made matters difficult for her and Samuel."

Honor had wondered why no friends visited the Cathwells in the week she'd been with them. Walking within the small circle of shade cast by her parasol, Honor pondered the end of her hopes. She had lost her home and her inheritance—and in the midst of very bad times. Everything stood against her. And intertwined with concern for herself and Royale was worry over Miriam, little Eli, and most of all, Samuel.

❁

That stifling afternoon Royale carried Eli to the back garden to play. Samuel's mother reclined on her chaise in the parlor, and at her request Samuel and Honor joined her.

Samuel resented his mother for including Honor. This woman had learned sign language, breached the barrier existing between him and everyone else. Also, she always looked him directly in the eye. Women ignored him. Why didn't Honor?

Her regard caused him to imagine impossibilities like having a wife and a family—things other men could possess, not him. The old, empty feeling dogged him.

The sheer curtains fluttered in the faint breeze. His mother began to sign and speak. "Samuel, I don't have much strength, so . . . please do not counter everything I say. I must settle matters . . . for thee and Eli, and soon."

Samuel's heart sank. *I waited too long.* Clenching his fist by his side, he felt like pounding his head.

"When we lost thy brother last year, the time was already too late for me to venture to the wilderness," Mother signed and said. "I have prayed and prayed, and now God has answered my prayers. He has provided someone else to go to Ohio with thee."

Samuel started at this, rising. "No." His fingers slashed the air.

His mother appeared to sigh. Then she rested her head on the back of the chaise and closed her hollow eyes.

Honor lifted her hand toward Samuel. "Please let her speak. She is so weak."

Samuel bent forward and touched his mother's hand. She opened her eyes. "I'm sorry, Mother."

She waited till he sat down again and continued. "I had thought of speaking to each of thee separately. But I have so little time left. Let us not argue. This is what I have to say. Samuel, thee cannot go alone to Ohio . . . with Eli still so young. Honor, no other recourse has opened to thee or Royale. Samuel, thee must consider offering marriage to Honor—" she forestalled his protest with a sharp gesture—"and, Honor, thee must consider accepting."

Samuel felt heat rising up his neck and face. He could not look at Honor, could not bear to see the rejection on her face.

Glancing finally from the corner of his eye, he saw that Honor was wiping away tears. Was she crying because his mother was dying? Or was she upset over the thought of being forced by necessity to consider marrying someone like him?

"Arranged marriages or marriages of convenience are not uncommon," his mother continued, her hand lowering as if she were losing strength. "My own parents met on the day they wed. And thee remembers the girl next door, Samuel. When her parents died at the same time we lost thy brother, her uncle came and took her home with him to marry a neighbor of his, a prosperous farmer. She has written to me that she is fine and happy. A couple can learn to love one another if there is trust."

Samuel watched his mother's slowing fingers, but he knew a woman would do almost anything to avoid being burdened with a deaf man. Now he would have to suffer through Honor's excuses as to why she couldn't marry him.

"I must rest now," Mother signed and said. "The two of thee should sit at the table and discuss this. I cannot force either of thee to do this, but I urge thee both to discuss it honestly."

Honor rose and spoke to his mother; then she complied, walking into the kitchen.

Samuel stayed where he was. This could not be happening.

His mother rapped the wooden leg of Samuel's chair.

He looked up, and she motioned for him to go to the table in the kitchen. He rose slowly, reluctantly, obediently.

At the table, he took the place facing Honor. "I did not know my mother would say that," he signed, trying to stop this before it went further. "I have never thought of marriage. Who would marry a deaf-mute?"

She dismissed this idea with a scornful expression. "Thee is hardworking and caring. Deafness means thee cannot hear. That is all."

Her proficiency in sign grew every time he talked to her, increasing his discomfort as the barrier between them lessened. "You cannot want to marry me."

"I do not want to marry, but there are no jobs for me or Royale. This house . . ." She gestured toward the For Sale sign and shrugged. "Thee plans to leave. What will we do?"

Samuel bowed his head and clasped his hands together. Her honesty shocked him. He'd been so wrapped up in his plans and his worry over his mother's health that he had not thought of what this lady was facing. However, marriage—allowing someone other than family to come so close . . .

❖

Honor could not sit and watch his distress. Her own doubt and hurt goaded her.

Outside, she collapsed onto the shaded garden seat near Royale. Royale glanced over her shoulder, then rolled a wooden ball to Eli, who was waiting across from her in the shade of another tree. Royale called out, encouraging the child to get it and roll it back. She turned to Honor. "What Miriam say?"

Honor closed her eyes, wishing she could block out everything she didn't want to face. Sadness twisted her heart. Drawing in a deep breath, Honor answered Royale. "Miriam suggested that Samuel offer to marry me and take us four to Ohio."

Royale's face opened with hope. "Will you marry him if he ask you?"

Honor looked away, resenting Royale's hopefulness, but honesty forced her to continue. Royale was counting on her, and the two of them had come face-to-face with a stone wall. "I don't know if I am in a position to reject his offer." Each word felt like a penance.

"Other men notice you at meeting," Royale offered tentatively. "I saw how they look at you." She accepted the ball from Eli and he ran back to his place, laughing.

"Yes, they might want to court me, but I'm in mourning. No one can court me or make an offer for my hand until a year passes. Where would we stay till then?" She thought of Darah, going to stay with Alec's aunt.

"Then how can you marry Samuel?"

"Samuel doesn't go about in society like others. I suppose we'd marry, then leave for Ohio."

Samuel entered the back garden, heading straight toward them. Honor fought panic, the urge to flee.

Eli ran to his uncle, showing the ball. Samuel patted his head and gazed uncertainly toward them.

Royale glanced between him and Honor, and without a word, she went to Eli and led him into the house.

❖

Samuel sat awkwardly beside Honor, overshadowing her with his large frame.

His discomfort crashed against her like the ocean tide. She stiffened herself against allowing her frustration to show. Reluctantly, she signed, "What will we do?"

Samuel rubbed his face with both hands, wishing he could roll back time. "Is my mother really dying?"

"Yes," Honor signed, her hand motion swift and sharp.

Samuel's heart clenched so tightly that he felt a moan deep inside. He looked away. He'd tried to avoid the fact, but it was undeniable now. How could he go on without his mother?

The woman at his side did not move. What was she thinking? The weight of what was taking place was crushing him. "You can't want to marry me." Samuel watched her hands, though fearful to see her reply.

Honor raised her eyes to his. "I do not want to marry any man. I'm still in mourning. I shouldn't marry this soon. But I can do nothing else."

She had been forthright with him, and he must not disrespect her by being less forthright. "If my mother dies, I will not be able to care for Eli and work and . . ."

"And be able to talk with others," she finished for him. "I understand. Both of us need someone."

Samuel nodded and, propping his elbows on his knees, buried his face in his hands. He steeled himself to face both their situations. He could not wish away what was happening. He weighed Honor's words.

It galled him that only at this point, the point of last resort, would a woman consider marrying him, but the world was the way it was. His mother had said that people could learn to love one another if there was trust. Was there trust between them? Could there be?

After a moment she touched his shoulder lightly.

He looked up, knowing that he must make this decision, hating that he must make this decision.

"We know each other little, but what are we to do?" she signed with effort. "Does thee know of a place for respectable unmarried women where I can stay?"

He shook his head.

"Is there anyone who will go to Ohio with thee?" She continued to point out the obvious.

Again he shook his head. No friends. No family left.

"Then . . . ?" She opened her palms in a gesture of helplessness.

His throat closed even though he never spoke words. Eli was depending on him, so what choice did he have? What choice did she have? The moment to accept the inevitable had fallen upon both of them.

He slowly dropped to one knee. "Honor Penworthy, will you be my wife and go to Ohio with me?"

Chapter 4

Honeybees buzzed around the flowering bushes as Honor stared at the man kneeling at her feet. A curious numbness gripped her, and a floating sensation untethered her mind like a flag drifting on the breeze. She tried to pull her thoughts together. How had God let her come to this?

But Miriam said she had prayed for her son, prayed for someone to go to Ohio with him and be his wife. Was Honor the answer to Miriam's prayer for Samuel? Even if she didn't want to be? *The man has proposed to me. I must not sit silent.*

She gazed upward at the limitless blue sky above the surrounding roofs and felt trapped.

Samuel had bowed his head, no longer looking at her. The humility in his posture touched her. He still expected her to balk, to refuse.

Why was she hesitating? Honor and Samuel had both come to a point non plus, no options left. She gently lifted his chin so their gazes met. "Yes," she signed, "I will be thy wife." Each heavy word jarred her like a blow.

Samuel's expression of disbelief told her she'd been right. He hadn't expected her to accept, not even as a last resort. Her sympathy heightened, drawing her toward him. She stroked his cheek. Samuel had suffered much just because he couldn't hear. She didn't think him less a man because of his deafness. She just didn't want to marry him, marry any man she didn't love. Now she must find out how to do this: marry here and move to the wilderness of Ohio.

In the bushes behind her head, a bird began whistling one note over and over as if prompting her, *Do it. Do it.* "Come sit. We must talk." She patted the sun-bleached bench.

He rose and sat beside her, not looking toward her.

She gathered her wayward thoughts like wisps of raw cotton drifting in the air. Propriety, a safe territory, presented itself first. She motioned toward her black dress. "The wedding must be private." That would be a problem since Quaker weddings had to be public. Without any ordained ministers in the Quaker religion, all the members present had to sign the marriage certificate as witnesses.

"My mother will know what to do," he offered.

Then a question occurred to Honor. "Why does thee want to go to Ohio?"

At this, he turned to her. "I want to have my own glassworks, my own workshop." His fingers were emphatic.

She nodded, understanding immediately why he would choose this. Still, she needed more details, more reassurance from him. She struggled to sign a more complicated sentence. "Does thee have funds enough for thy own shop?" Though heedless of wealth, she could not merely accept "poor" as a step up from "penniless." Living humbly didn't concern her, but poverty did.

Samuel looked her in the eye. "Yes. I have bought land near Cincinnati. It has a house and a large barn I can use for my work."

"Thee has enough funds for travel expenses for four? I cannot leave Royale." Another thought occurred. "We must hire and pay her."

"Very well. She is good with Eli."

She had to make something else clear to him. "Samuel, I do not know how to keep house. Royale can help, but she'll often be occupied with Eli. . . ."

He shrugged.

The short time she'd spent here had taught her how much she didn't know about keeping house. She doubted he understood completely. So she ventured another question. "Will we be able to pay for house help?"

He nodded again. "We will have enough to live comfortably."

She hesitated to press him. She could only hope her idea of *comfortable* corresponded to his.

"You will speak to my mother about the wedding?" he asked, looking restless.

Of course, *she* would have to be the one to take care of arrangements with Miriam. He was marrying her so she could be the one to take care of all the communicating with the speaking world for the rest of his life. And he had said, "Will *you* be my wife," not "*thee*," and he no longer attended meeting. She must broach that with him, but not now.

This arranged marriage. Samuel's deafness. The care of his three-year-old nephew. A suffocating weight settled over her, followed by something like escalating panic.

❖

SEPTEMBER 14, 1819

Two days later, the sun had finally lowered into twilight, golden rays gleaming through the parlor windows. It was his wedding day. Uncomfortable and hot, Samuel stood in his First Day suit, which Royale had brushed and pressed. Now Royale stood near the door, holding Eli in her arms. Samuel's mother reclined on her chaise, ready to act as witness. White-haired Jemima Wool had come to be the other witness.

Samuel felt trapped, yet something—some hope—stirred within him. Today he was getting a wife, something he had thought impossible. His bride, Honor, stood beside him, dressed in all he'd ever seen her wear—deep black—and her face was as fixed as if she were sitting for a portrait. He feared she would falter now.

Standing with them in front of the cold fireplace, a local Congregational minister who'd known Samuel's father had come to officiate. This minister would have to do, though neither bride nor groom shared his denomination.

The fact that Honor was still in deep mourning had saved him from the spectacle of a Quaker wedding and had persuaded the minister to come to his home to perform this private ceremony. But when it came to it, would Honor actually go through with the marriage?

The minister bowed his head in prayer. Samuel mirrored him but was unable to pray. God's latest treachery roiled inside him—he couldn't set aside his anger over his mother's illness. And his stiff bride looked as if she were facing the scaffold.

Honor's fingers shook as they signed, "Amen."

Now the minister looked to him. Samuel tried to read the man's lips and caught fragments of his speech. Honor touched his arm, and Samuel, glancing sideways, watched her laboriously sign the vows he was to agree to today. Quakers didn't take vows; they made promises or affirmations. He felt oddly guilty.

Again she nudged him, and he began to repeat the vows in sign to her.

Then she signed hers to him. "I, Honor, take thee, Samuel, to be my lawful wedded husband, to have and to hold from this day forward: for better, for worse; for richer, for poorer . . ."

He watched as her whole body shuddered, her hand trembling. She would surely flee from him now.

Instead she paused and mastered herself. She went on, steady and determined. ". . . in sickness and in health; to love, cherish, and to obey till death us do part, according to God's holy ordinance; and thereto I give thee my troth."

When the vows had been spoken, the two stared at each other. Dread gnawed at him. She could still back out.

Then Honor translated the minister's next words: "Where is the ring?"

Samuel lifted his grandmother's wedding ring, a cool, thick gold band, from his pocket. He repeated in sign the final lines of the vows: "With this ring I thee wed, with my body I thee worship, and with all my worldly goods I thee endow. In the name of the Father and of the Son and of the Holy Ghost. Amen."

In that moment his gaze and Honor's met, and the connection sucked all the air from his lungs. Even strained, even in Quaker mourning, his Honor was beautiful and possessed a fierce dignity that emanated from her core. Samuel had somehow gained not only a bride, but one of whom he knew he was unworthy. He expected her to shrink away.

But she didn't, and he placed the ring on her finger. Then she signed, "I have given thee my promises. I will honor them."

So the vow-taking had upset her too. Still buffeted within, Samuel replied, "I will also."

The pastor finished, "I now pronounce you man and wife. You may kiss the bride."

Samuel bent his head but could not make himself go the last few inches to touch Honor's mouth.

Honor rose up on tiptoe and pressed her cool, dry lips to his, then stepped back.

The touch sent shock waves through him. He held all reaction in, unnerved but unwilling to let it show.

He led Honor to the kitchen table, where he, Honor, and the pastor signed the marriage certificate, as did his mother and Jemima as witnesses. Jemima had baked a light French-style cake with creamy white frosting. They all gathered around the table to eat it. The sweetness nearly gagged Samuel as much as did everyone's attempts to appear cheerful.

He watched the faces around the table. No one looked truly happy, least of all his bride, who had withdrawn further from him—from everyone, really. And he didn't blame her. The wedding night loomed over both of them. He couldn't imagine that she would welcome him. *I can't believe this is happening to me.*

❁

As Royale cleared the table and began to wash the few dishes, Honor tried to keep a faint smile on her lips, show a serene countenance to all. Be the happy bride. However, her thoughts still floated through her head in a kind of daze. She had no idea whether her husband even liked her. And thinking of the wedding night scattered her thoughts further.

First the minister rose to take his leave. He paused to speak to Miriam. Then he bowed over Honor's hand, clapped Samuel on the back, and was gone. Jemima rose also, accepted their thanks, and left. The four remaining adults sat around the table. Eli was slumped on Royale's lap, nearly asleep.

Honor mentally drew herself together. "Miriam," she said and signed, "thee needs to go to bed. Samuel, please help thy mother."

Royale stood. "I'll get Eli into bed too." The overtired child whimpered as she carried him up the stairs, humming an old song.

By the day's last light, Honor followed Samuel as he carried Miriam to her first-floor bedroom. He set her down gently and left the room. Honor helped Miriam out of her dress and into her nightgown.

"Honor, I am so happy. I know this marriage is not what thee came to Pittsburgh to find. Yet even as I prayed for a wife for Samuel, I also prayed for that woman herself. God will bless thee. And my Samuel is an honest man with a kind, true heart."

Honor's strength was draining from her and evaporating, but she rallied. "I would not have married him if I didn't believe that." *And he will always need me, so he'll never betray me.* A bitter thought.

Honor helped Miriam lift her legs into bed and covered her with a soft, worn sheet. She set the handbell next to Miriam, who had flattened somehow, now appearing like a sketch of herself on paper. "Call me if thee needs me."

"I'll try not to."

Honor's body clenched. Yes, this would be her wedding night. How would she face it?

❖

Honor climbed the steps, feeling as if she were girding herself for battle. What did she know about husbands and wives and consummation? Royale had already moved her few things into the bedroom that Eli and Samuel had once shared. Now Royale would sleep with the child. And Samuel with Honor, his wife.

At the head of the stairs, Honor approached the room where her husband waited for her. The door stood open and her husband sat on the bed, his head bent and his hands hanging in front of him, folded. The very picture of dejection. She wondered if she looked as gloomy. *This is my husband.* Her heart went out to him. His mother was dying, and now he had been forced to marry a stranger.

Inhaling deeply, she entered the shadowy room, and he must have felt her step because he rose politely but wouldn't meet her eyes. As he seated himself again, she considered what to say. She nearly moved to the chair but changed her mind and sat next to him, drawing near. The bed ropes creaked; the bed dipped, sliding her closer to him. *This is my husband.*

Facing forward, she signed, "This is very awkward. We barely know each other."

He hazarded a glance toward her and nodded.

She kept her gaze directed at the open door but found his hand and took it in her left so she could still sign. Her heart beat like a man running on an uneven road. "Will thee give me some time alone?"

He nodded, rose in one quick surge, and was out the door.

Across the hall, Royale peered from her own door. "You need me to help you undress?"

The thought of asking Samuel to help with her many buttons and laces sent heat through Honor. "Please."

Royale proceeded to go through the nightly routine of assisting Honor and putting away her clothing neatly. As Honor sat and Royale unpinned her hair, she was tempted to ask Royale what she knew of the marriage bed but decided not to embarrass them both. "Oh, we will begin paying thee, Royale. I'm sorry I didn't start that earlier—"

"It be all right. I know you makin' sure I safe and got a place."

"It's different now. Samuel said we could afford to pay thee, and he appreciates how good thee is with Eli."

"I happy to hear that." When Royale finished, she squeezed both of Honor's shoulders. "You be fine." And she slipped from the room, closing the door behind her.

Honor did not know if she believed Royale.

Samuel opened the door and stepped inside. The last of the sunset glowed at the window.

Shaking, Honor stood from her seat and, not looking at him, went to the far side of the bed and slipped under the covers. Her heart beat so fast, she felt she could faint.

He sat down and the bed shifted.

This is my husband.

Then Miriam's bell rang, and another presentiment bathed Honor with sharp, cold dread.

❁

SEPTEMBER 16, 1819

Honor's wedding night had been Miriam's last evening in this vale of tears. So in her best mourning dress and stiff with grief, Honor stood at Miriam's graveside beside Samuel, who held a bewildered Eli in his arms. Royale stood a step behind Honor, weeping. Tall trees shaded them in the solemn place. Modest limestone markers dotted the green grass.

Honor realized now that Samuel's mother must have

been just holding herself together till Samuel had someone to speak for him, to go with him. Now she was being buried beside her husband in the Society of Friends cemetery. Honor gripped her frayed composure, stilling a deep trembling.

In the oppressive heat, one of the older Quakers stood at the head of the grave and read William Penn's soothing words in a deep, gravelly voice:

> "'And this is the Comfort of the Good, that the Grave cannot hold them, and that they live as soon as they die. For Death is no more than a Turning of us over from Time to Eternity. . . . Death then, being the Way and Condition of Life, we cannot love to live, if we cannot bear to die.'"

Honor craved the solace of these familiar words. She signed them to Samuel but couldn't tell if he was paying any attention to her or not. She had known Miriam so briefly; still the loss stung like an open cut.

Dressed all in black, Jemima Wool and other older members from the local meeting had come along to the interment. Now Jemima stepped forward to speak. "From girlhood on, Miriam was a blessing to everyone. A strong woman of faith, a good wife and mother. She will be missed."

The rest nodded and murmured their agreement.

As the men lowered the simple pine coffin into the earth, Honor bent her head and instinctively claimed Samuel's free hand, rough and dry even through her thin summer glove. "Ashes to ashes, dust to dust," she whispered, remembering her grandfather's funeral. She swallowed a gasp at a stitch of intense pain in her side.

Just as Honor, Royale, and their new family were about to get into a hack for the ride home, the land agent, a member of the local Quaker meeting, approached them. He handed Samuel a note with a solemn nod, then turned to her. "I hear that thee and Samuel were married?"

"Yes." *Two days ago.*

"May God bless thy union. I will come tomorrow with the papers to transfer the deed."

So the house had been sold. Honor felt as if someone had slammed a door against her. She let Samuel help her into the hack. Even in her extremity, she noted that he performed the same courtesy for Royale. She clung to that. Miriam had said her son was good and kind. Honor could only hope that would continue now that Miriam was with the Lord.

❖

Later that day, through the narrow, airless, grimy streets, Honor reluctantly accompanied Samuel to the manufactory where he worked so he could get his tools and quit. Why did they have to go there today, the day of Miriam's funeral? But, of course, the land agent was coming to complete the sale of the house tomorrow, and they must prepare to leave for faraway Ohio and the land Samuel had already bought.

Honor struggled to keep her mind focused on the present, not what might be coming toward her. *"Sufficient unto the day is the evil thereof"*—the Gospel of Matthew stated it well.

At the factory's wide double doors, the heat of the place hit her, wrapping itself around her face and smothering her. She stood gasping, watching men puffing into long-stemmed blowpipes, shaping terrifying molten glass into molds. And others fearlessly thrust tubes with the molten glass back inside small furnaces with open doors, alive with orange-and-blue flames. Honor had never seen anything like it. She fought the urge to flee from the hellish scene.

Samuel glanced into her face and tugged on her arm, prompting her to come with him. Still she held back. Then a few men did start looking her way, and this moved her forward. She didn't want to make a spectacle of herself here.

The unfamiliar, harsh odors of molten glass and coal-burning furnaces filled her nostrils and raised her gorge. She clung to Samuel's arm as he drew her toward what must be his place.

❖

Samuel's area sat empty. No one had turned toward him. The other glassblowers always ignored him. Yet even while intent on their dangerous work, they began to acknowledge his bride's presence, not his. He loved working with glass. But he hated this factory, though it was the place where the father who'd loved him in spite of his deafness had taught him his trade. His memory brought up an image of his father working here. Today he could leave it once and for all—a break he desired yet dreaded, too.

Feeling as if he were standing on the edge of a cliff, he led Honor along the side of the large, dim room to the manager's small office. Usually they communicated with brief notes, but now, with Honor translating, he introduced her as his wife. The man's expression at the announcement irked Samuel, but he supposed he might as well get used to it, if he ever could. Samuel explained to the manager that he was leaving the manufactory. The manager had risen for Honor and stood behind his desk in rolled-up shirtsleeves, now staring at Samuel. Then he addressed Honor.

"He says he'll give thee a raise if thee stays," she signed.

"Tell him we're going to Ohio, where I'll set up my own glass shop," Samuel signed.

The manager looked surprised, but then he startled Samuel by offering his hand.

Samuel accepted it. They shook, and after receiving the pay he was owed, Samuel and Honor left the office. They walked together to Samuel's station, where he methodically packed his long wooden toolbox with paddles, tongs, shears, hooks, metal blowpipes, and bellows.

The other men evidently started to notice he was packing up. One began talking to Honor and the manager, who'd apparently followed Samuel from the office. When Samuel finished and looked up, all work had stopped. The other glassblowers had turned, regarding him.

Samuel stood, frozen. Why were they acknowledging him now?

Honor signed, "I told them your news—about your mother and about Ohio."

One glassblower and then another raised his hand to Samuel as if in salute. Samuel stared at them. Most of these men had never even waved hello or good-bye to him. Today, for the first time, he felt a part of them, part of this band of men who worked in a hot, dangerous, yet useful and often-beautiful craft.

Then he, too, raised his hand to them. His throat thickened, clogged with his reaction to this tribute.

Honor and the manager accompanied him to the wide-open doors, and the manager shook hands with him again, thanking him for his work for the company. As Samuel turned his back, cold uncertainty flashed through him. He felt himself stepping into the dark unknown. Could he actually leave Pittsburgh, go somewhere he'd never seen, and set up a shop of his own?

The conflict between the known and the unknown sliced into Samuel like a knife. Sweat that had nothing to do with the heat of the forges or the summer day beaded on his forehead.

Honor walked beside him under a parasol, not looking toward him, appearing drained by the heat and by the events of the day.

He led her toward home, the heavy toolbox slung over his back, the weight of his isolation over his heart, bitter over his inability to connect with the other glassblowers. They might have been friends.

Honor stumbled over the uneven cobblestones, and he offered her his free arm. When she took it, he slowed to her pace. Sometimes when he looked at her, he couldn't breathe. But he had to hide his desire for her. So far their acquaintance had been one crisis after another, no time to get to know each other.

But did his wife want to get to know him? Would there always be this separation? He didn't know how to make friends, especially with a woman, a wife.

❖

SEPTEMBER 20, 1819

A few days later, Honor sat at Miriam's secretary desk in the parlor. She'd hunted through the pigeonholes and located a quill, ink, paper, sealing wax, and a seal. She had carefully laid out all of these on the fold-down desk. But she could not make herself lift the pen to dip it.

Never before had Honor resented the Inner Light. Never before had she felt a stronger prompting to do something. And of course, it would be something she did not want to do.

Father, I do not want to write a letter to Darah.

The prompting did not relent.

Already the day's heat was beginning to suffocate her. She closed her eyes and bent her head into both hands. "Father," she whispered, "my life in Maryland is over. I don't want to keep in touch with my cousin. She doesn't need me. She will probably read my missive with scorn or, worse, laughter."

Darah isn't laughing now.

Honor's eyes flew open. The words had come without a voice—just the words, just the feeling. She tried to discount what she'd thought. Tears flashed into her eyes at the memory of Darah standing with Alec Martin at their grandfather's graveside.

The prompting increased, demanding.

Blinking away the moisture, she picked up the quill and penned:

Dear Cousin,

I am writing to let thee know that I have married a Friend in Pittsburgh, Samuel Cathwell. He is a glassblower by trade. We are about to move to Ohio, near Cincinnati. Royale is going with us.

She knew she should add an inquiry about how Darah was, but she could not. Darah was doing very well indeed. She had inherited High Oaks and over a hundred slaves and was living comfortably with Alec's aunt while waiting for her mourning period to end so she and Alec could marry.

Honor ended the letter formally:

Thy obedient servant,
Mrs. Samuel Cathwell

Before her trembling hands could tear it up, she sanded the ink, heated the wax, and sealed the folded letter.

She rose, shaken. She hoped that Darah didn't read anything sad into the sparse words. She didn't want her cousin's pity.

Honor heard Royale opening the kitchen door; then a man's voice sounded. The land agent, no doubt. She entered the kitchen, where Samuel had risen in silent greeting. "Good day, Friend," she said and signed.

The three of them sat at the round table. Royale led Eli

outside to play. While Honor signed the agent's words to Samuel and he set his name to the documents, transferring the deed and receiving a bank draft for the price of the house, Honor studied her husband.

Going with him to the manufactory had increased her respect for Samuel Cathwell. How did he do such dangerous and exacting work? And even in the heat of summer.

Within a few minutes the transaction was done. The land agent departed.

As her husband rose to leave, Honor stopped him. Why didn't he tell her what she needed to know without being asked? "When do we leave for Ohio?"

"Within the month. We must go to the docks and make reservations on a steamboat to Cincinnati."

"A steamboat?" The idea of trying out this newest mode of travel startled her.

"I will help you pack," Samuel signed. "We will need the household items, but I have sold the house furnished."

Honor had trouble drawing breath and could only nod. Another deeply unwelcome packing up and leaving. She tried to think of something to say, but no thoughts or words appeared. Just the taunting image of Darah and Alec, stone-faced, staring at her across her grandfather's grave.

Chapter 5

OCTOBER 15, 1819

After nearly a month of preparation, Honor stood uncertainly on the Pittsburgh wharf with Samuel at her side. At her elbow was Royale with Eli in hand. This place marked the head of the mighty Ohio, where two rivers—the Allegheny and Monongahela—converged.

A trace of autumn chill chose this morning to appear, raising a billowing, cloaking mist. The murky, turbulent sky reflected her feelings toward her husband, toward this journey to a new home. She did not want to get on that steamboat.

A high whistle sounded, goading her. In the jostling but groggy crowd, Honor urged Royale and Eli toward the gangplank. Samuel strode forward and offered Royale his hand to help her onto the plank. Then he turned to Honor.

Honor hesitated. She felt as if she were about to step across some invisible but palpable line. Once on deck, there would be no turning back. She would be putting her whole trust in this distant, confusing man who had married her only out of necessity or obligation, not out of love nor even fondness.

He signed, "What's wrong?"

"Nothing." Her pulse thrumming at her temples, she grasped his hand. Still she glanced over her shoulder one last time. But why? Nothing, no one remained for her in Pittsburgh. With a deep breath, she stepped aboard.

While gaining control over her unruly emotions, Honor scanned the steamboat, the first she'd ever boarded. The craft looked shiny new, neat and imposing with its tall black smokestack. Two large cabins sat in the middle of the deck, leaving plenty of room to walk around. Through the mist, she saw the top rim of a large paddle wheel attached to the side of the boat. She tried to draw confidence from these signs of progress and attention to detail.

A uniformed man greeted them immediately, looking at a black ledger in his hand. "Name, please?"

For a moment Honor waited for Samuel, the man, to reply for them. Then she remembered she was Samuel's voice. "We are the Cathwells. I am Mrs. Samuel Cathwell." This was the first time she had given her new name aloud. She felt as if she were speaking of someone else.

The official lifted an eyebrow, no doubt at her replying instead of her husband. He jotted something in the book with a pencil. "You will be in Cincinnati tomorrow evening." And then he cocked his head as if waiting for her response.

"One night?" Honor echoed in genuine surprise, remembering to sign this to Samuel.

"Yes," the man said, beaming smugly. "We will arrive at Cincinnati tomorrow evening."

She gaped at him. "That quickly?" When she'd bought the tickets, she hadn't asked how long the journey would be. Her dread of traveling had rendered her nearly silent. But she'd expected she would have to endure days and nights of travel—difficult, but it would provide her time to think, to prepare, before they arrived at a strange new place. Instead the future was rushing forth to engulf her.

"The old keelboats sometimes took two weeks or more to reach Cincinnati." The official had been eyeing them as he spoke. "What's that you're doing with your hands?"

At the rude question, she primmed her lips. "My husband is deaf, so I speak to him in sign language." She did not sign this exchange to Samuel.

The official raised both eyebrows. "A good-looking woman like you had to marry a deaf-mute?"

The man's impertinent question made Honor bridle. She scalded him with a glance and moved them past. She didn't appreciate the way people deemed Samuel less than he was. She made sure she clung to his arm, letting it be known she didn't scorn him.

As more passengers arrived, she, Samuel, and Royale, with Eli huddled against her shoulder, gazed around. The newness of this experience dawned on Honor, lifting her spirits. Riverboat travel was not even a decade old. This was something to see, something she would remember all her life. A true adventure.

She felt a throbbing beneath their feet. "Can thee feel that?" she signed to Samuel, pointing to the deck.

"Yes. It is the steam engine that powers the wheel." He gestured toward the paddle wheel. "The engine burns coal, and the steam turns the wheel, which propels the boat."

"Thee has been on a steamboat before?"

"No, but I saw the first steamboat leave Pittsburgh harbor in 1811," Samuel commented as he squired her to the foredeck. Samuel's confidence and knowledge bolstered her.

She heard the order: "Cast off!"

Sharply she turned for one last glance of Pittsburgh, but now the mist concealed it. She moved closer to Samuel, needing his support. Royale huddled closer to Samuel also, Eli clinging tightly to her. The child had become more quiet and withdrawn over the past weeks. This disruption had affected him, too. The moment of departing united them. *Farewell, Miriam.*

The engine roared beneath them, and the paddle wheel began to turn, sending up water. The boat swooped forward, away from land onto the mighty river. Honor grabbed the deck railing, as did Royale. Samuel stood behind Honor as if ready to catch her. But soon the motion evened out, and as they headed west, the mist flew past them.

The die had been cast.

Under her feet, the motion was different from the rocking motion of the sailing ship they'd traveled on from Maryland to Philadelphia. She'd been afraid she might be seasick again, but no. Both the shock of leaving and the elation of the new experience evaporated at last. Fatigued, Honor sat down on a bench outside the cabin door marked

Ladies, and Royale sat next to her. Eli rested his head in her lap, content to be held.

Scanning the deck, Honor noted that she and Royale were among only a few women on board. She glanced around at the few other passengers. With an eye toward serviceability, not elegance, Honor wore her plainest mourning dress and bonnet. But a few of the men traveling with them sported expensive suits, intricate white cravats, and tall beaver hats.

A black woman dressed in a dark dress and a starched white apron approached her. "If you follow me, please, ma'am, I'll show you and your maid the ladies' compartment."

Honor signed this to Samuel and left Eli with him. Finally the child appeared interested in what was going on, though he stayed close to Samuel. The ladies' compartment, at the front of the nearest cabin, was furnished with a bench along one wall, as well as four berths, two on each of the longer paneled walls. In one corner stood a cabinet where the chamber commode was discreetly positioned behind a curtain. Beside it were a marble-topped vanity with a secured ewer and a mirror hanging on the wall. Everything was spotless and new.

"This is very well-appointed," Honor breathed. "I didn't think the accommodations would be so comfortable."

"Yes, ma'am." The woman looked at Honor and then considered Royale, her forehead wrinkled in concern.

"Yes?" Honor prompted.

"I think your maid best sleep with me in my quarters. I got an extra bunk for when the boat has more passengers and need another maid."

"That be fine with me," Royale spoke up. "Eli probably want to stay with his uncle anyway. He feel more safe."

The maid looked relieved, and Honor sighed, reassured. She had been concerned that there might not be any quarters for Royale and that she'd be expected to sleep outside, unprotected, something Honor would not permit.

"Anytime you need anything," the boat's maid continued, "you tell your maid and I'll get it." She left them, closing the door behind her.

Royale gazed around her, standing in the middle of the room. "I think I'm getting so I understand Mr. Cathwell better when he's signing. How do I sign 'Yes, sir,' again?"

Honor demonstrated the sign she'd made up for *sir*, a motion toward the head as if tipping a hat. She had found spelling out each word in the sign alphabet arduous and was trying to come up with simple motions for more of the oft-repeated words and phrases.

Royale imitated the sign and added a nod with it to denote "Yes, sir." Then she practiced "No, sir," a shake of the head with the tipping motion.

Honor had suggested that now that Royale was free and had revealed their blood connection to her, she should dispense with the use of *ma'am*, *Miss Honor*, and *sir*. But Royale had insisted that she was the hired maid and it wouldn't be proper. Something more than that lay behind it—something that Royale evidently needed—so Honor let her have her way. No doubt part of it was the strict line separating the races. Any breach of this would fall hardest on Royale.

Honor set her small traveling bag on one of the berths and sighed again. Since leaving Maryland, she had not slept well; after weeks of cleaning and packing, she was exhausted. She wished she could lie down here and now.

But Samuel might need her to communicate. So they went out onto the deck and sat on the bench again. Only two days and one night on this craft. Honor leaned back against the cabin wall and sent her husband a smile. He scowled at her, and it froze her in place. *I must speak to Samuel, find out more about where we will be settling. And why he's angry.*

❁

The swift, modern steamboat fascinated Samuel, but he hated being trapped in one place with a lot of people he didn't know. Worse, his new wife hadn't wanted to get on board the boat this morning, hadn't wanted to leave with him. He'd felt her reluctance.

When Honor and Royale came out of the ladies' compartment, he gave Eli to Royale's care and walked to the railing. Taking off his hat, he swiped his cuff over his forehead, wiping away the early mist collected there. Cutting ties with all he'd ever known had wound him up like a top. He couldn't settle down.

One of the men, well dressed and handsome, leaned against the rail near him and stared at Honor from under the brim of his beaver hat. Other men kept looking at Honor, some discreetly, some blatantly. But what could he do to prevent them from eyeing his wife? Was she returning their interest?

Samuel turned toward Honor, seated on the bench. Her face was shielded from him by her bonnet brim, wide and dark. He walked over and looked down at her. Her eyes were closed. But perhaps she had heard him coming and closed her eyes. Had she been looking back at the man by the railing?

Honor opened her eyes. Had she heard Samuel's footsteps? She patted a spot next to her on the red-painted bench. "Please, may we talk?" she signed.

The irritation of being with strangers, the unexpected homesickness, and the pretty wife who was a temptation to other men all combined to gall him. But at her request he sat, staring at the heavily forested shoreline they flowed past.

"Please tell me everything thee has planned for our home in Ohio. What kind of place is it?"

"The description of our property is a large barn, a house, and ten tillable acres."

"How far is this from Cincinnati proper?"

He shrugged. "The letter said half a day's ride to Sharpesburg."

Honor tilted her head as if wanting to see his face better around the confines of her bonnet brim. "Is it a large town?"

He shrugged again.

She touched his shoulder. "I need to know where we are going. What to expect."

He rose. "Later." He was a cur for leaving it at that. But how could he tell her the truth? That was all he knew.

❖

With the sun high overhead, Honor walked to the railing, claimed Samuel's arm, and signed to him that the dinner bell had just been rung.

An urgent shout—clearly nothing to do with the dinner

bell—went up from the passengers and crew. Alarmed, Honor swung around to see what was upsetting everyone.

What she saw shocked her speechless. A canoe with three bare-chested Indians had launched from a nearby island. They were paddling straight toward the steamboat. Stories of scalpings flashed through her mind. Would they be attacked?

On deck, crew members brought out concealed rifles, and some of the passengers drew pistols. All the armed men took aim at the Indians. One of the crew sent a warning shot over their heads.

Honor had heard a gunshot before, but not one aimed toward another human. She stood rooted to the spot.

Samuel yanked her closer and shoved her behind him. Royale hurried over with Eli and hunkered down behind Samuel too.

Frightened yet unable to resist curiosity, Honor peered around her husband's broad back, gripping his sleeves from behind. The Indians wore buckskin and feathers but were too far away for her to distinguish more than that.

Then the Indians held up their hands, showing that they held no weapons. They pointed to the boat, chattering to each other and yelling with obvious amazement.

"Oh!" she cried out, fearful but hoping to defuse possible violence. The Indians didn't look as if they intended to attack. They were merely marveling. "They just haven't seen a steamboat before!"

"That may be," the captain said, appearing on deck with a pistol in hand. "Still, keep those rifles pointed at them. But don't shoot unless they try to board!"

The Indians stopped coming nearer but kept pace with

the boat for about a mile or so, craning their necks to fully view the marvel. Then they turned their canoe aside and headed for another island.

Honor watched the entire time, her tension easing after the canoe disappeared from sight. Once the steamboat passed that island, the crew lowered their rifles, but a few remained at the rear, watchful, in case more Indians appeared.

Samuel turned and faced her, gripping her shoulders gently as if she might break in his grasp. Then he released her, signing, "Are you all right?"

After a morning of his surly company, his concern and touch now scattered her wits. She inhaled the clear air, tinged by the smell of burning coal. "I'm fine." She tentatively placed one hand over his and signed with the other. "I understand how the Indians feel, seeing their first steamboat. I had never seen a canoe with Indians." She grinned at her own whimsy.

Samuel looked mystified at her smile but moved his hand to the small of her back, guiding her to the long table and benches secured to the deck between the two cabins. Above, a canvas canopy fluttered in the breeze, shielding them from sun or rain.

Samuel's unexpected concern lifted Honor's mood. The sky stretched overhead so blue, and the breeze was so refreshing and fragrant with the scent of ham, the steamboat so unexpectedly comfortable. For the first time in many weeks, she found herself smiling naturally, not in a gallant attempt to hide her worry. She hazarded a glance at her husband.

❖

Uncertain over the meaning of Honor's unexpected smiles, Samuel now faced the ordeal of a communal meal. He didn't like sitting among others who conversed, excluding him. He also wanted to keep Honor away from the other men aboard.

As they neared the table, he saw the men standing, waiting. Manners dictated that they wait to sit until the ladies had been seated. Honor gripped his arm, and he helped her negotiate the bench, her narrow skirt constricting her movements. The other ladies followed her lead; then the men sat down.

One handsome young man wearing the finest suit and shiniest beaver hat Samuel had seen aboard—a dandy, all right—managed to shift into the place directly across from Honor. The dandy greeted Honor with many words and flamboyant motions. Samuel fumed, taking his seat beside his wife, ignored. Royale set Eli between his wife and him.

The two servants—one waiter and one maid, with Royale helping them—served the meal family style, passing around large bowls of boiled potatoes, sliced ham, thick pieces of bread, cheese, and a bowl of ripe apples. The food awakened his hunger, and he served himself from the bowls passed to him. He noted that Honor filled Eli's plate as she talked and smiled. This caught around his heart. She would be a good mother to Eli.

The irritating dandy addressed Honor. Samuel could sometimes read lips. He caught the word *husband* and stiffened. What was the man saying about him?

Honor touched Samuel's arm and signed the man's question: "What does your husband plan to do in Cincinnati?"

Why hadn't she just answered for him? Then he realized that she was attempting to include him in the conversation. But he really didn't want to converse with the dandy, with any of these strangers. Finally Samuel signed, "You may tell them I'm setting up my own glassworks."

Honor sent him a searching look, but she said and signed his words to the man. The dandy said something in response. Honor signed the man's comment: his name was Sinclair Hewitt, and he planned to find work as a journalist at the *Centinel of the Northwest Territory*, one of the first newspapers in the region.

Then the conversation went on without Samuel. He could only "hear" what Honor chose to sign for him. And she had to use her utensils to eat, so she couldn't sign everything said—though she obviously continued to include him and thereby called attention to him. He chewed his food and tried to appear unaffected.

He watched everyone laugh at something the dandy said. Samuel's stomach burned as he sensed not only their exclusion, but under it their dismissal of him as less than they were, invisible, unworthy of such an attractive wife.

Honor repeated the "amusing" comment to him, and he nodded like a puppet.

He glanced at the cabins, one in front of him and one behind. He and Eli would share one berth of the men's cabin. He didn't like that his wife would be in another room, not with so many strangers on board. He knew his mother wouldn't want him to doubt Honor's loyalty; however, men were unpredictable and would not see him as a barrier to getting closer to his pretty wife. They were mistaken, of course, but they didn't know that. And he didn't want to be forced to prove it.

His food churned in his stomach, hot and unsettled. Only one night and one more day, and they would arrive in Cincinnati. Then he could take his wife away from these men, away from temptation.

❖

October 16, 1819

The next morning, when Honor stepped outside the ladies' cabin, Samuel, holding Eli's hand, was waiting for her. She gazed uncertainly at her husband. Ever since they'd boarded the steamboat yesterday morning, Samuel had been acting very peculiarly. He'd either prowled the deck, hovered around her, or abruptly walked away from her and brooded. Could she get him to tell her why?

"Morning," Eli said, but Samuel signed no greeting.

Ignoring an unexpected urge to take Samuel's arm and draw him closer, Honor instead bent and cupped the boy's chin. "Is thee enjoying this steamboat trip?"

"I like the boat," Eli declared and signed, rising to his toes like a young cock crowing.

Eli's innocent words won her smile. As she talked with Eli, a silent Samuel steered them to the breakfast table. In the bright morning light, she noted once more how substantial her husband looked. She recalled how he'd quickly moved to protect her the day before. There was good in him, but why couldn't he relax and enjoy this fascinating experience just a little? She was trying to make the best of things.

The smell of fried bacon and buttered toast filled the

air around the table. Then, out of the corner of her eye, she noticed a figure in the distance. A woman on the high forested bluff was waving a white handkerchief.

Honor hurried to the railing and waved her own handkerchief in return, wondering who the woman was and how she liked living in the Ohio wilderness. Samuel moved to stand behind her again, protectively. Defensively?

Within moments, as the boat rounded a bend, the woman disappeared from sight. Again, a simple exchange had cheered Honor. She walked the last few feet to the table and turned to Samuel and Eli, smiling, only to see Samuel's face become taut.

All the gentlemen greeted her with more than average courtesy, and she blushed at their attention. Samuel helped her sit modestly on the bench once more. "Good morning," Honor wished the company in general. She bowed her head and said a silent grace.

When she looked up, the journalist again sat across from her. She smiled at him and opened her napkin. Beside her, Samuel tensed further.

Bowls of scrambled eggs, fried potatoes, buttered toast, and thickly sliced bacon passed from hand to hand. "I didn't think the food would be this good, Sinclair Hewitt," she said and signed, trying to include Samuel.

"I've been surprised greatly on this journey. The landscape is so much more striking than I had expected."

Signing his words, Honor tilted her head to one side, encouraging the young man, hoping Samuel might catch some of his enthusiasm.

"Look at these high bluffs." Sinclair Hewitt motioned

broadly toward them. "So high, and such a wild, a picturesque grandeur, which those who have never viewed nature in her primitive and unspoiled state can hardly imagine."

Honor continued signing the budding journalist's grand words.

Everyone else gave their attention to the young man, who continued to wax eloquent. "What dense and interminable forests." He raised both arms. "Trees of the most gigantic size. Did you notice the broad shadows they cast yesterday afternoon? And this river, so placid with meanderings and frequent bends, and all the wooded islands—"

Honor listened carefully, enjoying his elaborate words as she signed them. A glance at Samuel caused her fingers to falter. His face was set and darkened.

Several of the men chuckled, interrupting the poetic flow. One jested, "Well, you said you were a writer, and now we believe you!"

Hewitt grinned good-naturedly. "And which one of us could have believed that one could travel from Pittsburgh to Cincinnati in only two days?"

Honor signed this to Samuel, and she and the other people around the table—except for her husband—agreed with his observation. Steamboat travel was amazing. She glanced once more at Samuel and tried to gauge his mood. He frowned more deeply. Her own enjoyment faded.

"Can you imagine how steamboats will revolutionize trade from the Northeast to New Orleans?" Hewitt asked. "Cincinnati is going to become a great hub of trade, truly the Queen City of the West!"

Honor leaned forward to agree with the young man's contagious optimism.

Under the table, Samuel squeezed her thigh. Not enough to hurt her, but as an unseen command for restraint.

Her gaze flew to his face; his expression thundered at her.

She tingled with alarm. What had upset Samuel? She signed this to him, glad no one but Eli would understand.

Samuel didn't reply, merely glared at her.

Honor sent him a look that she hoped he read as notice of a coming discussion. He did not acknowledge her silent message with so much as a flicker of an eyelash, but merely began eating.

A lady across from Honor asked her if she was from the South, distracting her. But only for now. She would not be ignored. Her husband had avoided talking to her on this boat for the last time.

❖

Samuel found he couldn't evade his wife. As he roamed the deck, she dogged him. Finally, in a spot where they couldn't be easily observed, he stopped and faced her. "Why are you following me?"

"Because thee will not talk to me. Why did thee press my leg at the table?"

He folded his arms and tucked his hands under them.

"That won't work. I deserve an answer. No one is looking at us, and no one can read our signs. Why did thee press my leg like thee was upset?"

"I don't like that man, that dandy." His fingers snapped the words.

"We're only going to be on this boat for such a short time. What does he matter? I said nothing inappropriate to him, and neither did he to me. He is merely a talker, a man who amuses others. What's wrong with that?"

When she put it that way, he was left with nothing to say. "Sorry."

She plainly adjusted her expression, letting him see her set aside her irritation. "Very well."

He started to turn and begin pacing the deck again.

She stopped him by touching his arm. "I want to know more about where we are going."

So do I. He hesitated to tell her he didn't know any more. He was the man, the husband. He was supposed to have everything taken care of. But he couldn't put Honor off again. Better stick to the simple truth. "I have the name and address of the land agent in Cincinnati who arranged the sale. When we arrive, he will take us to our property and we'll see it. I only have the legal description, nothing more. What more could I have?"

She pressed her lips together. "Is that really all?"

"Yes," his fingers slashed. He was frustrated too. "I want to know more as well, but we will find what we find."

I hope we like what we find.

Samuel read these words on her face as clearly as if her fingers had signed them. And he could only agree. He had a wife and child depending on him now, and Royale, too. He would have to make everything work out. Worries he had buried bubbled up once more. He smoothed his hair back and situated his hat. And he began pacing again, dragging the heavy responsibilities behind him.

Chapter 6

SAMUEL'S COLD, possessive manner had ruined the rest of Honor's last day on the steamboat, and now the fiery sun hovered above the Ohio. She gripped the railing, assailed by a new uncertainty. The red-orange of the lowering sun reflected on the river, rippling toward land, toward their destination, toward Cincinnati.

The shoreline spread out flat. Then a steep bluff jerked her gaze upward. Honor craned her neck, glimpsing not the expected thicket of trees but a jumble of rows of houses, factories, and in the distance, church steeples. So big.

Breath rushed out of her. After miles and miles of uninhabited forest, now this—a fully grown city. Sinclair Hewitt had said Cincinnati was called the Queen City of the West, and now she saw why.

She turned to Samuel and signed something of her

surprise. He responded with a curt nod and turned away, another phantom slap in her face. She recoiled. Fresh aggravation washed away her reaction to Cincinnati.

She closed her eyes, praying for how to handle Samuel. She understood that he was still suffering from the loss of Miriam and from being forced to marry her. But neither excused his rudeness. She had also lost everything and been forced into this marriage. Tonight, when she and Samuel were alone at last, she would not let the sun go down on her wrath . . . or his.

The steamboat bumped the pier, jarring her. Shouts and whistles spurred the crew as they docked the boat. A few boatmen set two gangplanks—one for passengers and one for baggage—and others began unloading the luggage onto shore from the cargo hold like a bucket brigade.

She drew in a ragged breath and concentrated on disembarking and all it entailed. She wouldn't be able to relax and leave everything to her husband. *She* would be the one making their arrangements. After all, that was the main reason Samuel Cathwell had married her. The thought still stung.

Soon Samuel ushered her, Royale, and Eli down the gangplank. He stood by, brooding, while Honor gathered with the other men to claim their trunks and boxes. Wagons had appeared and lined up to receive the passengers and their bags. Amid the bustle, horses neighed and tugged at their reins. Honor spied a boatman pushing a cart loaded with her and Samuel's baggage. She beckoned him to come over.

Within minutes a drayman was helping the boatman

load their baggage onto his wagon. Many fellow travelers from the boat crowded around them.

"Mrs. Cathwell, I won't bid you and your husband adieu." Sinclair Hewitt doffed his curled beaver hat and bowed. "I'm sure we'll meet again in Cincinnati."

She smiled and thanked him, ignoring the ill humor wafting from her husband.

Several others also wished them well, the men bowing over Honor's hand. They all nodded to Samuel, and a few patted Eli's round cheeks. Their show of friendship in this strange place eased Honor's tension.

Samuel abruptly assisted Honor onto the wagon seat, looking grim. He helped Royale and Eli get settled on the bench behind them. Without a glance toward Honor, he climbed up beside her. She could have shaken him for his lack of tact.

"Where to?" the drayman asked, the reins slack in his large hands.

Honor signed the question to Samuel, who replied, "We need an inn for the night."

After receiving this instruction, the driver, a middle-aged man with a hat that had seen better days, slapped the reins. His horse moved slowly away from the wharf. Honor perched stiffly between the two men, both staring straight ahead. She tried to think of a gentle, diplomatic way to confront her husband later. But they were practically still strangers, and so far neither gentle nor diplomatic had answered her purpose.

Out of the corner of her eye, she caught a glimpse of two rough-looking men who were walking up the road behind them. One was staring toward her in a fixed way. When he noticed she was watching him, he turned to his companion and said something. Honor faced forward, unwilling to give credence to the shiver of wariness she felt.

The drayman drove past several inns but finally chose one on the high bluff overlooking the river. "This one's decent for a family. I'll wait to see if you get a room," he said gruffly.

As Samuel helped her down, Honor looked back and thought she saw the same men pull out of sight. Shaken, she paused on the wooden walk in front of the prosperous-looking inn. No one moved, and she shook her head at herself. *I am tired and upset; that's all.*

Honor marched inside and located the proprietor. She inspected the room he led her to and found that the sheets had been properly aired and everything looked neat and tidy. She secured the room.

In their lodgings at last, Honor looked out on deep-purple clouds draped over the last of the brilliant-bronze sunset outside the small window. Only a bed, one chair, and a ewer and pitcher on a stand by the door fit in their room. Suddenly exhausted, she sat down on the bed and looked at Samuel, who had sunk down onto one of their two trunks. The boxes occupied most of the space in the small room. She now felt unequal to the task of confronting him. "How long before we move into a place of our own?"

"We will shop in town tomorrow. First we need a team and wagon too. You can drive, can't you? Or do we need to hire a driver?"

Honor was taken aback. Men did not ask women to drive

wagons. But the reason came to her. City bred, Samuel had not needed to learn to drive a team. She almost suggested she could teach him, but then she thought of the voice commands used in driving a team. She would be unable to communicate the various commands to Samuel, and he likely could not speak them in any case. And would he want her, a woman, to teach him? Another touchy subject.

"Well," he prompted, "can you drive?"

"Yes, I can drive." *Until I have time to consider this.*

Royale knocked at the door and entered. She had been given a bed in a servant's room downstairs in the rear.

Samuel lifted Eli from Royale's arms and carried him out, not saying where he was going.

Honor wondered if he sensed her displeasure and was glad to escape even for a few minutes. Yet he would have to face her in the one bed in this small room. She motioned Royale to come nearer. Royale shut the door behind her and helped Honor undress. "So you sure we're not gon' live in Cincinnati?"

"Not right in the city, but somewhere close by, I'm sure." She added the last bit to bolster herself as much as Royale.

With slow, firm strokes, Royale brushed Honor's hair, no doubt trying to help her relax for sleep. "The innkeeper has a black maid working here." Royale's soft voice followed the brush soothingly. "I think the maid be able to help me meet some of my own people before we leave. Find an African church."

Honor gazed at Royale's reflection in the small wall mirror. Again their blood connection tugged at her. The reality that they were blood relations continued to seem unreal—yet God, who loved them both equally, had clearly marked Royale as her kin. Still, the world would ignore it and devalue Royale, who was so similar to Honor in intelligence and in what the world prized as beauty. Because Royale was born of a slave mother, she must sleep belowstairs. Grandfather's sins and lies—so scarring to both of them—stabbed Honor, cutting deeper.

Honor picked up the thread of their conversation. "I also wish to go to meeting here before we leave the city, meet some other Friends. I doubt the small village we're going to will have a place of worship for either of us."

Soon Royale set down the silver hairbrush and bid Honor good night. Honor forced herself to sit in the chair by the window in her nightdress and not hide under the covers. A married woman now, she must accustom herself to being in a state of some undress with Samuel. Besides, she didn't feel she could challenge him while lying down. And no matter her fatigue, she must.

Samuel entered with Eli. After one furtive glance toward Honor, he began helping Eli change his clothes. The glance told her he expected some grievance from her. She joined in assisting him with the child.

"I saw a horse," Eli volunteered. "I like horses and wagons."

Honor smiled. "Yes, the man with the wagon had a good horse."

Soon she slipped Eli into the bed where she and her husband would sleep together for the first time. After

Miriam's death, Samuel had escaped downstairs to his mother's bedroom.

With Eli between them, she doubted Samuel would claim his marriage rights. Honor now understood the word *limbo*. Somehow she must connect with this man she'd married, deal with his barbed moods. Bracing herself, she began, "Why did thee behave so rudely to me on the boat?"

He stared at her. No reply.

Her exhaustion pushed her to their raw bone of contention. "Did thee think I was encouraging the men? They were only showing me common courtesy. Nothing more."

❖

Samuel wanted to snap back at her, but he couldn't. For one thing, he had behaved less than politely to her. He was unsure about the common courtesy comment. "I apologize," he signed. *But you don't know how it feels to be ignored, belittled by their looks, deemed deficient.* "I'm tired." He motioned toward the bed.

"I am also, but I will not be mistrusted, and so I warn thee." With that, she slipped under the coverlet and shut her eyes.

He turned away to undress. For a fleeting moment, he wished he could sleep in a different room. Being in close quarters with Honor only intensified the separation that his deafness forced on him. No hearing person could comprehend that isolation; certainly no beautiful woman could. And now he must lie beside his lovely bride all night and not show how she affected him. A cruel penance for his offense.

❖

OCTOBER 17, 1819

Honor blinked herself awake to church bells ringing, chiming, calling the faithful to worship. Suddenly she was filled with anticipation. No Quaker meetinghouse rang bells, but the ringing was a signal to her nonetheless. She hadn't even thought about the day of the week last night, but now she realized why Royale had mentioned finding an African church. She had known the day.

Honor sat up and, reaching over the lump that was the sleeping Eli, shook Samuel's shoulder.

He opened his eyes and signed, "What?"

"It's First Day." She beamed. "We must get up and dress for meeting. The innkeeper noticed yesterday from my plain speech that I was Quaker and told me there was a meetinghouse just a few blocks away. I don't know how I lost track of the days."

"I'm not going to meeting." He rolled over, turning his back to her.

His refusal sent a cold wave through her. A verse of Scripture came to mind—*"Be ye not unequally yoked"*—and an inner alarm sounded. She rose, donned her robe, and crept barefoot to the other side of the bed. She shook her husband's shoulder again.

When his eyes opened in surprise, she signed with swift motions, "Samuel Cathwell, thee not going to meeting is unacceptable. Thee is a married man now and with a child to rear. How can our marriage prosper if we do not attend meeting as a family?"

Samuel stared at her. "Not this week." He tried to roll over.

She gripped his shoulder, stopping him. "But next week we may not be in Cincinnati."

Halted, he stared at her.

"Samuel," she began, needing him to understand why, "in Maryland, when Friends freed their slaves, they had to sell their land and leave. The other slaveholders despised them. When our meetinghouse closed because there were so few members left, I was still just a little girl." This explanation cost her.

Then the excruciating memory of leaving High Oaks burst in her heart. Her people—the slaves she would have freed—had lined the drive to bid her farewell. Some had wept; some had wailed; others had stared mournfully and lifted a hand in salute. She couldn't just forget them. She still yearned to set them free.

She must find others who thought the same, who would work toward the same goal. "I cannot be separated from the body of Christ in this new place. I must go to meeting, and my family must come with me. I cannot bear . . ." Tears overwhelmed her, and she couldn't go on. He couldn't mean that they would live cut off from other Friends.

Looking disgruntled, Samuel sat up. "Very well. We will go this time."

Honor nodded, but the words *this time* troubled her. She began praying that this meeting would welcome her husband.

A knock at the door broke the silence. Honor opened it a crack and found Royale there.

"I come to get your clothes to press for First Day. I ask the maid here, and she told me there an African church down by the river. She say I can go with her and her intended. Can I?"

"As soon as everything is pressed, thee is free for the day."

"Free for the whole day?" Royale echoed.

"Yes. On First Day, after helping me dress, thee can have the whole day off till sunset." After searching Samuel's coat pockets, Honor pressed a silver dollar into Royale's hand, her first wages.

Royale beamed at her and pocketed the coin. "Thank you, Miss Honor."

Honor opened her trunk, pulling out the family's First Day clothing. Royale rushed off to press the garments at the rear of the inn.

Honor rose and faced Samuel. Eli had awakened, and her husband was helping the little boy use the adult-size chamber pot. The sight of his gentle attention to the child reassured her. And he had agreed to go to meeting today. She would pray about his apparent reluctance to do so in the future.

Her mind alighted on another concern. Would there be others interested in abolition at this meeting? Or would they prove as unconcerned about slavery as the Quakers in Pittsburgh?

❁

Holding Eli's chubby hand, with Honor at his side, Samuel walked toward the meetinghouse just a few blocks from the inn. With every step they took, his stomach grew more and more unsettled. He had given in to Honor because of her tears. But he wouldn't be welcomed here either. After all, he had been stricken by God, hadn't he?

Ahead sat the meetinghouse, the plainest large building on the street. The three of them had arrived before everyone had gone inside. A tall, distinguished-looking Quaker stood at the entrance, greeting people. Samuel prepared himself for humiliation and felt his face freeze into his giving-nothing-away expression.

Honor, of course, sailed straight to the greeter and offered her hand. Clothed in traditional Quaker garb, the man wore a broad-brimmed hat, a coat and vest of dark-gray broadcloth, and antiquated knee breeches with long knit stockings. The mode had gone out of style decades ago. Samuel refused to dress as an old-fashioned Quaker.

She turned to Samuel and signed, "This is Friend Endeavor Lovelace, one of the overseers." She proceeded to introduce Samuel and Eli to Lovelace in both words and sign.

Lovelace sent him a searching look. However, he did smile and shake Samuel's hand in a welcoming manner, which was appropriate for an overseer, who was charged with encouraging the body and welcoming newcomers.

Honor signed the man's greeting to Samuel: "We are happy that thee has joined us today and hope thee will become a part of our body."

Samuel barely nodded, his closed expression unaltered. Just the usual empty words. Then he entered and, taking Eli with him, moved to the men's side of the meetinghouse. As was customary, the backless benches filled the open center area. The windows were wide-open, flies meandering aimlessly overhead. Everything was painted gray, gray, gray. Samuel shook his head. He was sure God liked color and wondered why Quakers preferred drabness. Who had decided gray was the color of sanctity?

Soon everyone had assembled, filling the benches. Honor sat directly across from Samuel, and though he resisted her, she kept catching his eye. Lovelace opened with prayer, which Honor signed to Samuel.

While everyone's heads were bowed, Samuel signed to her to stop it. He didn't want everyone watching them, as they would if she signed everything to him.

"Why dissemble?" Honor signed.

"I don't want to call attention to myself," his fingers snapped back.

"Will everyone ignore us? We're newcomers. We'll be introduced to the meeting at the close."

He shook his head sharply and glowered at her, the heat of embarrassment engulfing him in waves. Did she think anybody here would want to get to know a deaf-mute?

❖

Honor pursed her lips and tried to calm her spirit, to center herself in God's peace as her father had taught her. But Samuel's anger whisked up her emotions like a wire spoon whipping meringue. He didn't see that his resentment—though justified—made matters more difficult for himself. *Father, how can I help my husband not pull away—from me, from everyone, even from thee?*

A young man, wearing traditional Quaker clothing and

sitting near Samuel, rose to speak. "I have just come across a most interesting new publication, the *Philanthropist*, published northeast of here by Charles Osborn, a resident of Mount Pleasant, Ohio. Charles Osborn was born in the South and is opposed to slavery. He calls on all Christians to refuse to buy products that are produced by slave labor."

When this man hadn't just recited a verse or asked for prayer, Honor had identified him as a recorded minister, which meant he was acknowledged as having the gift of spoken ministry. He was also probably a delegate to the Quaker conventions in Philadelphia.

There was a rumble of approval. At this welcome sound, breath caught in Honor's throat.

A woman rose. "But how can we know which products are manufactured by slaves? Isn't all cotton produced in our Southern states?"

The young man bowed his head. "I do not know the answer to that." He sat down.

Honor sat transfixed. This meeting was openly discussing ways to oppose slavery. She closed her eyes and thanked God.

The rest of the meeting passed with prayers and with passages of Scripture read aloud and discussed. Then the overseer who had welcomed them rose and introduced Honor's family.

She stood and so did Samuel, though reluctantly. Eli spontaneously waved to the congregation, making many smile. She faced her husband, saying and signing, "My husband, Samuel, is a glassblower from Pittsburgh, and I am lately from Maryland. Samuel is deaf, and I speak to him with a sign language. I'd like to teach thee all how to say hello in sign so thee can welcome him." She proceeded to hold her hand high and demonstrate several times as she turned slowly in a circle so everyone could see.

At first only a few hands lifted and tried to copy the sign, but finally everyone's hand was moving in the simple gesture.

Honor beamed at them and sat down.

Samuel had kept his eyes averted during Honor's demonstration, but when he glanced up, he scorched her with his gaze.

She swallowed but did not quail. "I have done nothing wrong," she signed.

Lovelace prayed for Honor, Eli, and Samuel; then everyone was rising and chatting quietly.

Samuel came over, leading Eli by the hand. The boy was still waving and greeting anyone who spoke to him. Samuel jerked his head. "Let's go."

But everyone they passed greeted him with a signed hello. Honor halted, forcing Samuel to also stop. She didn't budge till she had spoken to everyone who greeted them. Samuel didn't like being ignored—she understood that. But evidently he also didn't like being noticed. He couldn't have it both ways.

On the short walk back to the inn, she could feel his increasing aggravation billowing over her. She decided not to show that she was aware of this.

Samuel was her husband, and she had promised to obey him. But submission did not mean letting a husband turn from the narrow way. Samuel would not prosper if he cut himself off from God and his people. And when she remembered how the young recorded minister at the meeting had spoken of refusing slave-produced goods, she glowed. *I have come to the right place.*

❖

Samuel seethed. Honor had blatantly disobeyed him. He'd told her not to put him on display.

His conscience corrected him. *She was right. Of course you would be introduced to the meeting. How could she hide you?*

He had no answer, and that stoked his anger more.

They arrived at the inn and found Royale and another black woman waiting for them near the entrance. The other woman was older and plump with a round face. Her clothing was simple, neat, and clean, and she walked on broad bare feet that had obviously seldom been confined by shoes.

Honor went forward to greet them, and Eli insisted on being set down. The child ran to Royale. "I went to meeting," he said and signed.

Royale responded with a smile and lifted him into her arms. She turned to Honor and gestured to the older woman beside her, apparently making introductions.

Honor signed to him, "Royale has found us a cook."

Samuel tried to bring his mind to this new topic. A cook? "Do we need one?"

His wife looked perturbed. "I cannot cook. Royale cannot cook. Can thee?"

Her tart reply set his teeth on edge. "What does she wish in pay?"

"She will work for the same as Royale, two dollars per month. Can we afford her?"

He stared at Honor for a long moment, then nodded. "But we will not need her till we move into our home. We need to go see what condition it's in, and soon."

She signed her words as she hired the cook, named Perlie.

Samuel waited impatiently and decided to show his disfavor by stalking upstairs to their room, simmering with unsaid words. His wife was not turning out to be biddable. He needed to take a stand as quickly as possible. Right now, however, he was too irritated to speak of it. Tomorrow would have to do.

❖

OCTOBER 18, 1819

As Samuel and Honor exited their inn the next day, heading off to buy a team of horses, she glanced back as if she recognized someone. He looked around but saw only two nondescript men. Neither looked like anyone his wife would give a second thought. "What's wrong?" he signed.

"Nothing," she replied. "I'm imagining things."

Samuel checked again, and the men had disappeared. He shrugged and trudged beside Honor for two miles to a small farm the innkeeper had recommended on the edge of Cincinnati. Eli had remained back at the inn with Royale.

Honor introduced herself and Samuel to the horse breeder and signed, "We need a team—an experienced pair for personal use and my husband's business. He was town bred, but I'm country bred. That is why he is asking me to choose some for his consideration. He will make the final decision, of course."

The horse breeder, a tall, well-dressed man, led Honor to a pasture, Samuel trailing behind. Honor stopped and rested a hand on the top rail of the fence, intently watching the horses. Samuel had to admit they were beautiful animals. From a distance.

Samuel's subordinate role still irked him, but he appreciated her suggestion that lack of experience, not his deafness, was why he was letting her take such an important role in this purchase.

The horse breeder nodded at him but spoke to Honor, leaning toward her, resting his arm nonchalantly on the railing near her hand. Samuel smoldered.

Then Honor turned to Samuel. "I think the bay team there—" she pointed to two horses standing nearby—"looks promising. Shall I ask him to bring them out for us to examine?"

Samuel nodded. What objection could he raise?

A groom held the reins of both horses. Honor asked the breeder to lead one apart. She walked around the horse and motioned for Samuel to come closer.

He didn't want to but complied anyway.

Honor pointed out various facts about the horse, lifting hooves and asking the groom to lead it up and down while she watched its movements closely. She repeated the process with the second horse.

Samuel found that he enjoyed observing how intent his wife was and how much she appeared to know about horses. He did not like the marked attention the horse breeder and the groom were paying her, however. He reined himself in, not letting this show.

"This is a good pair," Honor said. "Shall we begin bargaining?"

"Go ahead," he signed.

The dickering went on for several minutes. Finally Honor, Samuel, and the breeder agreed upon a price.

As the two of them walked back to their inn, Honor turned heads. Samuel glanced at her. She was leading the horses and totally unaware. Why didn't she ever seem to notice the attention she garnered? Maybe she just didn't show it, because she certainly couldn't be oblivious to it.

When their inn came within sight, Samuel saw the dandy from the riverboat lounging around the front of the building—like a bad penny. A fire lit in his stomach. The journalist raised a hand in greeting and hurried to join them. This man was like a burr Samuel couldn't shake off.

Honor greeted him with a smile.

Samuel gritted his teeth and raised a hand.

Soon Honor was showing the dandy the finer points of their new team of horses. Samuel felt like a fifth wheel on a wagon.

Yet his wife signed everything they said. Or he thought she did. He tried to ease up, let it pass over him, but he couldn't.

The hostler for the inn came to take the horses to the nearby stables for the night. The dandy followed them inside, and Honor let him kiss her hand in parting.

Samuel felt a muscle jumping at his temple. With the

barest nod to the journalist, he took his wife's hand and led her toward their room.

One look at Honor's fixed expression told him she did not appreciate his curtness. And she would not long remain silent about it. That much he knew about his wife.

Chapter 7

Upstairs, Honor was glad to find their room empty. Royale must have taken Eli for a walk. So now Honor would be able to say exactly what she wanted. Samuel closed the door behind them, and as the latch clicked, she turned to confront him. "Why does thee behave so rudely to me?"

Her husband looked away, hanging back near their stacked luggage.

She stamped her foot to insist on his attention.

He raised his eyes, resentful.

"Every time I am near a man, thee behaves as if thee doesn't trust me. I am not encouraging men to notice me, flirt with me."

Samuel stared at her and said nothing.

"Thee is my husband. I am not looking for . . ." She stopped, not knowing how to go on. What did she mean to say? *I am not looking for a lover*? Heat flushed through her whole body at the very thought of such illicit behavior.

She approached him and took the large hand that made hers feel so small. Touching him set off those unusual sensations in the pit of her stomach. If only they had been given time to get to know one another. Their forced and rushed marriage made everything harder. "I gave thee my promise. Is that not enough?" She searched his dark eyes and read his pain and shame.

An urgent rap on the door interrupted them. Before Honor could open it, the rap repeated, sharp, insistent, prodding her. She whipped the door open. "Yes?" she asked, flustered at the interruption.

The portly, red-faced innkeeper stood panting. "We got trouble. I found my laundress unconscious outside. And your maid and boy've been snatched."

For a few seconds the words didn't make sense; then Honor sucked in air and choked.

The innkeeper slapped her on the back.

Samuel gripped her shoulder and urged her to look at him. "What is it?"

Honor signed the man's words and returned her attention to the innkeeper. "How did this happen?"

Breathing hard, the man was having a hard time speaking. "I ran down the street, looking, and then up here." He bent, bracing his hands on his knees, panting. "Come." He motioned. "The laundress saw it all."

Honor signed this and grabbed Samuel's hand, pulling him toward the door. They followed the innkeeper down the narrow flight of stairs, through the dimly lit common room—eliciting surprised looks from the few men sitting there, including Sinclair Hewitt—then through the kitchen and out the back door.

In the small rear garden opening onto the alleyway, Honor saw a large, rawboned black woman sitting on a wooden chair, bent with her head in her hands, moaning. "Oh, Lord, Lord, have mercy."

The innkeeper sank onto another chair against the back wall of the inn. "Tell them what happened. Quick, girl."

The woman looked up and began wringing her hands. "Oh, ma'am, it was awful. Two men, two white men, come walkin' up the alley. Your maid, she was talking to me while I worked, and the little boy, he was playing with a ball."

The laundress suppressed a sob, and Honor resisted the urge to shake words from her.

"The men come up to us, and then one grabs your maid and clamps his hand over her mouth, an' at the same time, the other one hit me over the head with somethin'—a stick . . . I don't know. When I open my eyes agin, they both gone. Oh, Lord."

Honor could barely take this in. Nonetheless, she signed it all to Samuel, who looked aghast. "Why has this happened?" she cried.

Rocking back and forth in distress, the woman looked up. "Don't you see, ma'am? Slave catchers gone and took her to sell South. She pretty and almost white. They can get three, mebbe four times what a regular gal go for. They don't care that she got a manumission paper. Oh, Lord, save her."

Royale, kidnapped. Honor gagged. She turned her head and suffered a sudden bout of retching. Samuel hovered just behind her. She swiftly forced her fingers to sign the rest of the dreadful news. He pulled her against him, cradling her shoulders in his strong hands. She pressed a hand over his fingers and held a handkerchief to her mouth, forcing back the instinct to begin moaning with the other woman.

Her mind rioting with fear, she wrestled herself into control and addressed the innkeeper. "Why would they take Eli?"

"To keep her from calling for help," the laundress said, each syllable charged with outrage. "They can threaten to hurt the child if she don't do what they say. That's the kind of dirty trick people who kidnap free people do. God-forsaking, wicked men." The woman spit on the sparse wild grass near her bare feet.

"We must alert the watch," Honor said and signed.

"I already sent a boy for them." The innkeeper mopped his brow.

"Ma'am, you gotta work fast and find her," the laundress said, rising. "If they cross the river, you never find her again. She tole me about how you set her free. You gotta save her." The woman strangled Honor's arm. "The life they gon' sell her into ain't worth livin'."

Honor felt the urge to retch again and sucked in a deep breath. *Father, help. Keep my Royale safe.*

A uniformed officer wearing a badge strode up the alley with the messenger boy at his side. "What's happened here?"

The young officer's callow face did not reassure Honor. What could one man do against this evil that had come against them? She and Samuel must do more. "Innkeeper, please tell the law officer what has happened and describe Royale and Eli. I am going to get help and start looking."

"Yes, we need help," Samuel agreed. "But who?"

Taking Samuel's hand, Honor ran back into the common room. How could she get help from a town of strangers? She halted in front of the young journalist, exclaiming, "Sinclair Hewitt, slave catchers have kidnapped my maid and our little boy!"

The man leapt from his seat, as did the two other men who had been drinking ale next to him. "When did this happen, ma'am?"

"Just now! I don't know where to look!"

A voice hailed Honor from across the room. "Honor Cathwell, this is the hand of Providence." Honor recognized him—the recorded minister from yesterday's meeting. "We met yesterday. My name is George Coxswain. I just arrived to visit thee and thy husband to talk business, and I heard thy voice. What is this? Thy maid has been snatched?"

Faith leapt within Honor. God had known what wickedness was coming and had already dispatched help. The realization spun her whirling emotions.

Samuel stood behind Honor, one arm around her shoulders, his strength bolstering her, helping her go on.

Honor stifled tears. An emotional outburst would not help. "Yes, and our nephew. We must find them."

"Describe thy maid," Coxswain said.

All gazes turned to her.

The authority in the Quaker's voice galvanized her. "Royale is near my height, very light skin, golden-brown hair, and green eyes. Pretty. Very pretty." Her voice quavered on the last two words.

"The life they gon' sell her into ain't worth livin'."

He looked shocked. "Thee should have been more careful with her. She's worth thousands to unscrupulous men."

"That's right," Sinclair Hewitt agreed, gripping George's hand and introducing himself. "They'll be heading to the river." Hewitt turned to the other men. "Will you help find this woman and child?"

A chorus of agreement lifted Honor's hopes. "Ask anyone you see. Alert everyone. A young mulatta and a dark-haired white boy, three years old."

Hewitt gripped Honor's hand with one of his own and rested the other on Samuel's shoulder. "I'm going to start looking and spread the word. I'll notify the papers in town. Many eyes will be needed to find the girl. We must find her before these dastards take her across the river."

"We must find her before nightfall," George Coxswain amended. "I will alert the meeting. The old will pray and the young will search." He turned to join Hewitt. The other men hurried after them and out the front door.

The laundress appeared beside Honor. "I'm goin' to my preacher. There be free blacks here in this city, and they will look too. She come to our church yesterday. Everybody know what she look like."

"Stop!" The badged officer charged through the door

from the kitchen. "We can't have people taking the law into their own hands."

Suddenly furious, Honor swung on him. "I will do whatever it takes to find my maid."

The man looked aghast, his thoughts evident. *A lady, speaking so forthrightly?* "Your husband is the one who is responsible for the girl's safety, not you," he said harshly. "You're just a woman."

Honor had never been so tempted to slap someone. She held herself straight, unclenching her hands to sign what the man had said.

Samuel signed back. "Tell him if he talks to you like that again, I'll teach him manners." Then her husband raised a fist toward the officer.

The man stepped back but continued speaking belligerently. "Stop that black woman from leaving! We can't have free blacks running through town. Except for going to and from work, they're supposed to stay in their own neighborhood down by the wharf. This could start a riot."

Honor glared at him. "It should start a riot when a free woman and a little child are kidnapped in broad daylight and all thy men will do is try to prevent their rescue. Is it thy job to aid lawless men?"

The officer glared in return. Reddening, he shoved past her.

Samuel grabbed him by the shoulder, shook him, and signed, "Show respect to my wife or deal with me. Now do your job or else!"

Honor translated.

The lawman yanked free with a resentful expression and hurried out of the inn.

"We can't depend on him," Samuel signed.

Honor embraced her husband. He had defended her. Then, grasping his hand, she ran toward the street, praying with every step.

❖

Hours later, near dusk, Samuel still felt the weight of failure. Why hadn't he thought to keep Royale with them? Protecting his household was his job, and Royale was important to his wife. And Eli, his only blood kin left, had been taken too. He was just a little boy. Samuel's heart clenched. What if they never saw his only brother's only son again?

He now stood in a crude building near the wharf in a neighborhood called Little Africa. It was the African church Royale had attended, though nothing but a rough wooden cross hanging on the back wall looked church-like. At that moment he would have given anything to be able to hear what was being said. In the center of the room crowded with Quakers and free blacks, he and Honor were surrounded by a huddle of men, including that young Quaker, Coxswain, and the black preacher, Brother Ezekiel Langston.

Samuel focused on his wife's moving hand. She stood within the circle and tried to keep him included in the exchange. Samuel suppressed his feelings of being of little use. His own needs weren't important now. He had to focus on getting Royale and Eli back.

Honor turned to him, her expression one of despair. "Brother Ezekiel has called for men to hide in the shadows all along the wharf. They think that the slave catchers will wait till nightfall and then spirit her onto a boat to take her downriver to the Mississippi. She might be drugged, they say."

"What about Eli?"

"They may take him, too. He can identify them." Her fingers faltered. "I don't want to think it, but they might hurt him."

He felt sick. Did she mean—but couldn't say—they might toss him overboard when they were away from town, get rid of the only witness? Or keep him to continue to force Royale into obeying them? "What can I do?"

"We will also take our place in the shadows. George Coxswain says a group of Friends, both men and women, will join us, lurking around the wharf and sounding the alarm if they see anything suspicious."

"Why isn't the law officer here?"

Honor looked disgusted. "They have issued a warrant for the arrest of the men and have put up a few posters about the kidnapping."

"So you mean they have done nothing?"

"George Coxswain says the law doesn't like having free blacks in the city and does little to help them."

"What about Eli?" Samuel's fingers slashed the air. "He's not a free black."

"Brother Ezekiel says that's why the warrant has been issued and the posters put up at all. Otherwise they would do nothing to help."

Samuel let out a breath. He wished the officer were here so he could pound him into the dirt floor beneath his feet.

The dandy hurried in and waved a stack of single sheets of newsprint.

Honor accepted one and scanned it. "Sinclair Hewitt has brought broadsheets about the kidnapping from the *Centinel*."

Samuel took a sheet from her and read the brief account of the kidnapping. The paper called for all citizens to be on the watch for the mulatta with green eyes and the white boy of tender age. Samuel nodded his thanks to the man he had so resented.

One of the Quakers bowed his head for prayer and Samuel watched everyone do the same. A great heat roiled within Samuel's chest. *God, save them. Let us find them. Please.*

The gathering dispersed, Quakers and free blacks in groups of twos and threes. Samuel felt Honor take his hand and lift it to her cheek. Her tenderness caught around his heart.

"Have faith. We will get them back."

Samuel stared into her eyes and wished he could speak to her with words, pull her close, and reassure her. He'd been keeping himself apart from her, but suddenly that didn't matter. He drew Honor to him and embraced her, trying to express all the concern and caring he felt. They each might lose someone dear to them.

He felt her sob once and then regain control. He released her and, taking her hand, led her outside into the twilight. He couldn't pray. The fear and anger snuffed everything else out.

Night closed in, the shadows deepening, deepening. The cool, damp breeze flowing ashore from the river swirled around Honor's ankles. Her eyes and ears strained for any sight or sound that might be a hint of Royale's presence. Her stomach tightened into a knot of terror.

Samuel stood beside her, as tense as a tightly wound wire. She wished she could speak to him. But with only moonlight and the lamplight from windows along the quay and on board docked boats, she could not sign to him. They had already planned that if either saw anything, they were to shake the other and point in that direction.

A provocatively dressed woman walked past them and halted as if startled. Had she glimpsed Honor in the shadows of the alleyway? She leaned forward as if she couldn't believe her eyes. "What's a lady doing down here at this hour?"

Honor waved her arms, shooing her away. She couldn't let her presence be clarioned to the whole wharf. Indeed this was no place for a lady.

Down the street, a man burst out of a door as if propelled, tried to catch himself, and stumbled onto the wooden boardwalk. He began shouting in what must be a state of drunkenness. Two other men exited another tavern and headed toward Honor and Samuel.

The woman turned away and swayed in the direction of the two men. "Hey, gents, are you lonely?"

The coy invitation shocked Honor. A prostitute? She had never seen a woman of ill repute. Then Royale's voice played in her mind: *"Your grandfather be my father."* The reality that her grandfather had sexually used Royale's mother sickened her. And now Royale remained at risk.

"The life they gon' sell her into ain't worth livin'."

Honor pushed her senses up another notch, sorting through the sounds of inebriated laughter bursting from opening doors, of docked boats bumping against the wooden piers, of footsteps echoing on the planks. *Royale, Royale,* her mind chanted, *where is thee?*

The hours ticked by. Honor shifted on her feet and tried to stay alert. Her lower back began to ache. She blinked and drew in air. The night watchman walked past them, swinging a wooden baton. Honor didn't breathe until he moved far from them. She wondered if he was even looking for Royale and Eli.

More time passed and Honor fought harder to remain awake. She awoke with a start, a hand over her mouth. She struggled but realized that it was Samuel's hand. He put his fingers in front of her eyes. By the moonlight she could just make out the words. "You fell asleep."

She scrubbed her face with her hands. Had Royale already been spirited away, or were the slave catchers holding her till the outcry died down? Even the alehouses were quieting as the alcohol did its numbing work. Royale and Eli in the hands of wicked men. Dread had lain in her stomach ever since they had disappeared, but now it swallowed her like a tidal wave. She pressed a hand to her head. *Royale, why can't I find thee?*

❖

OCTOBER 19, 1819

Just after dawn, Honor stumbled up the last few steps to their room at the inn. Samuel grasped her waist, steadying her. She was holding in tears, but a night spent without rest and thick with worry and fear had sucked everything from her. She felt hollow.

Samuel unlocked the door. Honor staggered to the bed and fell facedown, the repressed tears pouring forth in sobs she couldn't contain. The bed dipped as Samuel lay down beside her and clasped her to him, and they wept together. She buried her face into his shirt, seeking his strength, his solace, sharing the grief.

❖

Samuel woke, disoriented. He looked to his right. Honor rested beside him on their bed at the inn. Gray smudged the skin beneath her eyes. Her discarded bonnet lay near her head. Her hair had come loose from its pins and framed her face. *My wife.*

He could not restrain himself. He gently stroked her soft cheek with the back of his index finger. So soft. Her pale-pink lips beckoned him. His own tingled at the memory of the kiss that had sealed their marriage promises.

Then the guilt over Eli and Royale reared up, nearly choking him with regret. He should have been more watchful, less involved in himself and his worries. They must be found today.

Her eyes blinked open. He read his name on her lips and then, "Any news?"

He shook his head.

She gripped his hands in hers and mouthed clearly for him to read: "We must keep faith."

Honor glanced toward the door and signed that she heard tapping. She rose, opened the door, and conversed with one of the maids. She turned to him and signed, "There's a man to see us downstairs."

She moved to the mirror and ran a hand over her hair, snatching out the pins and letting it flow down around her shoulders. She did her best to put it up again, but Samuel knew that Royale always did her hair, and the thought must have stabbed her as well. Turning away from this, she shook out her skirt and attended to Samuel, straightening his collar and smoothing back his hair. She took his hand and led him down the narrow stairs.

Samuel expected George Coxswain, but instead a white-haired Quaker of considerable age awaited them. He signed hello to Samuel. Then Honor signed what he said: "I'm an elder of the meeting and want thee to know we're behind thee. The women of our meeting are taking turns strolling down the quay with their older sons to run for help if need be. If they see anything suspicious, they will sound the alarm. The men will patrol tonight again. The kidnappers may think we will slacken our efforts with the passage of time. But they are mistaken. We will do all we can to find thy maid and boy. And we are united in prayer."

Honor gazed at Samuel, her broken heart in her eyes.

Samuel had trouble swallowing and signed, "My thanks."

The older man solemnly shook their hands and left them.

Honor walked to Samuel, and he wrapped his arms around her. Then she looked up and signed, "We will not give up till we have found them."

Samuel nodded. He had found a wife who didn't falter in the face of trouble. He bent and kissed her forehead. "We will find them." As they walked to the stairs, she nestled under his arm.

❖

OCTOBER 20, 1819

Another long night's vigil at the wharf was nearly over. Leaning against the wall near the opening of the alley beside Samuel, Honor was giddy with exhaustion. The sounds of the dock were slowly fading as another dawn glowed gray over the rooftops to the east.

Two men walked out from an alleyway. Each carried a sack over his back. They were joking and laughing, sounding loud in the relative quiet. Their manner was anything but stealthy. Wouldn't kidnappers try not to call attention to themselves?

Then Honor noticed one bag wriggling. "There!" she screamed. But she was not the only one who had seen it. Many voices shouted. A shrill whistle blew. Friends and free blacks poured onto the boardwalk.

The two men pelted toward a rough river craft, a small keelboat with a ramshackle cabin on it. Samuel sped past her and attacked the nearest man. A black man took down the other. Cursing. The landing of blows. Shouts of pain. A gunshot exploded.

Honor screamed. But she did not stop running. She snatched the smaller bag and tore at the ties. Another person, a black woman, rushed to help. She slit open the bag, and Eli tumbled free onto the planks. The woman sawed away the bonds from his wrists and ankles. Honor dropped to her knees and yanked the gag from his mouth.

Torches flared in the dim light as more help arrived from farther up and down the wharf. Eli wailed, and Honor crushed him to her. Then the commotion began to ease. The two men who'd been carrying the sacks lay on the wooden planks, one unconscious, the other dazed.

Honor struggled to her feet. "Royale? Royale?"

"She's here." Many voices echoed variations of this news.

Honor pushed her way through to where Samuel bent, panting. She came up against him, pressing Eli to him.

"Oh!" It was one of the few sounds she'd ever heard him make. And then he was hugging Eli and her. Eli repeated their names and grabbed handfuls of their clothing as if they might leave him.

She pulled away and gazed down at Royale, who didn't stir. "Is she breathing?"

"Royale," Eli whimpered.

A man in a doctor's frock coat had knelt by Royale and was holding her wrist. "She is alive, but barely. She's been deeply drugged."

"When will she recover?"

"I don't know. I'm always careful how much opium I give patients. One can be overdosed."

Honor dropped to the hard wood, which cut into her knees. She hugged Royale's limp form to herself and began weeping.

"What's all this?" a man demanded, pushing through the crowd. His polished brass badge shone in the dim light.

"These are the two kidnappers," George Coxswain said, pointing downward. "We just caught them carrying the child and his nurse onto this keelboat."

"We told you not to become involved," the officer barked. "We had more night watches on the wharf tonight. We were watching for the child."

Just the child. Honor glared at the man, pink dawn lifting behind him. "Then why didn't thee stop them before they got onto their boat?"

"I whistled as soon as the outcry went up. Help is on the way!"

"Well, we didn't wait for help that might come too late," Honor snapped, aggravation and anguish swirling in her voice. The man had as much as admitted he would have missed the kidnappers except for the vigilance of others.

"One of the kidnappers had a gun," Brother Ezekiel said, kneeling by the one who lay unconscious on the boardwalk. "I think he shot himself in the struggle."

Someone lowered the torch, revealing that blood flowed from the man's upper right chest.

Sickened, Honor turned her head away. "My maid needs to be carried to the inn."

The doctor rose also. "I will attend the wounded prisoner at the jail and then come to your inn. I know which one."

Hewitt emerged from the crowd and took Eli from

Samuel, who lifted Royale into his arms. Relief had weakened Honor, the starch draining out of her. She walked between her husband and Hewitt. Dawn was brightening the sky, and the nightmare would be over—if only Royale would wake. Soon.

Chapter 8

Honor paced her room around the bed where Royale lay, waiting for her to regain consciousness. Over the innkeeper's objection that a black maid could not rest in a room abovestairs, Samuel had carried Royale to their bed. Royale was barely breathing, still in a deep stupor. Honor could not stop worrying. Would Royale, her blood kin, suffer damage to her mind, her sanity, from the kidnapping and drugging?

In front of the door Samuel sat on the floor with Eli huddled on his lap. The child whimpered, weepy, clingy, and bewildered. Looking at his small, trembling lips cut Honor to the very heart. She ached to hurt someone. These men had hurt and terrified those she loved, and she yearned to see them lying at her feet, bleeding. Her hands gripped the phantom cane she wished she could use for their punishment. Never before in her life had Honor felt such a stirring to violence. She'd wanted to slap Darah, but that was no comparison to the rage she was experiencing now. She tried praying for calm, for God's peace. That soothed her need to strike back but did not ease the confusion and anguish she felt. *Oh, Royale, I let thee down.*

With effort, she paced back and forth, forcing down the chafing worries. Like a stallion out of control, her emotions reared up, raced. If she spoke, she didn't know what might burst out.

A knock on the door brought Honor to an abrupt halt. She motioned to Samuel, and he rose and opened the door, Eli tucked under one arm.

George Coxswain stood in the doorway. "I won't come in. I just wanted thee to know that the men have been charged with kidnapping and are in jail."

She moved toward George, hands outstretched.

Samuel caught her attention, and she stopped to translate the Quaker's message into sign. She added, "Friend, thank thee for telling us. We can never thank thee enough for thy help."

Bowing his head toward her, George clasped Samuel's shoulder and patted Eli's head. "A doctor from our meeting will call on thee later. I explained the situation, and he said not to lose hope. Keep faith." After bowing his head once more, he left them.

Honor tried to believe George but could not. Would Royale ever be herself again?

Samuel shut the door and placed Eli in her embrace. He rested a hand on her shoulder.

Honor looked up and pressed her hand over his. He'd been as concerned about Royale as about Eli. Perhaps that showed he had formed a loyalty to her, too. Then Honor recalled how he had held her and wept with her yesterday. Miriam had said her son was honest and kind. And perhaps this crisis had opened the way for more between them.

Honor claimed his hand and brought it to her cheek, kissing it and looking up at him. He leaned down, and for a moment she thought he was going to kiss her lips. She lifted her chin. But again he kissed her forehead.

Closing her eyes, she tried to tamp down her disappointment. She and Samuel had been forced closer to each other, but what would it take to move her silent husband out of his deep reserve? And with each minute that passed, Honor's worries over Royale leapt ahead. She began pacing once more. *Dear Lord, please let her wake. Soon. With all her wits.*

❖

Hours later, another knock came. Rising from where she sat on the bed, Honor hurried to answer it. Had the doctor come at last? Samuel was dozing in the chair, holding Eli as the boy also napped, still exhausted and stunned by his ordeal. Honor felt as if she were weighed down by boulders. She opened the door.

The innkeeper stood in the opening, wringing his hands. "Mrs. Cathwell, I'm sorry, but if you don't take the girl down to her own room, I'm afraid I will have to ask you to leave."

Honor stared at him, riddled with disbelief. "We're only keeping her here till she wakes."

"Three other guests have told me they will leave if this black girl isn't moved belowstairs immediately."

She wanted to snap at the man, but she saw that he appeared honestly torn between compassion and business. How could people be concerned only with Royale's color, not the ordeal she'd just survived? Honor glanced at her hand and saw that she'd worried it till it bled. She attempted to still her spirit. "Very well." She breathed in deeply. "I didn't mean to place thee in an awkward position. My husband will carry Royale down and I'll keep watch there."

The man mopped his brow. "Thank you. I'll make sure comfortable chairs are set there for you." He waited. "I'll lead you down."

Samuel had risen. She explained the distasteful situation. He made no comment, but his jaw tightened visibly. He set Eli in her arms. The little boy cried out, "No, don't hurt me!"

But he quieted when he saw Samuel lift Royale from the bed. Honor nodded to the innkeeper, who locked the door behind them and led them down the stairs, through the crowded common room and kitchen to the servants' quarters at the rear. Honor held her head high and did not deign to look at people so far from compassion.

Samuel lay Royale on her bed in the narrow room she and the other maid shared. The room was so tiny Samuel had to step outside with Eli. The innkeeper called for chairs, and soon Honor settled inside with Samuel and Eli right behind her, waiting for Royale to regain consciousness.

Sitting at Royale's bedside, Honor found herself

praying—chanting, really—*Lord, please wake her and comfort her and comfort Eli. And please let Royale be herself.*

❁

Late in the afternoon, Royale at last opened her eyes. Kneeling beside her, Honor clung to Royale's hands. Looking flattened and crushed as if she had been run over by a coach, the maid was too weak to lift her head. "They say you never find me," Royale mumbled with effort.

"Thee knows they lied. I would never have stopped looking for thee." Hiding her deep concern, Honor lifted Royale's head and shoulders and helped her sip from a glass of water. She turned to Samuel and signed for him to take Eli and tell the cook Royale had awakened.

He left, and for a moment all Honor could do was stroke the curly hair that had come undone from Royale's braids. Memories of them as children playing at High Oaks came to her. In her mind, she heard the rich and gentle voice of Royale's mother. Tears dripped from her eyes, and she swiped them away. Questions about Royale's ordeal jammed in her throat. She choked them back.

She helped Royale sip water again and gently laid her head down. "I'm so sorry." Honor's voice trembled in her throat. "We both are. It never occurred to us that someone would take thee by force."

"I didn't think 'bout it either." Royale closed her eyes and inhaled a shuddering breath.

A dreadful worry had plagued Honor. She voiced it now, speaking almost in a whisper. "They didn't *hurt* thee, did they?"

Royale sobbed without tears. “No. If I never know a man, they get more money for me.”

Relief mixed with horror shot through every nerve in Honor’s body. She gripped Royale’s hand. “I promise I will never let anybody have the opportunity to snatch thee again. Never.”

Royale nodded, gasping between sobs.

Grateful that Royale was able to speak sense, Honor helped her up to drink more.

“They kept me drugged. Did they hurt Eli?” Royale’s eyes were pools of dark suffering.

Honor smoothed back Royale’s tousled curls. “He’s frightened and has a few bruises, but he will be all right.”

Samuel opened the door, and the short, broad-hipped cook came in bearing a small tray.

“I made broth for her and some toast,” the cook said, looking around for somewhere to set the small tray. There was no place. Honor’s chair filled the only space left between the two beds.

“Here, I’ll hold it.” Honor rose and lifted the tray. “Thank thee.”

“We’re just so sorry this happened,” the woman said kindly, backing out.

Honor propped Royale up with pillows and helped her eat the broth. Each sip brought new life into her.

Samuel hovered in the doorway. Eli slipped down and climbed onto Royale’s bed. He patted her shoulder, whispering, “Royale, Royale.”

Honor repeated the name silently, comforted by the child’s affection for Royale.

When the meal had been eaten, Honor rose and handed Samuel the tray. "Royale, thee needs to rest now."

"Don't leave me," Royale implored, gasping.

"Mrs. Cathwell," the innkeeper's voice came from the hall. "If you please, the sheriff is here to speak to your husband about this case." The innkeeper peered around Samuel, who filled the doorway. "Don't worry about the girl's safety. The black preacher has been waiting out back. He says while your girl sleeps, his son will sit outside the door." Then the man spoke directly to Royale. "I took a look at him. He's a strapping young giant. No one will get past him."

Honor rose and, bending to kiss Royale's forehead, whispered, "If thee wakes while I'm gone, let the young man know so he can alert the cook. Thee needs to keep eating and drinking to gain back thy strength."

Then Honor greeted the young black man, who filled the doorway with his bulk just like her husband and had the same honest eyes. She had no doubt she could leave Royale safely in his protection.

Eli begged to be left with Royale, and the child lay down beside her and fell asleep. After being assured that the laundress would help with Eli, Honor left the room, and the preacher's son sat down on a chair, blocking the doorway. Honor drew in deep breaths, preparing to face the legal aftermath of the kidnapping. Had the sheriff come to advise them, or had something else happened? Had the kidnappers escaped? Had the wounded one died? She quickened her pace.

The innkeeper led them to his office, a small, neat

room near the entrance, across from the inn parlor. When Honor entered, a man in his forties rose, wearing a badge. The innkeeper introduced him as the local sheriff, Obadiah Blaine, then left the office.

Blaine, who stood a good foot shorter than her husband, studied Samuel, frowning. "They tell me your husband can't speak or hear."

Honor bristled. "He can do both if I am present to sign for him," she said, instantly disliking the man for the way he gawked at Samuel. "Do not think for a moment that my husband is lacking in any way." She hadn't meant to sign the last sentence, but she had become so used to signing all she said in Samuel's presence that she had begun before she realized what she was signing. Well, it was the truth.

Samuel touched her shoulder. She turned to face him. He said, "Tell him—I've been told that the men who kidnapped my maid and nephew have been jailed. When will the trial be?"

As if mystified, Blaine watched her hand as she signed and spoke Samuel's words. Then the sheriff frowned and shuffled his feet. "Well, we got a problem. The men say you sold the girl to them. And she ain't got her papers. Claims they burned 'em."

Honor gasped. *"What?"* She signed furiously what the sheriff had said. "How can thee believe that?" she demanded. "How could I sell a free woman—in a free state?"

Samuel moved closer to Honor and glared at Blaine. He signed with impatient fingers. "Tell him to stop talking nonsense. These two men kidnapped our maid and my little nephew and tried to spirit them away. We want justice. We will have justice."

Honor translated this with pleasure.

The man wouldn't meet her gaze. "Well, we don't have any witnesses—"

Throwing one hand up, Honor interrupted. "The laundress here observed the kidnapping."

"She can't testify in court. Blacks have no legal standing in Ohio."

"But this is a free state," Honor exclaimed again.

"Don't matter. They aren't citizens, and by the way, the girl broke the law coming into Ohio. She has to post a five-hundred-dollar bond like any other free black that comes into the state. Or she has to leave."

Honor stared at the man, speechless, then signed his unfeeling words.

Samuel stepped forward, nudging her aside, and faced the sheriff squarely. "Tell him this. I am Samuel Cathwell. My maid and my nephew were forcibly kidnapped by two lawless men. We caught the men at the docks. The men were trying to take them away, concealed in bags, onto a keelboat. I am going to hire a lawyer, and we will prove the case against these men." Samuel stepped farther forward, forcing Blaine toward the wall. "Justice will not be denied us. Or else."

His back against the wall, Blaine looked as shocked as if a mountain had just moved. "You don't need a lawyer," he sputtered. "The city will prosecute the men."

Honor moved closer to Samuel, signing Blaine's words and translating her husband's reply with relish. "We will hire a lawyer, and he will watch the proceedings. If these kidnappers are not prosecuted to the full extent of the law, we will appeal the verdict. I have funds enough to take it to the US Supreme Court if necessary."

Honor could hardly believe the words she was translating, but she reveled in them.

Blaine's face reddened. "Your husband doesn't need to tell me my business."

Samuel replied, "We will see."

"I need to leave," Blaine said, nearly pinned to the wall.

Samuel nodded but did not move for several seconds as if letting this man, this maddening excuse for an officer of the law, realize whom he was dealing with. Finally Samuel stepped aside slightly so Blaine could just squeeze around him. On the way out, the sheriff slammed the door.

Honor couldn't contain herself. Rising on tiptoe, she threw her arms around Samuel and hugged him. Then she stepped back and signed, "Thee was wonderful, amazing. I'm so proud of thee." And she hugged him again.

His arm came around her too. "We will not rest till those two are punished. And no one will take Royale from us again. I promise you."

"Thank thee. The sheriff will not treat thee that way anymore. He thought he could overwhelm us, bully us."

Samuel grinned. "You handled him very well."

Honor rose higher and began to kiss his lips. She waited, but though Samuel held her close, he did not return her kiss. She let the kiss end and remained resting against her husband in spite of his rejection. This was a man she was beginning to realize she could trust.

Someone knocked. Reluctantly Honor turned and opened the door. The innkeeper stood there. "Your maid is sleeping, and the young man guarding her is staying the night. I'm making sure your maid gets food and tea as needed."

Honor moved to the man and clasped his hand. "Thee has become a friend to us. We will not forget thy many kindnesses."

The man's face flushed. "You're good people, and I feel bad your maid was snatched from my property."

"The sheriff says the men told him that they bought my maid from us."

The innkeeper's mouth dropped open. "What kind of nonsense is that?"

"The worst kind," Honor said. She wrestled with her rampant anger. *I should not seek to do violence. My father taught me that I must control my emotions, not let them control me. The Inner Light cannot work in an angry heart.*

"Will thee have Eli brought up to us? I have only enough energy to go up to our room."

The innkeeper agreed and left them.

Honor led Samuel up to their room. As she mounted the stairs, her exhaustion made itself felt with each step. She wanted only to lie down. Samuel entered behind her, then drew her back to him and wrapped himself around her. Honor reveled in the comfort of the strong arms. She rested her head on Samuel's broad chest, savoring their intimacy.

But a moment later, another maid brought Eli to their room. This pushed them apart. "I was scared," the boy said and signed.

Honor sent her husband a look of regret over their having to part.

Shrugging, Samuel hugged Eli to him. Eli accepted this, then held out his arms for Honor.

Tenderness for the child filled her. She cradled him close and sat down in the chair. "My sweet boy," she murmured over and over, "thee is safe now. God protected thee. No one will ever take thee from us again." After several minutes of holding Eli and soothing him, he fell asleep.

Samuel lifted him gently and laid him on the bed. Then he sat on the bed, gazing at the boy.

Honor felt oddly keyed up again, as if she needed to walk, get fresh air. But she did not want to disturb this quiet moment together. Finally her restlessness and thoughts about its cause would not subside. She touched Samuel's knee and signed words she could not hold back. "Samuel, almost losing Royale has made me eager to work toward ending slavery." *More eager than before.*

"What?" Her husband looked puzzled.

"I am opposed to slavery and want it to end."

He sent her a look that said *impossible*. "The slaveholders need the slaves to work their crops. They will never let them go. They would lose their wealth."

Every word he said was the absolute truth, but that didn't mean she could not fight. She tried to think of another approach. "Even though she is a free woman, Royale was kidnapped. If there weren't slave states and free states, she would not be in danger."

"I don't like slavery. But the world is the way it is, and it isn't going to change."

His words were flat, and his fingers bluntly told her to let the subject go.

She held in more words she wanted to say. Yet earlier she had felt something in his embrace. Something had altered between them, some connection had formed. If they had been alone, she would have let the embrace go on, leading them to a more natural relationship for a husband and wife. But Eli had needed her. She only hoped Samuel would remember the closeness of that moment. She could not forget it.

❁

OCTOBER 21, 1819

The next morning Honor, Samuel, and Eli entered the common room, which was filled with the fragrance of bacon. Though Royale and Eli had been restored to them, Honor's spirits surged and ebbed. The sheriff's snide face kept coming to mind.

Rising, Sinclair Hewitt waved them over to his table. "I've been waiting for you."

Honor turned to Samuel, prepared to risk his reluctance. "He helped us find Eli and Royale. I am not flirting with him." Still, what did the journalist want from them? Or want to warn them of?

"I know," Samuel signed. She raised a brow at the unexpectedly cordial response. He sat down with Eli on his lap. The child twisted and turned, trying to see everyone around them. Samuel patiently shifted in his chair, accommodating Eli's movements. A servant girl brought coffee and went to get their breakfast.

Honor sat on the edge of her chair, focused on Hewitt.

"I heard from the innkeeper that the sheriff is not being helpful," Hewitt said, brushing crumbs off the white tablecloth.

Honor brought him up to date on what had happened so far. Each word raised her outrage toward the sheriff another notch. She finished with, "We are going to hire a lawyer today to represent us and Royale in this case."

Hewitt nodded and sat back. "I know where the law offices are. I'll be happy to go with you. I want to write up an article about this. I may not win popularity by it, but if the sheriff is not one to uphold the law regardless of a person's color or status, that should be known."

No doubt he was right. She'd thought people in a free state would bear more sympathy toward those who'd been freed. But might Hewitt's writing do more harm than good for Royale?

Honor studied the journalist. "I don't know if thee should write about it so soon. Blaine might have undergone a change of heart." *Especially after Samuel let him know how far he would go to seek justice.*

"I understand your hesitance, but I think having a journalist in attendance will cause everyone to do their duty more circumspectly, don't you?"

Torn, Honor signed this to Samuel and asked him to decide.

"Tell Hewitt to come along but not to write anything unless our lawyer says so."

Hewitt gazed at Samuel. "Show me how to sign yes."

Honor beamed at the young man and demonstrated the sign for him.

Samuel nodded to the journalist. Then the serving girl delivered their plates, filled with all a person could want for breakfast. If only Honor had any appetite. Royale appeared in the doorway to the kitchen, and Honor smiled at her. When she started to rise to go to Royale, her maid shook her head and mouthed, "I'm fine."

Royale appeared rested and was wearing clean, well-pressed clothing, so Honor merely nodded.

Still, worry over how this all might turn out twisted her stomach. She sipped her coffee and began praying for good outcomes. For Royale. And for her own future, here with her husband. Hope flickered, dimmed, but didn't die.

❖

After breakfast, Sinclair Hewitt led Samuel and Honor to the center of town, near the courthouse. All manner of people crowded the narrow streets. Honor let herself feel the bustle of the Queen City, trying to understand this place. She knew Samuel did not prefer to have the journalist with them, but they both agreed he could be of help in dealing with a lawyer. The innkeeper had recommended a young attorney, new to Cincinnati, who had stayed at the inn when he first came to town. The man's character had impressed the innkeeper favorably. Honor only hoped he would be willing and could help Royale get justice.

A collection of law offices filled the frame building, but it didn't take them long to find Alan Lewis in the attic, in the smallest of the offices. Lewis was young and thin with a large Adam's apple. His office was bare except for a few law books, two chairs, and a small, scarred desk.

"How may I help you?" Lewis asked as he seated Honor in the lone client chair. Then, since only his chair remained, he politely leaned against the wall. The other two men also stood out of courtesy.

Taking the lawyer's measure, Honor glanced to Hewitt, asking him to speak. She would be deemed very forward if she spoke to an attorney while men were present.

"I will speak for the Cathwells," Hewitt said with a nod to Honor. He proceeded to explain their situation.

"I have, of course, heard of this case," Lewis said, straightening from the wall. "I can well believe the kidnappers told the sheriff that cock-and-bull story. These men don't impress me with their intelligence. Their lie won't stand up in court. Even if you had sold them this girl, which would have been breaking the law and not a binding agreement, why would they take the boy? Why were the boy and your maid concealed in sacks? If he gives any credence to their story, the sheriff will look a fool."

"Thee will represent us, then?" Honor asked, then signed Samuel's question: "See justice done?"

"Since the city will be bringing the case against them and their own lawyer will defend them, I won't be able to do or say anything official in court. But I will attend the trial with you. If anything is not done according to the law, I will alert you and make it known upon appeal, if needed."

Lewis offered his hand to Samuel, who looked surprised but nodded and shook the attorney's hand.

"When will the trial take place?" Hewitt inquired.

"I'll go to the sheriff today and find out everything; then I will confer with you." Lewis looked to Honor. "Never fear. These men who took your nephew and maid against her will won't be allowed to go scot-free. We must make an example of them."

Honor hoped this would prove true. From what she'd heard so far, women and people of color rarely hoped to come out of a courtroom vindicated. Or that's how it seemed. Honor's resolve in the face of this inequity hardened. Her God was a God of justice and mercy, and she would serve him in both.

OCTOBER 22, 1819

Samuel wished he could have refused to come to the drab Quaker meetinghouse early the next evening, but how could he do that? The Friends had helped them save Eli and Royale. From across the room, he scrutinized his wife, a faint blush on her cheeks, her eyes glowing with eagerness.

He watched her closely. Her gaze did not follow George Coxswain or any other man. She was excited over this meeting of those interested in abolition. But all Samuel wanted to do was sit and stare at her. A dangerous temptation.

Samuel thought of last night when he and Honor had undressed Eli and tucked him into their bed. They'd been standing side by side, looking down at him. Then it had happened. After Honor had smoothed back Eli's hair and kissed his forehead, Samuel had felt a matching touch and kiss. She had turned, and he'd folded her into his arms.

He didn't know how much longer he could hold back from truly making her his wife. On the other hand, why did he hesitate to let her come nearer? They were married, weren't they? Stumped at his own reluctance, he diverted his thoughts from this thorny question.

George Coxswain had risen and was speaking to the group of around twenty men and women. Across from Samuel, Honor began to sign what George was saying. He should have known she'd do that.

But instead of cutting her off with a glare or doing what he wanted—gazing at her and ignoring everyone else—he forced himself to read her fingers. This meeting held importance for his wife, and he must follow what was said.

❖

Royale had first told Honor of this meeting when they had returned from consulting Alan Lewis. The black congregation wanted Honor to attend and report to them if anything of real value was discussed. Black Christians were not welcome in the meetinghouse.

Now Honor listened to George opening the meeting, and she began to sign almost without thinking. Would this body of Friends have ideas that could fight slavery?

"I have been concerned about abolishing slavery since I was a child in North Carolina—"

"I must interrupt thee before our conversation begins," another man said, holding up a restraining hand. He was very thin and sickly looking. "I don't think that we should involve women in this work. The fairer gender should not be troubled with such weighty issues, and what can they do to help abolish slavery?"

Honor sat aghast. She wanted to spring up and tell him that women were capable of much, but no lady contradicted a man, and never in public. She would wait to see how George replied.

George fixed his stare on the older man, but his voice was conciliatory. "I am sorry thee feels that way, Friend. I would think that the part played by women in the horrible kidnapping over the past few days would show what they can do. Often a woman can put off suspicion. As thee remembers, women from our meeting patrolled the wharf during the day when the men could not be away from their jobs or stores. And their presence did not alert the kidnappers that watch was being kept."

The thin man shook his head militantly and others joined in, protesting that the meeting could not continue with both women and men in attendance. This wasn't a worship gathering but a political discussion. And women had no part in politics. That realm was beyond their understanding.

Honor began shredding her lace handkerchief to keep from rising to debate.

Then George's widowed mother, Deborah, stood abruptly. "Ladies, I think we will move down the street to my kitchen—where, evidently, women belong—and have our own meeting."

As surprised as the few other women in attendance appeared to be, Honor wished to stay and argue the point. But she bowed to Deborah's suggestion and rose.

Samuel stood also and signed, "What's happening?"

Honor explained before following the other women toward the door. Samuel caught up with her. "Thee can stay here," she told him. *Thee wears pants.*

"Why? I won't hear a word said, and I'd rather be with you."

"I'd rather be with you." Honor tried not to read more into those words than she should. Of course Samuel would follow her. What choice did he have?

The women and Samuel marched down the street in the twilight and soon entered the neat parlor of the Coxswains' home, a two-story frame house. The dismissal still stung Honor. Men offered courtesy with one hand and insult with the other.

"Thank thee for opening thy home," Honor said as she settled herself stiffly on a settee with Samuel beside her.

"Thee is welcome—even thy husband. And I prefer we gather here in the parlor, not my kitchen." Deborah grinned. "I don't understand why a women's presence should upset Carter Fleming, but he is a curmudgeon of the first water."

The other women suppressed smiles. Honor thought of a few sharper terms for the rude man and scolded herself for this weakness.

"Of course I should not say so, but it's the truth, so God will forgive me," Deborah continued.

"I was surprised to see so few at the meeting tonight," Honor said, unable to hide her disappointment. "I thought all Friends opposed slavery." She signed the conversation to include Samuel, though he didn't look as if he were interested.

"Disapproving is different from taking action against slavery," Deborah said.

"But what *can* we do to help end slavery?" another woman asked. "Slaveholders have the law on their side. And wealth. And the vote."

The women looked into each other's faces, hoping for inspiration.

"Perhaps we should discuss why we're interested in abolition," Deborah suggested. "Honor Cathwell, we know that thy free maid was kidnapped and that thee is from the South. Are those the reasons thee wants to end slavery?"

"Yes, I am from Maryland. I don't think those who have never seen slavery understand how evil it is. Thee has a Southern accent too, Deborah," Honor said, offering the older woman a chance to reveal her past.

The ladies shifted their gazes to Deborah.

"Yes, I am from North Carolina. My family and I freed our few slaves. After doing so, we were forced to move north."

A rush of emotion clogged Honor's throat. Deborah Coxswain had suffered similar loss and dislocation.

"That must have been hard," another woman said.

"Indeed it was. My family became enemies to people we had called neighbors for two generations." Deborah shook her head sorrowfully.

Honor nodded, remembering her own bitter loss. Alec Martin's face flickered in her memory. He'd chosen Darah, not her; slavery, not emancipation. But her grandfather's querulous voice overwhelmed that memory. He had left his own blood—both her and Royale—vulnerable. A piercing like thorns twisted around her heart.

Deborah rose and drew something from a small secretary in the corner. "Has thee seen this? Read the title to all, Honor."

Honor accepted the one-page newspaper and read aloud its title. "'The Genius of Universal Emancipation.'" She scanned the page and devoured the impassioned plea for emancipation of slaves.

"Benjamin Lundy just published this in Mount Pleasant, Ohio," Deborah said.

"There is a new paper right here in town that speaks against slavery," another woman said. "The *Philanthropist*."

The others sat as silent as Samuel.

Honor sat forward. "I do not know how to change this evil, but I would suggest we begin with prayer."

"Excellent," Deborah affirmed. "Of course we should ask for the Inner Light to lead us."

The women bowed their heads, and each prayed in turn for guidance and inspiration to begin the work of ending slavery.

"Lord, inspire us with ways to end this dreadful bondage of our darker brethren and sisters," Deborah concluded.

"Well, at least we've held the first *Female* Anti-Slavery Society meeting," the youngest of the ladies announced. "I hope we will continue to gather."

The women around the circle nodded.

"Way will open," Deborah said, "if we pray and remain vigilant for any opportunity that presents itself. And if this be of God, the way to do it will come."

Honor and the other women murmured in agreement.

Honor's dismay had eased with prayer. God would show them the way.

A glance at Samuel's expression puzzled her. She couldn't decide if he was experiencing one of his bouts of wanting to be away from others or was pondering what had been said. But she hoped against hope that it was the latter. How could she proceed with working toward abolition if her husband opposed it?

Chapter 9

OCTOBER 25, 1819

Three days later, just after sunset, Samuel helped Honor down from the wagon bench when they arrived at the inn. The land agent had driven them to view their property. Even as Honor bid the land agent farewell, she did not appear pleased, and Samuel had wanted to please her. More and more, what Honor desired mattered to him. But he couldn't see how to give her what he did not want.

He opened the inn door for her, and they moved directly into the now-familiar common room, both of them chilled, hungry, and thirsty. Trying to show he cared about her comfort, Samuel offered his arm, leading her to her favorite table by the window. Honor spoke to the innkeeper, signing to Samuel that she was inquiring after Royale and Eli. The man assured her that they were safe.

But Honor's evident yet silent displeasure was still present, eliciting Samuel's concern.

Samuel waited impatiently till they had been served tea, then attempted to placate her. "I know our property needs work, but that can be done soon enough."

Honor gazed at him, her mouth twisted down at one corner. His wife did not mince words. "Why must we live so far out of the city?"

"Many reasons," he signed, not meeting her gaze directly.

She stared at him, telling him how inadequate this response was. "What are they?"

His own tension heightened. Honor deserved the best. Yet he knew this parcel of land was the best for him, not her. Words finally came. "I am going to build my business catering to other small businessmen who need glass products but are too small to interest the Cincinnati glassworks in designing something special for them. Our property is close enough to get what I need from Cincinnati and on the main road near the city."

"And we will not be near many people," she signed with sharp motions, showing him that his many words hadn't fooled her. She knew his true reason for wanting to live away from the city. And Honor herself had heightened his desire to escape.

Familiar hurts reared inside him as he recalled glimpses of how men here looked at his wife—as if they wanted her and couldn't understand why she had chosen to marry someone defective like him. He clamped down on these hot, unwelcome thoughts. "Our property is already purchased," he signed because he didn't have anything else to say.

She bowed her head in acknowledgment. Their supper was served and they ate in silence, her unhappiness robbing him of his appetite. Just as he longed to move closer to her, an issue once more put them at odds.

Then one positive point occurred to him. He put down his fork and signed, "Royale will be safer out of the city. I can keep closer watch on her—fewer strangers and farther from the river."

His wife considered this and replied, "That is right." But that was all she conceded.

Samuel's plan for his life had been completely altered. He had never thought he would marry, and here he sat with a wife—but one who hadn't wanted him. That alone kept him from reaching for her. And against his wishes, his wife persisted in trying to knit him into the hearing world. It was wonderful of her but still unpalatable to him.

The trial of the kidnappers, scheduled to take place tomorrow, hung over them both. They couldn't leave until it ended. Afterward he could find peace away from the constant irritation of people gawking at him as if he had three heads.

❁

On their way to the room, Honor considered what she wanted to say to Samuel. The thought of moving to the distant property on Lebanon Road left her feeling empty. Did she have a hope of persuading him not to live so far from the city? In such a secluded place, she'd be cut off from any chance to work for abolition. She'd be sitting amid the forest, isolated from everyone.

They entered the room. Honor sat on the chair, and Samuel slumped onto the bed. She had to make him understand, so she started with a point they agreed upon. "Royale will be safer outside of town. However, I cannot be happy so far from a meeting." She forestalled his response with a gesture. "Being part of the body of Christ is a necessity." *Especially the fraction who are antislavery.* "Will thee agree to bring us back to Cincinnati for meeting each First Day?"

"How could we do that? It's a trip of nearly four hours to our property." His fingers dismissed the idea.

"We could leave early in the morning or come into town Saturday afternoon," she urged. "We could do our shopping and stay at the inn Saturday evening. Is that possible? Do we have the funds?"

Royale tapped on the door and announced herself before entering. She set Eli down, and he ran for Samuel. As usual, Samuel carried Eli out while Royale helped Honor prepare for bed. Honor watched her husband leave. Even in the midst of this conflict with him, she wanted him to know she was ready for their limbo to end.

"How did you like our new place?" Royale asked, trying to conceal her obvious anxiety.

Honor sighed deeply. "It is a long drive from the city." Realizing that she sounded glum, she quickly brightened for Royale's sake. "Our cabin is in a very lovely meadow in the forest, and the air is clean."

"Cabin?" Royale gasped. In the silence they heard other guests walk past their door, talking quietly.

Honor closed her eyes and pictured the log cabin that

would soon be home. She sighed again and forced herself to appear content.

Glancing in the mirror, she recognized the strain in Royale's downcast expression. She touched her hand. "I've already spoken to Samuel about coming to town each weekend for worship and shopping. And thee will have our new cook, Perlie, for company too." Bleakness filled her.

Royale nodded, not appearing consoled.

But of course Royale was still recovering from the trauma of the kidnapping. And tomorrow's trial loomed over them all. Honor smiled at Royale, trying to convey her understanding and sympathy.

Royale returned a mechanical smile and concentrated on brushing Honor's hair.

Closing her eyes and giving herself up to the rhythm of the brush, Honor hoped Samuel would agree to her suggestion. She didn't know what she would do if he didn't. And living in a log cabin—she had never imagined that. How far must she fall from what she'd been born to?

Darah's face glimmered in her thoughts. Honor pushed it away.

Royale began softly singing, "'In that great gettin' up morning, fare thee well . . .'"

The familiar song comforted Honor but also mimicked her situation. *Fare thee well, Queen City.*

❖

OCTOBER 26, 1819

The land agent hastily entered the common room at the inn the next morning, just as Honor and Samuel were finishing as much of their breakfast as they could stomach. Eli sat on Samuel's lap, one of the places he most preferred since the kidnapping, looking frightened. The trial would begin in just over an hour. They would leave Eli at the Coxswain house with Deborah and several other Friends.

Honor sipped her bitter coffee, trying to keep what she'd eaten where it belonged. She found it almost impossible to believe the kidnappers would go free, but she couldn't be certain. Prejudice against free blacks ran high here.

Royale waited in the kitchen, dressed in her best and ready to go to court with them. She would not be allowed to testify. Her race and former enslavement rendered her invisible to justice.

The land agent looked distracted and harassed, his hair winging up as he swiped the beaver hat from his head. "I am so sorry," he began hastily. "I don't know how this could have happened."

Honor was so perplexed that she forgot to sign what the man had said till Samuel touched her arm. "What is thee apologizing for?" she asked and signed.

"I showed you the wrong property the other day."

Samuel watched Honor's fingers. He sat up straighter and glared at the man, who had taken a seat at their table. "What swindle is this?"

Honor placed a hand over his, silently asking for his patience. "This may merely be a mistake." She turned to the land agent. "Please explain what has happened."

To her, the land agent appeared distressed rather than guilty. "Somehow I mixed up the legal descriptions and the locations of two parcels of land. I showed you and your husband the wrong parcel yesterday."

Honor relayed this and watched red anger flush her husband's face. "Where is our parcel?" she asked, signing for Samuel's benefit.

"It is on Lebanon Road—we passed it on our way yesterday. I don't know why that didn't jog my memory. I am so very sorry."

Hope blossomed within Honor. "We passed our parcel yesterday?" That meant this parcel wasn't as far away as the other. Samuel would not be pleased.

"Yes," the man replied. "You noticed it, in fact. The property set back from the road about an hour outside of Cincinnati. The man who bought the land originally had the intention of breeding horses. That's why the barn is large enough to hold animals and leave a spacious work area. The house is a log one but with two rooms—one large common room and a large bedroom—and a loft, and there is also a detached kitchen. His wife was used to a frame house, so he tried to impress her with a larger log home."

"Did it work?" she asked, much in sympathy with the unknown wife.

The land agent chuckled dryly. "No, they only lasted a year and then moved back to town." He looked grim. "They died in the cholera outbreak this spring."

Honor's hand faltered as she signed this, knowing that cholera had robbed Samuel of his brother and Eli of his parents. The scourge of cholera appeared in cities every spring, and no one knew why.

Maybe Samuel was right. Living away from the city and its contagions might be the best course. After signing all to her husband, she waited to translate his reply. Several moments passed before she prompted, "Samuel?"

Her husband didn't conceal his irritation. "Tell him that we will view the property and deeds to make sure he hasn't made any further mistakes. We will bring our lawyer to go over the legal descriptions of both parcels. But it will have to be after today."

The land agent looked relieved. "I am in my office every day this week till seven. I will be happy to show you the parcel that is yours. Again, my apologies for the inconvenience." He rose, bowed, and left them.

Honor gazed at Samuel, his mask in place again. Her husband was a master at concealing his thoughts, his emotions. Even from her.

Before she could frame a diplomatic way to help him accept this unforeseen event, Sinclair Hewitt entered the common room. He headed straight for them.

At least Samuel had let his jealousy toward the young man ebb. Hewitt had proved himself a friend. Honor motioned him to take a seat at their table and waited while he waved to the serving girl, who brought him a drink and went to fetch his breakfast. "I am going with you to the trial if you will permit me," he began.

Her stomach clenched at his words, and she felt unable to go on with the meal. She put down her coffee cup.

"Sorry," Hewitt said. "I know this is upsetting, especially to a lady such as yourself."

Honor wondered why men thought that being a lady

made one more fragile or sensitive in regard to the harsher aspects of life. It didn't. Also, Royale's feelings weren't less than hers, just because she wasn't considered a lady. But of course, a lady wouldn't say that. "We are all doing the best we can. Eli is still very . . . frightened." *As is Royale.*

"I've been hired by the *Centinel.*" Hewitt stirred his coffee. "They liked the articles I submitted to them on the kidnapping." Hewitt frowned. "I find this city a strange mixture of North and South. It's in a free state, but free blacks are discouraged from settling here. And any mention of abolition is met with instant opposition."

There was much Honor wished to say in reply, but she held her tongue. Sinclair Hewitt might have abolitionist leanings. But this was not the time or place to begin that discussion, especially since her husband dismissed abolition and she was not sure whether he could ever be convinced otherwise.

Royale appeared in the doorway to the kitchen, wringing her hands and prompting Honor to rise. "Samuel, I can't eat anything else. And Royale needs me." The men rose, and she left them. She led Royale through the kitchen to a bench in the inn's small garden. In contrast to their tension, a robin hopped nearby, calling its mate. "I know thee is worried, but all will be well."

Royale was fighting tears. "I'm afraid."

"Of what?"

Royale didn't reply, just hid her face in her hands. Honor's mind proceeded to supply possible answers:

I'm afraid that I might be kidnapped again.

I'm afraid the judge will make me leave Ohio.

I'm afraid because, even though I'm free, I am unprotected by the law.

Honor knew the feeling of being stripped of protection. When she'd lost High Oaks, she'd lost a woman's only power in this world of men: inherited wealth. Now she was married to someone her previous neighbors would scorn, a deaf-mute who worked with his hands, not a gentleman. But Samuel was an honest man who defended her and provided for her. She turned back to Royale.

Words were of little comfort, but Honor spoke anyway. "Samuel will protect thee. It was our ignorance of thy danger that put thee in jeopardy."

Royale slid closer, and Honor slipped an arm around her shoulders. "We will face this together."

❁

The courtroom was stark, furnished with only the judge's high bench, two polished oak counsel tables facing the bench, the jury box, and the gallery seating. A railing with a center gate separated the tables from the gallery. An American flag hung behind the judge, a white-haired man with a scrawny neck above his black robe. The severity of the courtroom oppressed Honor.

As the afternoon trial commenced, Samuel, Honor, Sinclair Hewitt, and Alan Lewis sat behind the low oak railing on the prosecution side.

Sheriff Obadiah Blaine and another officer stood nearby. Royale watched from a balcony with the other free blacks who had come to support and protect her. The courtroom was crowded with other spectators—some well dressed, some in homespun. Honor recognized George Coxswain and several other Friends in attendance. The jury selected this morning now sat in the two rows of the jury box, at right angles to everyone else.

Honor tried not to look at the two kidnappers in shackles who sat beside their own lawyer. Whenever she glimpsed them, a sour sickness curdled in her stomach and a chilling perspiration bathed her.

As if sensing her distress, Samuel surreptitiously took her hand. Her husband was always kind, but that was all. Would he ever view her as more than a woman under his care—view her as his wife? She forced their uncertain relationship from her mind and tried to focus on the proceedings.

Lewis was taking copious notes with a pencil on a pad of paper. This seemed to distract the two prosecuting attorneys, who kept looking at him over their shoulders. Hewitt was also rapidly scratching notes along with another two newspaper reporters in court.

"The state calls George Coxswain to the stand," the lead prosecutor, a well-dressed and smooth-talking man, said.

George walked to the stand and, when asked by the bailiff holding the large, black leather Bible, affirmed that he would tell the truth.

"You were on the wharf on the night in question?" the prosecutor asked.

"Yes. I was helping look for the little boy, Eli Cathwell, who'd been kidnapped."

"And did you find the boy?"

Honor listened but primarily gazed at the faces of the

twelve men chosen to decide this case. Some of them kept glancing up into the balcony and glaring. Others listened with intense interest to everything that George said.

In her mind, the jury could do nothing but convict these evil men. But justice could be miscarried, especially because of Royale's involvement—which was not even mentioned in court except as an aside that the kidnapped child had been in the care of a nurse who had also been taken.

Samuel squeezed her wrist, reassuring her. She sent him a private smile, acknowledging his support, and continued to sign the testimony of each witness.

Several more Friends testified, identifying the two defendants as the men who had been caught on the wharf red-handed, with Eli Cathwell and his nurse secreted in bags near their keelboat. The prosecutor ended his case.

Then the defense lawyer, a squat man who kept casting dark looks at the prosecution side and at the balcony, brought some character witnesses to the stand who, in Honor's opinion, did the defense case more harm than good. The jurors looked aggravated at these testimonies, and she tried to take encouragement from this.

Samuel stroked the side of her gloved hand with his thumb. "I'm fine," she signed in return. He moved his hand away, but she drew it back next to hers. His thumb brushed the tender spot under her own thumb. His touch both distracted and comforted her.

The two kidnappers did not take the stand in their own defense. One sat grinning and cocky; the other, who'd been wounded with his own pistol, remained subdued and listless. Their lawyer ended his defense with an emotional appeal full of long Latinate phrases that made no sense to Honor. "All show to cover his lack of a defense," Alan Lewis muttered.

Then the jury left to deliberate in private.

Honor rose to stretch her legs, breaking contact with her husband, who also had risen. She slipped her hands around the crook of his elbow, leaning ever so slightly against his strength.

"I do not think this will take long," Lewis commented in a reassuring undertone. He rose and went to talk to the prosecuting attorneys.

Honor nodded toward him as she signed this to Samuel. She hoped for a quick judgment by the jury, hoped that Eli was not becoming fretful with Deborah. He didn't like to be separated from Samuel or Royale for long. She resisted the urge to crane her neck toward the balcony and call unwanted attention to Royale. The courtroom walls felt as if they were closing in, forcing out all the air.

Less than half an hour later, the bailiff came out, then the judge. Finally the jury paraded back to their seats. The judge addressed the foreman, who rose and announced the verdict. "Guilty as charged, Your Honor."

Shouts of victory went up in the balcony. The judge called for order. Thanked and dismissed by the judge, the jury left almost immediately. The other two newspaper reporters raced out the door to their offices, but Sinclair Hewitt hung back near Honor and Samuel. Relief drenched Honor, her tension releasing, leaving her weak.

Samuel pulled her into a one-armed embrace, and she wept a few tears against him. Friends from the meeting crowded around, congratulating them. Two officers marched the angry kidnappers out of the courtroom.

When the crowd had thinned, Honor and Samuel moved into the aisle. Sheriff Blaine walked up to them. "Well, that's done. Now I see your girl is here. Her bond has not been paid, so I'll take her into custody."

Samuel glared at the man. "Honor, tell him I am ready to pay her bond. No one is taking Royale anywhere I don't want her to go."

Honor translated this to Blaine with great satisfaction.

The sheriff appeared disgruntled but wary, more than once glancing up at Samuel, who towered over him. Honor took much comfort from this.

Alan Lewis rose and hurried forward to catch the judge, who was about to leave. "Your Honor, we'd like you to witness Samuel Cathwell paying the bond for his free servant Royale. Also, Your Honor, we need you to sign a new manumission paper for her. The kidnappers burned her original one."

Blaine looked as if someone had clubbed him. He turned and marched forward, blustering, "Yes, Your Honor, the girl entered Ohio and did not pay the bond as required by law."

Samuel ushered Honor forward, where he handed over a bank draft for the sum and accepted a scribbled receipt from Blaine, under the judge's order. They had gone to the bank the day before and had opened an account for this purpose. After the transaction was finalized, the sheriff stalked off, grumbling to himself.

Honor and the rest—including Hewitt, who'd stayed to get the whole story—moved to the judge's small, neat office, where Honor affirmed that she had been Royale's mistress and had freed her. The judge's clerk drafted a new manumission paper, which both Honor and the judge signed. The clerk notarized it also. The judge congratulated them on the guilty verdict.

They walked out of the courtroom and into the late-afternoon breeze. Honor clung to Samuel's arm at the head of the steps, still a bit shaky with relief.

"Is that all that must be done to protect our maid from the law?" Honor asked Alan Lewis, pausing there, ready to translate his reply.

"I believe we are done. I will accompany you with your land agent whenever you're ready to see the parcel he says you have purchased. I took the liberty of contacting a surveyor who will also come with us."

"Good." She thanked Lewis. Hewitt also bowed and left them. Honor and Samuel walked down the courthouse steps to where Royale, Brother Ezekiel, and his giant of a son, Judah, waited for them.

After greeting them, Honor touched Royale's shoulder. "We have paid thy bond, Royale, and the men will be sent to prison. The terrible episode is done. And here is a new manumission paper for thee."

Appearing only a bit relieved, Royale folded the paper into her concealed pocket. "I thank you. When we leaving Cincinnati, Miss Honor?"

So Royale would feel safer outside the city after all. "Soon. We merely need to make sure that we take possession of the land Samuel truly bought." Honor claimed Royale's hand. "Come. Let us go get Eli and tell him the bad men are going away for many years."

As the three of them walked toward the Coxswain house to fetch Eli, Honor's relief evaporated. Royale was still at risk—even in a free state. This must change, but she couldn't conceive how.

Soon she and Deborah, plump and pleasant in sober gray, sat in her neat, spare parlor alone. George had been called back to his shop unexpectedly. Escaping Deborah's company, Samuel had taken Eli out to play in the garden, and Royale was watching them, drinking her tea outside. Honor could hear Royale encouraging Eli to catch the ball.

"Thee is not cheered by the guilty verdict?" Deborah asked.

Honor glanced toward the nearby window and saw a faint reflection of herself there. She did indeed look downcast.

"The joy of the Lord is my strength." The words came unbidden to Honor's mind. But she felt weak and defeated. They'd won a battle, but what of the war? "Everything is against us, against Royale. She will always be in danger as long as slavery is legal in the South."

"We face a strong, entrenched evil," Deborah agreed. "But I was a girl when thirteen colonies took on Britain and won independence. At the beginning, all new causes must seem doomed to failure. Think of the twelve apostles and Paul taking on the Roman Empire. We cannot let the opposition intimidate us."

"But how can we end slavery?" Honor stared at her reflection, so transparent, so sad, so strained.

"By doing anything that comes to hand. By speaking out whenever the chance comes our way. We must be always ready to meet any opportunity that God sends our way."

Deborah's words stirred Honor from apathy. She gazed at her reflection a moment longer, then turned to Deborah, trying to hold on to the spark of hope. But surely she would not find many opportunities to work for abolition in the middle of the forested wilderness.

❖

Samuel entered their bedroom and locked the door behind him. Honor sat by the window. Soon they would spend their last night at the inn. Over the past few days, the lawyer, surveyor, and land agent had finally thrashed everything out about which parcel of land was theirs.

Samuel tried not to notice his lovely wife in her chair, backlit by candlelight. Eli was already asleep in the middle of their bed. Their wedding night had been delayed for so long, too long. So much had happened in such a short time, and everything seemed to conspire to keep them celibate.

However, they would soon move into their own home. Would Honor be willing, or would she hold back?

Chapter 10

OCTOBER 30, 1819

Honor and Samuel stood in the general store nearest the inn, its shelves lined with all manner of merchandise. The store smelled of fall's apples, a barrel of them at the end of one long counter. Royale and Eli had remained at the inn with Judah Langston, their guardian. Perlie had come with Honor to buy staples to take to their new property in a week or so.

Preparing to leave Cincinnati and move again was playing havoc with Honor's emotions. Her thoughts were trying to drag her back to that awful memory of the day before she'd left High Oaks, trying to pull her down to the same devastation. A discreet glance at Samuel told her that, in contrast, he was eager to leave. Perhaps moving away from the city would help her better comprehend him, help them grow closer. They still lived as polite acquaintances—in public as well as in private.

Perlie stood with them in the store bare of other customers, ordering what she needed to set up her kitchen. "I need a tub-a lard," Perlie said to the bald store owner in his white apron, who was writing down her list. "And a pound-a salt, five pound sugar, and . . ."

Sinclair Hewitt rushed inside. "Mrs. Cathwell!"

The urgency in his voice raced up Honor's spine and grabbed her by the nape. She whipped around. "Sinclair Hewitt, what is it?"

"They escaped. The kidnappers escaped from the jail last night."

Perlie gasped.

Honor staggered from the blow. Samuel gripped her arm, tucking her closer. She forced herself to sign the dreadful news to him. The storekeeper stood, gawking at her as she signed. Ignoring him, she looked to Hewitt. "How did this happen?"

"You the people whose boy was kidnapped, the family whose man is deaf?" the storekeeper interrupted. "Is that why you make those motions with your fingers?"

"Yes," Honor snapped, glaring sideways at the man. "More to the point, our free black maid was abducted. They only took our nephew to force her to obey them."

He raised his hands. "No need to get excited."

"They let them go," Perlie speculated darkly. "That sheriff . . ." The woman waddled a few steps away, muttering to herself.

Honor and Hewitt made eye contact. Could Perlie be right?

"She's got no call to say that," the shopkeeper said. "Those kidnappers were convicted, and—"

Honor swung on him, grateful for a target. "The sheriff believed the kidnappers when they lied, saying I'd sold my maid to them. He believed that I sold a free woman in a free state."

In the face of her fierce challenge, the shopkeeper moved back a step.

Honor's hands clenched. In her mind they were wrapped around a throat—not this storekeeper's but the sheriff's. Horrified at herself, she loosened her hands and drew in a deep breath. No matter what, she must control her emotions, not let herself go the way of violence. That wasn't the Friends' way, God's way. *Forgive me, Father.*

Taking another deep breath, she turned to Hewitt. "What's being done to catch them?"

"A posse was deputized to search for them, but I have no doubt the two are already across the river in Kentucky, among their confederates."

"Confederates?" Honor asked and signed.

"Other slave catchers. I wouldn't doubt that the two kidnappers were slave catchers who saw a chance for something more lucrative than a reward from a slaveholder."

"It's against the law to aid a fugitive slave," the storekeeper lectured them.

Honor swung on the man a second time. "What has that got to do with our nephew and his nurse being kidnapped?" She flung the words into his face with her voice and fingers.

"Well, if we sent all the free blacks back to Africa, we wouldn't have these problems. Colonization is the answer." The man's voice shook with his own intensity.

"I don't want to go to Africa," Perlie said flatly, shocking Honor and everyone else. "Who do I know in Africa? That's not where I was born."

The storekeeper grew larger in his anger. "We don't want blacks here in Ohio—free or slave. This country is for white people."

"Then what you bring us here for?" Perlie demanded, her hands propped on her ample hips. "My grandfather didn't want to come here, but they brought him anyway."

Honor signed as fast as she could, keeping Samuel abreast of the exchange.

"Are you going to let your servant speak out of turn like this to a white man?" the storekeeper demanded.

Before Honor could reply, Samuel tapped her shoulder and she spoke his reply aloud. "She is a free woman, and she can say anything she wants to anyone. And we will not be shopping in thy store again, since thee doesn't care that our nephew's kidnappers have gone free."

"The two matters are entirely separate," the man sputtered.

"No, they aren't. Our nephew wouldn't have been in jeopardy if lawless men hadn't kidnapped our maid," Honor said bluntly, "just to sell her back into slavery for the sake of greed."

Without a backward glance, Samuel guided her to the

entrance and waved her and Perlie to precede him and Hewitt. Speaking out had lifted Honor's spirits. Even more heartening, Samuel had defended Perlie.

Outside, she turned and, standing on tiptoe, touched her husband's cheek. If they'd been alone, she might have kissed him. "Thank thee. What should we do?" she asked.

Hewitt paused nearby. "I must go. I'm going to write this story up for the newspaper."

"Thank thee!" Honor called after him as he hurried away.

Samuel touched her shoulder. "Let's go to the lawyer and see what he says about this."

"And I know a general store that is better than this one." Perlie cast a scornful look at the offending storefront. "I shop there for my last mistress. It farther down toward the wharf."

Honor looked to the woman. "Go and order all thee needs to set up the kitchen. Tell the storekeeper we will pay him when he delivers the goods to the stable at the inn later today."

"I'll do that, ma'am." The woman frowned deeply. "But don't you go gettin' your hopes up about those bad men. If those catchers cross the river, you not gon' find them. All Kentucky will hide them." Perlie didn't wait for a response, just started walking south.

Needing to touch Samuel again for reassurance, Honor slipped her arm into his, and they headed for Alan Lewis's office. Perlie's words repeated in her mind. She'd hoped that a free state would be different from a slave state, be a safe haven for Royale. She'd hoped in vain—a hard truth. For a moment she rested her head against Samuel's arm.

"We will keep Royale safe no matter what," Samuel signed.

Honor squeezed his arm in reply, grateful for his support. But he was just one man—a good man, but just one. And as much as she longed to make life safer for Royale and the other free blacks, she was just one woman, unenfranchised and married—slighted by law, which granted no rights to a woman with a husband. She fought the crushing weight of helplessness.

❖

NOVEMBER 8, 1819

On a sunny fall morning about a week later, Honor drove toward their new property, which could be reached in only an hour—no doubt a blessing from God. As soon as they left the outskirts of Cincinnati, the forest thickened along the road leading to Lebanon. With each mile from the city, the road became rougher, more a matter of wheel tracks gouged into an opening, a trail between the trunks of towering pines, oaks, and maples. This made for difficult driving, and the horses were skittish in the midst of the trees, a new surrounding for them. Deer and small animals darted out, startling the team.

Honor stood many times to guide the wagon around blind bends through the forest. She kept up a constant flow of calm words, guiding the team and reassuring herself too. The farther from Cincinnati they drove, the less sure she felt, in spite of the balmy breeze and the closer proximity of their new parcel. She glanced sideways.

Samuel sat beside her, unusually cheerful. He'd decided

the second parcel was better than the first, with larger buildings and a good creek running through the property. He'd told her he needed plenty of water for his glassworks. So at least he was happy.

Behind them, their baggage and provisions and Samuel's tools were piled high and strapped securely into the wagon. Perlie rode on the tailgate of the wagon with Eli in her charge. A box of noisy chickens sat beside the cook. Behind the wagon walked Royale and Judah, leading the new milk cow and goat. Judah had offered to come help them unload and get settled in their new place, and accepting his help had been easy. Honor had not missed his partiality for her maid. Perhaps Royale would find love here in Ohio. The thought brought Honor joy for Royale but sorrow for herself.

They rounded a bend, and there was the small village of Sharpesburg. A blacksmith shop and two cabins ranged along the road, about a half mile between each building. Honor slowed the wagon, hoping to see one of their new neighbors come out before she drove around another bend and down the road at least a mile to their property.

Samuel, of course, asked why they were slowing, wanting to go directly to their cabin and begin setting up.

She didn't reply, just kept the team dawdling along. She needed to meet her new neighbors and find out what kind of people they were. A woman ventured out of the nearest cabin, and a man walked up from a cornfield carved out of the surrounding forest.

"Good day!" the small, white-haired woman from the

nearest cabin called out with a friendly wave. "Didn't I see you folk pass by before?"

"Good morning! We're the Cathwells. My husband has bought land near here."

The woman approached the wagon, glancing toward its rear. "I'm Charity Hastings. I live with my son and his wife here." Charity was speaking to Honor but gazing toward the rear of the wagon. "You bring servants with you?"

"Yes." Honor waited to see what the woman would say.

"I guess that's all right as long as they keep to themselves. There's a black town farther up the road, name of Bucktown. They keep to themselves pretty much too. We just see them passing once in a while when they go to and from the city."

Honor did not feel herself warming to this woman.

The young man from the field stepped forward, his face ruddy and his hair thick and red. "I'm Charity's son, Thad Hastings. My wife is lying in after our firstborn came last week. Welcome to Sharpesburg." Thad offered his hand to Samuel.

Honor signed the man's greeting and was not surprised to see the consternation on their new neighbors' faces. "My husband is deaf," Honor explained. "I talk to him with my fingers."

"And you're both in mourning," Charity Hastings said, still assessing them.

"Yes, thee is right," Honor said politely but felt herself tighten inside. "We both lost close relations recently."

"Oh, my!" Charity exclaimed, her face registering surprise and displeasure. "And you're Quakers, too."

"We are not a usual couple; that's true." Honor gazed at the woman and her son, assessing them as they continued to do the same. Not the welcome she'd hoped for. *But maybe I hoped for too much.*

Another man joined them, obviously the blacksmith from his leather apron and sooty face.

Samuel signed to Honor. "Tell the blacksmith that I'm a glassblower and will set up shop soon. I will need some blacksmithing from time to time to repair tools and such."

Everyone looked to Samuel, in apparent disbelief that a deaf-mute could be a trained artisan. Honor gritted her teeth.

The blacksmith, named Micah Smith, took off his battered hat and shook Samuel's hand. A few more comments were exchanged.

Bidding them a curt adieu and slapping the reins, Honor decided that the meeting was enough for now. These people would be their neighbors. Time would tell if they would be good neighbors or not. But thus far they had not impressed her.

❖

Down the road and around a bend of trees, Samuel gazed with satisfaction at their new home: the two-room cabin, the roomy detached kitchen, and the large barn. The long delay had finally ended, and he could start his business, do things his own way. Samuel glanced around him, suddenly missing his mother, an intense, gripping feeling of loss.

He'd always imagined arriving here with Mother, his brother, and his brother's family. Now there was only him and Eli. But that was foolish. He had Honor, Royale, the cook, and Judah along to help. Still, he wished his mother could have lived to see this day, be here. And he still didn't know how to reconcile his wife to their new life outside the city. Would she hold this move against him?

Honor halted the team outside the cabin door. Samuel got down and waved for Judah to help him unload the wagon. He turned back to assist Honor. She stared at him for a moment, and he recalled her hesitation before boarding the steamboat. He searched her face for any sign she cared for him, trusted him.

Without showing any, she accepted his help. On the ground, she paused, gazing around her. Again he was hit by the fact that he'd brought a Maryland lady to live in a cabin in the wilderness.

"Samuel, please will thee and Judah bring the trunks and boxes inside? Then the kitchen boxes to that building so we can be working while thee two set up thy workshop."

He nodded.

His wife marched toward the two-room log cabin and opened the door. The day before, Samuel and Judah had driven out with the new furniture, swept the buildings clear of cobwebs and dust, and cleaned the windows.

Over the past weeks, Samuel had insisted on paying Judah for protecting Royale whenever they had to leave her alone at the inn. And when the man had offered to help him set up his glassworks and new home, Samuel had promised to pay him for that as well. Judah had begun to learn signs too, so Samuel could work with him. It was good to have a man along.

That idea startled Samuel. He couldn't recall any men except for his father and brother whom he'd wanted working beside him. But Judah was quiet and efficient. Samuel realized with surprise that he liked Judah. This prompted another thought that caused him to hurry after Honor. He caught her elbow.

She turned, a question on her face.

"Do you think Judah would work for us?"

"As a handyman?" she asked.

"No." He thought of laboring alone in his glassworks. "He could work as my apprentice. I will need help in the shop."

A smile lit Honor's face. "An excellent idea. Shall I ask him?"

Samuel nodded. "We'll make a room for him in the barn for now—if he wants the job."

Honor turned and waved to Judah. She offered him the job, then signed his reply: "I don't know if I can be a glassblower, but I will do my best, sir." Judah was beaming, shaking Samuel's hand, and thanking him.

Samuel felt a sudden joy. He'd always thought he'd prefer to work on his own. But now he realized not only that he was unable to do his best work alone but also that he didn't want to.

❁

Pondering this new development, Honor directed Royale and Perlie as the three began unpacking the household items. They would start in the main cabin and help Perlie set up the kitchen next, which would also be the living quarters for her and Royale.

Samuel's job offer for Judah cheered Honor more and more, and she noticed it put a smile on Royale's face too. Honor drew in the clean, pine-scented air. She sent a prayer, thanking God for bringing them out of the city yet not too far. She had Royale and Perlie for company, after all, and Royale would be well protected with two men at hand.

The only thing that didn't please Honor was that Royale, Perlie, and Judah had insisted that they eat in the kitchen, separate from the Cathwells. They feared the potential backlash from those who lived nearby. Blacks and whites did not sit at the same table, and Royale and Perlie were paid as servants. Certainly the neighbor's comment today about their servants keeping to themselves proved that Royale had been right.

Yet Honor would make this place home. And perhaps here she and Samuel could become a true husband and wife. The last thought wavered inside her. All they'd gone through had shown her that Samuel was a man of character, in spite of his faults. Misunderstandings and disagreements stood between them, but as she considered his honest and kind nature, a new tenderness drew her to him.

❖

At sunset Samuel gazed around their cabin—now filled with their possessions, even the clock from his mother's kitchen—and knelt to bank the fire low for the night. Eli had insisted upon sleeping with Royale in the large bed at the rear of the kitchen instead of his pallet in the loft above their room. That left Samuel and his wife alone for the first time since their wedding almost two months ago. He didn't know where to look because everywhere he glanced, he saw his wife.

His mind went over every time she had reached for him during the past weeks. She had sought comfort from him when Royale and Eli were missing and again at the trial. And she always let others know his deafness didn't make him less than other men. She included him in every conversation. All of this was encouraging, but would she welcome his advances?

In her nightdress already, Honor was blowing out the extra candles. He followed her every move with his gaze, unable to look away. Then she carried one taper into their bedroom. He finished with the fire and rose, dusting off his hands. The faint glow from the candle drew him toward the bedroom. Along with the fact that his wife was waiting for him in a soft, white flannel gown.

When Samuel entered the bedroom, he found his wife sitting up in bed, reading her Bible. His mouth went dry. In the shadows he shed his day clothing, hanging each piece carefully on the pegs by the door. His heart was thumping in an odd gait. He pulled on his nightshirt and slipped into the far side of the bed. His wife's gaze never left the page she was reading.

Then he noticed that the Bible trembled ever so slightly in her hand. Did she fear him? He wanted to tell her he would never hurt her. He tried to tally his feelings for her. Did he love her? *I need her.* That, of course, was not the same, not enough to justify taking her into his arms. Or was it?

She closed her Bible and turned to him. "Good night, Samuel."

He responded in kind. Honor blew out the candle and slid farther under the covers. His heart began thumping harder and more unevenly. He could not make himself move closer to her. *She can't want me.*

Then he felt Honor take his hand. He imagined folding her into his embrace, kissing her. But the fear of her rejection held him in place. He pictured her pulling away and how that would cut into him. He could barely breathe. *She must make the first move.*

❖

NOVEMBER 9, 1819

After a long, sleepless night, Honor sat at the breakfast table. Their first night alone as man and wife had been an agony of indecision and rejection. She could barely look at Samuel. What did she know about the secrets of the marriage bed? She was the wife. The man must act first, not the woman.

"Hello the house!" An unfamiliar man's voice called the greeting outside their door.

Honor rose from the table, signing to Samuel that they had visitors. Stepping outside with Samuel and Eli behind her, she saw that a wagon filled with strangers—a man, a woman, and six children—had arrived at her door. What did they want? "How may I help thee?"

Her question seemed to make the man and woman mute.

"May I help thee?" she repeated.

"You're Quaker," said the man, who looked to be in his thirties.

"I am." Honor waited.

"Is your husband the glassblower that's deaf?" the man asked, taking off his hat politely. "The one whose nephew got kidnapped?"

Honor sensed something wrong. The woman, her face hidden by a ragged poke bonnet, sat with her head bowed, and the children stared at Honor. "Yes, he is."

"Is that him?" the man asked, staring at Samuel. "He looks normal."

"He *is* normal," Honor snapped. "He just can't hear due to a childhood fever."

"I see," the man said, setting his battered hat on the wagon brake.

This blunt man strained her politeness. Why were they here? Honor wished they would get to the point. But one couldn't demand people to state their business or leave.

"When his nephew was kidnapped and all, we read stories in the paper about him and his being a glassblower and how he talks with his hands." The stranger watched as Honor signed this to Samuel. Honor knew that Sinclair Hewitt had written articles about them during the kidnapping and trial.

The man motioned toward the woman beside him. "See how she does that with her fingers?" he said. "It's clever." Then he turned back to Honor. "I just married this widow, and together we'll have five children, my three daughters and her two sons."

Honor looked and saw that there were six children, all

who looked to be twelve years and under. So why had the man said they had five children together?

"My son," the woman said in a low voice, not looking up, "also suffered a severe fever early this year. It took his hearing as well. And robbed me of my husband, too." The woman pressed a hand over her mouth.

Struck with sympathy, Honor signed this to Samuel and said aloud, "Oh, I'm so sorry." The woman looked as if she was about to begin weeping. Honor thought she might know why they had come. "Did thee want to learn sign language?"

"No, we want to give her son to you," the man said. "I'll keep her other sons. They can hear. But I don't want a deaf kid. I told her I'd marry her, but I won't take the boy."

Honor could hardly believe what she was hearing. She swallowed twice before she could speak. "I beg thy pardon. Thee won't take her deaf son?"

"No, it's not safe to have a kid around that can't hear," the man said. "Besides, people will think he's strange, that we got bad blood. And we're on our way farther west. I'm looking for land in Illinois. I hear the soil's better there, and no trees to clear before plowing."

The widow was wringing her hands and weeping silently. She muttered, "I don't want to leave him, but what can I do? I had to marry again. I have myself and two other children to think of. We have nothing." She turned, revealing the suffering in her face, which implored Honor's understanding.

Honor was shocked into silence. She could barely move her fingers to sign the gist of the conversation to Samuel.

Sitting high in Samuel's arms, Eli watched, looking confused. He pushed to be released, and Samuel let him down.

"Well, will you take him?" the man demanded with obvious frustration. "You can teach him how to do those signs with his hands, and maybe he can learn your man's trade. We can't tarry. We got to drive back to Cincinnati now in good time to make it to our boat."

As Honor signed these words, Samuel gripped his fists as if to keep from attacking the man. He signed to her, "This man is asking us to take in his wife's son like a stray dog?"

Honor responded urgently. "We must take this child. If we don't, this man might abandon him somewhere. We can't let that happen."

Samuel nodded, still clenching and unclenching his fists. "Tell him we will keep the child."

Honor translated this, and the woman began to sob openly.

The man got down and lifted one of the boys from the rear of the wagon, pushing him toward Samuel, then turned to climb back on the wagon.

"What is his name?" Honor asked over the woman's sobbing, her heart racing. This was all happening too quickly.

"Caleb. His name is Caleb Mason," the man said. "His father was John Caleb Mason." Regaining his place on the wagon, the man tried to prevent his wife from getting down. But she leapt to the ground.

She dropped to her knees and clasped the child to her, weeping. "Please, Thomas, isn't there any way—?"

"We agreed before we went to the preacher. I need a

wife. You need a husband. But I can't do anything for Caleb. These people can. I know it's hard. But it's for his best too."

She continued to sob, holding Caleb tightly. The boy looked to be nearly eight. He was thin with brown hair and eyes and dressed in ragged clothing. His expression mixed fear and confusion.

Slowly his mother regained her composure. She turned to Honor, rising. "When Caleb is able to understand you, please explain to him. I can see you're good people. I got the newspaper saved. When we get settled, I'll write to you so I can keep in touch with my son."

Honor didn't know what to say. They were going to leave this boy here with them. How would she explain this to a child who didn't hear and hadn't learned to sign? Panic fluttered to life within her.

She moved forward with the woman, who let her husband pull her up onto the wagon. "Is thee sure this is what thee wants to do? Stay with us and learn to sign, and then—"

"I can't have a deaf kid," the man said without a hint of apology. "People will think we're odd. Treat us as peculiar. I can't do it."

Honor tried to think of an argument, a persuasion. Judah had come out of the kitchen and was heading toward them.

"Much obliged. She'll write!" The man slapped the reins, backed up the team, and made a wide turn in front of the barn.

One little boy sitting in the back of the wagon cried out, "No—don't leave Caleb! No, Ma! No!"

Caleb screamed, "No!" He ran after the wagon. "No! Ma! Chad! Seth! Ma!" he wailed in a strange-sounding voice as he ran.

Lifting her hem, Honor ran after the child, his screams going through her like icy needles. *Dear God, help!*

The man sped up the team, shaking them off.

Finally, farther down the track, both Caleb and she gave up the chase. The little boy collapsed on the ground, face-down, shaking, sobbing.

Honor dropped to her knees. She didn't know whether to comfort him or just sit and wait for him to exhaust himself. What had just taken place in this quiet setting had shaken her to the core. Sympathetic tears coursed down her face. After her father had died, she'd felt like this child in a way.

And now she feared in some tight place in her heart that Samuel might never accept her as his wife. It was irrational, she knew, but it was real. This boy's anguish and rejection were hers. She swallowed her own sobs.

Eli came near and sank to his knees on the other side of the boy. He too looked bewildered. Samuel and Judah joined them, standing over Caleb.

Samuel touched her shoulder but made no sign.

She pressed her hand over his. Why did he only touch her when she needed comfort? Still she touched her cheek to his hand. What were they going to do?

Honor looked up at Samuel and saw in his eyes that he was suffering along with this child. She nodded and signed, "This is Caleb."

Finally the boy lay still. Eli touched him. Caleb turned

his head toward Eli. Eli pointed to himself and, with his chubby little fingers, signed and said, "I am Eli."

Honor pointed to Caleb, saying and signing, "Thee is Caleb." Eli repeated the sign.

The child stared at him.

Honor picked up Caleb's hand and helped him move his fingers to say, "Eli." Then she lifted Eli's hand. "Keep showing him thy name, Eli, till he learns it. We must teach him how to speak with his hands."

Obediently Eli followed her instruction.

Honor sat back on her heels, watching. Would Eli be able to open up communication with the boy?

Chapter 11

CALEB REFUSED TO be distracted by Eli and refused to get up. Honor did not want to give in to tears again. The child needed her to be strong now. Weeping with him would not help him face this awful parting, this slicing of family ties.

"Can't just leave him in the middle of the road, ma'am," Judah said. Approaching the boy, Perlie and Royale paused, concerned. "He might try to go after them, get lost," Judah continued. "It's not safe out here for a child alone. Bear and wolves around."

Eli looked troubled, and she didn't know how to reassure him. He'd just been through a terrible ordeal himself.

Honor covered her face with her hands, her heart torn in two. Grandfather had betrayed her just as this child had been betrayed by his family. When would this stop happening? One parting, one sorrow, followed another. At an outcry from the boy, she dropped her hands.

Samuel had picked the boy up and was carrying him toward their cabin. Caleb screamed, beat and kicked Samuel, but the child's fighting didn't deter her husband. He marched onward. When he arrived in front of their door, he set the boy down.

The child looked up at the big man, knuckling his red, swollen, tear-clogged eyes.

Samuel knelt in front of him, eye to eye. He gripped Caleb's thin shoulders but in a sign of acceptance, of affection even. Then Samuel signed to Eli, "Play here with this boy. Help him."

Eli obeyed, sat down beside Caleb, and showed him his carved wooden horses. "You can have this one," Eli said and signed. He shoved one into Caleb's hand and galloped the other horse down his own leg, demonstrating how to play with the toy.

At this act of generosity, Honor blinked back tears. Royale edged closer to her, offering silent comfort.

Caleb finally grasped the horse but only stared at his new toy.

"We must go about our business," Samuel signed. "Let Caleb have time to accept us as we are. But he needs Eli as company."

The sentence, so insightful and wise, raised Honor up onto her toes so she could put her arms around Samuel. Once again the man's instinctive kindness came to the fore and drew her near. Then, embarrassed in front of Judah and the others, she pulled away.

Samuel motioned for Judah to follow him to the barn. The men left her with the boys, sitting by the door. She wanted to hover over Caleb, make him welcome somehow. But she trusted Samuel's instinct.

Caleb must face this cruel abandonment. Perlie reached into her white apron pocket and held out two oatmeal cookies, one to each of the boys.

Caleb let his lie in his lap while Eli started eating his immediately.

"Eli, stay with Caleb and try to teach him to sign *horse* and thy name. If he tries to leave, call me."

"I got a brother now," Eli said, still nibbling deftly.

"Yes, now thee has a brother," Honor agreed. Caleb wasn't the first child who had been sent away from his family. And though she didn't like Caleb's stepfather, in a way he had acted in the boy's best interest.

Samuel would teach this child what he needed to face the world as a deaf person. But how could she communicate this to an abandoned child who couldn't hear her comforting words, whose heart had been broken?

❖

Honor came awake abruptly and sat up in bed. Cold night air blew around her face and ears, chilling her. The faintest moon glow peeped in through the window and the open door. Why was the door open?

Instant fear shot through her. Instead of sleeping with Royale in the kitchen, Eli had decided to keep Caleb company in the loft above their bedroom. Honor threw back the covers and hurried to the ladder outside the bedroom door. She climbed up and found Eli sound asleep, wrapped in a quilt. But Caleb was not in the other quilt. *Oh no.*

Honor let herself down the ladder, nearly falling in her haste. She shook Samuel awake. When he sat up, rubbing his eyes, she pointed toward the door. "Caleb isn't in the loft," she signed, then realized he couldn't see her hand in such dim light. She moved and held her hand in front of the glow from the low fire, signing it again.

She heard rather than saw him get out of bed. He clambered up the ladder as if checking her statement. She didn't blame him. She could hardly believe a small boy would venture out alone into the black night. When Samuel came down, she heard him pulling on his clothing. She hurried to do likewise, donning her dress over her nightgown and tugging on shoes and a shawl as quickly as she could.

He passed by her and lifted the candlestick from the mantel, lighting the taper from the fire. The candle illumined his face, where she read his concern. He handed her the candle and signed by the light, "We must go after him. I will light the lantern and get my staff."

Before he moved, she signed and said, "Where will we look?"

"The road. His mother went down the road."

She signed her agreement. Within minutes the two of them stood just outside the door, the chill hitting her full in the face.

"Caleb!" Honor called, then felt foolish for calling a deaf child.

With the lantern, Samuel went out back to make sure the boy hadn't gone to the necessary. He peered into the window of the kitchen before coming back and shaking his head, letting Honor know Caleb wasn't with Royale. Then he paused. "I'll check the barn."

He returned within minutes and again shook his head no. Judah hurried out of the barn, joining them. In the thin light from the high quarter moon, Samuel grasped Honor's hand, and she his. Samuel must be as afraid as she of their losing each other in the dark. But he released her in a moment, bowing to the necessity of signed communication.

"How far do you think he could get?" Samuel asked her, holding his free hand in front of the lantern light.

"I don't know." Judah had mentioned wolves and bears, but a child could die of exposure just by getting lost among the myriad of trees and not finding his way out. The surrounding forest loomed, impenetrable and threatening. "But we must find him."

Judah stood nearby, shivering a little. Samuel paused and told Judah in sign to stay—to protect Royale and Perlie, check on Eli from time to time, and watch for Caleb. The boy would likely head toward Cincinnati, not away. Honor interpreted to ensure the message was clear, and Judah hurried to the kitchen. Honor accepted Samuel's decision. She could only be grateful that he didn't send her to wait while he searched alone, for she couldn't have borne that.

Samuel moved slowly forward on the rutted road, the pool of lamplight before him. Honor stumbled, saved from falling by Samuel's hand. In the silence of night, she could hear her heart thudding in her ears.

Their slow pace countered her desire to run down

the road, calling for the child. Another fear reared up in her—not just that they might not find Caleb tonight in the dark. Maybe he didn't want to be found. Sometimes people couldn't bear the changes that life forced on them.

Maybe Caleb had wandered into the forest, unthinking, in a despair as deep as death. She swallowed a moan. *Lord, help us find Caleb.*

They pressed on, straining against the almost-complete dark that kept them cautious. The lantern in Samuel's hand became her guide. What must have been a bat swooped over them. Honor tugged her shawl up over her head and clasped it tightly under her chin.

The chill of the crisp fall night soon worked its way steadily through the layers of her clothing. She shivered. Cold on the outside, terrified on the inside. A wolf howled in the distance and others of the pack joined in, sending chills through her. Had they detected the scent of the boy and his fear? Or hers and Samuel's?

How long had they been walking? Honor glanced up and saw that the quarter moon had lowered against the starry sky. Her perceptions had become altered: her eyes could detect more and her ears had become sharper, picking up the rustling of every small creature through the forest, the low hooting of every owl, and the rush of unseen wings.

Halfway to Cincinnati, they halted. Honor moved her hand in front of the glow of the lantern to sign. "How far could he go?" Even as she signed, she knew Samuel could not answer. Only God knew.

In reply, he pulled her to him, pressing her cheek against his wool coat, and she welcomed his touch.

Then he signed by the lantern light, "We must go home. We can do nothing more now."

She held in her crushing despair. They had failed this child. Nonetheless, she turned around with Samuel and began the cold, despairing trek back over the rutted, uneven road. The pointless journey home felt shorter in spite of the miles and even bleaker than before. Would they ever see Caleb again? *Oh, Lord, please.*

After stopping to tell Judah they hadn't found Caleb, Samuel led her inside their cabin and shut the door behind them. Chilled to her marrow, Honor stirred the fire, added kindling and a few slender quartered logs. She rubbed her hands near the awakening fire, trying to warm up. Yet the heat of the fire did nothing to the ice inside.

Behind her, Samuel set the lantern on the mantel and shed his jacket.

Suddenly Honor could bear their separation no longer. Rising, she flung her arms around his neck and pressed her face against him, weeping for the child who had lost his family and was now lost himself. Weeping for all they too had lost.

❖

Samuel froze in place. His wife's despair over not finding this boy, a deaf boy who'd been with them less than a day, touched him, moved him. He nudged up her chin, intending to comfort her with an understanding gaze. But in the flickering shadows he glimpsed her soft, perfect lips, barely parted.

And in one swift motion Samuel's mouth claimed hers.

He tried to end the kiss, but instead he deepened it. Any second she'd push him away. But he drank in this stolen moment, yet not tightening his hold, letting her know he'd release her.

Then he felt it, her lips answering his. Exultation roared through him. His wife wanted him. He swept her up into his arms and carried her to their bed. He laid her down gently and went to his knees. He let his mouth hover over hers, asking her permission.

She reached up and guided his head downward, his mouth meeting hers, drawing in her breath as his own. Tears clogged his throat as he chanted silently, *Honor, my Honor.*

❖

NOVEMBER 10, 1819

Honor woke the next morning, aware of a lush, sweet warmth. Samuel lay against her, his face on her shoulder and one arm over her. Morning light shone brightly through the windows. She knew she should get up. Perlie would soon bring coffee and breakfast. Instead she gazed at her husband's handsome face, half hidden against her. She trailed her fingers through his thick, springy hair. Now she knew how it was between a husband and his wife. She blushed, remembering.

Eli clambered down the ladder. "Where's Caleb?"

Her bliss evaporated. She shook Samuel's shoulder.

He looked into her eyes, a slow smile registering on his face.

"Eli is awake and wants to know where Caleb is," she signed.

His smile vanished. He rose and signed to Eli. "Caleb ran away last night. After breakfast we will try to decide how to look for him."

"He ran away?" Eli echoed. "I want him here."

"We do too, Eli," Honor said soothingly. "Now go wash thy hands and sit down at the table for breakfast. There's a good boy."

Eli moved to obey, and Samuel rolled away from her and donned his trousers and shirt.

She followed suit, quickly slipping on her clothing, gathering her loosed, tangled hair over her shoulder. After Samuel stoked the fire, she turned and caught him watching her. They exchanged sweet glances.

Samuel moved to her, wrapped his arms around her, and kissed her. Then he left to help Judah take care of their stock.

Honor blinked away tears of relief, of joy. She and Samuel could not be parted. They had become truly husband and wife.

Then she recalled a little deaf boy lost and alone in miles and miles of forest, hungry and feeling unwanted, and she blanched. *Father, protect him. Help us find him.*

After breakfast, with Judah at his side, Samuel headed to the barn. He nearly had his shop set up. While Honor drove toward the city to search for Caleb, Judah would help Samuel lay the groundwork of his forge and its chimney. Having someone working beside him who was learning to communicate through sign gave him a feeling he hadn't experienced since his brother's death.

Uppermost in his mind, however, was what had happened last night when he and Honor had arrived home. He didn't know how to feel, how he was supposed to feel. But making love had altered matters between them.

She'd been sincerely distressed over the child's abandonment and his flight. That had drawn Samuel to her in a way he hadn't expected, made her approachable, open to him. Why didn't she look at Caleb and despise him for his deafness as others did? Despise Samuel as others did, for that matter?

Samuel kept reliving moments from the night before. Holding Honor in his arms had been an experience like no other. He'd waited for her to hold back or to stop him. But she had welcomed his touch with a shy eagerness he'd found irresistible. He still had difficulty believing that Honor, a lovely woman of strong character, really wanted him as her husband. But the facts appeared to confirm that she did. The only worry now was, would they find Caleb?

He entered the barn and, with his hands propped on his hips, surveyed all the progress they'd made. A metal-topped workbench, buckets necessary for water to keep wooden tools from igniting, and in the center of the room, the beginnings of the mighty forge that would melt sand into liquid glass.

Nevertheless, his concern for Caleb overlaid both his satisfaction with the workshop and his joy and confusion about last night. The boy had suffered the same fate he had.

Distant memories of the morning Samuel had himself

wakened to a silent world flickered in his mind. He'd been angry and terrified, frustrated that he couldn't hear his mother's voice. But both his mother and father had loved him enough to hold him close and find a way to communicate with him. *I was blessed.* The thought startled him.

Judah tapped him on the shoulder, also startling him.

Samuel grinned. "Let's get started."

Judah nodded with understanding.

Samuel's mind shifted back to Honor. He wished he could have asked her why she'd welcomed him last night, let him become her husband in the most intimate way. But he couldn't frame the words, couldn't bring himself to test the still-uncertain waters between them. And for now he was content to be accepted, whatever the reason.

❖

Before Honor left to search for Caleb, Royale came in to gather the breakfast dishes and halted, giving her a thorough look-over. "Something different about you."

Honor blushed, hot and no doubt vivid red.

"I see," Royale said with a knowing expression. "You know Judah is courting me?"

"I like him."

"Me too." Like girls again, they both giggled. Then just as suddenly they stopped. "I pray you find that poor boy."

Royale's heartfelt sympathy poured through Honor. She paused, pressing her lips together to keep them from trembling. "Thank thee." Honor helped Royale with her chore and walked her to the door, discussing the day's work ahead of them. "I must go and alert people that the deaf boy belongs to us. If somebody finds Caleb, he couldn't tell them where home is."

Royale nodded solemnly. "I be praying." She left with the tray of dishes to wash.

Honor prepared herself to face the world and soon was driving the team away from home. After alerting her neighbors about Caleb, Honor drove down Lebanon Road, first away from the city and then toward Cincinnati.

At the few cabins she passed, Honor climbed down and asked if anybody had seen a boy around Caleb's age. No one had. Each regretful comment and promise to watch for Caleb brought her nearer to tears. How could she have foreseen that he would actually run away?

Finally she had to turn home. She couldn't believe that the child could have walked in either direction this far in the dark last night. She'd been terrified with a lantern and Samuel at her side. She returned, hungry and thirsty, to Sharpesburg.

As Honor passed their neighbors' cabin, Charity ran out. "Did you find the boy?"

"No." Honor wrestled down her own despair. "I feel so helpless."

Charity clasped her hands together. "I'm praying he'll come back."

Surprised by the woman's sympathy, Honor tried to smile but was afraid she did a poor job. "Thank thee. I have to get home."

When she arrived, Samuel and Judah came out of the barn and Royale, Eli, and Perlie from the kitchen. She knew from their expressions the boy hadn't returned while she was gone. She choked back helpless tears.

In spite of everyone watching, Samuel helped her down and clasped her to him, comforting her. She clung to him. They'd done all they could. She knew God held Caleb in his hand, and she prayed he would guide the child home to them, safe. *Please, Lord.*

❁

NOVEMBER 11, 1819

"Hello the house!" A deep, unfamiliar voice called from outside, summoning Honor. She stood at the table, gathering up the tableware from breakfast. Another night and a new morning had come since Caleb had run away. Her pulse quickened. Had someone found him?

"Coming!" she called. She stepped outside and halted in her tracks, her welcoming smile dying on her lips.

Two rough-looking men with rifles at their sides sat on the bench of a wagon. One appeared older, with gray in his unruly hair and beard, and the other much younger. A grandfather and grandson? Caleb sat between them, his hands and feet tied.

She stepped forward and the boy's name died on her lips. Not only couldn't the boy hear her, but another sight shocked her to silence. In the back of the wagon, two black men slumped, shackled hand and foot to iron rings embedded in the wood.

Slave catchers. A silent gasp filled her lungs. Two of this brand of wicked men had kidnapped her Royale. And now two others had come to her door. Her heart plummeting, Honor couldn't find her voice.

Eli ran from the cabin. "Caleb!" He halted. "Why you tie him up?"

"We're slave catchers, boy," the older one said. He had one eye whose lid stayed half shut. "We found this kid by the side of the road," he said around the wad of chaw in his cheek. "We asked around and heard a boy gone missing. Everybody said head this way, that the boy was deaf and wanted here in Sharpesburg." He spit over the side of the wagon.

"The blacksmith sent us to your door. What do you want a deaf kid for?" the younger man with long, greasy hair asked, looking at her boldly.

She ignored his inappropriate attention. One glance at the battered and beaten slaves told her these two knew nothing of compassion. She'd heard people say their skin crawled when encountering something extremely distasteful, and now she felt it herself. "Caleb was left with us by his parents. Eli, run and get thy uncle, please."

Honor did not feel safe around these men. She didn't like the way they looked at her, and Caleb appeared terrified. Had they hurt the boy? She had no way to ask him. Honking geese flew overhead in a V, filling the frustrated silence between them.

Samuel and Eli joined her. She noted that Judah, Royale, and Perlie remained inside. "Thank them for bringing Caleb back," her husband signed. He moved to lift the boy down.

"Not so fast," the younger slave catcher said, shifting between Samuel and Caleb. "We spent half a day—"

"More'n half a day," the older interrupted, "carrying the kid round, looking for this place."

"Yeah," the younger agreed. "And time is money."

Though signing what they said to Samuel, Honor stared at them, aghast. Previously they'd said they found Caleb beside the road. No doubt Caleb had finally given up and come to the roadside, and these two opportunists had snatched him up. And they were demanding a bounty.

Samuel signed for Honor to ask how much they wanted.

Honor did so numbly.

"Two bucks," the older one said, belligerent.

Samuel signed for her to go inside and bring out his purse. She did so and handed it to Samuel, who unclasped it.

Then he opened his palm, revealing the silver coins, and motioned for them to hand him the child.

The older slave catcher grabbed the money, and the other moved so Samuel could lift Caleb into his arms.

Honor stepped closer to her husband, still uneasy.

"We heard your man was deaf," the younger slave catcher said, actually leering at her now. "Couldn't you do no better? A pretty gal like you?"

Honor flushed hotly at the question, though she'd heard it before. "Thee is impertinent. Our business is done. Leave."

They laughed as if she'd told them a joke. The older one slapped the reins and turned the wagon.

Honor stood with her hand tucked into Samuel's arm and watched the wagon drive away. The black men in the back looked crushed, their eyes staring at her without hope.

Honor had trouble breathing. She'd been able to rescue Royale but was powerless now. She and Samuel were no match for the slave catchers, who were armed and protected by law.

The wagon disappeared around a bend. "Untie him, please," Honor said.

Her words proved unnecessary since Samuel had set the boy down and was already undoing the knots.

Caleb began weeping, and the desolate sound tore at her heart.

She dropped to her knees and wrapped her arms around the boy, careful not to block Samuel's efforts. When Caleb was free, he clung to her and she to him. Only then did she notice that Caleb had fresh bruising and a cut by his eye. Reacting without thinking, she signed, "Did they hit thee?"

Samuel growled in his throat, a menacing sound, something she'd never heard him do before.

Honor glanced at her husband's face, contorted in rage. Heartened by his similar reaction to the slave catchers' unfeeling behavior, she touched his hand and signed, "Take him inside so I can examine him. He might have other bruises or cuts."

Honor followed as Samuel carried Caleb into the house and sat him on the bench. She ran her hands over him, watching to see if he showed pain at her touch. The little boy sat silent and morose, tears washing his dirty face. "He doesn't seem to be hurt other than the bruise."

The boy's stomach grumbled, and he peered at Honor with hesitation.

"Yes," Honor said and signed. "I'll get something for thee to eat right now."

Stepping outside, she called Perlie, who was already bringing corn bread and fried salt pork. Judah and Royale stood just outside the door, watching Caleb.

Honor and Royale exchanged glances filled with horror over what had just come to their door. Turning away so Samuel couldn't read her lips, she said, "I couldn't do anything for the two men."

Royale nodded and didn't object when Judah put an arm around her shoulders. The sight lifted Honor's mood, but only a mite. What a sad world sin had caused.

The boy inhaled the food and drank several cups of sweet coffee. When he finished, he fell asleep on the bench where he sat.

Samuel caught him before he slid under the table and carried him up to the loft.

The six of them stood together outside in the crisp autumn day, facing each other. "We must make Caleb welcome in every way we can," she signed and said.

"I'll play with him," Eli volunteered.

"That's good, Eli," Honor said. "I don't think he'll run away again." After being caught by those hard men, who would? Her whole body clenched with outrage at the callous pair. The desolate eyes of the escaped slaves in the back of the wagon flickered in her thoughts, bringing a tide of sympathy and overcoming her caution. "I wish I could have gotten the slaves away from them."

"That is not our business," Samuel signed. "Those men are merely carrying out the law."

Samuel's hand sought hers. But even as she accepted his touch, Samuel's unsympathetic reply about the slave catchers caused her heart to pull back. Royale, Judah, and Perlie excused themselves and headed off. As they walked away, Royale repeated Samuel's words aloud to Perlie, who was having trouble learning to sign. Perlie shook her head. Honor felt their dark response to Samuel's words.

Still, he was only giving the same opinion about runaway slaves that most everyone else would give. Only a few—and most of them Quakers—thought slavery should be abolished. Another belief that distinguished the Society of Friends and caused others to mock and distrust them.

Honor recalled how her neighbors in Maryland, people whose great-grandparents had known her great-grandparents, had shunned her for her belief in abolition. How Darah and her own grandfather, two she had loved, had forsaken her. She tried to wash her mind of these thoughts.

She had married Samuel Cathwell. Now she must continue drawing closer to him—even though he didn't share her belief in abolition. Still, she couldn't forget what she'd seen this day. Would never forget her own powerlessness. There must be something she could do.

Chapter 12

NOVEMBER 25, 1819

Roused, Honor blinked herself awake. Careful not to interrupt her husband's sleep before she knew what had disturbed her, she sat up in bed. Moonlight shone through the windows.

Royale, wrapped tightly in a shawl, waited beside Honor's bed. What had brought her out in the middle of the night?

Trying to wake fully, Honor began turning to Samuel.

Swiftly Royale claimed her arm. "No," she whispered and motioned for Honor to come out into the larger room.

Confused but trusting, Honor slid her feet into her slippers. Royale already held her dressing gown and helped Honor into it. When they reached the outer door, Royale offered her a wool shawl, hanging on a peg there.

Royale led her out into the chill night under faint moonlight. A few feet from the house, Honor halted. "What's wrong?" Then she noticed that Royale had brought the medicine chest along. "Is Perlie or Judah sick?"

"Somebody sick."

Honor wanted to question her, but the brittle chill hurried them toward the kitchen. Within seconds Royale was waving Honor inside, where the fire glowed bright. Inside the door, Judah stood, watchful.

Perlie sat on the bench at the small table. Beside her slumped a stranger, a woman of very dark complexion. In the low light, Honor saw the woman was barefoot, clad in only a thin, tattered dress, and without even a shawl against the cold.

With this one glance, Honor knew all. A runaway slave. An invisible hand clutched her stomach, fear of lawbreaking, fear for the woman. "What is amiss?"

The stranger began weeping. "She gon' turn me in, give me to the catchers."

"No," Royale said, "I told you she would help."

Royale's confidence tore something inside Honor. For a moment Honor hated her white skin, hated that this woman would fear her on that basis alone.

Turning to the practical, she had to see what was needed. "Judah, please draw the curtains," Honor directed. "Perlie, please light more candles on the table." As the cook lit candles, Honor asked the stranger, "What ails thee?"

The stranger rocked back and forth in her distress.

"Trust me," Honor murmured, touching the woman's

bony shoulder. "Thee can trust me." No one on earth could make her turn this woman in.

"You a Quaker. Thank the Lord. Please, can you help me, ma'am?" the woman whispered. "I cut the side of my foot on a piece of glass. It infected."

The desperation in the voice rattled through Honor. "Of course I'll help." She fell back into a role she'd been raised for—the lady caring for her people. Throwing off her shawl and wrapping it around the woman's bent shoulders, Honor knelt down and opened the chest that Royale had placed at her side. "Royale, I'll need warm water."

"We already got it warmin'," Perlie replied.

"And rags."

"Everything too new for that," Royale said.

"Then tear up a clean dishcloth into squares. And another into wide strips as a bandage."

Quickly Royale obeyed, and soon Honor was bathing the woman's foot in warm salt water and dealing with the infection that had caused the foot to swell. The woman made no sound, but Honor felt her despair lap like cold waves of water against her heart.

Finally she bandaged the foot with the clean linen. "That should begin to help the healing. Can thee walk?"

"I got to, ma'am." The woman's voice shook with fear. "I hide during the days. Run all night."

Honor looked to Perlie. "What can thee feed her?"

Perlie rose. "Got some leftover corn bread, milk, and syrup."

"I overhear some passerby sayin' there be a Quaker

along here. So I prayed God would lead me to that house," the runaway said, her voice still quavering.

Honor grasped the woman's work-worn hand. "Thee isn't running till tomorrow night. Thee must rest."

"Oh, ma'am . . ." The woman began weeping, no doubt from exhaustion, from terror. "I hate to put you in danger of the law. I come across from Kentucky. Been runnin' four nights." Her words gushed out like a pent-up dam, all her anxiety and loneliness spilling over. "I been afraid to ask for help, even when I saw other blacks in Cincinnati. Then I see this little cabin and thought servants might be in here." She wiped away tears with her fingertips. "I look in the window and tap on it. I couldn't go on without help."

Honor squeezed the woman's hand, her mind racing. "Judah, I think it best she hide up in the barn loft. Nobody else uses the barn but thee and Samuel, and he can't hear her. And before she leaves tomorrow after dark, I want to check on her foot. An infection untreated can result in amputation."

"Your people tole me you was a good white," the woman said, accepting a bowl of milk and corn bread drizzled with sorghum. "Bless you, ma'am."

"I am doing very little for thee," Honor said, the truth of this cutting deeply into her soul. "I only wish I could do more." A worry intruded. "I don't know my husband's views about runaways. Royale, thee was right not to waken him."

"He not a Quaker?" the woman asked.

"He was, but . . ." Honor didn't know how to go on. "Life isn't always easy to explain."

The woman replied with a harsh, mirthless laugh. "Life ain't easy at all; never easy."

Honor agreed silently. "Royale, Judah, Perlie, I'll leave her in thy care." She noted that Judah had rested his arm around Royale's shoulders again. And Royale looked less anxious than before.

No doubt this woman's plight had brought back Royale's own recent trials. In passing, Honor pressed her cheek against Royale's. Royale pressed hers in return. This gesture was common between women who were relatives or close friends but not between mistress and maid. But at this moment Honor needed to show comfort and reaffirm her undeclared relationship with Royale.

In the half moon's light, Honor hurried toward her bed, hoping Samuel hadn't wakened to find her gone. Slipping inside, she waited by the door, listening. Had she roused anyone else? But only Eli could have heard her movements. No sound from the loft. She tiptoed to the bedroom and saw that her husband still slept, unaware.

Should she wake him and tell him what she was doing?

Surely Samuel would want to help this poor woman.

But I don't know that.

The image of the two slave catchers who had returned Caleb flashed in her mind, and she recoiled from taking a chance on Samuel. He'd said the slave catchers were just carrying out the law. Indeed, Honor had heard the Fugitive Slave Act would make Samuel liable if he did not turn the woman in.

But what would he do when faced with an actual woman in dire straits? Honor knew he was a kind man—wouldn't he show mercy on her? But she knew it wasn't that straightforward. Whether from ignorance or plain prejudice, most people thought of slaves as less than whites, less than completely human. If she hadn't been raised by her father, wouldn't she have also been tainted by this?

Wrestling with these questions without answers, she quietly took off her robe and slid between the now-cold sheets.

I can't take a chance with this woman's life, she decided. When the slave catchers had been at her door, she'd sensed their ruthlessness. What would they do to this poor, unprotected woman? Rape loomed as a real possibility and terrified Honor as much as the woman's being returned to an angry, probably cruel master. This runaway must have been in a desperate situation in Kentucky to chance escape.

Samuel's warmth beckoned Honor, but she resisted. If he woke and asked why she felt like ice, why she had been out of bed for so long, what answer could she give? Oddly, now that the separation between them had finally been breached, going against his wishes made her long to feel his strong arms around her and his lips coaxing hers apart.

Another thought slammed her. She'd just broken the law, a federal law. She was a criminal now. Was that how Samuel and the neighbors would view her if they found out? And it wasn't only their opinion of her at stake. What did God think of her lawbreaking?

❖

The next day Samuel watched his wife as he and Judah gathered stones to continue work on the forge. For some reason she was teaching Eli and Caleb how to groom a horse. To him, the creatures were too big, too unpredictable for the children to be around. But she'd tethered a horse to a tree, and now she stood between the two boys on one side of the animal. All three were brushing it down.

It seemed, as usual, that Honor knew more about people than he. She'd found something Caleb wanted to do. The boy was stroking the horse with a large brush he had to use two hands to grip. Sometimes he would lean his cheek against its side as if showing affection.

One of their neighbors, red-haired Thad Hastings, sauntered up the road, carrying something small in each arm.

Surprised, Samuel stopped his work. Judah also paused and moved a few steps backward, behind Samuel.

Grinning, Thad waved and greeted them. Samuel drew closer, trying to see what he carried.

"What has thee got, Thad Hastings?" Honor asked and signed, wondering if this signaled a change in their neighbors' opinion of them. Or had the man come with suspicions about the runaway hidden in the loft? She gripped the brush more tightly. He couldn't possibly know, could he?

Thad held up a pup in one hand and a kitten in the other.

"Hey!" Eli said, dropping his brush and rushing to the man. "Kitty . . . puppy!"

"Well, the pups and kittens are weaned now and need a home," Thad said to Honor with a nod to Samuel. "I was thinking that one of your boys might want a pup for a watchdog and one a kitten, to do the mousing. That is, if you think it's a good idea, ma'am."

"How kind," Honor replied, and it was. And Thad hadn't so much as glanced at the barn, though Judah did just once before she saw him force himself to look forward.

Honor controlled her expression, caught between Thad's unexpected kindness and her anxiety over the runaway's safety as she watched Caleb stare at the animals. Though holding himself aloof, Caleb couldn't hide his interest.

Thad knelt down and set the pup and kitten on the ground. "Let's see if they like you boys."

Honor signed all to Samuel, still compelling herself not to glance toward the barn.

Eli motioned for Caleb to draw near. The older boy handed Honor his brush and walked slowly to join Eli, who was on his knees now.

Caleb stood, looking down at the animals. The brown-and-white, long-eared puppy woofed and scampered over to the boy, wagging his tail and wiggling with excitement. The pup jumped high against his knees—irresistible.

Caleb dropped to the ground and lifted the dog into his arms. Then he froze and looked up. Samuel nodded, so Caleb cuddled the pup, who began licking every part of his face within reach.

The kitten wandered over to Eli and rubbed her head along his leg.

Honor thought their nephew might prefer the puppy, but Eli lifted the kitten and began to pet the little gray-and-white fur ball. "Kitty. Pretty kitty."

Samuel gently draped an arm over her shoulders, and together they observed Caleb responding to his pup. Judah remained a few steps behind, vigilant. Honor could sense his tension and hoped she was the only one who could.

Caleb scooted closer to Eli and let the puppy onto the grass. Eli followed suit, and the pup and kitten, evidently old playmates, began to roll together on the dry, wild grass.

Honor watched Caleb's face relax into a smile. She offered her hand to Thad. "Thank thee. They are perfect for the boys."

Samuel also signed his thanks.

Then Thad surprised her by asking her how to sign, "You're welcome." Samuel watched, amazed by Thad's gesture.

Honor inquired after Thad's family, relaxing somewhat as he spoke of his new baby. But she couldn't pull her thoughts far from the woman in the barn. She hadn't come up with any way to help the woman further with the long, dangerous journey ahead. During the recent war, runaway slaves had been welcomed into Canada by the British. Was that still true?

If only she knew more Quakers north of here, on the route to Canada. She didn't even know if any Friends lived north, let alone if any supported abolition. She must find out from the other women in the Female Anti-Slavery Society. Would they countenance abetting runaway slaves? Or recoil from lawbreaking? She needed to discern whether she could share this secret with any of them. *I must be as gentle as a dove and as wise as a serpent.*

❁

DECEMBER 4, 1819

Saturday morning, with his usual courtesy, Samuel helped Honor onto the wagon bench for their weekly trip to Cincinnati. Judah already sat with the reins in his hands. After a cold night, she'd crisscrossed and tied herself into one wool shawl and wrapped herself in another against the early-morning chill. The sun peered over the horizon, glistening on every frosted leaf. Samuel fastened the top button on his plaid wool coat as he took his seat beside her. He swung a lap robe over them.

Royale, with Eli on her lap, and Perlie, holding Caleb's hand, sat in the wagon bed, all dressed warmly and covered with blankets. Judah drove slowly down the rutted trail. The runaway had left days ago, but the experience still weighed on Honor's mind.

Later today she would visit Deborah's house for the planned Female Anti-Slavery meeting. While needing information about any other Quakers in Ohio who might help runaways, she had decided not to give away the fact that she had hidden one. She couldn't take the chance that one of the women might let it slip and draw slave catchers to her door. Taking a deep breath, Honor tried to let anticipation over a day in the city lift her tension as she considered this meeting, fraught with both possibilities and traps.

❁

On a crowded Cincinnati street, Samuel climbed down from the wagon at their first stop, the general store that

Perlie preferred. He steeled himself for other customers' probable reactions to his sign language—gaping and rude comments. He had an important errand in town today, one that would further his business, and being deaf would not stop him. But first they must do the necessary shopping.

He helped Honor down, Judah helped Perlie, Royale, and the boys, and they all entered the general store. Judah and Royale took the children directly to the Franklin stove in the middle of the large room to warm themselves while Perlie bustled up to the counter. The bald storekeeper in a white apron greeted them with a jovial grin. At their first meeting some weeks ago, the man had looked at Samuel as if he were on display at a fair. But his original curiosity had dimmed, and now he treated Samuel as a regular.

The fragrance of cinnamon and cloves spiced the air. Perlie spoke to the man behind the counter, handing him the list Honor had helped her write. Eli gravitated toward the sweets, nearly drooling on the glass case of lemon drops and horehound candy. Wary, Caleb didn't leave Judah's side. When Perlie had all the items she needed and Honor had bought some cloth and buttons to make new clothing for Caleb, who had been left with no winter garments, and Eli, who was growing so fast, Honor signed the total cost.

Samuel noticed that as usual Honor had not chosen anything for herself. He didn't like that. From the sale of his parents' house and his inheritance, he had more than enough to care for her. "Don't you want something for yourself?"

She looked surprised. "I don't need anything, Samuel."

"I didn't ask that. I asked, do you want anything?"

She gazed at him for a moment, her expression lifting and a blush tinging her cheeks. "Nothing here, but I'd love to visit a bookstore and buy some books for the winter. Poetry—perhaps Robert Burns. Maybe a few children's Bible storybooks for the boys. I could read to us in the evenings."

Samuel took pleasure in the way she smiled at him. He turned to the others. "The three of you, choose something today, here or at another store. You've all worked hard and deserve a gift. And, boys, how about some sweets?"

After a moment's pause, Perlie hurried over to the fabric section and selected two new colorful kerchiefs for her hair. Royale immediately chose a packet of pretty buttons and then joined Perlie by the fabric. She waved Judah over, a bolt of cloth in her hand. Samuel imagined it would make a good shirt for the younger man.

Samuel suddenly recalled that Judah lacked something every man needed. "Judah, choose a pocketknife for yourself."

Judah beamed, and the two of them surveyed the display of knives. Judah tried to pick a less expensive one, but Samuel insisted he choose the one Samuel thought was the best in quality. When the men turned, everyone was smiling. The joy of giving warmed Samuel in a way he hadn't felt for a long time. With distinct pleasure, he drew out his purse and paid the proprietor.

Another thought came to Samuel. "Ask the storekeeper if he'd be interested in stocking some of my bottles and jugs for sale."

Honor did so.

The man looked startled but interested.

"He read Sinclair Hewitt's article about us too," Honor said. "And he says if the quality is good, he will stock your bottles. He could use some gallon jugs himself for molasses and such."

Samuel offered the man his hand to seal the bargain.

The storekeeper shook it, smiling suddenly.

"Tell him I'll be back sometime soon with bottles for him to inspect."

Honor and the storekeeper spoke briefly before the man bowed them out of his store. They all boarded the wagon, and Samuel directed Judah to the establishment where he could order supplies for the forge. After this had been accomplished, Judah drove to his family's home in Little Africa, where he, Royale, and Perlie would visit for the weekend. Caleb refused to be parted from Judah, who carried the boy inside his father's house. Eli, gripping his bag of candy from the store, insisted on staying with Caleb. Samuel promised Judah he'd come back and take Eli with them to the inn for the night. Whether Caleb would insist upon staying with Judah for the duration of their trip, remained to be seen.

With the boys safe in Judah's care, Honor took over the reins since she had yet to come up with a way for Samuel to drive a team, something he really didn't want to do anyway. He directed Honor to head for the *Centinel* office. Honor looked surprised but drove there. It was small, most of the space taken up by a large printing press in the middle of the room.

A man was working at the press, setting lead type. The scent of some oil, probably a lubricant for the press, hung in the air. An older man sat at a cluttered desk in front of the press while Sinclair Hewitt, whom Samuel still thought of as a dandy, sat at a desk behind it. Samuel's jaw tightened reflexively at the sight of the handsome young man, though he chided himself for the reaction.

Upon seeing the Cathwells, Hewitt sprang up. Samuel saw his mouth open in exclamation. Hewitt hurried forward, his hand outstretched. He bowed over Honor's gloved hand, then reached for Samuel's.

Samuel forced himself to clasp the man's hand and smile. Though he knew Honor had no interest in this man, irrational jealousy stirred like sluggish bubbles in a pot of oatmeal.

Honor translated Hewitt's question: "What brings you here to see me?"

Yet again Samuel wished he could hear the man's tone of voice, but he had to content himself with reading his face. Hewitt's countenance was friendly and open, and he had proven his loyalty and generosity. If he glanced repeatedly at Honor, Samuel could not blame him. His wife merited a second look, even a third.

"Tell Hewitt that I need to take out an ad for my glassworks," Samuel signed to Honor.

As soon as Honor had spoken, Hewitt's expression registered approval. He clasped Samuel's hand again and motioned for them to come to his desk. He seated Honor there but looked to Samuel, who stood beside her.

Samuel read the unspoken question and withdrew a folded piece of paper from his pocket. He'd worked over what he wanted to say and had it memorized:

Cathwell's Glassworks
Sharpesburg, Ohio
Glass Bottles, Jugs & Sills available for pickup
or delivery
Custom Orders for Size & Lettering Available
Contact Samuel Cathwell, Owner

Hewitt read it and looked up. "Excellent," he mouthed. Then he turned to Honor and asked, "When does your husband want this to appear, and how often?"

Samuel read Honor's fingers and replied, "The first business day of every month for the year."

"Excellent," Hewitt said again. He gestured and spoke to the older man at the front, who came over and shook Samuel's hand. Honor conveyed the man's thanks on behalf of the *Centinel.*

Samuel nodded, holding in the pride of this moment. Now his business would officially start. He paid for the year's worth of advertising and received a receipt. Samuel and Honor were escorted outside, where Hewitt bent over Honor's hand in farewell before letting Samuel help her onto the seat. Samuel climbed up after her and, in Hewitt's presence, felt his disadvantage at not being able to drive the team.

Honor drove them toward the familiar inn for luncheon. She planned to visit Deborah Coxswain's house for the afternoon meeting of the Female Anti-Slavery Society. She thought that meeting with other women over tea would end slavery. Foolish idea.

But if it made her feel better, why not? He agreed

slavery was wrong, but he'd long ago become resigned to it as an ancient practice. Nothing would ever change how society viewed people with dark skin. And slaves were too valuable to merely let go. The world was the way it was, and a small group of women in a frontier town could do nothing to change it.

❖

Honor perched on the edge of a rocker across from Deborah in the Coxswains' snug parlor, a fire in the hearth warming the room. She had read something in one local paper recently that had buoyed her hopes about abolition, and she looked forward to sharing it when the meeting began. Clouds now hung in layers outside the window. Samuel had settled himself comfortably at the table in Deborah's cozy kitchen with several newspapers to read.

But Honor's luncheon sat on an uneasy stomach. How could she gauge this group's disposition toward aiding runaways without giving herself away?

During a brief time of silent prayer, Honor considered each woman present. White-haired Deborah presided by the fireplace in a winged chair. The other ladies ranged in a semicircle facing the fire, each with some handiwork in her lap. Cordelia, a dark-haired young wife and mother of two, generally looked peeved. Anna, a fair-haired new bride, sat beside her. And May, an unmarried, bookish girl who wore spectacles, rounded out the group. That was all she'd learned about them over the past few weeks—in addition to the fact that they were interested in pursuing abolition.

"We have formed our society," Deborah began when they were finished with prayer. "Now we need to begin to formulate ways to further our cause. Does anyone have any suggestions?"

Yes. We should help runaways who come to our doors. Instead Honor cleared her throat and said, "Our geographic location provides us a special opportunity as a path to freedom."

The other women looked to her, Anna and May encouraging, Cordelia frowning.

"Freedom? Just coming into Ohio doesn't grant a slave freedom," Cordelia snapped.

Honor continued. "I have read in a recent issue of the *Philanthropist* that Canadian Attorney General Robinson has openly declared this year that residence in Canada makes American slaves free. And according to the article, Canadian courts will protect those who flee there for freedom."

"But slavery still exists in England and all English territories," Anna blurted and blushed rosy pink.

"If thee recalls," Honor said with outward calm, "during the recent war, the British offered transportation for anyone wanting to leave the United States, including slaves. Many slaves fled and were transported by ship to British Canada." Honor experienced a jolt of memory. Her father's death had come during that violent time. She blocked out the emotions evoked. She must concentrate on persuading these women to take action.

"So might Canada be doing this to make America seem unfeeling by comparison?" Cordelia suggested in a sly tone.

"I think that's safe to say," Deborah said wryly. "We'll free *thy* slaves, but not our own."

"My point is," Honor said, "that Ohio lies between Kentucky and Canada. We are a natural conduit for those seeking freedom."

The other women stared at her.

Honor gathered her courage. "Steamboats dock here every day. Isn't it possible that runaway slaves might use them?"

"How could they do that?" Anna asked, pausing with her needle in the air. "Wouldn't they be apprehended, traveling on public conveyances?"

"Not if they had forged manumission papers," Honor said, setting down her needle. "Aside from their papers, who can tell if a black person is slave or free? And how many people would ask to see their papers anyway—except for slave catchers?"

Deborah gazed at Honor intently. "What is thee suggesting?" she asked. The other three women bent their heads as if avoiding the issue about to be broached.

Honor had prepared for this question. "If thee was a runaway slave arriving in Cincinnati, where would thee turn for help?" Honor asked.

"I'd find other people of my color and ask them to help me," Deborah said without hesitation. "I would not easily trust a white person."

"These slaves are fugitives from their rightful owners. We're bound by law to turn them in. Should we countenance those breaking the law?" Anna asked earnestly, her cheeks turning pinker.

Anna was right, Honor knew. Scripture said Christians were to obey the laws. But Honor had come up with her own defense, a defense she felt was equally in line with the teachings of the Bible. "In Christ, we know there is no distinction between slave and free. Did the patriots who dumped tea in Boston Harbor rather than pay an unjust tax break the law? Are we to obey God or man?" Honor let the silence following her question grow. In the days since helping and hiding the runaway, she'd decided to do whatever she could, short of shedding blood, to continue this work. These women must decide for themselves.

"I believe I am constrained to help the oppressed," Deborah stated with quiet authority. "If any one of thee disagrees, then I think thee should reconsider whether thee wants to be a part of this group. Slavery is the law of the land, but we oppose that law. I believe God opposes that law. Breaking the law peacefully may be a way to serve him."

A second silence vibrated in the neat parlor. Flames crackled in the hearth. Honor realized she was holding her breath and released it as quietly as she could.

Bespectacled May spoke for what seemed like the first time ever. "I'm staying."

Though her face glowed red, Anna nodded once in a show of decisive agreement.

"Exactly what is thee proposing?" Cordelia demanded.

Honor braced herself. She'd come up with a way to help without directly exposing her aid of a runaway slave. "What I'm proposing is that we offer help to the African church in assisting runaways."

"What kind of help?" Cordelia looked guarded.

"Funds for the runaways for their long trip north?" Honor ventured.

Cordelia's mouth thinned to a line. "But we are not in control of our *husbands'* money. Is thee?" she asked with an edge to her voice.

The woman's reply revealed much about Cordelia's life to Honor. "Perhaps we could sell something to earn money?"

"All our income belongs to our husbands or fathers," Cordelia snapped, her thread breaking with the force of her emotion.

Honor lowered her eyes. *Samuel always gives me anything I ask.* And today he'd insisted on giving her gifts. On the way back to the inn, they were going to stop at a bookstore. She hadn't considered before how unusual that trait might be among husbands.

Yet Cordelia spoke the sad truth. Every law seemed to be against women taking any real action, just as every law seemed to oppose Royale and every other free black, not to mention slaves who wished to be free. The laws were unjust. But . . . laws could be changed.

Electrified with a new idea, Honor lifted her head. "We need to draft a letter to our state legislature."

Every chin snapped up. The three younger women gawked at her while Deborah tried to hide a grin. "What does thee want to say to our state legislature?"

Honor's mind raced. What would be a good first step? "Royale, my maid, was kidnapped here in a free state. Wouldn't a law penalizing other nefarious men who try this be appropriate? Royale's incident was broadcast widely, and people were upset that Eli was put at risk by those kidnappers—"

"Who went free after all," Cordelia said bitterly.

"That does not matter," Honor said, facing her. "Did thee come here just to sew?" *And argue?* "Yes, we have few rights, but we can still speak. The US Constitution gives us that right in the First Amendment. We can also approach the government for redress. Slave catchers ought to be forced to at least consider the consequences if they kidnap free blacks to sell them back into slavery. And the furor over Royale's kidnapping is fresh in everyone's mind."

"Yes, popular opinion is important to politicians," Deborah said. "We must not let this opportunity pass by. I think that thee should write the letter here today, Honor, and we will all sign it. This no man can stop us from doing, and it costs us only postage."

When none of the other three women responded to Honor's suggestion, Deborah continued more boldly.

"If we do nothing, we should just change our name to the Society for Females Vaguely Concerned about Slavery. Will we just sit and sew and bemoan the terrible fate of our darker brethren and sisters? Or will we act?" Deborah's passionate speech galvanized the meeting.

"Cordelia," Anna said, "thee has not even given thy answer. Is thee staying part of this group or leaving?"

"I apologize," Cordelia said. "I had a . . . difficult week, and I was taking it out on all of thee." The woman composed herself visibly and glanced from one to another around the half circle. "I hate oppression. I will do whatever the longing for freedom calls me to do."

Honor leaned forward and touched Cordelia's hand. "Deborah is right. We can't do much, but what we can do—"

"We will do," Anna finished and grinned.

May, again quiet, nodded vigorously, the brown curls over her ears bouncing.

Honor smiled back, and a sigh of relief winnowed through them all. One action had been agreed upon. Honor felt her inadequacy to affect the lives of thousands enslaved, but she had won support for runaways and free blacks with this small group.

"One step at a time," Deborah murmured, evidently gauging Honor's mood. "Every journey is just a series of steps forward."

Chapter 13

DECEMBER 5, 1819

The last of the First Day sun glimmered low on the horizon before quiet little Sharpesburg came into view around the bend of forest. Honor's fatigue lifted. This place had become home. The only thorn this day was the way Caleb had misbehaved while visiting Judah's family.

According to Royale, the child had thrown a tantrum worthy of a two-year-old. Caleb had tried to run away. Judah had prevented him, thereby triggering the tantrum. The boy didn't know his mother had left Cincinnati. He must have thought he could find her. The cruelty of this world pressed in on Honor.

Royale must have been thinking the same thing. "We got quite a job with this boy. How we ever gon' get him signing?"

Shivering from the cold, Honor turned to her. "I've been praying for inspiration. But he must want to learn."

"He is so sad and so . . . closed off, someway. And I don't mean because he can't hear," Royale said.

Judah tied the reins to the set brake handle, and Samuel climbed off the bench and reached up to help Honor down. Then she realized he didn't meet her eyes.

She thought over what Royale had just said about Caleb. It could be said of her husband, too. Honor felt a wave of despair. She mentally shook herself—after all, Samuel was much more approachable now than when she'd first met him. Grasping her husband's chin, she forced him to look at her, then released him to sign. "Somehow we have to think of a way to get Caleb to want to communicate with us."

Samuel looked grim. "That stepfather ought to be horsewhipped."

Honor nodded in agreement. She'd like to add to that list all the people whose ignorance and lack of compassion had wounded her husband. Should she tell him about the letter to the legislature she had drafted and signed? Would he object to her doing that?

Honor helped Perlie and Royale carry the smaller parcels inside. Samuel and Judah unloaded the larger ones for the house and kitchen, and Judah led the team to carry others into the barn. Soon Royale helped Eli and Caleb wash their hands and directed them to the table. Perlie delivered a cold supper of biscuits, bacon, and fresh hot tea. Honor thanked both of them, so glad they were here.

The kitten played on the floor with a bit of string. The

pup sat beside Caleb on the bench. Honor saw the little dog begin to squat. Crying out in dismay, she jumped up, grabbed the pup, and set him outside in the grass. Caleb ran after her, wailing for the pup and ratcheting up Honor's exhausted nerves another notch.

When the pup was finished, Honor motioned to Caleb to take him inside. As she followed him in, she tried to come up with a way to involve Caleb in training his pet.

At the table again, she held her cup of steaming tea and pondered this situation.

"I name my cat Candy," Eli said and signed.

"Why?" Samuel signed, the first comment he'd made since coming indoors.

"Because she sweet like candy." He waved what was left of his peppermint.

Honor grinned in spite of her irritation. "That's a good name for her." But Caleb's downcast face dampened her good humor, as did the fact that Samuel had been more withdrawn than usual.

"Eli," Samuel signed, "ask Caleb what he's named his pup."

"He don't sign. I sign to him, but he don't sign back."

Honor knew the rejection Eli experienced. Caleb lived beside Eli day and night, but the older boy refused to speak to him.

"Then we will have to give him a reason to sign." Samuel looked to Honor. "He loves the pup. He will learn sign to keep him, won't he?"

Honor looked at him. The pup could be their vehicle to reach Caleb. What did they have to lose?

"Eli," she said and signed, "tap Caleb, and then sign your name again."

"But I already do. He won't."

"Let me finish. Then point to us and sign our names and your cat's."

Eli appeared puzzled but obeyed.

"Now lift up Caleb's pup and look at him as if thee wants to know something. Samuel and I will too."

Grinning as if it were a game, Eli obeyed again. She and Samuel rapped the table and pantomimed the same question. "What is the pup's name?"

Eli set the pup down and pointed to him. "Name?" he signed.

Caleb ignored them and tried to take back the dog. But Eli retrieved him too quickly.

Samuel rapped the table harder, and Caleb turned to him.

Honor watched as her husband signed each of their names, then Caleb's name, and finally pointed to the pup and lifted his hands in obvious question.

Caleb glared at them and folded his arms in unmistakable stubbornness. He sometimes reminded her of Samuel in more ways than one.

Yet in a way this reaction reassured Honor. His refusal to obey was a child's response, a normal child's retort at being asked to obey when he didn't want to.

Samuel reached over the table and lifted the pup by the scruff of its neck, away from Eli. He petted the dog and signed, "This is a good dog. His name is . . ." Again he made the clear questioning motion.

Caleb slapped the table and just as obviously demanded the pup back. He yelled in that strange-sounding voice of his, "Mine! My dog!"

Samuel signed the question again. "What's his name?"

"Mine!" Caleb yelled.

"His name is Mine?" Samuel signed. "Mine?"

Caleb stared at him belligerently. He stood on the bench and reached across the table.

Samuel refused to give him the dog, moving it out of Caleb's reach.

Caleb began huffing with his aggravation. "Mine!" he yelled and pounded the table with the flats of both hands.

Samuel signed back the word. "Mine?"

Caleb threw himself on the floor and yelled, "Mine! Mine!" He kicked and screamed the word over and over.

Honor's neck tightened. "Samuel, he's working himself up into a fit."

"Wait."

Eli picked up his kitten, stooped beside Caleb, and signed, "I name her Candy. Candy." He offered Caleb the kitten.

Caleb stopped yelling and kicking. He petted the kitten and then held out his hands toward Samuel, asking for his pup, looking piteous.

Samuel asked for the name again.

Honor's stomach clenched, and she felt the tension radiating through her whole body. The boy's struggle over whether to give in and sign the pup's name was visible. Anger and frustration and mulishness all figured in his expression.

"Pal," Caleb said aloud finally, holding out his hands again. "Pal."

Honor interpreted with a hopeful glance toward Samuel.

"No, you must sign it," Samuel responded. Then he signed the three letters for the boy. *P-A-L.* He pointed toward the pup and pantomimed returning it to Caleb.

Eli also signed the three-letter word, and Honor nodded in encouragement.

Caleb glared at Samuel but said aloud, "Do that again."

Samuel formed the signs again, and Caleb did each one after him.

Samuel handed the pup to the boy. "Pal," he signed back. "Your dog is Pal."

Caleb wrested the dog from Samuel and turned around, hugging the pup to him and pouting, his body radiating frustration.

"He signed it! He signed it!" Eli crowed.

Honor drew in a deep breath. Caleb had just learned his first word in sign. She squeezed Samuel's arm.

Samuel rested his hand over hers, another moment of family. He gazed into her eyes, then sent Caleb a troubled glance.

Honor felt his compassion for the child and signed, "We won't give up on him."

❖

After supper had been devoured, Honor rapped the table and signed to Caleb and Eli. "Time for bed. Take thy animals out once more; visit the necessary."

As the boys passed her going to the door, Honor kissed Eli's forehead. When she tried to do the same for Caleb, he pushed her away and slammed the door behind him.

She and Samuel shared another moment of mutual concern. She walked over to him and bent her head to rest upon his. With one arm he drew her close, soothing her unsettled nerves. She kissed his upturned mouth. Their efforts for the boy brought them together more and more, but Caleb would need so much in order to heal.

❁

DECEMBER 6, 1819

Honor woke and lay silently, listening. A muffled knock sounded against the door to the outside. She knew what it must signify.

She slid out of bed, pulled on her robe and slippers, and tiptoed to the door. Hoping not to wake Caleb's pup in the loft, she leaned close to the door and heard the soft tap again. Her heart throbbing, she opened the door only a narrow slit.

A pair of eyes stared back at her. After a moment she saw an outline in the glow of the gray dawn just lightening the chilly night. A black man in tattered clothing. God had sent her another escaped slave to help. A mix of fear and excitement electrified her.

Snatching down her shawl, she held a finger to her lips and breathed, "Shush . . ." She stepped outside, making him back up. "Go to the barn," she whispered, shutting the door with exquisite care and throwing on her shawl. "Hurry."

The two of them hastened over the frozen grass to the

barn. In the small room at the rear, she woke Judah, who lit his lantern. Judah pulled on his coat and boots and ran to the kitchen to get provisions for the man. Honor swept one of the blankets from Judah's bed around the runaway's shoulders. Soon Judah returned with a jug of water and a plate of cold leftovers. The man ate ravenously.

"Thank you. Thank you," the man said at last.

In the dim light she could see little of him or his face. "Thee can sleep up in the loft. But my husband is not sympathetic to runaways, and we have neighbors who occasionally visit," she said in a low voice. "Please be careful not to make a sound during daylight."

"Thank you. A black man in Cincinnati told me people in Sharpesburg would help me. To look for a large log cabin, large barn with a small cabin behind. An' I ask God to lead me to the right door. An' he did."

"I will pray for thy safe journey north also. I must return before I'm missed." She hurried outside and shut the door behind her. The cold quickened her step as much as the dread of discovery. She slipped back into the cabin, shrugged out of her robe and slippers, and slid under the covers again. Her heart beat fast from hurry and fear.

She hoped Samuel hadn't noted her leaving and returning. She listened to his breathing, which sounded normal, and slowly her body warmed again as she fell asleep, praying for the runaway in her husband's barn.

❖

Samuel watched Honor at the table the next morning. Where had she gone in the early hours of the morning?

She generally didn't use the necessary at night, so why had she gone out into the cold? Uncertainty swirled inside him; insecurity simmered in the pit of his stomach. He swallowed coffee. *I should just ask her. She'll tell me.*

But he couldn't. What if she had left his bed to . . . to what? Whom could she be meeting? They had only two close male neighbors, and it was obvious to everyone that Thad loved his wife. That left only the bachelor blacksmith, Micah. But he and Honor had never been more than polite to each other.

Samuel reminded himself that Honor had done nothing to deserve his mistrust—on the contrary, she'd proved loyal at every turn. He gripped his mug of fragrant coffee, trying to come up with some honest reason that his wife had left his bed in the dark. Maybe she'd heard a noise from the animals and slipped outside to see what was wrong. Or . . . "Have you heard from that newspaperman?" he signed.

Perlie had just delivered scrambled eggs and a pan of hot biscuits. Honor was melting butter over the biscuits one by one. Her hand faltered. "What? Why would thee ask about him?" she signed.

He shrugged without any answer.

Honor sent him a look edged with irritation. "I am thy wife, Samuel Cathwell."

Samuel felt foolish. Honor was everything a man could want in a wife. That's what caught in his craw. Sometimes he still couldn't believe he was enough for her.

Eli and Caleb climbed down the ladder from the loft and came to the table, their pets trailing behind. Surely if something had occurred out of the ordinary, Eli would have woken. And Pal already promised to be a good little watchdog.

Samuel rose and stood next to his wife, signing for her eyes only. "I'm sorry I asked about Hewitt."

She turned to kiss his cheek and went on with her buttering.

The tightness in his chest eased, and he sat down and began signing to Caleb, encouraging him to sign back. But the worry and doubt deep inside him had rekindled.

❖

"Today I will fire up my forge for the first time," Samuel signed at the end of breakfast.

"Is the forge done now?" Honor asked, glancing up.

"Judah and I finished it yesterday with Thad's help. Micah will bring me some coal. I have some good clean sand that I've dug from nearby. I will try to melt some in the forge. Make my first glass in Ohio." He beamed at her, a rare display.

On her part, Honor tightened with sudden fear for two reasons. After her visit to the glassworks in Pittsburgh, she was all too aware of how dangerous glassmaking might be. Tremendous, fearsome heat alone could melt sand into liquid glass. And Samuel had told her that glass could explode, shatter into piercing shards.

Then the second worry reared up on its hind legs. What if Thad came to see what his help had made possible? Would the runaway in the loft make any telltale sound? "Thad Hastings is helping thee?"

"Yes, he's coming today." Samuel paused. "He's learning to sign more and more."

Startled, Honor stared at him. She had kept her distance from Thad's family. But she had noticed that Thad came over often and spent time in the barn. "I'm glad." She began to realize more fully how her mission would separate her from her neighbors. Tight with fear, all she could say was "Be careful."

"I'm always careful." Samuel wiped his hands on the finger cloth lying on the table.

Honor picked up her coffee with both hands and drained the cup. Someone knocked on the door, and her guilty nerves jerked.

Eli jumped up and opened the door.

The blacksmith, Micah, had arrived. "Morning."

Beside him, Thad signed the greeting and asked aloud, "Samuel, done with breakfast? Micah brought coal."

Both men tugged the brims of their hats, nodding toward her, grinning like children about to get a treat.

Honor signed Thad's question to Samuel, who rose and waved a greeting to the men. Her husband seemed more relaxed in their company than she'd often seen him. This small community seemed to be the right place for her husband.

"Shall we fire up that forge?" Micah rubbed his hands together with anticipation. Judah appeared behind the other two, looking just as hopeful.

Samuel's broad smile could have lit the room. After finishing his coffee, he kissed her cheek, grabbed his hat and jacket, and headed toward the door.

Eli finished scooping in the last bite of his eggs and motioned for Caleb to follow him. Caleb slid off the bench and picked up his pup to pursue the other males. Bringing up the rear, Eli's kitten chased them all outside.

Honor stared at the door with a bit of puzzlement. Firing up a dangerous forge frightened her, but evidently it was highly entertaining to the male sex. Her amusement was short-lived. She bowed her head and prayed that the glassblowing would go safely and that the man in the loft would not give himself away.

❖

As the morning progressed, Honor learned that another neighbor had stopped by the blacksmith's shop yesterday and had evidently spread the news of today's event. Men she'd never seen crowded around the entrance to the barn. Honor couldn't help herself. The barn also drew her like a magnet. And her worry over the runaway kept her heart thudding against her breastbone.

She stayed near the men but somewhat apart, watching as Samuel repeatedly tested the temperature of the forge's heat. Finally he signed that the sand he'd poured inside the forge was ready to be worked. He thrust a long metal tube into the forge and began to twirl it slowly, gathering the molten amber glass around the tube. Honor was torn between fascination over the process and worry that it would go wrong. The men watched in intense silence.

"Remember," Micah said to the other men, "stay back. That forge is as hot as mine when I'm working iron, and glass can explode. Do not touch Samuel or get too close."

In response the surrounding men stepped back a bit farther. Honor's fear wrapped more tightly around her, and it was all she could do not to glance up into the loft. Was the runaway awake and aware of the danger? Or would he snort in his exhausted sleep and betray them?

The men remained serious and focused on Samuel's movements. She understood the import of this event for her husband. Today all of the surrounding neighbors would view Samuel's skill. Her husband's face showed no emotion, but she read tension in his spine and the way he held his jaw.

Judah and even Thad narrated for Samuel as the others watched in fascinated silence. Eli stood near Honor, peering through the legs of the men in front of him. Caleb sat by the door of the barn, playing with the pup and kitten, teasing them with a string Honor had given him. Ignoring them all.

Honor watched Samuel, who had chosen not to use a mold, twirl the molten glass on the tube, then roll the blob on a slab of marble on his workbench.

"Mr. Cathwell is marvering the glass," Judah informed them in a quiet, respectful tone. "That means cooling the outside of the glass. That marble is called the marver."

Then Samuel began to puff into the blowpipe, creating a bubble in the glass. The men reacted in unison, exclaiming in wonder. Honor shifted for a better view. How did he possess the courage to come so close to having his flesh seared?

Samuel thrust the glass back into the furnace, orange-and-blue flames licking the sides of the glass on the cane.

"Mr. Cathwell is reheating the glass so he can work it more. That opening in the furnace is called the glory hole," Judah said. The men were obviously puzzled by Judah's presence and knowledge, but no one commented on Samuel's free black apprentice. Honor drew in a deep breath and prayed again for the runaway's silence. Still, her husband's skill captivated her.

Samuel withdrew the rod. With Judah's deft assistance, Samuel used wooden paddles and pads that had been soaking in water for days to shape the glass vessel. Again her husband's demanding craft drew Honor's respect. The wooden pads Samuel wielded were all that separated his flesh from the molten glass.

He went through the same blowing process, and the shape grew larger, fuller. Finally she could see the bottle he was making, a sill or jug about a foot high and a foot in diameter at the base. Judah stepped forward and lifted a rod to Samuel's sill, taking it from the blowpipe.

Then with quick, deft movements, Samuel created the neck and lip and fashioned a finger handle on the side. He held up the finished bottle still at the end of the rod.

One man reached out toward the jug.

"Don't touch it!" Micah roared. "It's still burning hot!"

The man staggered back in surprise. Honor inhaled sharply.

"Sorry. It will take some time before it can be touched." Micah's voice sounded tight. "And it could still shatter. Keep back."

The man wiped his forehead with a navy-blue handkerchief. "Much obliged. Never seen anything like this before."

The rest murmured in agreement with him.

Samuel cut the glass from the rod, set it in another compartment of the forge, and shut the door.

Judah latched it. "That's the annealer. The glass needs time to cool so it won't shatter from cooling too quick."

Honor flushed with pride at her husband's ability. The jug was practical, of course, but in a way beautiful. Samuel had taken sand and coal and created this. Peering through the tiny gaps between the men's shoulders, she beamed at him. He smiled almost shyly at her. She was so glad for him, for this day. She savored his new pride and the respect he had won. And the runaway had not betrayed his presence. If only she could think of a way now to draw everyone away.

"Miss Honor," Royale said in the doorway of the barn, "Perlie made cookies and a fresh pot of coffee for your guests. If they come to the house, she set up on your table."

Honor sighed with silent relief at this clever ploy. "Please, gentlemen, come to our home for a small celebration of the beginning of Cathwell Glassworks."

The men trooped after her, toward the cabin and away from the barn—away from the runaway.

"That was very thoughtful of Perlie," Honor murmured to Royale.

Royale winked. "We just want to do you and the mister proud, Miss Honor."

Chapter 14

DECEMBER 17, 1819

Samuel woke up in the dark, chilled room. Honor was sliding between the sheets. He grabbed her hand. A little over a week had passed since this first happened. Where had she gone again?

She turned toward him, not trying to free her hand.

He couldn't see clearly enough to know if she was signing with her other hand. He felt for it and claimed it as well.

She rolled toward him, cuddling close.

He felt how cold she was, but the way she came into his arms of her own accord distracted him from suspicion. In the darkness, as the scent of her rosewater enveloped him and her soft form pressed against him, his desire for her overcame his misgivings. He leaned forward and kissed her. And when she kissed him back, he forgot everything but Honor in his arms.

❁

DECEMBER 18, 1819

Against the mid-December chill, Honor added another log to the fire in Deborah Coxswain's neat, plain parlor and sat down to continue sewing the sleeve of a winter coat for Caleb. Honor had driven alone to Deborah's for this afternoon's Anti-Slavery Society meeting with something concealed in her pocket. Anna and May were already sewing near the windows, making the most of the winter sunlight. The meeting had begun with a time of quiet meditation, and then everyone had taken up their handwork. Honor hoped Deborah or one of the other women would begin the discussion. She hesitated to share her latest attempt.

And overlaying all her thoughts, last night Samuel had caught her coming in from helping another runaway. She'd used passion to distract him and felt guilt about that dishonesty. A Christian wife shouldn't employ passion as a shield or weapon. Yet at the time it had been the only choice that came to mind.

The fire crackled on some sap, flaring up. Honor glanced around, apprehensive over what these women would say if they knew she was harboring escaped slaves, breaking federal law. Did she have the courage or the right to reveal this? The folded paper in her pocket nudged her.

"I . . . have something to share." Honor pulled out the paper.

"Deborah, it's me." Cordelia's voice came from the front hall. They heard her shedding her shawl and scarf in the foyer before she entered the parlor, breathless. "I had trouble getting away. I'm sorry." Pulling off her gloves, Cordelia took the vacant seat and smoothed back her straight, dark hair.

Deborah smiled and nodded. "Honor was just going to share something with us, and I have something too."

Everyone looked to Honor, who now wished she had kept this to herself. But perhaps this new way of furthering the cause came from God too. "I tried my hand at some poetry."

"Poetry?" Cordelia sounded uncertain.

"Yes. I was thinking that people are often touched by poetry, and this might be a vehicle for our cause. Perhaps it could persuade some."

"Please read it, Honor," Deborah encouraged. "We will give thee our honest but loving opinion."

Honor cleared her throat. "It's a child speaking to his mother." She smoothed out the creases of the paper on her lap.

> *"What is a slave, Mother?—I heard you say*
> *That word with a sorrowful voice, one day;*
> *Methinks I have heard a story told,*
> *Of some poor men, who are bought and sold,*
> *And driven abroad with stripes to toil,*
> *The live-long day on a stranger's soil;*
> *Is this true, Mother?"*

Honor felt her throat clogging with emotion, but she pressed on.

> *"May children as young as I be sold,*
> *And torn away from their mothers' hold—*
> *From home—from all they have loved and known,*
> *To dwell in the great wide world alone,*
> *Far, far away in some distant place,*
> *Where they never may see their parents' face?*
> *Ah! how I should weep to be torn from you!*
> *Tell me, dear Mother, can this be true?"*

Shaken from reading her own words aloud, Honor glanced up, almost afraid of their reception of her poor attempt to portray the evils she had witnessed firsthand. "And finally the mother replies, 'Alas, yes, my child.'"

"Oh," Anna said, a hand to her mouth. "I hate to think of those poor children."

May was dabbing her eyes under her spectacles with a handkerchief.

Cordelia was merely staring at Honor.

"A worthy effort," Deborah said with sad confidence. "I think that thee should submit it to the *Philanthropist*. I'm certain they would welcome it."

"A poem by a *woman*?" Cordelia said with grievance in her tone. "They will say it is unladylike and—"

"Anne Bradstreet's Puritan poetry has been published for years," Deborah interrupted. "Some men belittle women, but not all."

Samuel never belittles me, Honor thought. She glanced

at Cordelia and wondered again about how her husband treated her. "Cordelia, I know I am not a great poet," Honor said, "but it's the cause that matters. I never thought to write poetry, but . . . I must let out what my heart feels about the suffering of my African sisters and brothers."

"Let the editor of the paper decide," Anna said. "If it's God's will, this poem will be published and move hearts to our cause."

May nodded enthusiastically, the curls over her ears bouncing as usual and her spectacles slipping down her nose.

Cordelia drew in a deep breath. "I agree."

Honor found she couldn't stop a smile.

"Now for my news," Deborah said. She drew a letter down from the mantel. "We have received a reply to our letter to one of our local legislators." She read a flowery, condescending letter from the man.

Honor buried clenched hands in her lap. "So he thinks a pat on the back for our concerns about free people of color is commendable, and that's all. Humph. Does he think we will give up after a polite dismissal?"

"I'm not about to be dismissed," Cordelia stated. "Let's write him again and also a letter to another legislator."

Every lady turned to stare at Cordelia. Honor couldn't hide her shock.

"What?" Cordelia responded. "I'll write the letter this time. I have a few things to say!"

Spontaneous applause greeted Cordelia's words. Honor clapped hard. Perhaps this group was about more than freeing only slaves.

By the end of the meeting, a reply to the first legislator

had been penned, a second to another one, and Honor had copied her poem and planned to mail it to the newspaper office before leaving the city.

She drove away, chilled in the late-afternoon twilight, warmed by the efforts of their group. Though what they did might amount to a teardrop in an ocean of misery, at least they were trying. And though she hated lying to Samuel, she could not stop helping runaways who found their way to her door. *God, help change his mind. I know I can't.*

❁

DECEMBER 24, 1819

Samuel awakened to find the bed beside him empty once more. Why had Honor left him? Where could she be? Invisible fists of jealousy grabbed his heart and twisted. He would find out this time.

He sprang out of bed and clambered up the ladder, though he knew she wouldn't be in the loft. Caleb's pup opened an eye at him, his tail beating the floor, but then went back to sleep.

Samuel dragged clothes over his nightshirt. At the door, he yanked on his wool coat and knit hat and gloves. Where would he look first?

The only place he could think of was the kitchen. Was someone there ill? He could make no sense of her going out into the cold night, and jealousy clawed him—even though he knew it to be irrational. At least he would learn the truth tonight, for good or bad.

He shut the cabin door quietly but firmly behind

him. The crescent moon was still in the eastern sky, so it was before midnight. The scant moonlight glimmered on the inch of snow on the ground, and he saw them. Footprints—large running beside small. Who could be with Honor?

He took off at a run, disbelief and hurt surging with each step. He reached the kitchen. Candlelight shone from the window. He charged inside.

The scene that met his eyes shocked him into immobility.

With a candlestick in hand and her back to him, Royale stood beside the bed, opposite Honor on the far side. In the bed a black woman with a full womb writhed in the obvious pangs of childbirth.

All faces in the darkened room turned to him.

Honor looked horrified and darted forward. "Samuel, she's a runaway and needed help. Please just go back to our cabin. I'll explain later, but I can't leave now. I'm needed."

His mind stumbled in shock. "What are you doing here?"

Honor glanced over her shoulder. "I am helping this woman. She is about to give birth. Something's wrong. Thee shouldn't be here."

Samuel stared at her. A runaway? Childbirth? His mind scrambled as if slipping on ice. He stumbled to the bench at the small table. "Go ahead. Help her."

Then every head swung to the woman. Samuel couldn't hear the woman's distress, but he could see her face and body contorted with pain. His fingers shouted in panic, "Help her!"

❁

Honor almost staggered with relief. She hurried forward and spent the next hour helping Perlie, who had some experience as a midwife. Finally Honor held a tiny infant, swaddled in a pillowcase and a linen towel. "We must get them into the barn loft before daylight. I never know when those two slave catchers could appear at our door."

"They might even come on Christmas Day," Royale said bitterly.

The fact that this child had been born on the eve of Christ's birth vibrated through Honor. Friends didn't celebrate Christmas lavishly, but she was struck by the thought of Mary giving birth in a stable.

"I can carry her and hide her in the loft," Judah said and signed, staring at Samuel. "But will you permit me, sir?"

All of them turned as if connected by thread to look at Samuel, who still sat as if dazed on the bench.

With the child in her arms, Honor sank to her knees in front of him and signed, "Please, Samuel, let us hide her in the barn. If the catchers come . . . Traveling now, alone in the cold, might kill her and the child. Please." Honor rested a hand on his knee, her heart in her throat, its beat nearly deafening her.

She couldn't imagine the Samuel she knew sending this woman and infant out into the cold. But then she'd seen otherwise-generous white people inflict unthinkable cruelty on those with black skin. Now came the moment she'd dreaded, the moment she would learn whether Samuel's kindness was only for people with skin like his. Whether he would obey the law of man or of God.

Samuel appeared to shake himself. "Hide her." He rose. "I'll help Judah carry her."

Honor rose as he did and tried to put her free arm around him.

Samuel shied away from her.

Her heart shattered. Samuel was aware of her secret now, but it might cost her all the progress they'd made to being husband and wife.

❖

DECEMBER 25, 1819

Late that morning, Honor tried to continue sewing new, larger clothing for Eli. Samuel had barely looked at her since he'd burst into the kitchen in the hours just before midnight. After a breakfast eaten in tense silence, he'd fled straight to the barn without a word about what had transpired. *Dear Lord, what will happen now?*

She heard the blacksmith, Micah, call, "Hello the house! I'm back, and I've got someone for you to meet. Come out!"

Along with her anxiety, she folded up her sewing, smoothed down her hair and apron, donned her wool shawl, and stepped outside. Already outside playing in the snow, Eli and Caleb came running too. Micah had left for Cincinnati two days ago. Honor halted in surprise. All four members of the Hastings family—the baby included—had accompanied Micah, and a plump, pretty young woman in a fine navy-blue dress and bonnet stood beside him.

"This is my bride—my Christmas bride, Amanda."

"Whoop!" Eli shouted and dashed toward the barn with Caleb at his heels, presumably to fetch Samuel.

"Amanda," Honor said, trying to hide her surprise and her caution. "Welcome." She grasped the woman's hand. "Please come inside, out of the cold."

"We came for our wedding celebration," Micah said, not letting go of his bride's hand. Honor stared at him, unsure what he meant. "We were married this morning in Cincinnati, as I told Samuel last week, and I've brought a large apple cake with us to gather and celebrate with our neighbors. We knew that your husband's barn would be warm because of the forge, and it's larger than any of the cabins around here, so Samuel told us we could hold a party there. I've invited everyone to come celebrate our wedding and Christmas today in your barn."

Honor's heart fell. How could Samuel have neglected to inform her of this? A wedding celebration in their barn—with a runaway and her baby in the loft? She felt the blood drain from her face. It wasn't possible.

Samuel had exited the barn, pulling on his wool coat as he walked. Eli and Caleb followed him. Any hope that Samuel would draw on his usual standoffishness and somehow dissuade Micah from staying here disappeared with one of her husband's rare smiles. Nodding, he clasped Micah's hand, then released it and signed, "Congratulations! Let's bring the cake into my barn!"

When Honor didn't translate this, Samuel nudged her and she quickly relayed his words to Micah. She tried not to make another sound or motion so no one would note her rising tension. What was Samuel thinking? He couldn't have forgotten the woman hidden there. Was this his way of teaching her not to aid runaways? Her stomach twisted into a cold knot.

As Micah, Amanda, and the Hastings family headed for the barn, Samuel pulled Honor aside, communicating with her at last. "I am sorry I forgot to tell you about offering Micah our barn, but this calamity is of your own making." With that, he strode away from her, toward his friends.

When Honor caught up to them, Amanda sent her a nervous glance, and she summoned up a smile. This woman would be a close neighbor, perhaps for the rest of their lives. "Of course I'm just taken aback. This is all so sudden."

Micah seemed to misinterpret her. "Well," he said, sounding shy, "I been writing letters back and forth with her over the last year, and I finally persuaded her to marry me."

"Where is thee from, Amanda?" Honor asked.

"A town across the river from Cincinnati. Covington, Kentucky," Amanda said. "I met Micah at a horse sale. I was living with my uncle."

So this bride came from a slave state. The band around Honor's lungs tightened. How would this all end? Would her secret lawbreaking become public knowledge today?

❁

Within an hour, all the local families had arrived for the celebration. Nearly twelve chattering adults and a pack of noisy children gathered in the barn, which Thad had helped sweep clean. Honor had changed into her best mourning dress for the occasion, and the rest of the women had come in their finest also. The forge radiated a comfortable heat. And many had brought lanterns for the ride home and for lighting the dim, cavernous barn during the short daylight hours.

Judah had warned the runaway to be quiet at all costs. He'd managed to hide the sleeping baby in a bucket and carry it to Perlie in the kitchen, unnoticed. No one would go there, so if Perlie could keep the infant quiet, all would be well. Honor tried to turn over her worry to the Lord, but it refused to budge. Amanda proved to be a soft-spoken, friendly girl. But Honor's constant worry put her on her guard.

The men had set up a makeshift table using leftover wood slats on top of sawhorses. Honor draped two of Miriam's embroidered tablecloths over it to add to the festive air. Every woman who'd come had brought dishes to pass, so Samuel's last-minute notice of this party didn't require undue effort from Perlie or Royale. Soon heavy pottery bowls filled with a variety of breads, stews, and vegetables covered every inch of the starched white tablecloths. The mouthwatering aromas of rich food mingled in the air. In the center of it all sat the fragrant apple cake, tantalizing them. Honor wished she could have enjoyed this first community party.

She schooled herself not to look toward the loft. God forbid that anyone should detect the woman trapped there because Honor slipped. But the compulsion to look upward bedeviled her moment by moment.

As soon as everyone assembled, a beaming Micah formally introduced his bride to each family, one by one.

When he finished, everyone applauded and the men insisted he kiss his wife for all to see.

Even Honor, as stressed as she was, smiled at the big blacksmith, who was now blushing.

One of the older children ran toward the ladder, followed by Eli and several others. "Let's play in the loft!"

"No!" Honor objected, frantically searching for a reason. "I don't want anyone falling. Come here, Eli."

The boy looked startled since he often played in the loft. But he obeyed her and turned from the foot of the ladder.

Honor tried to think of another place she could have hidden the runaway. But there was nowhere else. And no chance now.

The festivities continued. Soon the women were sitting on the benches and chairs they had brought, eating, while the men leaned against the walls and ate. Honor couldn't concentrate on the conversation going on around her. What if the woman in the loft sneezed? Honor felt as if someone were sawing at her insides, as if she were a piece of wood nearing the point where she would snap apart.

"You must not be hungry," Charity commented.

"Oh, just thinking," Honor apologized and began to try to eat her food. Her unsettled stomach, however, threatened to refuse to keep it down.

Then she saw Caleb climbing the ladder to the loft. She couldn't call him back. He wouldn't hear her.

He mounted the top rung. He would see the runaway! She leapt up, her heart racing so fast she could barely breathe. Stars burst before her eyes.

❁

Honor heard Charity's voice from above her. She blinked and opened her eyes. Charity knelt beside her, chafing her wrist. "Mrs. Cathwell, wake up."

Honor's thoughts remained scattered. "What happened?" she muttered.

"You fainted," Amanda said from Honor's other side.

Even in the dim light, Honor saw that she was surrounded by the women. All of them were staring down at her. Her mind came back into focus. At all costs, she must not give the woman away. But Caleb had been at the top of the ladder. Had he seen the runaway? Revealed her? "Caleb?"

"Eli, she wants Caleb," Charity said.

"No," Honor protested, not wanting to call attention to the loft. "He just came to mind. I think I can sit up."

Samuel moved forward and gripped one hand to help her rise. "Are you all right? Should I carry you to bed?" he signed.

"No, I'll be fine," she replied.

"Take it slow, Mrs. Cathwell," Charity said. "We don't want you fainting on us again."

Samuel set her gently in the chair Charity had vacated.

When she was situated, Honor gazed around. The women ringed her, and the men encircled them. No one looked upset, so the runaway must not have been discovered. Had her fainting drawn all attention away from Caleb? Had he come down before actually gaining the loft? Or seeing the runaway?

"I'm fine. Really. I don't know why I fainted like that," Honor repeated.

Assured of her recovery, the men began talking again and left the women, going to where the jug of home brew sat in the corner. Samuel lingered, but Thad tugged his arm and led him away.

"Are you increasing?" Charity asked in a low tone.

"No—or I don't think so. I don't know why I fainted," Honor repeated the half-truth. Terror at the thought of the runaway being exposed here—here, in front of people who would send her back to slavery—had caused her to faint.

"Well, you just sit here and watch," Charity said.

So Honor obeyed, observing the wedding celebration and secretly fretting but trying not to let this show.

About an hour before dark, everyone began to pack up to go home to bed. Dawn and another day of work would come all too soon.

"It's too bad we don't have a fiddler in the neighborhood," Thad said as he carried a basket of food remnants out the barn door. "We could have had dancing."

Caleb came to her while everyone else bustled around. He signed slowly. "Why is there a woman?" He pointed upward.

Honor blanched and her fingers flew. "Slave catchers chase her. Don't tell anyone. Please."

Caleb stared at her in the low light. He drew close and whispered in her ear, "They are bad men."

She took his face in both hands and nodded. "A secret," she signed and put a finger to her lips.

The boy whispered, "I hate bad men."

Honor knew how Caleb felt. Hatred for the slave catchers surfaced every time they passed. *But I'm not supposed to hate anyone. Or break the law. I cannot give way to violence or hatred—no matter what.*

Now Caleb knew of her secret, and she'd made him an accomplice. How long could a boy keep a secret? An old saying taunted her: "Two can keep a secret if one is dead." And it wasn't just two—now her entire household knew, Eli the lone exception.

Why had her husband put her through this torture? She understood that their neighbors would have been suspicious if Samuel had canceled. But surely he could have done something to keep them away.

❖

In the flickering candlelight, Honor bent over the runaway and gently closed her eyes and raised the sheet to cover her face. After dark, Judah had gone to carry the woman back to the kitchen for food and care, but he found that she had expired. He'd carried her over anyway, not knowing what to do. The thought that a woman had died alone in her loft while a wedding party took place just below ripped at Honor's heart; her chin trembled.

A shocked quiet pervaded the kitchen. All the others stood back from the bed, staring at the still form. Samuel looked crushed, battered. Honor longed to draw near him. Yet the way he'd burst in here last night so angry still left her uncertain. But this sad death would melt even a heart of stone, and Samuel's heart wasn't stone—usually.

"Poor woman wasn't strong enough to make it through a hard labor," Perlie murmured.

"I've never seen a pregnant woman so thin and worn," Royale said. "What kind of master did she have to fail her so?"

"A cruel one," Honor said darkly, trembling. "But all masters are cruel. Owning another human alone is cruelty enough." She wiped away a single tear.

"What are we to do about this child?" Judah said. "We can't keep him. People will want to know how we suddenly have a baby. But I'll die before I let him go back to slavery."

This had been the woman's only desire, repeated over and over through her labor: to have her child grow up free. Honor watched her husband, waited for him to join in.

"I give her my promise too," Royale said. "We got to find someone to nurse the child till we find him a home."

"He doesn't look black," Honor said. "Yet. The skin will darken over time."

"Unless the father was white," Royale said in a harsh tone. "The child might not darken much."

Another silence greeted this suggestion.

"I'm old and too tired to do much more than fall into bed," Perlie said from the chair by the fire with the infant in her arms. "Royale, can you take care of getting the poor woman ready for burial? Judah, we'll need us a grave in the woods. Even though we got a dusting of snow, the ground isn't frozen solid."

Honor gazed at her husband, imploring his cooperation. She hoped for his help, but . . .

Samuel moved toward her, though hesitantly. "I'll help Judah bury her."

Did this mean Samuel supported Honor's work, or was he bowing to necessity? "We need to talk about this," Honor signed.

Samuel looked away. "We need shovels," he signed to Judah. The two men left.

Royale came to Honor and wrapped her arms around her. "Is he gon' let you help runaways? Your man say anything about all this?"

"No, nothing." *He has barely looked at me.*

"Judah and me talking about getting married and moving to Bucktown, a few miles up the road."

"No," Honor said, unable to stop herself.

"If we can't help runaways here, we got to go where we can. That's why Judah's father gather the church in Cincinnati, so he can give cover to runaways and help them. The same with places like Bucktown. There be a few more black settlements around Ohio, and all stay here to keep free blacks safe in Ohio and give cover and help to those on the way to Canada."

This was a long speech from Royale. Honor wept a few tears onto Royale's shoulder. "What will I do if Samuel forbids me to help escaped slaves?"

"I pray he don't."

Chapter 15

THE COLD MOON shone over the thick forest. Samuel and Judah had just finished digging the woman's grave. A small lantern sat beside Samuel's feet, barely illumining the open patch in the woods. Royale stood beside Judah at the head of the grave. On the opposite side of the grave from Honor, Samuel stared at her, and she met his eyes with fear and something like hostility—as if he were another slave catcher. Her expression pricked him.

They'd left Perlie in the kitchen, weeping and rocking the orphan in her arms. Fortunately, after the excitement of the wedding party, Eli and Caleb had already fallen sound asleep in the cabin loft and knew nothing about this.

Judah touched Samuel's arm. "Will you pray for her?"

"You pray," Samuel signed. Then, by the moonlight and his lifted lantern, he watched all that Judah said and signed:

"Father, we commend to you our sister. We don't know her name, but you do. She died nameless so no master could claim her child. We thank you that you brought her to us. We know that she is with you since we heard her call upon your name as Savior."

Judah lowered his hand. He had tears running down his face, no longer able to speak. Royale leaned over and put her arm around his waist in support.

Samuel wished this grave, this death, did not separate him from Honor. He longed to hold her, reassure her, and in a way feel the comfort himself. Her pale hair and face shone in the dark, a beacon. Death had again robbed a life. This scene dragged his mind and heart back to his mother's graveside. He forced back the gloom closing around and within him. *I didn't even know this woman,* he tried to convince himself.

In a few moments Judah began again. "Now no one can hurt her. She is safe in your arms, Lord. Free at last."

The simple words etched themselves onto Samuel's heart. But his mind was still dazed. Now he guessed that this woman wasn't the first runaway who had been hidden in his loft. That's what had taken his wife from his bed. Why would escaped slaves come to his door? Was it because Royale had been kidnapped in Cincinnati? How could they know that Royale lived with them or that they would be helped?

He and Judah began shoveling dirt over the blanket-wrapped form. It bothered Samuel that they hadn't had time to build her a coffin, but the body must be hidden as soon as possible for the child's sake. No one must know that a runaway had died in his loft—while they made merry over a wedding cake. The morbid situation whipped his thoughts and feelings into a tumble. He felt queasy, as if the apple cake wanted to come up.

As Samuel shoveled, he glanced up at the shadows from the surrounding trees flickering over Honor's lovely but stricken face. He tried to go over what had taken place in the past twenty-four hours since he'd awakened to find her gone. But too much had happened. He just felt sick and sad.

Soon they were packing down the earth over the fresh grave, replacing the sod, and scattering dried autumn leaves and pine needles to hide it.

The scene was like something in a bad dream. The scent of pine needles filled Samuel's head, and he wondered if he'd ever be able to smell them again and not think of this dreadful happening. He led the way back to the cabins with the lantern. Honor plodded beside him.

"How can thee have forgotten to tell me about the wedding party thee agreed to host?" she demanded suddenly, her fingers accusing within the pool of lantern light. "And why did thee let it go on when thee knew the runaway was hiding in the loft? Did thee want her to be discovered?"

Samuel paused, galled. "How could I refuse Micah without giving a reason, without causing gossip? I sometimes forget that people can hear," he signed. "I didn't realize what a risk it was till everyone started arriving. Of course I didn't want her to be found and captured. She was too weak—"

"But if she became well again, would thee have turned her over to the slave catchers who keep coming around here?"

Her accusation sliced into him. "This isn't the first escaped slave you've helped without telling me," he signed, fighting back.

"No, she wasn't." Honor's lovely face was drawn with worry lines, but her eyes remained fierce. "Samuel, I must and will help any runaway that comes to my door."

"Our door," he corrected.

"Is thee forbidding me to help those who need my aid?"

He saw a fresh flash of anger in her eyes. "You are breaking the law."

"An unjust law that keeps one race enslaved to another." She slashed the air with emotion.

"I don't support slavery—"

"If thee does nothing to stop it or to aid those who are fleeing it, then thee does," her fingers snapped, judging him.

Indignation billowed inside. "There have always been slaves and will always be slaves."

"I refuse to accept that."

"Miss Honor," Royale interrupted as they approached the barn, signing and saying, "we got to take the baby to Bucktown tonight. We need find him a family, and there must be at least one nursing mother there."

Honor agreed.

Royale continued, but her gaze was directed at Samuel. "We need you to come with us, ma'am, so we don't get in trouble with any catchers that might be out."

Samuel did not want Honor to go into the cold night,

but he knew there was no way to stop her. "Go ahead, Honor. I'll stay and keep the boys and Perlie safe."

Honor nodded to him, going toward the barn with Judah to get the team harnessed.

Samuel walked away toward the cabin, feeling very alone. Why did Honor have to go against the law, against their neighbors? Wasn't it enough that he and Caleb were deaf? Didn't that separate them, make them stand out enough?

❁

In the freezing night, Honor sat on the wagon bench beside Royale, who held the swaddled infant. Both were huddled in shawls and covered with lap robes. In the scant moonlight, Judah drove the team to Bucktown, which was some miles north.

After staying up two nights in a row—helping the woman through her labor, hosting the wedding party, and now burying and mourning the nameless runaway—Honor slumped against the back of the bench, exhausted. She and Samuel had not had enough time alone to talk over what had happened, find common ground. Still she hoped, trusted that they could come to some sort of understanding. One thing had become clear to her—she wanted not only Samuel's cooperation; she wanted his approval, his affection, his love. Did that mean she loved him?

Necessity had forced her to leave Samuel with so much unsettled between them. She ached to have his strong arms around her. But she, Royale, and Perlie had all agreed that finding a wet nurse for the baby could not be put off. The newborn would begin to be really hungry soon. And there was only one place safe to seek a home and help for the orphan. Going into the city to Judah's father's house would increase the distance and the danger.

The baby's unnatural quiet worried both Honor and Royale. The mother had been so weak. Would this child live?

"He should be crying with hunger soon," Royale said. "The sugar baby Perlie makes ain't enough to satisfy him for long."

Honor nodded, gazing at the child sucking sugar wrapped in a cloth plug. "If only we can find a nursing mother in Bucktown, one willing to take the child."

"I can't see any woman turning away a baby," Royale said, rocking the infant against her and crooning softly.

The icy landscape passed in silence then, except for an occasional whimper from the swaddled baby, the screech of an owl, the rustle of the wind through dried oak leaves. The horses' breath sent up plumes of white vapor, and the chill in the air seeped through the layers of wool and flannel till Honor felt like ice.

Finally, around a bend of trees, a settlement of several cabins and a few fields carved from the surrounding forest came into sight. A tall black man loomed out of one cabin, holding a lantern high. He strode to the middle of the rough road leading to the huddle of cabins, a challenge in his stance.

Honor tried to hope but failed.

Judah reined in the team and lifted one leather-gloved hand. "I'm Judah Langston. I'm apprentice to the glassmaker in Sharpesburg. This is my intended bride, Royale, and the glassmaker's wife, Honor Cathwell. We need help. Can we come inside and talk?"

"I'm Hank Clifton." The man motioned for them to get down and held the lantern high for them. A young boy hurried out of the house and led the team into a nearby barn.

Inside the neat, warm cabin, Honor and Royale crowded close to the fire, trying to warm up. One younger woman and one older sat at the table, wrapped in shawls over nightdresses, watching them.

"Hank Clifton, I'm glad to meet thee," Honor said when she could stop shivering. "We need a nursing mother. Is one living in this town?"

Hank studied her in the firelight. A man of powerful build, he looked to be in his forties with threads of gray in his dark, curly hair. He took his time assessing her and then the baby. "That baby isn't white."

"No, the poor babe's been orphaned and needs a family," Royale spoke up. "You don't need to be afraid of Mrs. Cathwell. She set me free."

"She's a Quaker?" the man asked.

"Yes, I am a Friend," Honor answered for herself. "And Royale is my blood kin."

A kind of shock went through the room.

"There's many of us with white kin," Hank said finally in a dry tone, "but none that will claim us."

The younger of the women rose and offered Honor her hand. She had an almond-shaped face and a kind expression—beautiful. "I'm Hank's wife, Keturah. And this is my aunt. I'll go get the nursing mother that lives nearby. I know she'll help."

Hank waved for Honor and Royale to sit on the bench, and Judah came in with the boy who'd helped with the horses. "This is our son," Hank said. "Now how did you get this baby?"

Honor let Royale tell the sad story.

"Well, God bless you for helping her," Hank said to Honor.

"How could I turn her away? And how could I blame her for wanting her child born into freedom, not shackles?"

The door opened again, and a plump young woman entered, carrying her own baby on her hip. "Where's that poor orphan child?"

Within moments the young mother sat by the fire and coaxed the runaway's baby to begin nursing. "He's half starved."

"I know. We weren't sure how cow's milk would affect a newborn," Honor explained, drenched in relief. "Perlie, my cook, kept giving him sugar wrapped in cloth to suck. Thank thee. I am so grateful, so grateful." She fought a rush of emotion. "I was so afraid we might get here too late or not find a nursing mother." Honor burst into pent-up tears.

Royale folded her in her arms. "Miss Honor been carrying a heavy load. Her husband didn't know she was helping runaways till this baby's mother showed up."

"Still he let you bring the baby here?" Hank asked.

"He wouldn't hurt anyone, least of all a child," Honor said through her tears. "But he doesn't believe abolition will ever come. I don't know if he'll let me help others in the future."

"Well," Keturah said, "that's better than it could have been."

But not what I want. I want Samuel to share my passion to set the captives free. I want him to see these people as I do.

❖

DECEMBER 26, 1819

At luncheon the next day, Honor and her family all sat around the table. Upon returning last night, Honor had explained everything about the baby and his new family to Samuel. He'd merely nodded, not showing any reaction. Did he feel that she was being disloyal to him, her husband? She had kept her illegal work a secret, and she would understand if he resented her for it.

Now she faced the wearying routine of sharing a meal with Caleb. She and Samuel had begun to insist that Caleb ask in sign for his food. Honor gestured toward an empty bowl and signed to Caleb, "Spell *stew* so I can give thee some."

Caleb stared at the table.

She sighed. If it wasn't Samuel puzzling her, it was Caleb. She knew their prickliness flowed from their deafness. But she never treated them as less than they were because they couldn't hear her. She didn't see why the boy still resisted her efforts to teach him sign language.

She signed this question to Samuel, adding, "Did thee resist learning?"

He shook his head no. But he didn't give any other response.

She ignored another token of his pulling back, withdrawing from her, and signed again to Caleb, instructing him to spell *stew*.

The boy grudgingly signed, *"S-t-e-w."*

Honor dished him up a generous helping, then served herself. She'd just lifted her fork when she heard the jingling of a harness and a deep voice calling, "Hello the house!"

She signed this to Samuel and rose to open the door. She stepped outside and immediately wished she hadn't. The slave catchers had returned. All that had happened the night before flashed through her like ice and flame. "What does thee want?" she demanded, flushing with unwelcome anger.

"To see if you got a runaway in your barn, Quaker," the older one retorted. "We're lookin' for a pregnant slave."

"Thee is not welcome here," she said, gratefully aware that her husband had come up behind her. The dead woman's face came to mind, her thin body and tattered clothing proof of dishonor and mistreatment. Honor gripped herself tightly and kept the outrage at bay. *God, help me not to hate them.*

"Don't matter if we are welcome here or not. We got a right to search for runaways. Dan, head into that barn and see if they got that Negro we're looking for in their loft."

Honor glared at the men. She didn't know if the Fugitive Slave Law gave them the right to search or not. She would ask Alan Lewis when next she went to town. She signed the slave catcher's words to Samuel, who raced off after the younger man.

"My husband said he better not touch anything in his glassworks."

"I heared your man could work glass. That seems funny. Him being deaf and all." The older man itched the side of his nose.

"One doesn't need to hear glass to work with it," she shot back. She knew there was no trace of the runaway having been here—except for her unmarked grave. Could they somehow track the footprints there?

"Oh, I riled you." He chuckled. "You Quakers get so upset about us returning property to its rightful owners. These runaways cost plenty."

Honor did not deign to reply to this. Greed, not a zeal to enforce the law, drove these catchers. She pinched the bridge of her nose and tried for calm.

Samuel stalked back beside Dan, the younger slave catcher.

"No slaves, Pa," Dan announced and swung up on the bench.

"I'm gonna be watching you, Quaker," the older one said.

"And I will be watching thee," Honor returned, her impotent fury boiling over. "Do not try to kidnap a free person of color." This was the only retort she could think of.

The dart hit the mark. The older man's face boiled red in an instant. He slapped the reins and turned around. As he drove away, he roared, "Watch your step, Quaker!"

Honor seethed, watching till they were swallowed up by the forest, hating that they could stir her to such anger. She tried to release the hot flush, the tight neck muscles. She shook her hands to loosen her arms.

Eli appeared in the doorway of the cabin. "Caleb's hiding. He won't come down. He saw those men and hid."

With Samuel at her heels, Honor hurried inside and up the ladder. But with her skirt, she couldn't easily crawl into the loft above their bedroom. She called Caleb's name, scolded herself for forgetting he couldn't hear her, and rapped the floor to gain his attention. "Caleb," she signed, "those men are gone. We will not let them take thee. Come down."

The boy crouched in the farthest corner of the loft.

When those two catchers had found him, what had they done to him to cause such fear? Anger tried to boil up higher inside her. She closed her eyes, praying for God's peace. Human wrath was against the will of God and only gave Satan influence over a soul. Honor must leave these evil men to God's justice. She took deep breaths as if forcing the anger out. The tightness in her chest eased enough for her to consider the pressing problem of comforting Caleb.

She couldn't reach Caleb without raising her skirts to an immodest height. So she waited till she breathed normally again. Perhaps Caleb would sense her anger and think it was directed toward him. If he wouldn't come down, she must let Samuel deal with him. Once again Caleb needed her, but she couldn't reach him. That was true, so achingly true.

Caleb didn't budge, just stared at her, cringing against the wall.

Heartsick, she carefully stepped down the ladder, as ladylike as possible. The boy's fright had quenched her frustration over the catchers' visit. "Samuel, thee must go up and reassure him."

Samuel climbed up the ladder, and soon she heard Caleb yelling in inarticulate anger. Samuel came down the ladder with the screaming and kicking boy over one shoulder.

Before Samuel put him down, Honor clasped Caleb's face with both hands and shouted, "Caleb, stop fighting us! We'll protect thee!" Then she felt foolish again and guilty, yelling at a child who couldn't hear. But desperation prodded her. She didn't know how to help him.

"I don't want to learn to talk with my fingers!" Caleb yelled back. He must have read her moving mouth or interpreted her face, twisted with irritation. "I don't want to be deaf!"

Her throat thick with emotion, she signed this to Samuel as he set the boy on his feet.

Samuel dropped to his knees and gripped Caleb's shoulder, signing, "I didn't want to be deaf either. This is the way it will remain. For both of us. Fighting us won't help you."

Caleb stared into Samuel's eyes, which were nearly level with his. Then he leaned his head back and moaned loud and long like a wolf howling.

The sound cut Honor in two. She felt like throwing her head back and joining in. She didn't want this child to be deaf and to lose his parents. She didn't want poor runaways to huddle in their barn, fleeing God knew what. She didn't want slave catchers to search their property. She didn't want Samuel to believe slavery would never be outlawed. She didn't want the world to be the way it was.

She knelt and wrapped her arms around Caleb and Samuel. She felt Eli come alongside her and join the circle they had created around the older boy. Tears fell from her eyes, covering her face like a mourning veil. Caleb had been with them over a month. And only now was he at last expressing all his despair. Was that why the boy affected her emotions so deeply? She wanted so much to feel Samuel's touch, to feel close to him the way she did when words and circumstances didn't get in the way. Now so much had come between them—between them all.

Chapter 16

JANUARY 3, 1820

On an unusually cold January morning, Honor heard hoofbeats followed by a forceful, peremptory knocking on the door. Setting down her sewing, she hurried across the room. Samuel had just left for the barn. When she looked out the window, she saw that her husband was already halfway there, his back to her. She wished she could call out to him.

But first she must find out what the person at the door wanted. The man was so wrapped up against the cold, she could see only his eyes. He tugged down a scarf, revealing his face, and asked, "Is this the Cathwell house? Cathwell Glassworks?"

"Yes?" Honor said hesitantly.

The man turned and from his saddlebag lifted out a

packet of letters tied with string. "I'm the postal rider hereabouts. Got three letters for you. The charge be five cents."

Honor gaped at him in surprise. Letters? From whom? They hadn't yet received any post in the few months they'd lived here. Then, shivering from the cold, she asked him to step in and closed the door behind him. Inside, she eyed the packet of letters in the man's hand.

"Much obliged," he said, heading straight for the roaring fire to warm himself.

"Would thee like a cup of coffee?" The pot sat on a trivet on the hearth, keeping warm. Hospitality hadn't prompted her but the need to delay him, to collect herself before the mail was in her possession. What if Darah had written her? The thought was excruciating, like a fine needle piercing her heart. She wanted desperately to hear from home, yet she wanted to forget High Oaks and everyone there.

"Yes, ma'am. Coffee would warm me, and I thank you."

Dumbly she poured it and added sugar at his request, handing it to him where he stood, still thawing himself. "I must go get my husband to pay thee." Anything to distance herself from the letters in that packet.

Wrapped in her wool shawl, Honor walked across the yard, not hurrying over the crunchy frozen grass to the barn. There in the light from the windows and the already-fired-up forge, Samuel was obviously teaching Judah some technique before they tried it with actual molten glass. Usually she enjoyed watching her husband working at what he did best, but today's unwanted visitor had unnerved her. And an uneasy truce still lay between her and Samuel. Neither of them had mentioned runaway slaves or abolition in the days since she'd returned from Bucktown.

She waited anxiously till Samuel looked up. "A letter carrier needs payment for postage. We have mail."

Samuel signed a few more instructions to Judah and hurried beside her to the house. His large form so near always made her feel protected—even now, when they'd been at odds for days. Inside the cabin he lifted down his leather purse from the mantel and handed the man the exact postage.

Gawking at them as Honor signed to Samuel, the postal rider had frozen where he stood. Then, with a start, he gave her the letters. "One's all the way from Maryland," he said, still staring at Samuel.

"All the way from Maryland." What she'd dreaded.

"That's the one that cost you the most. Do you have anything you want to mail?"

Honor recognized the handwriting on one of the letters. Darah had indeed written her. She blanched, and her hand trembled. It had been months since she'd written Darah of her marriage and her move to Ohio. She'd accepted the fact that Darah would not reply, and had been somewhat grateful for it. So why was her cousin communicating with her now?

"Ma'am?"

With effort, she brought her mind back to the present. "I have nothing today, but if thee comes near here in the future, please stop so I can send a reply." *If I can send a reply. I don't even know if I can bear to read this.*

"Will do. Be back this way within a week." The postal

carrier set his empty mug on the table and adjusted his scarves to confront the cold again. "I'm hoping for a break in this weather. I pray spring starts early this year. Well, I wish that every year." He waved farewell, something close to a salute, and headed out, pulling the door shut behind himself.

Honor handed Samuel the letter addressed to him. With her mother's silver letter opener taken from the mantel, she sank into the rocking chair by the hearth. She moved Darah's letter behind the second letter, from a stranger named Mrs. Thomas Iding. She carefully opened the wax seal on this letter.

December 12, 1819

Dear Mrs. Cathwell,

I am Caleb's mother. I'm writing to you to let you know where we are now. We have settled in the small town of Beardstown, Illinois, on the Illinois River. We have land that my husband bought from a veteran who wanted to move farther south.

I try not to, but I weep every night over having to leave my Caleb with you. I try to keep from blaming God for taking both my husband and son from me. Is Caleb well? Is he learning to speak with his hands? Again, I thank you and your man from the bottom of my heart for taking Caleb in. Please write to me. I long for news of my son.

Your obedient servant,
Mrs. Thomas Iding

Again bitterness gnawed at Honor, not against this woman but against a husband who would force her to abandon her son. At Samuel's touch on her shoulder, she glanced up. "Caleb's mother has written us from Illinois."

He acknowledged this with a nod; then a grin spread over his face like the dawn. "I've received an order for bottles."

Excitement for him lifted her to her feet. "Thy first order?"

Samuel handed her the businesslike letter, trying to hide his own jubilation. Someone had placed an order at last, likely prompted by the advertisement in the *Centinel.* Fortunately Samuel's substantial bank account had carried them through this start-up time for his business. God had provided for all their needs.

As Samuel had predicted, it wasn't a big order, such as one that would have been given to the larger glassworks in Cincinnati. This order came from a farmer who kept bees and wanted to start filling bottles with his name on them and distributing his honey to stores. Samuel's first order specified four dozen bottles.

As Samuel went to the door and donned his jacket and hat, Honor could not mistake the lift in his step. She closed the distance between them. Stopping him, she took his hand, so large within hers, and looked him in the eye. "I'm so glad."

He stepped closer to her, beaming now. "I first must carve a mold with the farmer's name and town to appear on the front of the bottle. And perhaps something more—a picture of a honeybee?"

She stood on tiptoe and leaned in to kiss his cheek, then cupped his chin in her palm.

Haltingly he bent as if to kiss her cheek in return.

At the last moment she moved forward, her lips meeting his. *Samuel, I don't want this distance between us.*

He stood very still, not breaking their connection. His lips caressed hers.

Honor savored their closeness, his touch. She stepped back and signed, "I'm sorry I've angered thee."

"I'm not angry with you."

She signed the same words back to him.

He smiled once more, looking bashful, before he left her, shutting the door behind him and the biting cold.

Honor stared at the closed door, glad she'd bridged the gap that had kept her from Samuel. Still, the unopened letter from Maryland nagged her. She began pacing before the fire, tapping the letter against the palm of one hand.

Letting in another blast of icy air, Royale hurried inside, huddled in a shawl. "Judah say you got mail. Did Darah write back?"

So Honor could no longer delay reading the other letter. Taking up the letter opener, she slit the seal open. The outside of the missive appeared only a little worn. Inside, the words were written in Darah's elegant copperplate hand.

December 1, 1819

Dear Honor,

I apologize for not replying sooner to your letter announcing your marriage and your intention to depart for Ohio. I have been slowly becoming accustomed to not having you and Grandfather with me. Even though my full year of mourning had not been observed, I was married October 14 in a private ceremony at High Oaks. Alec was eager for us to marry, and his aunt said no one will think it precipitate, as I needed a husband to oversee my affairs. I hope you and your new husband are well and happy. Greet Royale for me.

Your obedient servant,
Mrs. Alec Martin

Sinking into the rocker once more, Honor read the letter to herself again before handing it to Royale. Married? Already? She had expected much more time to prepare. Images of Alec, his lazy smile as he leaned against the old oak in the garden, gazing at her. Alec, galloping his black stallion up to her door and swinging down with his customary flourish, his lips coaxing hers—

A log broke on the hearth, sending up a plume of sparks, jolting Honor from her daze. She tried to remind herself of the man she knew him to be—Alec, gripping her arms in the garden and berating her for doing what she knew was right and just.

"They got married in October?" Royale said with disapproval, holding the letter away from her like a snake. "That don't sound right to me. Was Mr. Alec afraid she marry someone else and he would lose the land?"

Honor could not come up with an answer. She realized

she was chewing the inside of her cheek and stopped. Why had news of the marriage so taken her aback? She'd known that Alec and Darah would marry at some point. Darah had gotten everything—Grandfather's favor, High Oaks, and now Alec. All was complete. They were married.

Honor accepted the letter from Royale and resisted the urge to toss it into the fire. "At least Darah mentioned thee."

Royale snorted. "She probably wish I still belong to her. Darah wasn't like you. She don't see slaves as people."

Honor rose and tucked the letters behind the Bible on the mantel, closing the discussion. Then she told Royale of the letter from Caleb's mother. She rubbed her arms, chilled in spite of her long sleeves, and voiced a familiar question, the uppermost question, the one she'd asked Royale every day since they'd buried the runaway. "What are we going to do if another escaped slave comes?"

Royale shrugged. "Your man let us take the baby to Bucktown."

Honor rubbed her arms again, then tucked her hands into the bends of her elbows. "I wish," she murmured, "that I could make him understand how important abolition is to me."

Reaching out, Royale smoothed back wisps of Honor's hair from around her face. "Judah and I planning a spring wedding."

Honor concocted a smile. "I'm glad."

Royale frowned.

"What?"

"I know how much you give up and went through to

get us here—to set me free, keep me safe. I just wish I could do something for you."

Honor realized that Royale was obliquely pointing out that while she was able to marry a man of her choice, Honor had been forced into a marriage of circumstance to save both of them. Tears threatened, and she tugged Royale close, pressing their cheeks together. She didn't trust her voice to tell Royale all of what it meant to have blood kin still a part of her life. "Just having thee near is payment enough," she managed. "I lost everyone and everything but thee."

As if also unable to voice her feelings, Royale embraced her, a rare moment revealing and reaffirming the bonds that made them important to each other. Royale broke away first, hurried to the door. Drawing on her shawl, she became practical. "We both got work to do today. No time for tears. God will bless you, Honor. He blesses the faithful."

"Then he will bless thee, too." Honor swallowed down emotion. "I'll bring my sewing into the kitchen. I don't want to be alone today. And it's time we called the boys indoors to warm up. They've played in the cold long enough." She gathered her sewing box and a half-finished shirt for Eli. As she wrapped up against the cold, another bleak realization dawned on her. After their moment of sharing joy over his first order, Darah's letter had heightened her feeling of separation from Samuel. She'd been reminded of the life that had been hers and the one she'd foolishly thought might be hers. *Alec and Darah, husband and wife so soon . . .*

❁

JANUARY 24, 1820

Three weeks later, Honor was preparing to drive Samuel to deliver the bottles he'd crafted for the beekeeping farmer. Alone in the cabin, she added layers of clothing before putting on her dress: a pair of long wool socks over her cotton stockings, a second pair of pantaloons, and another two petticoats. Then she wrapped her thickest wool shawl around her, found her fur-lined driving gloves, and donned a wool scarf and her bonnet over it. On top of everything else, she wrapped a muffler around her neck.

Last week a southern wind had brought the first breath of spring, but earlier today as she'd walked to the kitchen to discuss the day with Royale and Perlie, she'd seen her own breath. Though the snow had melted, remaining puddles now had a skin of ice over them. A vicious wind whipped the treetops.

Royale knocked and entered Honor's bedroom. "I wish the weather was better. You'll be frozen within miles."

Honor ignored this. What could she do about the weather? About her husband's continued reluctance to discuss her desire to help future runaways? "The wagon is already loaded," she said. "Judah is hitching the team, and we'll be off straightaway."

Royale pushed a sack of lunch and two leather-covered canteens wrapped in layers of wool cloth—one of water and one of coffee—into Honor's hands.

Samuel rapped the outer door as he opened it, motioning for her to come outside.

Snagging the thick lap rug hanging on a peg, she and Royale hurried into the front room and bent to wrap heated bricks to put at their feet. Honor turned to the boys, playing with their pets near the hearth. "Eli! Obey thy elders. Tell Caleb to do the same. We'll be back before dark." The strong, bitter wind buffeting her, she strode outdoors and toward the team waiting in front of the cabin.

Samuel was checking one last time on the boxes of bottles, cushioned with straw and already strapped into the wagon. Judah had secured a rug over the seat back to shield the Cathwells somewhat from the wind. With Samuel's help, Honor mounted the wagon. Settling beside her, Samuel covered their legs with the thick rug. Royale slipped the bricks under their feet.

Clucking her tongue, Honor slapped the reins, and the restless team started off at a quick pace. They too appeared to want to be away, to get this trip done quickly.

Wind stung her face like needles as she passed the Smiths' cabin and the Hastings', smoke billowing from their chimneys. Then they were free, heading down Lebanon Road with the letter in her pocket providing directions to Weymouth, where the beekeeper lived.

With a commanding "Gee!" she turned the team around a curve, the sharp wind battering them from the west, the sky gray and foreboding. Thad Hastings had assured her they should make the round-trip journey before dark without any problem.

Glancing sideways at her husband, Honor wished she didn't have to wear thick gloves and keep her hands on the reins. There was so much she wanted to discuss with him now that they were alone for a day. The weeks since the baby was born and the mother had died had passed as normal on the surface. But the inner turmoil she felt at pursuing her mission against her husband's wishes had taken its toll. She wasn't sleeping well and had a hard time concentrating.

Honor slowed to navigate an especially rutted part of the road amid the forest. This stretch must have been exceptionally muddy last summer, and the ruts had frozen once winter set in. She could hear the bottles rattling behind her. After she negotiated the rough patch, Samuel patted her back.

A simple show of concern from him, a boon. As much as his formidable physical presence, Samuel's honest goodness powerfully attracted her. And he always protected her, backed her—except where runaway slaves were concerned.

She turned her head and smiled tremulously. If she and Samuel had enjoyed a normal courtship, they would have spent time together with both of their families, sharing meals and parties and carriage rides—time to talk, to become familiar with each other's likes and dislikes, each other's beliefs.

But circumstances had brought them together in a hasty marriage, and before they had met, their lives were totally different. Slavery had never been an issue in Samuel's life—he'd rarely had to think about it. This realization suddenly struck her. If she shared what she knew of this awful institution, would that make a difference?

How could she portray slavery as she'd experienced it to someone who had never seen it or known it? Honor closed her eyes for a moment. She had never revealed her grandfather's betrayal to Samuel. The deep wound still ached within. Even now, she felt the shock of it as if someone had yanked a dressing from a half-healed scab.

Honor braced herself to bring the matter out into the open. Her husband had a right to know how she'd ended up nearly penniless in Pittsburgh. She'd revealed the bare facts to Miriam but had not spoken of it to Samuel. It must have taken great forbearance for him never to inquire, she knew. She had to explain why she could not turn a blind eye to slavery.

The road evened out and the team had calmed down, so she could safely hold the reins in one hand. The deer were all hunkered down in the forest out of the wind, and she doubted any would be leaping into their path. Now was the time. She couldn't put this off any longer. She tugged off the glove of her right hand.

"What are you doing?" Samuel signed.

Ignoring his question, she began signing. "Thee knows that before this century began, the Society of Friends Convention decided all Friends must free their slaves."

He stared at her, looking puzzled, wary.

"But my grandfather refused to free his slaves. He parted from the Quakers instead." Her fingers stiffened with the cold, the hurtful memories, but she went on. "My father intended to free our people, but he died before my grandfather, before he could inherit our plantation, High Oaks. Grandfather knew I intended to free our people and sell High Oaks, so the week before he died, he disinherited me. He left everything to my first cousin Darah."

Who promptly became engaged to the man who had courted me. And who has now married him. This bitter thought she would not share with a husband prone to jealousy.

"He disinherited you?"

Honor read sympathy in his eyes and saw that he grasped how this had cut her to the marrow. She tried to take a deep breath of the freezing air but could not. "Yes. He extended his hold over his slaves—held on to them beyond the grave." Her heart clenched afresh as she recalled how he had treated Royale. "I wish I could say something good about him, my grandfather. But owning people changes a person, hardens their conscience." She glanced at Samuel and was heartened to see that he was really considering her words.

"Thee did not grow up with slavery. Thee doesn't know how it tears at the souls of not only the slaves but their masters."

"I don't understand."

"Slave owners know it's wrong to own human beings, so they hide behind Bible verses about slaves obeying their masters and ignore the ones that condemn those who deal in human flesh."

She forced her fingers, aching with the cold, to go on signing. "Because I disagreed with him—" her fingers paused, then went on—"he only left me Royale and one hundred dollars. He'd always claimed he loved me, and perhaps he did in some way. But he was corrupted by three generations of slaveholding."

Samuel reached for her hand but did not grasp it, seeming to ask if she wished for his condolence.

She closed the distance and took his hand. For a moment she rested a cheek on his mittened palm, then released it to go on with her story.

"Yet that is not the worst I can say about him." She stared straight ahead, gathering her courage. "I have never told thee, but Royale is my blood kin. My grandfather fathered her."

She could not make herself glance toward Samuel. "Royale's sweet mother was the nurse who raised not only her own child but me and my cousin. My grandfather forced Royale's mother into being his mistress—the same woman who nursed me and raised me and who died still his 'property.' My grandfather, who I thought would never sin so blatantly, did." Sorrow over her grandfather's hypocrisy welled up inside her, and she gripped the reins with both hands, holding on.

Samuel moved closer to her and slipped his arm around her waist.

Nearly tearing up at his gesture, she raised her right hand again. "He made no effort to liberate his own child except to leave her to me, knowing I would free her. He left Royale—his own blood—nothing, not a word or a penny. And he had treated the woman I loved as a mother like a concubine or worse. What choice did Royale's mother have in anything?"

Samuel might still not understand why this alone was enough to make it impossible for her to ignore slavery and its cruelty. But perhaps he could comprehend that a man she'd loved all her life had broken faith with his granddaughter and his own daughter.

Now Honor must make certain her husband clearly grasped her intentions, though she did not know what she would do if he forbade her from acting. She turned her face to him. "I do not wish to go against thee, my husband, but I cannot bring myself to turn a blind eye to those fleeing such evil. I must continue to work toward ending slavery. And I cannot refuse any runaway who comes to me for help. I just can't."

She had stated her case. Now she must make clear all the stakes. "I think thee needs to know that Royale and Judah are planning to marry in the spring, and she told me they will leave us and go live in Bucktown if we don't let them help runaways at our home." Maybe if her own suffering were not sufficient, the potential loss of his apprentice would sway her husband. She waited.

Samuel tugged her closer beside him and kissed the bit of her face visible. He signed, "Very well. I still doubt your measures will bring about the end of slavery. I saw how hard things were for that woman and her child, however, and I'm glad you saved the baby's life. I will not try to stop you or Judah or Royale. I will aid you when I can. But we must be very cautious. I don't want anybody to know what we are doing. I don't want to call any attention to us."

With one brief nod, Honor donned her glove again and stared at the steady movement of the rumps of the team and the billowing vapor from their breathing. She rested her head against her husband's arm. He pulled her closer to him, reinforcing their bond.

She couldn't ignore how her husband's words poured over her; most lifted her, but some cast her down. He would not stop her—he would help her, even—but he, a good and kind man, still didn't fully understand. She could say no more. For now.

FEBRUARY 7, 1820

Spring was whispering its promise in little bursts. Today the cabin door stood open while Honor tried to keep Eli and Caleb sitting at the table with her, continuing to print the alphabet on their slates. Eli had already learned the finger alphabet and signs, and Caleb had been taught his alphabet and how to spell words before he came to them, but both needed practice writing. Perlie also sat at the table with a slate, practicing the letter *G*.

The sound of hoofbeats brought Honor to her feet. *Dear heaven, not the catchers again.* She hurried to the door while Perlie put down her slate and rose from the table, distancing herself from evidence that she was learning the alphabet so she could read and write like Judah and Royale.

Honor hated Perlie's fear, which sprang from past abuse. But she understood it. She stepped to the door, cracked it open, and a smile burst inside her. "Deborah! George!" Her spirit soared but soon sank. "Is anything amiss?" She could think of no other reason George would leave his shop midday.

"Nothing! Something wonderful has happened, and we couldn't wait to share it with you," Deborah said, nearly dancing as she spoke.

"Here," George said, handing Honor a newspaper rolled in his hand.

It unrolled as she accepted it, and she saw that it was a copy of the *Philanthropist*, folded open to the second page. And on that page her poem had been printed. Honor sat down on the bench at the table with a plump. "Oh, my. I . . ." She stared at the words she'd penned and read the byline: *By Honor Cathwell.*

A shadow fell across the threshold. Honor looked up to see her husband quizzing her with a glance. She rose, suddenly cautious. What would he think of her writing antislavery poetry? But it was already done and in print.

"Samuel, our friends George and Deborah have brought me good news." Honor handed him the paper, her index finger directing his gaze to her poem.

Samuel bent his head to read it.

Honor waited on tenterhooks for his response. But of course he kept his reaction hidden. He nodded and smiled at George and Deborah, greeting them with a lifted hand.

Perlie curtsied, said she would make tea, and hurried out.

Honor motioned for Deborah to sit in the rocker by the hearth. Samuel didn't want anybody to know of her passion for abolition—didn't want her calling attention to them. Would he be angry with her?

"No, Honor, please. Both George and I would like to see thy home and Samuel's glassworks."

Honor signed this and began the tour. She showed Deborah the bedroom off the large main room. Then Samuel led them to his barn, where Judah was waiting to blow glass into molds.

Honor translated for Samuel. "My husband has carved a mold for a man who makes maple syrup. See, it has a maple leaf on it along with the man's name. This customer saw the bottles Samuel had designed for a beekeeper in Weymouth."

George drew nearer to where the molds lay ready for glass. He stepped back when Samuel and Judah tested the molten glass. Both men, standing at opposite ends of the workbench, started it into molds, blowing, forcing the glass to fit the mold's shape. George and Deborah watched with interest. And when the mold was full, they applauded.

"Amazing!" Deborah said. "I've never seen glass being made."

Perlie appeared at the door of the barn with Royale behind her. "The tea and refreshments are on the dinin' table, ma'am."

"Royale," Deborah said, "how good to see thee looking so well. What does thee think of Honor having a poem published?"

Royale bowed her head politely. "I'm not surprised, ma'am. When we was girls in Maryland, she sometimes wrote poetry."

"Please come to the table," Perlie said. "The tea will get cold."

George and Deborah followed Honor to the cabin, where she entertained them. Samuel came in a few minutes later and apologized for his delay, saying he'd had to finish the glass bottle he'd begun in the demonstration. Out of the blue, he asked their guests, "Why do you think slavery can end?"

Both George and Deborah stared at the bald question.

George cleared his throat. "Ending slavery will not be easy, but establishing a democratic republic has not been easy either. Sometimes one must work for what is right, even when the odds of victory appear small."

"What do you think of people who hide or aid runaways?" Samuel asked.

Honor translated but felt her pulse speed up. She had not revealed her involvement with runaways to anyone outside the household, not even to Deborah. Was her husband trying to show her she was wrong? Or expose her wrongdoing?

Deborah spoke before her son. "I would not turn an escaped slave over to a catcher. I've seen the kind of men who do this nasty job. They are the sort of people who kidnapped Royale and your nephew."

Samuel looked startled at her response.

"My mother is bold in her cause," George said. "We have never had a runaway come to our door, but I too would help him. My mother and I were forced to leave North Carolina when we freed our slaves. The anger our former neighbors and friends turned on us told us much. When a person does what is right, it stirs the rage of those who will not turn from doing the same evil."

Samuel nodded slowly but did not give away what he was thinking. Once again he had shut them all out, including Honor, his wife. She absorbed his withdrawal, praying that someday her husband would cease hedging out the world, walling himself away.

Soon after the tea had been finished, George and Deborah left the Cathwells' for the drive home. Honor stood at the door, waving them off in the bright sunshine. When they disappeared around the bend, she turned to face her husband, finally able to ask him, "So is thee angry about my poem appearing in the press?"

"You might as well have put a sign on our door for all the slave catchers around to see."

The truth of what he said settled within her like a cold rock. "I should have asked to remain anonymous."

"Our only hope will be that slave catchers only read the classifieds, not poetry. But this kind of paper—" he pointed to the newspaper lying on the table—"is just the kind of thing they would read for leads."

Honor sank into the rocker, weak with regret. "What should we do?"

"Hope that it goes unnoticed." With that, he left her.

She rocked beside the low fire and tried to come up with a way out of this trouble. She recalled the pride she had felt when she'd first seen her name in print. Well, *"pride goeth before destruction, and an haughty spirit before a fall,"* and Honor had the safety of others to consider, not just what people might think of her. Anonymity would have been a small price to pay if it had kept the slave catchers away. If only she'd considered that earlier.

❖

FEBRUARY 8, 1820

Once again Royale hovered by Honor's bed in the early hours of the morning. Honor rose and, this time, shook Samuel awake too.

"We got a whole family in the kitchen," Royale said,

shivering slightly in her robe and shawl. "Where we gon' hide a whole family?"

Honor threw on a dress and shawl over her nightgown, and Samuel dragged on his trousers and jacket. They hurried through the gray light of dawn to the kitchen, where they found a man, his wife, his mother, and their two children, both around Caleb's age. They were huddled near the fire, eating leftovers and gulping water.

"Boss, the loft won't hide this many," Judah said. "And what if the catchers come?" They'd all been on edge since the poem had appeared in print the previous day.

"We must take them to Bucktown. Now," Samuel replied. "Judah, go get the team harnessed. We'll leave immediately."

Honor could hardly believe her eyes. Her husband was taking action for these runaways.

He turned to her and signed, "Think up some reason for us to go to Bucktown so early in case anyone asks. We'll come back at once."

As he passed her on his way to the door, she gripped his forearm. "Thank thee, Samuel. I know this seems an imposition."

He shrugged and pulled free, leaving her.

Honor smiled at the runaways, but her thoughts were on her husband. A desire to keep their neighbors from finding out what they were doing might explain his quick actions. But he could be acting out of respect for her—or even out of a growing compassion for runaway slaves themselves.

❁

Samuel and Judah returned well into the morning. They entered the kitchen, where Honor waited with Royale and Perlie. Eli and Caleb played with their pets and small leather balls in front of the fire.

"They're safe," Judah said under his breath, hanging back by the door. "We met no one on the way, and the people of Bucktown took the family into hiding right away."

Samuel nodded toward Judah, obviously prompting him. "Mr. Cathwell says we got to build a better hiding place than just putting people in the loft."

As if nudged sharply, Honor sprang up from the bench to join them. She schooled her voice to avoid drawing Eli's attention. "What?"

"We planned it on the way home. We're going to get started on it right away. If you see anybody coming, give us a shout and we'll hide our work. Mr. Cathwell doesn't want anybody to know what we're building."

Honor nodded, stunned. When the two men left, she turned to Royale and Perlie. "Does thee think my husband has come around to our way of thinking?"

"No," Royale said laconically. "I think he don't want to stick out and be noticed."

"The mister never like people to come or to look at him," Perlie joined in. "I think that's what this is about."

Honor didn't contradict them, but a flicker of hope flared, hope that Samuel was drawing nearer.

Chapter 17

APRIL 4, 1820

Honor blinked herself awake to a tapping. She sat up, glad of spring, glad to wake without a cold nose. The feeble gray of predawn lightened the window. The tapping at the door sounded again. A caller before dawn? No, it would be another runaway.

Jolted fully awake, Honor rolled out of bed and donned her robe. She hurried to answer before the noise woke Eli this early. She opened the door and saw in the barest light two women, hunkered under shawls in the morning mist.

"This be the Cathwell house?" one asked.

Alarm quivered through Honor. Usually the runaways didn't know or ask their name. "Yes," she replied in a cautious whisper. "I am Honor Cathwell."

"Honor." The one word was spoken in a voice she had never forgotten, fixing her in place, her blood frozen.

"It is me, Honor." The woman lifted the shawl she wore over her head and shoulders, revealing her familiar pale face surrounded by brown curls in disarray.

"Darah," Honor gasped, her heart throbbing within her.

"Can we come in, Miss Honor?" begged the other woman, who was rounder and whose skin was the color of brown sugar.

Not recognizing this other young woman, Honor fell back, dazed. She closed the door behind them, shutting out the early mosquitoes. She stumbled to her chair and sat down, feeling she might faint. Was she having a dream? Could this be real?

His nightshirt tucked into his trousers, Samuel came up beside her and touched her shoulder.

Honor looked up at him in the shadows. Even in her shock, his presence strengthened her. Samuel moved farther to the side, evidently so she could see his fingers by the faint light from the window. "What's wrong?"

"This is my cousin," she signed, unable to go on.

❖

Samuel tried to read his wife's face but saw only taut suffering. Her cousin? The one who'd inherited the plantation instead of Honor? He drew near his wife, who sat as stiff and still as wood.

He motioned for the two women to come farther inside. They didn't move, remaining huddled by the door. The pale skin of one shone in the low light. What was going on?

Honor did not move to hurry the early morning visitors to the kitchen or barn as she usually did—but then, these weren't typical runaways. If indeed they were running at all.

The two women still did not move.

Reaching over, he gently touched his wife's arm. She didn't respond. Increasingly worried, he lit a candle.

Finally Honor held her hand high in front of the candlelight and signed her words as she spoke. "Darah, why has thee come here, and in this way?"

The pretty but drawn-looking white woman buried her face in her hands. "You must hide us, Honor. We're headed to Canada."

Samuel read the reply from Honor's fingers and could not make sense of it. Why would a white woman need to go to Canada?

"I thought—" Honor said. "Thee wrote me of thy marrying."

Following the conversation through Honor's fingers, Samuel watched the woman called Darah bend over, shaking, sobbing. "What troubles her?" he asked Honor.

"I don't know. I don't know why she's here. She should be in Maryland."

"Miss Honor," the maid said, "I'm Sally. I know us comin' is a surprise, but there be two catchers on our trail. I think you better hide us quick."

Though Honor signed the woman's words, she still didn't move.

Catchers. Samuel motioned for the women to follow him. When Honor rose at last, the two strangers obeyed him. His wife trailed them, lagging behind the quick pace he set.

Soon, in the first true glimmers of the dawn's light, Samuel and Judah led the women to the secret room they'd built in the rear of the barn near Judah's bedroom. Royale and his wife followed them, both looking confused. Inside, with the touch of a hidden lever, Samuel opened a wall covered with bottles on shelves.

The women behind him appeared surprised. But they walked into the secret room, obviously noting the blankets neatly folded there as well as the jug of water. Honor set down a bag of bread, turned away, and started back to the cabin.

Quickly Samuel showed the women how to open the door from the inside in case of emergency, then shut them in. Even now, just before dawn, the day promised unusual heat and humidity. He had drilled holes high and low in the wall for ventilation, but still it would be warm, stuffy inside.

Bewildered, he hurried after his wife. Sunshine already lit the sky, though the sun still had not cleared the horizon. Inside their cabin, she sank onto the rocking chair, folding in on herself.

Samuel sat down in the chair opposite her. He didn't know what to say. He'd followed the conversation but couldn't see why her cousin had come here. And why was the woman running away with her slave? "I don't understand," he signed, moving his chair closer to hers.

Honor raised her hand. "I don't either."

"Is this the cousin who got your inheritance?"

Honor turned her face away and buried her hands in her lap as if refusing to reply, her anguish plain to see.

He tapped her arm, insistent, concerned. "Talk to me."

"It is hard for me to talk about her, but yes, she's the one who inherited our plantation," Honor signed. "I can't believe that my cousin is here. And why is she heading to Canada? It makes no sense."

Over the past months since he'd built the secret room for runaway slaves, their life had evened out. As long as she kept her activities secret, he'd accepted his wife's need to help runaways, and helped them himself, as he had by building the secret room. He had begun to see first-hand the ravages of slavery on humans like himself. The world had rejected him, but it hadn't beaten him, branded him, or dragged him away from his family. And Judah was as intelligent and skilled as Samuel himself, but his skin color—like Samuel's deafness—marked him as of less value to the world. It didn't make sense.

When Honor put her hands over her face, her pain pricked him. She was always good to him, faithful, respectful. . . . But Samuel longed for more. He yearned to be closer to this beautiful, tenderhearted woman. He'd begun longing to see his wife sign the words, *I love thee, Samuel.*

But they'd married out of necessity, and he'd accepted that he might never see those words. He was lucky just to have Honor, a good wife, an exceptional woman. He had no right to expect more from her.

❁

Later that morning, Honor was pouring fresh coffee while the rest of her family sat down, ready for breakfast. For the boys' sake, they must masquerade that this day was like any other. Her stomach clenched, and she doubted she'd be able to eat anything. Darah, here. She couldn't imagine why.

Then Honor heard an approaching wagon.

"Quaker!" the familiar yet unwelcome voice called. "You got any runaways for me today?"

Honor choked, gasping for breath. Ever since Darah had arrived, Honor had felt like someone had put a loaded pistol to her head and fired. She couldn't think. And now she must face the catchers, who never passed without stopping. The two had been here almost monthly ever since they'd returned Caleb.

She signed the catchers' arrival to Samuel and went to the door, which already stood open to let in some breeze. Darah and her maid were hiding in the barn. That wasn't an illusion, and never had she feared these two men more. The situation and its implications about her own understanding of the past nauseated her. She forced down the waves of sickness.

"Good morning, Zeb, Dan." She hoped her calm and polite words hid her turmoil.

The older of the two, Zeb, cackled sarcastically at her cordial greeting. "You Quakers are a funny bunch. We're chasing two women this time. You wouldn't have seen them, I suppose?"

Her wits scattered, she couldn't spar with them as usual. Nothing was usual today. Her mind continued to scramble as words she never expected passed through her lips. "Would thee like a hot cup of coffee?"

Zeb cackled again. "Yeah, you're going to give me a cup of coffee. Whatcha gonna do, spit in it?"

His response goaded her. "If thee doesn't trust me, come in and watch me pour it." She backed against the door, opening it wider. She must keep them busy, throw them off the scent. Or was something else prompting her to offer this odd invitation?

The older man eyed her distrustfully. "I'm still gonna look around your place."

"Does thee have a search warrant?" She had recently learned from Alan Lewis that they could not search her home without invitation or a valid warrant.

"No, we got no warrant," Zeb admitted. "You gettin' too knowing."

Inviting them in had not come from thoughtful consideration. But she had no time for reflection, and she couldn't rescind her invitation, whatever ensued. She turned to sign to Samuel and Caleb that she'd invited them in so the boy wouldn't be surprised into flight.

Samuel gawked at her.

She didn't blame him.

Though casting her sharp, distrustful glances, Zeb tied the reins of the wagon to the brake handle and got down. His grandson looked surprised but followed him.

"What you up to, Quaker?" Zeb asked before stepping inside.

"I'm offering thee hot coffee, hot biscuits, and gravy."

"Why?"

"'Love your enemies. . . . Do good to them that hate you,'" she quoted, the familiar words coming to her without thought. Now, however, she felt the weight these words carried. Rarely was she tempted to do good to those who cruelly returned slaves escaping harsh masters. Instead she had often wished harm upon them. *"Do good to them that hate you"* lay like burning iron over her heart. She dragged in a ragged breath.

The old man fumed. "Don't quote the Bible to me. It's writ in there that slaves are supposed to obey their masters."

"Yes."

"Then if you follow the Bible, why are you helping runaways?"

She looked him in the eye. "Thee has never proved such a thing. And I could explain why slavery is wrong, but perhaps it is something thee should ponder thyself. Does thee want biscuits and gravy or not?" Her already-tight stomach twisted again.

The two neared the table awkwardly and doffed their hats.

Honor motioned them to sit down, her throat struggling to hold in the truth.

"Don't they got to wash their hands first?" Eli complained, having been chastised for forgetting to do this just minutes before.

"Eli, do not correct thy elders," Honor scolded without heat.

Caleb hurried around the far side of the table to sit beside Samuel. Signing, Honor tried to reassure him that these two would not hurt him. Caleb finally trusted Samuel and Honor to keep him safe, but he still feared these two.

After the slave catchers sat down, Samuel signed, "Good morning."

Honor could tell by his bemused expression he also wondered what she was doing. And she wondered too. But something had prompted her. It might have come from an irrational reaction to shock or panic, or it might have come from the Inner Light. She felt as if she were being led into the dark, following a distant candle.

Mechanically, she poured the men coffee and set two more places, serving gravy made from fragrant sausage and drippings over Perlie's light, buttery biscuits. All the while, her mind whirled with feelings, thoughts, unable to focus.

Honor bowed her head and said her silent grace, adding a plea for God to keep Darah and her maid from these men. She took her seat beside Samuel. As they ate, the strained silence around the table expanded moment by moment. Even Eli, who usually chattered at breakfast, stayed silent.

Finally, desperate to fill the gaping silence and escape her thoughts, she asked, "Where are thee two from?"

Zeb gave her a distrustful look. "Virginny."

"I'm from the South too—Maryland, Tidewater."

"We're from the mountains," Dan said in between bites.

"Tidewater is rich with tobacco plantations. You come down in the world," Zeb said, pointing his finger at them. "And you two are breaking the law, hiding runaways."

"Has thee ever found a runaway here?" Honor asked innocently. Her leg jumped as if giving her away.

Zeb cut into his biscuit. "No, but you people are gettin' clever about hiding them."

"We were already clever," Samuel signed, and Honor spoke it.

This forced a laugh from Dan. "You are clever, knowing how to talk with your hands and such."

Zeb looked disgruntled and spent the rest of the meal brooding, silently finishing two full helpings of biscuits and gravy and four cups of coffee with sugar and fresh cream, all the while glaring at Honor.

Honor managed to eat a little and prayed for calm.

When their plates were clean, the guests rose. Zeb stared at her. "We thank you. Good victuals. But we're going to look up in the loft here. We can 'cause you invited us in."

Honor tilted her head to one side and bowed it. "Thee is welcome to look, but only in the house, Dan, Zeb. We didn't invite thee into any other building on our land."

Her mind still buzzed. From nowhere, she recalled how the angel had set the apostle Peter free when he'd been jailed in Jerusalem and how the maid Rhoda had been so shocked to see him freed, she'd left him outside the door. Now Honor understood Rhoda's reaction. She'd felt the same way when she first laid eyes on Darah and her maid.

"Thank ya for the meal, ma'am. It was good," Dan said.

Honor nodded. She certainly had learned little about them except that they too had started life in her part of the country.

Unreasoning fear rolled through her. She resisted an urge to run to the barn and fling open the secret panel. *I'm not thinking rationally.*

Samuel waited at the door and signed to her.

"My husband says he'll escort thee to thy wagon," she said. She didn't follow, couldn't trust her legs or herself.

Dan left, but Zeb paused at the door, glaring at her as usual. Then, for a moment, his face softened.

Honor looked at him, glad he didn't ask her another question about hiding runaways, but wondering at the change in his expression.

"You stuck with your man," Zeb said in a low tone for her ears only.

Honor gazed at him, uncomprehending.

"After a while, I figured you'd up and find somebody better than a deaf-mute."

Hot indignation shot through Honor. She stiffened.

"Don't get riled. You're a pretty woman. I'd understand if you wasn't satisfied."

"I gave Samuel my promise," Honor replied with brittle courtesy, recalling that she had nearly given Alec the same promise before he turned on her. She rose, walking forward, forcing Zeb outside.

Zeb climbed up on the wagon and looked down on her. "I misjudged you. You didn't turn out to be a false-hearted love. I give credit where credit is due."

Honor merely nodded, unable to think what to say. "Good day, Zeb, Dan."

Then, as he started the team, she barely heard Zeb's final comment. "Wish I'd chosen as well."

She watched the two men drive off. Zeb's phrase *"false-hearted love"* repeated in her mind. Her own hurt stirred. She pressed it down.

A long, uncomfortable day of work in the unusual April heat lay ahead. She and Royale would be doing the weekly laundry and ironing today. She looked down at her hands that had become callused in places over the past months. She was fortunate to have a man whose business prospered more and more and who could afford a cook and maid. But no longer was Honor the lady of the plantation. She worked with her hands too.

"*You can always tell a lady by her hands,*" Royale's mother had said. Honor refused to allow any more memories. Her life in Maryland was long ago and far away—except that Darah had brought it all back by running away from Alec and hiding in Honor's barn. A churning started in the pit of her stomach. Why had Darah left Maryland, left Alec?

❖

As soon as the catchers went on their way, Royale hurried inside the house. "Samuel say Darah and her maid are hiding in the barn. What happened?"

Honor had retreated into her chair, trying to recruit her strength. "I don't know. But Eve isn't with her. A new woman is her maid."

Royale dropped into the chair opposite. "What? Eve was raised to be her maid for life—just like you and me." Royale's face twisted with confusion. "Why is Miss Darah here? Her letter say she married Mr. Alec last year."

Honor lowered her head into her hands. "Darah didn't seem to want to talk, and we had to get them hidden before dawn. And then the catchers came."

"What did you give those two breakfast for?" Royale's voice vibrated with her disapproval.

Honor shook her head. "I wanted to distract them." *To distract myself. I don't know why.*

Several minutes passed before she looked up to find Royale staring at the wall, frowning. "What is it?"

Royale worried her lower lip. "I heard things . . . in Maryland. Slaves talk about their masters."

Honor straightened up. "What did thee hear?"

Royale ignored her question and still gazed past Honor. "I never worry about you and him 'cause I never thought you would marry him."

This distracted Honor. "Thee didn't? Why?"

Royale shrugged. "I knew you intended to free your people. If you did that, Alec Martin wouldn't want to marry you. No land."

Ice went down Honor's spine. "Thee means that he only wanted me for what I'd bring him."

"I didn't say that," Royale amended. "Mr. Alec want you because you were the prettiest and you got special style and wit. But land and money are important to him."

Royale's confidences had only stirred up Honor's emotions more. "To a lot of people."

Royale let loose a sound of dry agreement. "I wish we could go out and talk to them, but with the catchers nearby, we can't till way after dark."

"I know." Honor reached for Royale's hand, seeking reassurance that she could count on her not to have changed, lied. She wanted to press Royale for more insights about Alec, but suddenly fearful, she asked, "Why is life always so unpredictable?"

Royale squeezed her hand. "I don't know, but I do know we got a lot of laundry to do before it gets any hotter."

Yes, better to concentrate on reality. "Go ahead. I'll be right out."

Honor watched Royale walk outside and tried to focus her mind, but her thoughts bounced around as if she were driving down a rough road. And that seemed to be an apt comparison. No matter what Darah had to say, this would be a rough road.

❁

As the day passed, Samuel tried several times to get Honor to speak with him about the two women. She refused to discuss them and withdrew from him. He felt her absence keenly. How had he missed how much he'd come to prize her constant thought and effort for him, toward being his helpmeet?

Night loomed ahead, and he asked if she wanted to take the women their meal or let them come in. She blinked away tears. He had rarely seen his wife so distracted, so downhearted. It shook him. But he had no idea how to reach her.

After sundown and supper, he headed for the kitchen with his silent wife, who'd agreed to take the meal to the barn. Perlie dished up two more plates of food and put them in a water bucket in case the catchers had circled back in secret. Royale and Judah came along as well. The two couples walked out to the barn, side by side without exchanging words.

In the barn, Samuel lit a lantern and felt his wife withdraw further. Judah worked the lever on the wall, and with a rattle, the panel of bottles swung open. Within, the two women looked wilted from the day's heat. Samuel hadn't fired up the forge today, but that didn't look like it had helped. He hoped a cooling rain would drench the land soon and break the humidity.

Honor and Royale stood back as if not wanting to get too close. Wondering at this, he lifted the two plates out of the bucket and sent Judah to fill their jug with fresh water. Before they ate, the two hurried through the dark shadows to the necessary and back again. They sat down on the floor to eat their cold meal.

Samuel watched them eat, baffled as Honor stood like a statue, staring at her cousin, barely blinking. Even with the conflicted past that stood between them, he would have thought Honor would try to get answers out of this woman.

Royale also stared at the visitors as if she couldn't believe her eyes. But she was the one who began the conversation. "Where's Eve? Why she not here with you?" she asked, signing it too.

Darah glanced up and down and spoke. At her answer, Honor visibly reacted as if someone had struck her, but she didn't reply or interpret for Samuel.

Royale also appeared shocked, but she gathered herself and signed what Darah had said: "Alec sold Eve south—without even asking me."

Sending worried glances toward Honor, Royale explained to Samuel, "Eve raised with us to be Miss Darah's maid. What call would make Mr. Alec sell Eve?"

"So Miss Darah be all alone," the new maid said.

Royale signed this and let her hand fall. She moved closer to Honor as if shaken.

Samuel stood, watching, trying to figure out what this all meant and how to help his wife.

When the two women were done eating, Samuel needed to gauge their intent. Unwilling to disturb his wife or Royale, he asked through Judah, "Are you planning to go to Canada?"

The two women assented with nods.

Samuel watched the cousin's drawn face for any betrayal of motive for this flight all the way to Canada. He saw only fear and worry and suffering.

Judah relayed their question. "They want to know how far Canada is from here."

"Over a week, I reckon, by wagon." Samuel knew that the other runaways had also headed to Canada, the only safe place for a slave to go. But what about Honor's cousin? What was she running from?

Judah asked this question for Samuel.

"The maid will only say they won't be safe till they both are in Canada." Judah turned and signed, "I don't understand either why a white woman is running away."

Was this woman in her right mind? Taking her maid and running away like a slave herself? Something worse than he could imagine must have happened. But he wasn't sure it was his place to dig deeper and wondered why his wife didn't talk to her cousin. None of this added up.

He realized then that he must act. Honor was evidently not able or willing to take action, to face whatever her cousin's appearance had triggered. He'd let other runaways go off by themselves. But he refused to entertain the idea of letting these two defenseless women go north alone. Regardless of what had happened in Maryland, this woman was his wife's blood kin. No matter what, one didn't abandon family.

"Judah, tell them," he signed, "that we will leave for Canada tomorrow at first light. We can just behave as if the maid is a servant traveling with us."

His wife's cousin vehemently shook her head no and began speaking rapidly.

"She says," Judah translated, "that while her husband away, they traveled together as a veiled lady and her maid. They arrived in Cincinnati together but slipped out of the city in the dark because they were afraid that Miss Darah's husband would come seeking a lady and her maid. They don't want anyone to see them here with Honor or traveling with her so their trail dead-ends.

"They want to just disappear, leave no trace. You see, in Canada the maid can refuse to return to her master and the court will uphold her. But a wife would not be able to refuse to return to her husband. No one would stop a man from carrying his wife off."

Samuel stared at them a long time, struck by this truth, wondering at this arrangement, waiting for his wife to speak. Finally he gave up and assured the women that they would be transported in secret. Raising a hand, he bid them a wordless good night.

Judah again shut them up in the secret room. Usually runaways only stayed one night. What if the catchers had gone back to Cincinnati to get a warrant?

Outside, Judah walked Royale back to the kitchen while Samuel and Honor headed toward their cabin. Honor drifted beside him as a silent stranger into their bedroom. The boys were already asleep in the loft above. He turned to his wife, trying to think of some way to reach her.

"We will have to leave Judah to protect Royale and Perlie and the boys," she signed abruptly. "I will have to drive."

He agreed. Hovering near, he longed to hold her, something which had become more natural to them of late, but he hesitated to touch her now. Somehow the arrival of her cousin had distanced her from him in a way he couldn't breach. And now they must face the journey to and from Canada with her. Samuel did not understand why a wife would flee her husband. He tried to imagine Honor running away from him, but that was impossible.

APRIL 5, 1820

Early the next day, Samuel opened the concealed door. He waved the women out of the hidden room and toward the wagon, parked in the barn. In the dim light, he whipped back the tarpaulin and showed them the empty bay in the middle between boxes of bottles. He'd strapped the boxes onto secured shelves so they would not fall on the women when the wagon rocked.

Samuel helped them into the wagon, pointing to a pallet they could lie on to soften the ride. After securing the tarpaulin again, he overcame his reluctance with the horses and led the team out of the barn and to the house.

At the cabin door, Eli and Caleb stood rubbing their eyes, still in their nightshirts.

Honor stepped outside as well, dressed in her boots,

gray dress, and bonnet for the journey. "While we're away, boys, help Judah with the animals and mind thy elders," she signed and said. "We'll be back as soon as we can, but it will be a while."

"Do you got to go?" Eli said, appearing a bit worried. Caleb stood close to Eli, also looking strained.

"Yes, we do," Honor said. "But we will return." *God, help us.*

Samuel stooped and hugged each boy, reassuring them. Caleb looked like a lost lamb. Samuel stroked his hair and kissed his forehead. Then he rose.

Judah, Royale, and Perlie arrived and stood near the boys. "Don't you worry," Judah said. "I'll make sure everyone stays safe."

"If any catchers make trouble here, go to Micah or Thad," Honor said. "They will stand up for thee."

Then she let Samuel help her up onto the wagon, noting a rifle, which Judah had taught him how to shoot, resting at his side. No wonder. Shawnee and Wyandot still roamed the state. And bandits and slave catchers.

The round trip would take at least two weeks over routes that were more wheel tracks than roads. As she grasped the reins in her leather-gloved hands and slapped them, heading down Lebanon Road, Honor's nerve nearly failed her.

She didn't know if she had the courage or the strength to do this. But Darah was her blood, and something must have gone very wrong in Maryland. What could Alec have done? She wanted to know, yet she hoped she would never find out.

⁂

The trees crowded close to the wheel tracks on the crude road to Dayton. Honor slumped on the hard bench, weary of holding the reins, stiff from the day of driving. At least the past weeks had been dry, so mud didn't slow or stop them. The front wheel hit another deep rut. As the horses struggled with the lines, Honor encouraged them forward with care. "Easy."

Ahead, Honor glimpsed a break in the forest. She urged the team over the ruts. They still had a few hours of sunlight, but her stomach rumbled with hunger. All day her unruly mind had brought up memory of home after memory of home. Would it let her sleep, let her forget?

When they reached a clearing, Honor turned the wagon off the road. She drove in as far as possible. A log cabin, perhaps one from a long-gone French fur trapper, had fallen into partial ruin there, and she heard a brook running nearby. "Whoa!" She hauled back on the reins and halted the team. "Hello the house!" No one responded. "We'll stop here tonight," she told Samuel.

He nodded, getting down and walking to the rear.

Irritated that her husband went to help her cousin first, Honor moved slowly and eased herself off the bench and down to the thick spring grass. She limped around to the rear also, trying not to have uncharitable thoughts.

Samuel was already lifting out the boxes of bottles that hemmed in the hidden women. Both of them were lying down, and they slowly clambered out when Samuel cleared an opening. While Honor had sat on a hard bench, controlling and guiding a team of horses over a narrow, rutted road, Darah had lain all day on a pallet. Resentment curdled in Honor's stomach in spite of herself.

Samuel turned to her, signing, "I was coming to help you. They have been trapped, cramped all day."

His explanation didn't change the way she felt. She turned and stiffly walked away, heading toward the creek, where she could drink and splash away the sweat and grit on her face and neck.

"Honor," Darah called, "don't run from me. We need to talk. I was too frightened and tired before to try to explain, but you need to know."

Honor didn't stop, didn't slow. But she heard her cousin pursuing her through the tall grass, crunching pinecones underfoot. She felt like outrunning Darah, but suddenly her resolve wilted. Darah caught up with her.

Honor didn't turn to acknowledge her. She slipped through the trees and hurried the last few steps to the creek. Removing her shoes, she lifted the back of her plain gray skirt and tucked it into her thin belt. She waded out into the chilly water and bent to splash it on her face and neck.

"I know you don't want me here," Darah said, following her into the water, not bothering to tuck up her skirt of fine cotton.

Honor stared at her cousin, who stood erect and defiant.

"I know what kind of man Mr. Alec be," the new maid spoke up. She must have trailed Darah to the creek. "I born on his land. I see what he did to my mistress."

Honor wanted to ask, *Did what?* She couldn't form the words.

Darah rolled up her sleeve and held out her bare arm. "See what he did to me."

When Honor saw a pronounced lump between the wrist and elbow, she gasped and nearly slipped on the slick creek pebbles.

"This happened only weeks after our wedding. Alec threw me against the fireplace and broke my arm. My maid, Sally—" she nodded toward the other woman—"bound it as well as she could, but . . ."

Honor looked into her cousin's eyes. She pulled back at the stark suffering she saw there. Revulsion over the injury hit her and she bent, gasping against waves of nausea.

Sally waded farther into the creek. "White folk didn't know, but Mr. Martin's slaves did. He got a mean streak."

"It is true," Darah affirmed. "I couldn't believe it either at first. But sometimes it's like he goes mad. It's terrifying what he does in a rage."

Honor tried to put this together in her mind.

"Honor, I am not lying." Darah grabbed her hand. "I can't go back to him. He threatened that if I tried to leave him, he'd have me locked up as insane. If he finds me and takes me back, my life won't be worth living. I'll kill myself first."

Honor's pulse skipped and jumped with emotions she didn't want to confront. What was true? The memory of her last conversation with Alec in the garden of High Oaks returned. How he had slashed the air with his cane and gripped her arms. She'd thought it was due to the intensity of his feelings for her, but now she was forced to admit she had been deceived.

Chapter 18

APRIL 12, 1820

A week later, the four of them had passed through busy Detroit and ferried across the Detroit River to prosperous Windsor, Canada. Now in a cozy log inn, they sat at supper in a private dining parlor so Sally could eat with them. Though already partway into the evening, golden sunlight flowed through the open windows. Finely woven cheesecloth hung over each, keeping out most of the mosquitoes yet letting in the evening breeze.

Honor sat beside her husband, trying not to look at Darah, across from her. Even though the horrible truth of Darah's marriage had been revealed, Honor's sense of hurt and upheaval festered. Still, Samuel's solid presence bolstered her. She might not be certain her husband would ever love her, but she couldn't imagine Samuel ever turning his strength against her. Once she'd believed Alec loved her, but she'd been proved wrong, and in so many ways. Maybe Alec didn't know what love meant. She recalled their last conversation. He'd started it with, *"What about me?"*

They'd ordered an evening meal of smoked grouse with a delicious cranberry sauce. Honor, drained in every way, just picked at her food, trying to revive herself. Even though it would mean another day of driving the team, she couldn't wait till the day after tomorrow when they could leave Darah here and head back to Sharpesburg.

The servant girl came in, removed their dinner plates, and set a platter of sliced cheese and rhubarb pie on the table. One forkful and the tart rhubarb tingled on her tongue.

"Honor, I need you to ask your cousin some questions," Samuel signed.

Every bone in her body ached from many days of driving the team. She sighed and signed, "Do we need to talk now?" *To my cousin who robbed me of everything and didn't care?*

He nodded. "We must have our plans in place because we leave for home at first light in two days. I have work to get home to."

No mention of Honor's distress, just his work. Selecting a slice of cheddar cheese, she quelled a grimace and signed, "Very well."

"Ask your cousin if she has any skill that she might use to make money."

Honor thought of how ludicrous this question was. Darah had been raised to be a lady, just as she herself had. The skills they had been taught—elegant manners, beautiful needlework, and the pianoforte—did not have any market value. In her deep fatigue, even the idea of lying down here on the floor started to have appeal. Ever since Darah had appeared at their door, Honor had been prone to crave sleep more than usual—only to wake to nightmares.

Pushing these thoughts aside, she delivered Samuel's question, hoping to end this as soon as possible and go to bed.

Darah didn't look surprised. "I can make lace, fine lace."

Now Honor did recall this. Both of them had been taught this ladylike skill, but unlike Honor, Darah had excelled in it.

Samuel nodded. "Good. Tomorrow we will rent you a shop with living quarters. I will pay the rent for a year. And I will deposit a hundred dollars in an account at the bank for you."

Honor, in the act of reaching for another slice of cheese, halted her arm in midair. Samuel had to nudge her into relating his words.

Darah gasped.

"Thank you, Jesus," Sally murmured, clasping her hands together.

Honor stared at her husband, unable to speak. A hundred dollars? She pulled back her hand from the cheese board, suddenly short of breath. One hundred dollars was what she'd been left in her grandfather's will. The irony of this wrapped around her throat. "We're leaving High Oaks in Alec's possession, then?" she demanded sharply.

Every face turned to her.

"What can we do about that, Honor?" Darah asked. "Upon our marriage, High Oaks became his. As a married woman, I have no property rights."

Honor chewed on this unpalatable legal fact. Though why she should experience afresh the loss of High Oaks baffled her. Even before Darah married Alec, Honor's home had been wrenched from her. Had she in some secret part of her heart hoped to somehow free her people even now? Impossible.

"The hundred dollars is a loan, which I will expect you to repay over time, Darah," Samuel signed and Honor translated. "But not till you've established your business in a few years and are making a steady income."

Darah murmured a bewildered thank-you.

Honor lifted a slice of cheese but couldn't eat it. She still couldn't look at her cousin. She believed what Darah said about Alec. No sane woman would flee as Darah had unless she had cause. But Honor's own situation was fraught with such uncertainty. She and Samuel had come so far, but would they ever be completely one? Would her devotion to abolition continue to separate them? Worry tied her up inside into tight, hard knots. She set the cheese on her plate.

Samuel turned to Sally. "What can you do?"

"I can sew and mend. I could hire out."

Samuel nodded. "I will give both of you money for new clothing so you can look presentable to apply for work. You need new shoes and will require warm clothing for winter."

Honor continued to share his words, the mistreatment by those she trusted still souring her unsettled stomach. Of course Samuel would be generous; he had been generous with her. It stirred something unpleasant within her nonetheless, something she wished she didn't feel. Their meal finally ended, and soon they retired to their reserved rooms upstairs. Honor could barely wish her cousin good night.

In their room, Samuel shut and latched the door. Honor sank into the comfortable chair by the cold hearth. The last rays of the sun lit one wall, reflecting her low mood. She wanted to lie down and sleep, and she wanted to spring up and run from the room.

Samuel stood motionless, gazing at her. She tried to read any trace of love in his expression, his eyes. As usual, he excelled in masking his emotions. Above all, she needed reassurance of their bond. She needed him to hold her, but she couldn't ask for it. He must do it without prompting or it would mean little.

Everything in her life had been turned upside down. Alec was a monster. Darah was reduced to fleeing him. The people she would have freed were at the mercy of a man with an ungovernable temper. Samuel had proved practical and charitable, while Honor was barely able to speak a civil word to her only cousin. Hot tears flowed down her cheeks. And she was totally helpless in the face of this disruption—of her life now and of what she'd believed about those she'd left in Maryland. Her soul cried out to God, not in words but in confusion and hurt and exhaustion.

❖

When Honor and Samuel left Canada, riding the ferry over the Detroit River back to the American shore, she stayed near her husband for protection among the strangers, some very rough-looking. Even a few bare-chested Wyandot in buckskin and feathers stood nearby.

On the ferry dock at the Canadian shore, Darah and Sally stood in the morning sunshine that glinted on the water. Watching the ferry leave, Darah raised her hand in farewell.

Honor wanted to ignore the gesture, forget all the shattered illusions, but she could not. She raised her hand. Would she ever see Darah again? The blue water flowed underneath them as she left her kin on another shore, in another land. She had never felt so alone. Samuel never spoke of love but protected and provided for her. Alec had vowed his love for her, but then he married Darah and savaged her. Honor's turmoil continued to plague her, leaving her weak, bewildered.

Soon, with a bump and groan of ropes, the ferry docked, and Honor led the team and wagon onto the American side. They left bustling Detroit behind, driving south again for another week on the crude trail. Her arms ached as they never had before, her fatigue deeper than ever.

Honor leaned against the bench, her lower back complaining. If Samuel were able to drive, they could take turns holding and guiding the team. While it was true that being unable to voice commands for the team was the main obstacle, she sensed that Samuel's refusal to learn had more to do with how he still viewed himself—an unwelcome thought.

And she must do all the driving without the diversion

of spoken conversation. Slow tears slid down her cheeks. She couldn't recall being this physically and emotionally tormented and exhausted. The sun rose higher, higher, and the heat of the day grew cloying, breathless.

"Why are you so upset?" Samuel signed.

Incapable of explaining what she didn't understand, she brushed his question aside with a wave of her hand.

He stared at her, brows drawn together, then folded his arms and turned away.

Lost in her inner misery, Honor did not attempt to ease their impasse. Some time slipped by before she became aware of a change in the wind.

Samuel rested a hand on her arm. "Are you angry with me? All I've done is help your cousin and her runaway maid."

She shook her head, glancing skyward.

The wind began to gust, and she realized the moisture in the air had climbed also. Honor looked to the west. Thunderclouds were building into ominous, murky-gray mountains. She glanced around in alarm.

Samuel touched her arm again. "What is wrong? Is there something you haven't told me?"

No shelter anywhere. And Samuel questioning her about the real issue—now, of all times. She slapped the reins, hurrying the team forward. Maybe around the next bend they would find a clearing. If there were thunder, the team could hurt themselves in their panic or run away with the wagon, crashing and injuring her and Samuel. And sitting up so high off the ground, the two of them and the horses would be targets for lightning strikes.

"Whoa," she said in a reassuring tone while slowing the

team so she could free her hand. She nudged Samuel with her elbow and signed, "Look for a clearing or a low place away from the trees. A storm is coming."

With the swift spring storm sweeping toward them, the horses became more and more restive. No clearing was in sight. The horses danced, nervous of the change in the wind.

Samuel tapped her arm once more.

Honor swung to face him. "I can't talk now!" she bellowed. The barest hint of thunder rolled in the distance. The team fought the lines. "Whoa!" She hauled back on them, and for once Samuel reached over and helped her restrain the horses. She couldn't wait another moment. She turned to him and mouthed, "Hold them!"

Scooting down from the bench, Honor quickly unhitched the team and took off their harnesses. She even tugged off their bridles, which she worried could attract lightning with their metal parts. Then she released both horses, clicking her tongue, urging them to go. At first they looked around, agitated as if they couldn't figure out what was happening. When lightning crackled in the distance, the team charged forward, racing headlong down the trail—as they would have even if harnessed to the wagon. She'd acted just in time.

She swung back to Samuel, who sat with the slack reins in his hands, looking astonished. She gestured to him to follow her as she raced toward the rear of the wagon. She signed for him to open the tailgate and then clambered up into the narrow wagon bed under the tarpaulin.

Samuel hesitated. Then, with a cold gust, the rain

poured down like a bucket tipped overhead. He shouted in surprise and scrambled under the tarpaulin, crowding up against her.

The world around them detonated. Lightning flashed. Thunder pounded. She panted and shivered from the sudden chill, from wet and from fear. Hail battered the tarpaulin and wagon around them. Thunder pounded without interval. As if he could save her, she gripped Samuel's shoulders, cringing with every flash of white lightning.

The fast-moving storm swept onward, leaving them panting from the exertion and worry. She still clung to Samuel, grateful for his presence and strength, but her feeling of being tossed in a blanket by recent events hadn't lessened. She didn't trust her own heart and mind. Her husband was physically here to weather this storm. But since Darah had come, the similarity between what she'd felt for Alec in the past and what she now felt for her husband shredded her peace. Had she ever loved Alec, or had it been something completely different? Did she love Samuel? Did that matter in their life together? She fought tears of frustration.

Samuel finally slid toward the foot of the wagon bed and down to the earth. Honor lay on the pallet, smelling the stale sweat left by Darah and Sally. Now, on top of everything else, she and Samuel were stranded far from anyone, with barely any food. And who knew where their horses had run to?

It was too much. Honor lay curled on the pallet, bereft. She rolled onto her back and smelled the wet, low-hanging tarpaulin overhead, steaming. She couldn't summon the strength to face this, too.

Samuel touched her ankle. Closing her eyes, she squeezed back tears. She mustn't just lie here till dark came. Life had to be faced. She slithered down, and he helped her out. She leaned against the wagon and gazed at him.

Samuel met her eyes, his brows raised. "We're stuck here without our horses. Why did you let them loose?"

"Didn't thee see how they bolted at the first thunder and lightning? I had no choice but to let them run free." Frustration and hurt billowed inside her. She leaned back against the wagon and folded her arms, refusing to talk further to him.

Samuel touched her shoulder. "We must find the horses," he signed.

"I know that!" she shouted and signed.

"Why are you so upset?" he asked. "You're angry about something."

She went around and lifted their traveling bag and cloth bag of supplies, seething at the situation, at the husband who remained oblivious. She slung the lighter bag over her shoulder and handed him the other. "Let's go." She strode away.

He hurried after her. "Are we just going to leave the wagon behind?"

"What can we do? Can thee pull the wagon thyself?" Thinking of the plight of her lost team, she felt her irritation dissolve into worry. "Let's hope neither of them was injured or struck by lightning. I think they will stay together.

I hope." Shrugging her uncertainty, she stopped and looked heavenward. "God, help us. We need our horses."

But no hope flickered within her. She plodded beside Samuel, occasionally whistling for the horses but with little hope of finding them. She stared down at her muddy shoes and her mud-spattered hem in despair. Was there no balm in Gilead? Or Ohio?

❁

In the midst of the endless, brooding forest, Samuel trudged through the mud and puddles beside his wife. He was at a loss for how to shake Honor from her dark mood. And now they were slogging up a miry, slippery track, looking for horses. Would they have to abandon their wagon this far north and buy another team somewhere?

He glanced at Honor from the corner of his eye. He could see her anger. But it wasn't due to the storm and their situation—he understood that. She should be angry at the man who'd hurt her cousin, and perhaps even at Darah herself—but not at him.

Another mile passed and his own frustration increased. Finally he tapped his wife's shoulder. "Tell me why you are so angry."

She scorched him with her gaze and kept walking.

He hurried after her. Here in the uninhabited forest, absolutely alone, at last he would demand the truth.

He grasped her shoulder and halted her. "Stop. I want you to explain to me why you are so upset. And don't tell me it's about the horses."

She glared at him, slashing the air with a question. "Thee doesn't know?"

"No!" he signed back, not hiding his frustration.

Ripping off her driving gloves, she held out her hands before her. In spite of the gloves, they were painfully red, swollen, and callused from driving the team. The sight unsettled him, shamed him. He should have been the one driving.

"Look at my hands! Isn't that enough to be upset over?" Leaning forward, she began to sob, appearing to have trouble catching her breath.

This alarmed him. He drew her close under one arm and signed, "I'm sorry, but that isn't all. You have been upset since your cousin came."

"Yes!" Her expression confirmed that he was missing something.

"Because she inherited the land that was rightfully yours?"

"No! Because Alec courted me first!" She jabbed a finger at herself. "Then married my cousin. How could I have believed such a false-hearted man?" She averted her face, yet her fingers went on signing. "He just wanted the land. Why didn't I see that? Am I blind?"

Samuel jerked backward, stunned by this revelation. Such a man deserved to be horsewhipped.

Honor turned away from him and began marching down the road again.

He rushed after her, stopping her by grasping her arm. "I still don't see why you are so angry. He courted you, but you didn't end up married to him. You married me."

"Yes, and I'm glad, but that doesn't change the fact that I was betrayed by everyone—my grandfather, Alec, and my cousin. It hurts. I can't help that. I hurt." She pressed a fist to her heart.

He moved to catch her hand.

She evaded him and stalked away.

Baffled, he bent and braced his hands against his knees, gasping for air, for a way to help his suffering wife.

When Samuel was able to look up, he saw that she must have fallen. And she wasn't trying to stand. His anger was quenched in a second. Was she hurt?

He hurried forward. "What's wrong?"

She gazed at him but made no effort to reply. The knapsack she'd been carrying had fallen so it supported her head. Lying on the muddy road, she was weeping.

Terror for her ripped everything else from his mind. He dropped to his knees. "What can I do? Tell me!"

She wouldn't look at him but just lay there, inconsolable.

He ransacked his mind but could think of nothing to do. They were alone in the middle of nowhere.

Then Honor turned her head, and he saw her mouth form an O.

He followed her gaze and saw a wagon rounding the bend through the thick fir trees. He couldn't believe who was coming toward them. The slave catchers. What help would they be?

The older one, Zeb, hauled up on the reins. Looking as though he were shouting, he jumped down.

Samuel sprang up and stood in front of his wife, ready to protect her.

❖

Honor could not believe her eyes. Their horses were tied to the rear of Zeb's wagon. She grabbed Samuel's hand before he stirred trouble. "They caught our horses," she signed.

Samuel looked as disbelieving as she felt.

"What's the matter, Quaker?" Zeb asked, coming to stand in front of her.

"I stumbled," she said, still too done in to rise. "We're walking because a storm came and we had to set our horses free for their safety. Thee found them."

"I thought the horses looked familiar." Zeb regarded Honor, worry creasing his forehead. "We were lucky enough to find shelter in a clearing. When we started out again, we found these two on the road. Where's your wagon?"

"Not far." She pointed behind them.

"Are you ailing?" he asked.

Honor sighed. "No, I'm just so tired, and I'm sick every morning, and—"

"Sounds like you might be in the family way," Zeb interrupted.

A jolt went through Honor, and she counted back the weeks. She had missed two monthly flows now. Darah—coming, upending everything—had pushed any suspicion out of her mind. She rubbed a hand over her eyes, trying to feel something besides exhaustion.

"You look like you been cryin'." Zeb frowned deeply, eyeing Samuel as if he'd done something to upset her.

Zeb's concern lifted her spirits. "I was," she admitted

but didn't elaborate. She tugged on Samuel's hand, and he bent to help her up. She was sweaty and muddy and miserable. But somehow she didn't care about herself any longer. Samuel's strained, unhappy expression pierced her. Memories of his past mistrust of her returned. *I should have been kinder, more diplomatic, when I told my husband about Alec courting me. Or held my tongue. After what he did for Darah, I shouldn't have lost my temper and taken this out on him.* She tried to smile at him but failed.

"Well, let's go find your wagon and get your team hitched up again," Zeb said. "Dan, you get down and let the lady sit up here."

Dan obeyed and helped her up on the bench.

Zeb took his seat beside her and set the wagon in motion.

"Zeb, I admit, I am glad to see thee," she said.

"Never thought you be sayin' that, did ya?"

She found it in her to grin. "No, I didn't."

"You ain't been home for a spell. We were followin' a slave and lost him."

Thank God the runaway had eluded them. Honor glanced at him sideways. She knew he and Dan hunted slaves for money, but what kind of life was that for anyone, even men who furthered a system of oppression she hated? "Doesn't thee ever tire of roaming around?"

"No, I got Dan and this wagon. We get by."

If there were anything she could say to change the man's mind, she would have said it. But now she merely patted his rangy arm. "I thank thee for catching our horses. I'm exhausted and just didn't know if I could face trying to find them or buying a new team."

"What are you up this far north for?"

"Samuel had bottles to deliver, and we carried a friend on the way. She's starting a lace business near Detroit." Honor chose her words carefully, not wanting to lie but neither able to tell the entire series of events.

He squinted at her. "You telling me the truth?"

She was glad to be able to say yes.

"You sure this ain't about a runaway slave?"

Honor drew in the clammy, cooler air left by the storm and again selected her words with caution, avoiding his question. After all, the maid had not run away from her mistress; she had helped her mistress run away. "My friend is fleeing her husband. He beat her and broke her arm in a rage. She had no family to protect her. Now I suppose thee will tell me that a wife should submit to her husband and that we shouldn't have helped her."

"No, I ain't gonna say that. A man who's got a good wife should count himself lucky and treat her right."

Grateful, she turned her face to Zeb. "Thank thee, Zeb. She was a good wife. It's been very upsetting. And I'm so exhausted from traveling."

"And you might be in the family way. Women get emotional then. More than usual, that is."

Still uncertain about this, Honor went over all she'd gone through in the past days. Expecting or not, she'd had plenty to be emotional about. She'd thought that she and Samuel had come to an understanding of each other. But learning the truth from Darah had upset everything.

After her grandfather's death, she and Royale had been hard-pressed to find a way to survive with some dignity. No time for reflection or acceptance. Finding a way to live, a safe place and provision, had overwhelmed them. They were secure now, but the turmoil of Darah's arrival had thrown Honor back into that awful time.

Honor knew that Samuel was a good man, that Alec could not begin to compare. But even if she tried to frame this into a defense, she wondered whether her husband would believe her after her hasty words about Alec's courtship. *His suspicions may start all over again. God, help me.* She and Samuel had been married for months and might have conceived a child together—a true blessing—but in her distress, she feared she had done harm to their marriage, lasting harm.

❖

The journey home went easier and faster than expected. Samuel didn't like being in the company of the catchers, but he said nothing. Honor seemed at ease with them, something he couldn't understand. Dan, the young one, took over driving the Cathwell wagon so Honor could walk or ride. When they reached Dayton, the older one saw a poster about a runaway, and the two wagons separated.

Now Honor sat beside Samuel on the wagon bench, again driving their team. Since they'd had company most of the way home, they had interacted very little. Trying to reconcile himself to Honor's past with Alec Martin, Samuel had not wanted to engage with her. And evidently his wife had been of the same mind. They had only communicated about the merest practicalities.

Finding out that the man had courted Honor had reignited a trace of Samuel's former jealousy, though when he thought about their situation rationally, he could not imagine Honor possessing feelings for a man who had betrayed her and mistreated her cousin. Yet the revelation had cut Samuel deeply, and the wound didn't go away. Honor had pressed her hand to her heart and said, *"I hurt,"* and Samuel felt the same.

Honor was an upright woman and a praiseworthy wife, but she'd only married him out of necessity. That was the sticking point. Would she ever feel any love for him?

Chapter 19

MAY 5, 1820

In the weathered building where the African church met, Honor sat between Samuel and Caleb, Eli on Samuel's other side. Over her shoulder, Honor glimpsed Royale and Judah in the open door at the rear. The wedding couple's radiant faces told the truth. Royale loved Judah, and he loved her. Everyone rose in honor of the bride and groom as they entered.

Tears rolled down Honor's face. She could not stanch the flow and did not try. Beside her stood the husband who had barely spoken to her since they had returned from Canada. Not even when she revealed she was probably expecting their first child, though she'd hoped this good news would break the impasse between them. Samuel had said the right words but with no emotion or spontaneous gladness. He had guarded himself as he always did. He was extra careful of her and concerned about her overdoing it, but that was all.

From the rear of the room, a woman with a rich, melodious voice began singing a song familiar to Honor, bringing her back to this special event.

"Fare thee well, fare thee well.
In that great gettin' up mornin'
Fare thee well, fare thee well."

Holding hands and dressed in their best clothes, Judah and Royale walked—no, nearly danced—down the aisle together. The whole congregation clapped and joined in the song.

"In that great gettin' up mornin'
Fare thee well, fare thee well."

In her memory, Honor heard Royale's mother's rich voice, lifted, singing the same song. Emotion raced through her. Face forward, Honor hid within her bonnet and made no telltale move to wipe away her tears.

An image from her own very different wedding, of Samuel's closed face as he'd affirmed his commitment to her, released long-denied despair, welling up inside her. Every day since they'd returned, she had tried to smooth matters over, but he remained aloof. All the headway she'd made in her marriage had evaporated, mostly because of her rash words on the drive home. Would the child she carried be born into a house empty of love between its parents?

After the song died down, everyone sat, and Judah's father, Brother Ezekiel, stood between Royale and his son, speaking to them of love and commitment. Honor's mind raced with flashes of memory of her home in Maryland, the green fields of tobacco, and the sad faces of her people—faces she would probably never see again in this life. The images felt as sharp as pinpricks, and her tears rolled downward. She'd wanted to free her people, but now they lived under a master more unfeeling and volatile than his predecessor.

Judah and Royale said their vows loud and strong.

Honor's own vows echoed in her head. *"I promise, with God's help, to be unto thee a loving and faithful wife until it shall please the Lord by death to separate us."* She'd made that promise and would live up to it, but she hadn't counted on how difficult the road would be. Just weeks ago, she and Samuel had been united by something near to love. Would it ever return? She wanted what everyone wanted: to love and be loved by someone.

Brother Ezekiel tied Royale's and Judah's wrists together with a rough cord. Then Judah kissed his bride.

Following a round of cheers and applause, the wedding couple turned unexpectedly to Honor, who was sitting in the front row as requested. "I got something more to say," Royale announced.

Royale drew Honor up to stand beside her. "This lady is Mrs. Samuel Cathwell, the woman who freed me. Mrs. Cathwell wanted to free all her people, and because of that, she lost everything. I just wanted all of you to know what kind of lady she is."

Honor could no longer hide that her face was drenched in tears. Maybe tears at a wedding would be overlooked. Still, she pressed her handkerchief to her mouth, hiding her quivering lips. Royale still did not want to reveal their blood tie in public, and that was her prerogative, but Honor felt their bond more than ever.

Drawing up Judah's hand, still tied to hers, Royale motioned for quiet, until silence loomed over them, broken only by a baby's cry.

A man with a rich, deep voice began singing.

"The Lord, by Moses, to Pharaoh said:
Oh! Let my people go.
If not, I'll smite your firstborn dead—
Oh! Let my people go.

"Oh! Go down, Moses,
Away down to Egypt's land,
And tell King Pharaoh to let my people go."

Emotion electrified the room. Honor felt the thrill vibrate through her, and the hairs on her neck prickled. She'd never before realized that this song meant freedom to these people. Royale drew nearer, and Honor wept again with her friend's arm around her.

The song ended, and Royale released her. Honor returned to Samuel's side and watched as Royale and Judah walked up the aisle to jump the broom at the door of the church.

A thorn pierced Honor's heart. Unlike Royale, she'd

married a man who didn't wed her out of love. She rose and left the church on Samuel's arm, Eli and Caleb alongside. She knew that Samuel was capable of faithfulness, goodness, and kindness. Maybe it would have to be enough.

❖

After the wedding and luncheon, Judah and Royale stayed at his father's home. They planned to spend their two-day honeymoon visiting friends and shopping to furnish the new cabin that would soon be built between the barn and the kitchen. Perlie had also decided to spend the days visiting friends. She had taught Honor how to cook a few simple dishes in recent months, and Honor assured her she could manage on her own.

As Samuel and Honor passed Thad's place in Sharpesburg, Eli and Caleb asked to stay behind to play with Thad's son, who was starting to crawl. Honor declined to linger for conversation with Charity and her daughter-in-law. She insisted upon returning home. She didn't feel ill, just tired, as she told Charity.

At last, she and Samuel approached their house. Samuel signed that he was going to check on the cow in the meadow before heading inside.

Being alone like this only accentuated the barrier between them. She nodded, realizing that he did not want to join her in the cabin any more than she wanted to be with him. She wondered if, for him, the wedding had stirred up all the undercurrents that she had felt. Untying her bonnet ribbons, Honor walked into the cabin.

And halted. Her breath caught in her throat. She couldn't move.

Alec Martin turned. His handsome face was flushed in the heat, yet he wore an impeccable riding suit, his white cravat still stiff and perfectly tied. He rushed to her and clasped her hands in his. "Honor, you're more beautiful than I had remembered."

She fell back, bumping up against the wall. "Alec!" she finally gasped. "Why is thee here?"

He had released her and now stood and stared at her. "My wife's been here! I can see it in your eyes. That deranged woman has been here, telling her lies about me!"

Honor could not think. She recalled that Darah and Sally had both testified to Alec's rages. His fury ignited before her, and cold fear trickled through her.

"Darah is insane!" he ranted, pacing up and down. "How could I have been so deceived by her? She falls and hurts herself and then blames me!"

Every exculpatory word he uttered only convinced Honor that Darah had been telling the truth. Alec was the one who appeared deranged. Alarm ignited in the pit of her stomach. Would he vent his anger on her?

They were alone. She could call for help, but Samuel could not hear. She must run to him. She edged toward the door.

Alec blocked her way. "Tell me you believe me. I can't bear for you, my sweet Honor, to think ill of me. It's all lies! I am going to find Darah and take her home and lock her up. She's a danger to others! To herself!"

Honor skirted to the side, trying to ease past him to

the door. She nearly said, *I don't know where she is.* But she couldn't tell him a lie, nor would she tell him the truth. "Alec, I cannot help thee."

He ignored her. "I should have married you and been happy. I could have talked you out of freeing your people. Darah . . . You don't know the way she threw herself at me. If I had been older, more experienced, I would have seen her stratagems. You cannot imagine how I've regretted my actions that hurt you, my dear Honor."

Is this the man over whom I once felt such anguish? Any lingering resentment Honor might have held toward Darah was extinguished by Alec's presence. This type of confrontation did not fit in her life. Honor continued to inch away from him. The open door was just a step farther . . .

He moved forward and captured her by the shoulders. "To see you living here in this humble cabin. Oh, what have I done?" The words sounded artificial, as if on the way here he'd practiced all these phrases in an attempt to ensnare her. They only repelled her.

Honor shrank from him, her fear racing, nearly making her light-headed. "Let me go, Alec!"

"You should have been mine!" He bent to kiss her.

She turned her head to the side and tried to pull away. Alec held on to her, gripping her tighter. Honor panicked and shrieked. If only Samuel could hear her!

❁

Striding toward the cabin, Samuel looked through the open door and gasped. A finely dressed man was trying to kiss his wife. Honor was attempting to get away. Fury shot through Samuel.

"Stop!" Samuel roared, the first word he'd said aloud in many years. He charged into the room.

His wife turned her head toward him. "Help me!" The words were plain on Honor's mouth.

Samuel grabbed the man with both hands and threw him backward. The intruder hit the wall and fell to the floor.

Honor signed that the man was Alec, looking for Darah.

Darah's husband—the man who owned land that was rightfully Honor's! Samuel's hand itched to make the man hurt.

Alec regained his feet and came at Samuel, his riding crop in hand.

Samuel yanked the crop from him and tossed it away.

Alec aimed a punch toward Samuel's face.

Samuel dodged it easily. He pummeled the man who'd hurt his wife, his Honor. Then it wasn't just Alec he was hitting; it was all the men who'd ever looked at him as if he were a freak or dolt. A red haze filled his eyes. He felt his throat contract with rage.

Then slender arms closed around his neck from behind. *Who, what . . . ?* Honor had wrapped her arms around him, pulling at him. He gasped, awakened from the haze.

He reeled backward and looked down. Had he gone too far?

Alec Martin slid to the floor, and Samuel realized that he'd backed the man against the wall and nearly beaten him senseless.

Samuel staggered to a chair and collapsed.

Honor bent to look at him. "Is thee all right?" she signed.

He nodded, gasping, his knuckles aching and stinging.

His wife bent forward and kissed his forehead. Her fingers flew. "Thank thee. I was so frightened. How did thee know I needed thee?"

"I noticed a strange horse tethered behind the kitchen." Still panting from exertion and the mindless rage, he swallowed and leaned back, resting his head against the chair. He noted she made no effort to go to the man who sat on the floor, his head in his hands, and found satisfaction in the fact.

❖

Honor took a deep breath as Alec rose shakily to his feet. He stared at Honor and Samuel side by side, confronting him—united again, Honor realized. Alec's split lip bled, and his shirt was disheveled and bloodied, one eye already showing bruising.

"I see you believed that lying, insane wife of mine," Alec said in an ugly tone she'd never heard him use before today.

She signed this for Samuel and replied, "Yes, we do. Please leave. And don't return."

"Where is Darah?" Alec demanded.

Samuel grabbed Honor's arm. "Tell him he will never find her." She did.

Alec swore violently at them.

Samuel must have sensed this and moved to his feet,

approaching Alec. "Tell him to leave before I throw his unconscious body off my land."

Honor took satisfaction in repeating this.

Alec cursed her again, picked up his battered hat, and passed her with a sneer. "You deserve this, Honor Penworthy. Living in a sty with a deaf pig."

Honor didn't deign to reply, merely stared at him with all the disdain she could muster. Soon she heard hoofbeats and, from the doorway, saw Alec speed away.

Though tears flowed, she turned and poured water into a basin. She motioned for Samuel to pull the rocker close to the table. With trembling fingers, she washed the blood from his hands and applied iodine to his broken skin. Alec had barely touched her husband. Only a faint bruise on his jaw appeared.

When she'd finished caring for him, she leaned over and kissed his mouth, something she hadn't done for weeks. The feel of his lips caressing hers drew her closer. "Thank thee. He terrified me."

To soothe her, Samuel urged her onto his lap, nestling her softness against him. They had been apart so long. Feeling how she still shook, he wanted to say something calming to her, really speak to her, let her know how deeply he felt for her at this moment. But aside from his outburst at Alec, he never spoke words aloud. Could he say what he wanted? Would his unusual voice repel her, as it had others when he was a boy?

He closed his eyes and asked God for strength, courage. "Honor," he said slowly, hoping the word had been audible, understandable. "I'm sorry."

Her expression showed her shock. She signed, "Thee can speak like Caleb. Why doesn't thee speak to me?"

"My voice sounds odd," he said, hanging his head. Speaking words exhausted him as always.

She nodded slowly, putting a hand on his arm. "It sounds wonderful to me," she signed.

"No matter what you say, it sounds strange." Samuel lapsed into sign. "That's why I don't speak. I don't know why, but a person has to be able to hear his voice to sound like himself." Rampant emotion roiled through him with every word he conveyed. He felt each nick and cut to his knuckles. He was clumsy and inadequate. But his wife had resisted her cousin's husband—even though he was handsome and whole.

Honor waited, her expression soft.

"I'm sorry about my jealousy," he went on. He'd plainly seen her revulsion as Alec had pressed his attentions on her. In that moment, all traces of his jealousy had vanished, burned up. His only regret was that it had taken so long—Honor had proved her faithfulness time and again. Samuel leaned back into the chair, spent. "I'm sorry you had to suffer . . . seeing him, having to witness a fight."

Honor shuddered. "I finally saw Alec as he really was. I realize now that both Darah and I were too young, too innocent to understand his true nature, what kind of man he actually was."

A profound gratitude filled Honor. She rested her palm on Samuel's cheek. "I felt betrayed by Darah, but I see now God was protecting me. He would have protected my cousin, too, but she did what she knew she shouldn't. Yet in the end, he gave her a way out." She bowed her head, letting all the old hurt drain out only to be replaced with relief. *The Lord saved me.*

Samuel exulted in her gentle touch. "I'm sorry," he signed.

Being done once and for all with the past, she even felt lighter. God had brought her a good and kind man to be her husband, and the Lord had made so many other provisions through their marriage as well. Their union had eased Miriam's passing for Samuel, provided care for Eli and Caleb, brought security for herself and Royale, and connected Samuel with the hearing world and brought about his dream of his own glassworks.

She stroked his face and leaned forward, placing another kiss on his mouth. She remembered not his jealousy but his kindness to the runaways they hid, his exceptional benevolence to Darah and her maid. "I am glad thee is my husband."

"I am grateful you are my wife," he signed. Then he did something he had wanted to do but had not allowed himself. The jealousy and resentment had kept him from touching her so intimately, touching what connected them so deeply.

Samuel laid his hand upon his wife's abdomen, fully aware, perhaps for the first time, of the new life within. The wonder of it brought his face up to hers. She too looked amazed. She laid her hand on top of his and kissed him again, then rested her forehead against his.

Suddenly the courage he needed rose in him. "I love you, Honor," he said aloud. "I love you."

She moved her head so their eyes met. Her gaze delved

deeply into him as if reading his very soul. "I love thee." She spoke the words so plainly it was as if he could hear them. She said the words again in sign.

Tears rose in his eyes, joy overflowing. "I love you, Honor," he repeated.

Once again her lips dipped to his. Her kiss was slow and thorough and thrilled him to his marrow. Then she rose and latched the door. When she turned, he saw a light in her eyes he'd never witnessed before.

He stood and opened his arms.

She took her time reaching him, all the while smiling at him, promising him her love. Then she was in his arms, so soft, so yielding, a miracle.

He savored what he hoped would be the first of many moments like this—he would remember it all his life. *Thank God. Thank God.*

Epilogue

Honor laid her tiny napping daughter into the cradle by the crackling fire, warming them both against the December chill. She had just finished her two weeks of lying-in and was so happy to be free of the bed. Now she had a letter to write. Micah would be driving into Cincinnati tomorrow and could mail it for her.

Over the past few months, her life with Samuel had changed. A week after Alec had come here, his badly beaten body had been found dead near the Cincinnati wharf. The night watch had found Alec's ornate calling card on the body, and the sheriff had traced him back to the inn where he'd been staying. The innkeeper had recalled that the dead man had asked about the way to the deaf glassblower in Sharpesburg.

So the sheriff had sent a deputy to them. Samuel had identified the body and paid to have Alec buried in

Cincinnati. Samuel's theory was that Alec went back to the city boiling for a fight and started one with someone he shouldn't have. Honor had written Darah and enclosed a clipping from the newspaper about Alec's murder. Unfortunately, through correspondence with the lawyer Bradenton, Honor had been informed that Alec had left his whole estate, including High Oaks, to his nearest cousin. So Darah was disinherited but free. And prospering in Canada.

Honor now had a happier letter to write. She brought out her box of stationery, the wax and seal, a writing pen, and ink. She trimmed the quill and began writing.

December 15, 1820

Dearest Cousin,

I am happy to announce the birth of Blessing Miriam Cathwell two weeks ago on November thirtieth. She is plump and healthy, and my neighbor Charity agrees she is a most content and beautiful little girl.

I was glad to receive thy letter. I think thy decision to remain in Canada is wise. Though I grieve over the plight of our people, we are helpless except to pray for their safety and future freedom. Let the Martin land go to Alec's cousin. I agree thee is better off to make a new life far from unhappy memories. Both Samuel and I were encouraged to hear that thy lace business is thriving. And that thy maid had found a good husband.

Samuel and I will visit whenever he has a delivery to make north of Dayton. He is learning how to drive the wagon and is speaking commands to the horses. He still speaks very little with his voice otherwise, but I see this as a good sign. So we are doing well, and I hope to see thee in the spring.

As always, thy loving cousin,
Honor Cathwell

She folded and sealed the letter with hot wax, marveling at how God had brought her, Royale, and even Darah through the past year. Honor had not been able to free her people, but she was helping others to freedom. And the letters they had written in Deborah's parlor perhaps had some influence. The law penalizing anyone who kidnapped a free person of color in Ohio and tried to sell them back into slavery had come up for a vote in the state assembly and had passed. This had excited the members of the Female Anti-Slavery Society and proved that women could do something to oppose slavery. It was a start, at least.

❖

Samuel entered, shutting the door against the cold behind him. He took off his hat and mittens and warmed himself by the fire before he bent over the cradle. He couldn't look at his little daughter enough.

His wife moved to stand beside him.

He put his arm around her and kissed her cheek. "She is beautiful. You are beautiful."

The baby began to fuss. Honor lifted their tiny daughter from her cradle and set her to nurse. He loved watching her hold the little one that belonged to both of them, linking them forever.

They had come through so much. And now they had little Blessing. He had chosen this name for their daughter, hoping that Honor would realize it was a tribute to their love and how he felt about their marriage.

He tickled the baby's chin, and the child sent him an angry look for interrupting her nursing. He watched a smile crinkle Honor's face as she laughed at him. Then he leaned closer and savored a kiss. He had more than he ever thought possible: a home, a thriving business, and a loving wife and family.

Eli and Caleb burst inside, rosy from the cold, playfully punching each other.

Honor turned to scold them, but Samuel couldn't help himself. He let the laughter rumble up from deep inside him. Life was good. God was near.

HISTORICAL NOTE

To THOSE WHO have read my previous historical series, it will come as no surprise that when considering a new series, I looked for an area where great social and political upheaval and conflict had taken place. In my earlier Texas: Star of Destiny series, I chose Texas, which changed from Spanish colony to Mexican territory to the Republic of Texas and finally to the state of Texas, all between the years of 1820 and 1847. The period also included the Texas Revolution ("Remember the Alamo!") and the Mexican-American War.

That done, I next turned my attention, of course, to Ohio. Ohio?

Yes, during the same years, Ohio simmered and at times boiled as a hotbed of conflict and activism over the issue of abolition.

While in Texas, the winds of change and social upheaval were acted out in open conflicts, in Ohio, the revolution took place behind doors and within secret rooms, only rarely breaking forth into race riots. The

Underground Railroad started spontaneously, many say, with John Rankin, a Presbyterian minister who moved to Ripley, Ohio, in 1822. When Harriet Beecher Stowe was asked after the Civil War, "Who abolished slavery?" she answered, "Reverend John Rankin and his sons did."

But actually, the Underground Railroad was not any one man or woman's idea. It was a spontaneous, uncoordinated response to the plight of runaway slaves. It began with free blacks in Ohio, such as Judah and Royale. There were several black settlements in Ohio; some groups of them were made up of slaves freed and resettled by their former owners. These settlements consciously saw themselves as havens for runaways. John Parker, Henry Bibb, Charles Langston (the inspiration for Brother Ezekiel and Judah's surname), and many more free blacks in Ohio sheltered and then moved escaped slaves toward Canada.

However, because of the Black Laws of Ohio (1807), people of color had no legal status and could not testify in court or vote. White abolitionists came forward to stand up for and assist their black cohorts in these situations, often providing funds. Keith Griffler states in his landmark study, *Front Line of Freedom: African Americans and the Forging of the Underground Railroad in the Ohio Valley* (Lexington, KY: University Press of Kentucky, 2004, 60):

> The movement that came to be called the Underground Railroad would never have gotten off the ground without the dedicated group of whites who hailed from the South, providing the African Americans engaged in

> the life-and-death struggle with American slavery indispensable allies in their frontline struggle. If the South had bequeathed to the Ohio Valley much of its proslavery animus, it also ironically supplied it with some of its most ardent and militant antislavery white activists—willing to risk their reputations, their fortunes, their freedom, and even their lives. It might not be too much to say that the Underground Railroad in the region would have taken much longer to initiate without the zeal they brought to the cause they espoused. Their fervor was equal to that . . . which the love of slavery inspired in leaders of the South. Having witnessed—and learned to hate—slavery at close quarters, they brought not only a passion but also the willingness and desire to work closely with the African American communities whose existence on the northern bank of the Ohio defied both Northern and Southern public opinion.

Honor is not a heroine who truly lived in history, but many with her passion took an active part in the antislavery movement. The poem I let Honor take credit for—"What Is a Slave, Mother?"—really belongs to Elizabeth Margaret Chandler, who wrote many antislavery poems and who started a Female Anti-Slavery Society in Michigan about a decade after the fictional one in Deborah Coxswain's parlor. The full poem can easily be found online. Chandler participated in national discussions and debates through her articles and poems about abolitionism. She also edited Benjamin Lundy's abolitionist journal, *The Genius of Universal Emancipation* (which actually began in 1821).

Also, the inequity of property laws pertaining to widows at this time might have been a surprise to some readers. This was, of course, demonstrated by the fact that Alec could leave his whole estate—even the part that Darah brought into the marriage—to whomever he wished.

Usually a third of the estate was saved for the widow's portion or dower (even in the United States). However, this had to be specified either in the prenuptial marriage agreement or in the husband's will. I think Alec's decision not to provide for Darah in his will, along with her lack of a male relative to protect her interests in a prenuptial marriage settlement, fits both Alec's character (or lack thereof) and the story.

The next story in this series will be about Blessing Cathwell, Honor and Samuel's daughter. You'll see how the conflict over abolition and the advent of the women's rights movement will affect her life. What challenges will she face? And what man will find her too fascinating to ignore?

DISCUSSION QUESTIONS

1. What if doing what is right cost you everything—fortune, friends, and family? This is the concept that is central to the novel *Honor*. At the beginning of the story, Honor tries to do what is right, but she has no way of foreseeing the repercussions to come. Have you ever experienced or seen a decision like this in your own life or in the life of someone close to you? What was the outcome?

2. Some characters in the novel misunderstand, avoid, or scorn Samuel because of his deafness. How is today's society different from Samuel's in its treatment of people with disabilities? In what ways is it the same?

3. Soon after marrying Honor, Samuel becomes irrationally jealous whenever she interacts with other men. Why does he feel this way? How does his character develop throughout the story, and what causes this development? If you could give Samuel one piece of advice, what would it be?

4. Were you surprised at how few choices women could make to support themselves in 1819? Why do you think this was true?

5. Why does Honor chose to marry Samuel? Did she make the right decision? What would you have done in her place?

6. Throughout the novel, Honor struggles to control her angry impulses. What does she do to contain her anger? Read James 1:19-21. What steps can we take to strive for the righteousness of God without giving in to angry actions?

7. Looking back, it is easy to think that if we had lived in Honor's time period, we would have helped runaway slaves and worked for abolition. Abolition became popular in the decade before the Civil War broke out, but in the 1820s, abolitionists were considered odd and subversive to society. Would you break a federal law to seek justice for others? What would be the hardest part of doing so?

8. Though many Quakers opposed slavery, most meetings insisted that members of color sit in a separate section of the meetinghouse. Why did they do this? Can you think of a parallel in today's church?

9. The Quakers are a distinctive sect of Christians. What did you learn about them from this novel? What is most appealing to you about the Quaker lifestyle? What would be most difficult?

10. Honor works passionately to bring light into the lives of people marginalized and mistreated by her society. What can you do personally to add light to this world rather than darkness?

ABOUT THE AUTHOR

LYN COTE, known for her "Strong Women, Brave Stories," is the award-winning, critically acclaimed author of more than thirty-five novels. Her books have been RITA Award finalists and Holt Medallion and Carol Award winners. Lyn received her bachelor's degree in education and her master's degree in American history from Western Illinois University. She and her husband have two grown children and live on a small but beautiful lake in northern Wisconsin. Visit her online at www.LynCote.com.